MW00928889

DUNGEON OF THE GODS

LEGENDS ONLINE BOOK TWO

JONATHAN YANEZ

ROSS BUZZELL

CONTENTS

STAY INFORMED

Get A Free Book by visiting Jonathan Yanez' website. You can email me at jonathan.alan.yanez@gmail.com or find me on Amazon, and Instagram (@author_jonathan_yanez). I also created a special Facebook group called "Jonathan's Reading Wolves" specifically for readers, where I show new cover art, do giveaways, and run contests. Please check it out and join whenever you get the chance!

For updates about new releases, as well as exclusive promotions, visit my website and sign up for the VIP mailing list. Head there now to receive a free copy of *Shall We Begin*.

http://jonathan-yanez.com

Enjoying the series? Help others discover *Legends Online* by sharing with a friend.

REUNION

ILLUME, Nari, Victor, and the dragon Trillian rode across the fields before Cryo's Quarry toward the army that stood in place. Illume stopped his party fifty yards from the army's front line and glanced at Trillian. He didn't seem on edge or in an aggravated state. This brought a slight sense of relief to Illume.

"Victor, what scents are you picking up on?" Illume asked.

The werewolf sniffed the air. He leaned forward and sniffed some more. After several moments of pensive silence interrupted only by Victor's sharp inhalations, he shook his head. Victor huffed, unable to speak in his fully changed form.

"Victor, Trillian, you stay here," Illume said. "If anything goes wrong, we'll need you to be able to move into play. Nari, let's go negotiate terms."

Nari and Illume moved toward the center of the field as a small contingent of heavily armored men began to march at them. Their formation was that of a square. They were protecting someone in the center.

"You want to tell me how the terms of combat system works?" Illume asked.

"I don't know," Nari said, shaking her head. "I was only responsible for coding the plains region of the map. This army looks like they're from the marshlands. Things are different there."

"Well then, let's hope we don't get ourselves into too much trouble," Illume replied.

Illume and Nari came to a stop. He heard Trillian let out a low growl that rumbled over the plains like thunder. Illume put his hand up. Trillian stopped. He glanced back over to Nari as the squad grew closer.

"Have you ever been outside of your own domain?" Illume asked.

"No," Nari replied, shaking her head. "Too many variables. But mostly, I didn't want to risk a glitch."

Illume nodded as he dismounted. He walked over to Nari and helped her off her steed. Thomas took his horse by the reins and took several more steps forward. The squad before them stopped moving.

Their armor seemed to be made from wood. It appeared lightweight, but Illume noticed several gashes that were reminiscent of heavy axe cleaves. They had only left minor marks. Moss held their pieces of armor together and the teeth and claws of mysterious animals decorated some of the higher ranked officers.

A loud *CRACK* erupted into the air. One of the commanders peered at Illume with dimly-glowing yellow eyes from behind a helmet that covered his whole face. A massive whip struck at the air again and let out yet another crack. It was barbed like that of an iguana. It was only then Illume noticed massive scaly hands with claws that rivaled Victor's at the end of each finger.

"Our leader wishes to speak with the Lord of Cryo's Quarry!" the lizard man announced.

"Your commander can speak to this!" Victor replied while giving a rude gesture.

Another crack rang out. Victor staggered back and held his face. Illume noticed a bit of blood under Victor's eye. Shaking his head, Illume whispered, "That was a mistake."

Victor's features tightened as he snarled at the commander. In a blur, Victor dashed across the field and tackled the commander to the ground. Both hit with such force, they bounced and tumbled over one another.The other soldiers stepped back and made room for the fight. Victor slashed his claws at the commander's chest. The wooden armor almost completely deflected his attack.

A tail lined with spines swung up Victor's back and wrapped around his neck, pulling him off the commander. With the precision of a surgeon, the werewolf sliced the tail between the commander's scales.

With a hiss, the commander released Victor and drew his sword. Both beings lunged at each other once again, this time more animal than anything else. Illume stepped forward. He focused his frost mana into his hands. He gave both beings a quick blast of frost to cool them down.

"Victor, stand down! I am Illume, Lord of Cryo's Quarry!" Illume announced. "Who brings their armies to my doorstep?"

"The commander of the Barnogian armies, Obscuritas!" the commander announced.

Illume's brow furrowed. That name was familiar to him, but he couldn't quite place it, almost as if it had appeared to him in a dream. Illume peered through the ranks that stood before him to try and get a glimpse of the commander.

Obscuritas, Obscuritas, where have I heard that name before? Illume thought to himself. His eyes widened as it all came back to him, plowing into him like a semi-truck.

"No," Illume whispered in disbelief.

"Remember when I hit you that time and cracked your head open?" the familiar voice asked.

The guards parted. Between them stood a man in forest green robes that draped from him like Gandalf's and yet had a hood like an assassin. Human hands slid from the baggy sleeves and pushed back the hood. A man about five years older than Illume smiled at him. He had long hair that hung almost to his shoulders. It was held out of his face in a long ponytail.

"That was hilarious!" the man added.

"You said that you'd buy me ice cream if I didn't tell mom about it," Illume replied.

Illume's heart skipped a beat. The spitting image of his older brother stood directly in front of him. He couldn't be sure if it was his brother or just the game's projection of his memories.

"And I never did!" the man replied.

"That's really you, John!" Illume's voice came out in a weak whisper.

John walked over to Illume and nodded. He slammed his chest into Illume's. He felt his brother's arms coil around him like a snake. They squeezed him tightly. Illume's eyes began to sting with tears as he wrapped his arms around his older brother. The Cryomancer lost his breath as a silent tear of joy rolled down his cheek.

Illume couldn't breathe. Not because of his brothers

vice-like hug but because he never thought he'd see John again. John was the first to break the embrace. He leaned back and wiped one of Illume's tears away.

"Wow, crying over your big brother?" John teased. "You baby."

"How?" Illume stammered in a whisper. "How are you here?"

"Mr. Matsimoto reached out to me after your accident," John explained. "He said your consciousness was still alive on their servers. They offered to give me unlimited access to the game so I could see you!"

"What about my body?" Illume asked. "You're a doctor. Is there any way you could save it?"

John released Illume. He grimaced as he shook his head. John removed his heavy flowing robe and revealed a form-fitting one underneath. John tossed the robe to one of his soldiers.

"I'm sorry, Ray," John replied. "But from a medical standpoint, your body is crispy bacon. There's nothing anyone can do."

Ray nodded. He figured this would have been the case. He accepted the news with a resolute disdain and scratched the back of his head.

"No need to be upset," John said. "You're still alive and in a world most people could only dream of!"

"A world that is not mine!" Illume retorted, raising

his voice. "A world that is meant for temporary visits, not permanent residents!"

"So who might this be?" Nari's voice echoed from behind Illume. By her tone, Illume could tell the woman was less than amused by being left out of the conversation.

Illume went silent for a moment. Collecting one's thoughts in this situation wasn't exactly easy. It wasn't every day you got to introduce your video game girlfriend to your brother.

"John, this is Nari," Illume introduced. "Nari, this is John, my older brother."

John bowed slightly, as did Nari.

"Whoa, it is quite the pleasure to meet you!" John said with innuendo in his voice. "Can you tell me where to find an NPC like that?"

"Not an NPC! You heathen." Nari corrected. "I'm guessing the whole foot-in-mouth thing runs in the family?"

Illume laughed as John went as white as a sheet.

John shook his head, opening and closing his mouth as if he were trying to find the right words to say. When he couldn't, he just closed his mouth altogether.

"No, he's actually the smooth one," Illume said.

"I am so sorry," John apologized. "I didn't know

there were other humans here. I mean, real life people."

"It's okay," Nari interrupted with a giggle in her voice. "I was only being half serious."

"How are you logged on?" John asked.

"I'm not," Nari replied. "I'm stuck here like Illume. I was the programmer for the plains portion of the map and when I decided to beta test the gameplay… Well, you've seen the results."

"I'm really sorry to hear that," John replied.

"Don't be. I have everything I need here in Valka," Nari said as she nudged Illume.

"Come on!" Illume commanded as he waved his hand. "I'll show you Cryo's Quarry."

John walked at Illume's side. Everyone, army included, began to make their way back toward Cryo's Quarry.

Illume's army almost seemed disappointed they had prepared for battle only to walk back into their own castle without swinging so much as an axe.

Illume understood that.

All dressed up and nowhere to go, Illume thought to himself as he saw his warriors re-enter their city gates.

"Why are you here with an army?" Illume asked.

"Well, when I logged in, I was dropped into the middle of a village on the outskirts of a massive tree that doubled as a city," John explained with a shrug. "They called it Moot. It was under attack by these really weird beasts. I stepped in and helped fight off the invaders and they made me the captain of their armies."

They continued to walk toward Cryo's Quarry. Victor fell in line and took his human form before he greeted the Barnogians.

"Since my main goal was to come here and find you, I decided it might be best to take a portion of the army before setting out into a world that I don't know," John continued.

"It's good to see you," Illume admitted. "Is that your old avatar from college?"

"Yeah!" John laughed. "Mr. Matsimoto let me upload this character with all my abilities into the game."

"So what kind of character do you play?" Nari asked.

John, Illume, Nari, Victor, and Trillian began to walk up the land bridge. John's army stayed behind since their numbers would have put Cryo's Quarry's capacity above its current 350 limit.

"I'm a..." John started.

"You should wait and see for yourself." Illume interrupted.

Nari lifted her eyebrows at Illume. Illume nodded

with assurance. "Trust me, it's much better that way. Let's get something to eat."

Victor's children ran past them and leapt onto their father. Victor knelt and gave them big hugs and kisses. Kassandra walked over to Victor and gave him a kiss as well before she made her way over to Illume. John was frozen, his mouth gaped open as he watched Kassandra and her children.

"I'm Kassandra, Steward of Cryo's Quarry," she introduced herself. "Who may I ask brings an army to our doors?"

"I… uh… um," John stammered. He leaned over to Illume and spoke out of the side of his mouth. "How did THEY get in here?"

"When my consciousness was being uploaded, it filled the world's random NPCs with the faces of people who I know to help me acclimate to the world's immersion," Illume explained. "Mindy, Sara, and JJ happened to be part of that auto fill."

"I'm sorry, Lord Illume. Did I do something to offend our guest?" Kassandra asked.

"Not at all, Kassandra," Illume said. "You and your children bear a near identical resemblance to my brother's wife and child, that's all."

"Oh!" Kassandra exclaimed as her eyes widened. "Well, Lord Obscuritas, it is an honor to have you grace our city. Dinner is ready in your home whenever you are ready, Lord Illume."

Kassandra turned and walked away with her family. Illume nodded to Victor, as he left as well.

Illume called out after them, "It's just Illume. Not a Lord!"

"How'd she know my name?" John asked. "And if they thought we were going to attack you, why is dinner already ready?"

"You're a player," Nari replied. "You're not like Illume and me. The NPCs are programmed to know your gamer alias. And as for dinner. I like food. I wanted to make sure it was always available in my portion of the game."

"Always some sort of meal time," Illume added, slapping his belly. "I know it's just a game, but I can still taste it."

"Now if real life were only like that," John cooed.

Illume waved for John to follow him and Nari. He led his brother to the large structure that was his home.

"Wow!" John exclaimed. "This is beautiful."

"Thank you," Nari replied.

Illume opened his front door. Everyone, Trillian included, entered his house. Illume closed the door as his brother looked around and investigated every little part of Illume's main entryway.

"There is something else I should probably tell

you," John said, finally breaking his silence. He still investigated every little fantasy piece of paraphernalia that Illume had adorned in his house.

"What is that?" Illume asked.

"Well, there is something in the swamps that has been growing in power," John explained. "It seemed to come out of nowhere one day and outclassed everything that went up against it. Since you were stuck in here, that means this... THING posed quite the threat to you. I've fought its force, and I'm telling you, Ray, you need to come with me and take care of this beast before it decides to march here. If you don't, I'm not sure if you'll be able to stop it."

Illume's brow furrowed. He glanced at Nari. She shook her head and shrugged as she leaned against one of the pillars.

"What is this thing you are talking about?" Illume asked.

John gave a little figurine a gentle push. The eyes glowed for a brief second then faded just as quickly. John turned to Illume and put his hands behind his back.

"How familiar are you with Cthulhu mythos?" he questioned.

2

ANOTHER ADVENTURE

Quest Added:
Stop the threat to Moot and its surrounding lands.

JOHN, Nari, and Illume ate together. Nari and Illume shared stories about Trillian and the Dark King. Illume spoke of the Order of Light and their activities. He warned that they would probably be all over the Barnogian people. Nari spoke about her forging. Night pressed on and weariness grasped Illume and Nari. John's avatar stared blankly at the wall for a few moments. He snapped back and stood from the table.

"The wife's home," John said. "I've got to go and get dinner ready for the kids. Do you want me to say 'Hi' for you?"

"That's probably not a good idea," Illume decided. "Don't get me wrong, I would like for you to send my love. But do you think that the kids would understand what was going on? Or that your wife would even believe you?"

"He does have a point," Nari tacked on.

"Okay. I've been given a week off work for bereavement," John informed Illume. "From what I understand, that's quite a bit of time here. I'll log in tomorrow and we can head towards Moot then. It's good seeing you. I'm glad you're not gone. I mean, not really."

When John logged off for the night, his avatar simply vanished into thin air. Illume stood up and offered Nari his hand. She took it and rose to her feet as well.

"What does your brother do for a living?" Nari asked.

Illume gathered the dishes. Just because they were in a cyber world didn't mean they could live like slobs. He took them to a bucket of water and began to clean them.

"He's a surgeon," Illume answered. "He did general for a while then specialized in neuro."

After washing the dishes, Illume propped them up on the table to dry before he turned to Nari.

"And what did you do again?" Nari asked.

"I was a video game journalist," Illume remarked as he made his way over to Nari.

"Wow!" Nari teased in a sarcastic tone. "Your parents must have been so proud!"

"Oh yes! One child is a world-renowned surgeon. The other is a video game journalist," Illume replied in nearly as sarcastic a tone. "I'm the child my parents were proud of."

Both laughed as Illume moved closer and kissed Nari. He took her hand and proceeded to go to bed. Both of them could have used the *wait* mechanic to pass the time until John returned, but there was something refreshing about actually getting sleep.

Illume woke up first. He donned his armor and weaponry before he left his bedroom and went to the main hall. Nari was still asleep, sprawled on the fur bed. As Illume entered the main hall, he saw that John had already logged back in.

John tossed a battle axe across the room. Trillian galloped over to it, picked it up, and ran back to John before he sat it at John's feet. Illume pulled up a seat next to his brother. Trillian sat next to Illume and set his chin on Illume's lap. Trillian gazed up at Illume with his big blue eyes as if he were begging to be pet. Illume scratched behind his adolescent dragon's ears, which made his wings twitch.

"You do know how dangerous this place is, right?" Illume asked.

"I've seen my fair share," John replied.

John pulled a map from his cloak and set it on the table. He unfurled it to reveal a detailed map of the Swamplands. In the center was a massive city marked as Moot. Southeast of Moot was a port town in the marshes that acted as a border to the swamp. It was labeled Mire. To the northwest, on the opposing coast, sat another port city named Traders Bay.

Locations added to your map:
New land added to your map: Swamplands
New city added to your map: Moot
New city added to your map: Mire
New city added to your map: Traders Bay

Illume entered his menu. He pulled up his map, and sure enough, the entire lower half of Valka's map was now visible. Just to the north, the mountain range acted as a barrier for the fog of war. All three cities were clearly marked on his map.

As Illume looked closer, his map had far more detail than the one John showed despite it being in black and white. Illume noticed lots of water and dark forests that encompassed this new portion of the map. He zoomed in as best he could to inspect the border and saw dozens of what he could only assume were boats. The entire top half of his map, however, was still hidden by a thick gray fog.

"Looks like we'll be traveling by boat?" Illume asked as he closed his map.

"Some of the way, yes," John confirmed. "If you're stuck here, it's important that we make sure there is nothing in the game that could cause you harm. I don't want to lose you—I mean, not for real. If you were to have to use your third and last life—"

"That's not going to happen," Illume said, cutting off his brother. "I'm stronger now. Nothing is going to kill me. I'll find a way out of this game. Without a body waiting for me in the real world, that might be hard, but we'll figure out a way."

John's eyes glistened. He wiped them in a hurry then looked back at the map. "It is a swampland after all. The humans who live there have set up a series of channels that will help us navigate, but one thing is for sure. That armor is not going to do you any favors there."

Illume glanced down at the armor Nari had helped make for him. He let his fingers run over the scratches that had been put in it over his many fights. It wasn't a heavy armor, but when water was involved, it would more than likely prove heavy enough to drown him.

"You're probably right," Illume acknowledged with a sigh. "I don't have anything lighter than this that wouldn't cause some form of corruption."

"That's okay," John said. "We'll get you some

proper equipment for the kingdom we're about to go to."

"You ladies going to keep talking or are we actually going to head out?" Nari asked. "I'm not getting any younger here."

She exited the bedroom. She was fully clothed and armed to the teeth. She offered John a wave as she ripped a piece of bread free from its loaf and took a bite.

"That is an incredibly insensitive thing to say." John scoffed.

Illume's brow raised. He shot a look at his brother, the man he'd heard mock people who got offended over every little thing.

"Seriously, John? You're one of them now?" Illume gaped.

"No, I'm just messing with you," John snapped back with a laugh. "Let's clear out any threat so my little brother can be safe in his video game world. Whoa, when you say it out loud like that, it sounds kind of crazy."

John offered the map to Nari. She looked at it for several seconds. After she was finished, she rolled it up and handed it back to him. Both John and Illume rose to their feet. Illume grabbed a piece of meat from the table and tossed it on the floor.

Trillian approached the treat. He sniffed it then

rolled it around with his nose. It was a little on the raw side. Too raw for Trillian, apparently. He picked up the piece of meat and tossed it into the fire. He took a deep breath after several seconds and blew ice into the smoldering ashes and froze them. Trillian leaned into the fireplace and pulled the meat free before he ate it.

"He's a picky eater," Illume explained. "Come on, Trillian!"

Nari walked out of the front door and left it open. Illume and John were close behind as Trillian finished his food and trotted out of the house as well. As he was every morning, Illume was greeted by Kassandra.

"Good morning, Illume," she greeted with a toothy grin. "I imagine you will be leaving again soon. Before you do, is there anything you'd like us to do to build Cryo's Quarry up?"

Cryo's Quarry had grown quite a bit since it was founded. Dozens, if not hundreds of people came from Mobrebalku, Lapideous, and countless other outlying villages that Illume hadn't discovered yet. Some came for trade, others to see the city built by the Cryomancer. Cryo's Quarry would soon be far too small for the growing population and visitors.

"Don't just use our people for this," Illume said softly. "Offer pay to anyone who is willing to stay and help relocate the outer wall. I want it pushed out another two hundred yards. Have the masons build stairwells from the base of the quarry all the way up here so those who live and work down there won't have to take the land bridge every time. Put the main gate out past the land bridge. I know it's more easily defended, but with the stairs, that is no longer a security issue should anyone get within our walls."

"You might want to seek out more vampires and werewolves," Nari suggested. "They are stronger and much faster and can work through the night. It'll allow construction to come to a quicker end if you work round the clock in shifts."

"That's a good suggestion, milady," Kassandra replied.

"We will need to bring a few traders with us too," Illume said. "We are going to a new land and we would miss quite an opportunity if we didn't establish trade. Have Urtan and three of his best meet us past the gates. As for accommodations, taverns and shops, you know what is going on far better than I. I will let you choose what else needs to be built within the walls."

"Of course," Kassandra replied.

She had taken notes in her book before she made her way to the markets.

Illume walked toward the front gates. As he did, he greeted several people warmly and helped move a few logs here and there. He even cast a fire spell to help get an oven up and running. Illume stopped as he saw Halfdan and Abdelkrim. They stood next to Khal, who was sitting on the ground with a basket. Inside were a few polis, but nothing of value.

"Khal!" Illume called as he approached the boy. "What are you doing out here?"

Khal looked up at Illume. He was filthy and looked both hungry and tired.

"The woman who took care of me died when she tried to protect me from Buthrandir," he explained. "I ran out of potion supplies and all my potions went to defending the city."

Abdel and Halfdan's men stood up straight as Illume's gaze fell on them.

"This boy saved our lives with his potions," Halfdan said.

"We have invested far too aggressively in the marketplace," Abdel added. "With no money to spare, we offered our services of protection to the boy."

A pang of guilt struck Illume. He had been responsible for telling the boy to spare what he could. He didn't expect the boy to give it all away. Illume kneeled before Khal and picked up the basket. He looked inside before he glanced at Nari. Almost as if she could read his mind, she nodded in approval.

"Khal, do you know how to take care of yourself?

Feed yourself, bathe yourself, all of that stuff?" Illume asked.

"Yes, sir," Khal whispered with a nod.

"Okay then, you may stay at my house for as long as you'd like," Illume said.

Khal looked up at Illume, his face beamed with joy.

"Really?" he asked.

"Really," Illume confirmed.

Khal lunged forward and threw his arms around Illume, who returned the boy's hug. A soft *ding* rang in Illume's ears.

Trophy Earned.
Name: Heart of Gold
Type: Gold
Requirements: Adopt a child of Valka that needs it
*   most.*
Well done! You're on Santa's nice list this year!
Just be sure to find a good babysitter.

Illume couldn't help but scoff at himself and the trophy. He released Khal and looked at the twin brothers.

"You two, unless instructed by Kassandra or Victor this boy is now in your charge while I am gone," Illume said. "Maybe invest in his potion business and train him how to fight."

Both men nodded in unison and slammed their hands on their chests together.

"Yes sir!" they said as one.

Khal scrambled to his feet and ran as fast as he could toward Illume's house. Halfdan picked up Khal's basket and followed the boy.

"Aren't you a benevolent lord," John teased.

"There's nothing wrong with being kind," Nari admonished.

"Ignore him," Illume said he began to walk to the front gate. "He's the kind of guy who will kill everyone in a game just to see if he can. Then reload it and do it again."

"Oh come on!" John protested as he started after Illume. "I bet you still haven't looted a body yet, have you?"

"I'll have you know…" Nari started to get riled up.

"Ignore him, Nari. He's just looking for a response," Illume called. "And besides, we have an adventure to go on."

He approached the front gates, which opened for him. On the far side, Urtan and several other traders stood in wait for Illume. The Barnog army was unmoving at their back.

3

ACHERI

"YOU HAVE AN ORC?" John mused upon seeing Urtan. "How did you land an orc?"

"Illume was kind to Urtan," Urtan revealed before Illume had a chance to speak. "Illume let Urtan pursue passion instead of business. Urtan forever grateful to Illume. Urtan pledge his services to Illume."

"Well then. I'm glad you're on our side, big guy," John replied.

Illume approached Urtan. The massive orc offered an outstretched fist to Illume. He bumped his fist with Urtan's.

"How's business been going?" Illume inquired.

"Urtan hired shopkeeper, business goes well," Urtan responded. "Now Urtan proper entrepreneur, give employees great benefits package and retirement plan. Make Urtan feel good about himself."

"Good. Hopefully, this trip will prove fruitful for you," Illume said. He looked out over the other merchants. "For all of you. John, can you leave twenty-five of your men here?"

John hesitated for a moment. The question had clearly caught him off guard. John looked at his army for a few seconds and shrugged.

"Sure, why?" John asked.

"Urtan is a skilled fighter. Nari can take out an entire squad without blinking and you'll see what I am capable of later," Illume explained. "Cryo's Quarry has fifty places open for citizens. With the three of us gone, all fifty will need to be fighters."

"But you asked for twenty-five," John replied.

"The other twenty-five will be coming back with the merchants," Illume imparted. "They will be needed as trade guards to prove we are friendly to the Barnogian people."

John nodded and walked before his men. He clapped his hands three times and let out a strange series of hisses. After several minutes of silence, numerous hisses responded. Twenty-five Barnogian soldiers stepped forward.

"They will help. They are more than just soldiers, though," John explained. "They are builders, hunters, and trappers. They are pretty adept at poisons as well."

The twenty-five soldiers walked past Illume and

toward Cryo's Quarry. Nari watched them with a close eye as they passed.

"What are you? Speaking in parsal tongue these days?" Illume proclaimed good-naturedly. Without waiting for a response, he addressed his party. "Let's go!"

They walked southwest. The path John was leading them on passed between Lapideous and Tanner's Folly. As they made their way through the fields, Illume took notice of the organic feel each soldier's armor had. Some appeared to be made of wood, others of scales.

All of it moved so lightly that Illume thought for a moment that the armor might just float if they fell into the water. Their weapons were the same. Swords made of green glistening metal and staffs that were made of a black wood with bone and metal attached to the ends for spears. As the hours slipped by, Illume noticed none of the Barnogian soldiers removed their helmets. It was warm, and if Illume had a helmet, he would have taken it off at this point.

"They're cold-blooded creatures," John explained. "Their armor is designed to hold heat in. If they take it off, they could die here."

John moved up next to Illume. Trillian dashed between both men, making sure no one got too close to Illume.

"I'm that transparent, huh?" Illume asked.

"I'm your brother. I know how to read you," John stated. "Is there anything my men need to know while we move back through your lands?"

"Yes, do not attack any centaurs we come across," Nari blurted out.

She was several yards away. Her face was mere inches away from one of the foreign armor sets. Her interest as a master blacksmith piqued as she inspected it for any secrets it may have held.

"Centaurs, check," John repeated.

"We're going to be stopping near Acheri territory," Illume relayed softly. "If your men hear anything rustling in the fields at night or see a set of glowing eyes or hear a growl as if made by death itself, they are not to attack. It's a being called an Acheri. They are mostly invisible and they have a bad temper."

"Thank you. I will let them know," John replied.

John broke off from Illume and moved through the ranks. He hissed at the soldiers as if having a conversation. They hissed back. John's errand took most of the rest of the day, and by the time he'd returned to Illume, the sun had already begun to set.

The map filled Illume's view. They had made pretty good headway. Had they gone straight west, they would have been able to see Lapideous by now. Illume set up a fire, as did the soldiers. Nari and Urtan assisted everyone, and by the time night had fallen,

Illume had begun to make his rounds, lighting each firepit.

He took the first watch that night, armed with only his bow. He wasn't worried about bandits or other monsters attacking the small army that was with him. Several of the Barnogian woke up in the middle of the night and would wander into the fields. Probably to relieve themselves. Most of them returned within a few minutes.

Something didn't sit right in Illume's gut. He did a quick head count and found that three soldiers were missing. Illume gave one of the soldiers a kick in the bottom of their boot. It woke him up. Illume mimed for the soldier to stand guard before he walked toward the firepit, where John, Nari, and Trillian slept.

Folding his lower lip back, Illume let out a loud whistle. Trillian jumped up in the blink of an eye. He was ready for action. Nari gave off a soft groan and John didn't move. When Illume snapped his fingers, Trillian whipped his head around and looked right at Illume. He pointed at John, and without hesitation, Trillian trotted over to John and licked his cheek. He still didn't move.

The Cryomancer knelt down by Nari and gave her a gentle shake. She groaned once again and opened her groggy eyes just wide enough to see Illume. She reached up and tried to push him away so she could sleep some more.

"Nari, three men are missing," Illume said softly. "I'm going to go look for them I need you to keep watch."

"Okay," she mumbled. "One minute."

Illume grabbed his sword and fastened it onto his back as Nari got herself up. Illume looked at John, who still hadn't moved.

"They're just probably going to the restroom. Keep an eye on him, and if he wakes up, let him know I'll be back," Illume said.

Nocking an arrow, Illume entered the fields of wheat that stood much taller than himself and snuck as best he could through the stalks of grain. The soft breeze masked what noise he did make.

He heard movement ahead of him and to his left. He drew his arrow and followed the noise. Illume could have easily closed the gap in a blink of an eye, but if the noise was danger, he'd rather use the broken stealth/sneaking strike mechanic skill.

Illume stopped at the edge of a clearing. He recognized this kind of clearing. The wheat was matted down in a large oval and massive claw holes had punctured the wheat and ground. Illume immediately dropped his bow. He drew his sword and stuck it blade first into the ground.

Ahead of Illume were the three missing soldiers. They had their weapons out and were back to back. He couldn't see their faces, but the shuddering of their armor said more than a facial expression ever could. Illume emerged from his cover. All three soldiers turned to face him and held their unsteady spears out toward him.

"Drop your weapons!" Illume whispered in a harsh tone.

The soldiers didn't obey. How could they? They couldn't understand him. Illume pointed at the weapons then at the ground before he stepped aside and indicated at his bow and sword. The soldiers shook their head.

"You will all die if you don't put your weapons down—" Illume was interrupted by a deep and terrifyingly familiar growl.

A cold chill ran down his spine as a pair of glowing red eyes flashed into his field of view. They peered at Illume and the soldiers from behind several stalks of wheat. A second glowing set of eyes moved out from behind the first. They began to circle the clearing.

The soldiers moved back to back once again. Illume let out a hiss. They all looked at him momentarily. Illume drew his dagger and threw it on the ground. The soldiers shook their heads for a second time. That was when Illume felt it. A warm breath shot down his back, angled from somewhere above him.

Turning and looking up, Illume's heart pounded as his mouth went dry. He could feel his hands grow cold as his body prepared to defend itself. It took everything he had not to attack out of instinct. Two glowing red eyes stared down at him.

Illume forced his breathing to be even. The Acheri exhaled once again. Its hot breath smelled of a rotting corpse. It moved ever so slightly. The movement allowed Illume to see it for what it truly was.

A tall, pale, emaciated being stood before him. It had the form of a humanoid woman covered in tattered cloth. It was so thin, Illume could nearly count its bones. Its arms were elongated and almost touched the ground. Thick, long, razor-sharp black fingernails protruded from each finger, any one of which was long enough to skewer a man. It had long matted and tangled hair that fell down its scaly-skinned body while rows of anglerfish-like teeth protruded from its dessicated lips.

Illume took a small step backward. The Acheri glared at him from under an eyebrow-less Neanderthal brow. Its forehead had bony protrusions that pierced the skin across its skull's ridges. The Acheri let out a blood-curdling scream that sounded like a woman being murdered. Yet Illume stood his ground.

His knees wobbled, but he didn't move as the beast's foul breath washed over him. Illume could feel his body grow colder and colder with each passing second of the unending scream. After what felt like several minutes, its shout died off. Illume held up his forearm and revealed the blessing bestowed upon him by the centaurs. The Acheri drew back its claws in response.

Illume allowed his cryomancy to break through. His hands smoked as they dropped in temperature. Frost formed up his arms as he poured mana into his spell. Illume took a deep breath and roared back at the Acheri while he made himself appear as big as he could.

The Acheri's breath became visible as Illume channeled his magic through his vocal cords and infused his shout with the deep cracking sounds of ice. Illume dropped his hands as his breath ran out. He exhausted his mana stores to put up a wall between this Acheri and the soldiers. Yes, there were two on the other side, but they were smaller.

The Acheri huffed. It shook its head and stepped back. As it backed away into the wheat, it gradually vanished until it was just a set of glowing eyes once again. Illume glanced over his shoulder, past his waist-high wall. The other two Acheri backed away into the darkness. A soft *ding* filled Illume's ears.

New Power Discovered

Shout: Imbues voice with an elemental magic to great
> *effect.*

Level one: Intimidation +60

Level two: Intimidation +120

Level three: Intimidation +300

Cost: 5 skill points to unlock level two

10 skill points to unlock level three.

Another *ding* rang out.

Trophy Earned.

Name: Staring down a barrel

Type: Bronze

Requirements: Stand up to a legendary creature that
> *could kill you in one swipe and make it back*
> *down.*

Looks like you're becoming quite the tough guy.

Illume exhaled. His mana bar blinked for a few seconds before it started to fill once again. *How was that only a bronze?* Illume asked himself as he turned and vaulted his ice wall. He marched toward the soldiers. *Should have been a silver at least!* He grabbed the spears out of the soldiers' hands and threw them to the ground.

"What's going on here?" John's voice called out.

John, Nari, and about half the army emerged from the wheat. They had their weapons ready and pointed at Illume.

"Your men just almost got us all killed because they couldn't listen to orders and drew their weapons on the Acheri," Illume pointed out.

"Where have I heard that word before?" John wondered.

"In that supernatural show we used to watch. Remember that demon from the end of season two?" Illume reminded him, trying to jog his brother's memory. "'All Hell Breaks Loose' was the episode's name. The creepy little girl?"

"Oh my gosh!" he exclaimed. "I do remember that. She's in this game?"

"No," Illume replied. "The Acheri here are much worse. Now tell your men to put their weapons away before I do it for them!"

John gave another hiss. This time, it seemed more forceful and deliberate. Immediately, all the soldiers dropped or sheathed their weapons. Illume approached his brother and placed a gentle hand on his shoulder.

"John... I don't know how it is in the swamps, but if these men can't follow orders, we're not going to make it to this Hastur," he cautioned softly. "Are there more disciplined armies we may have access to?"

John shook his head. He glanced around at the soldiers, who had begun to fall into formation.

"These are it," John replied. "These are all that is left from Moot's standing army."

John's avatar paused for a few seconds. Illume waved his hand in front of his brother's face. No reaction. He sighed and began to flick his ear over and over again.

"What are you doing?" Nari snickered as she approached Illume.

"Growing up when we'd ignore each other, this is what we would do," Illume explained. "Flick the other person's ear until they broke down and addressed the situation."

"He won't feel that, you know," Nari explained.

"I know, but it makes me feel better," Illume grinned.

John's avatar twitched. Illume took a step back as John re-asserted control over himself.

"Sorry about that. My... Why did my health drop?" John asked.

Illume laughed. Nari chuckled as well. John just stared at both for a few moments in silence.

"I thought we'd grown past that," John huffed.

"Nope!" Illume replied.

"I have to go pick the kids up from school," John explained. "Keep moving forward to the boats and wait for me. DO NOT go into the swamplands without me accompanying you. Okay?"

"Okay. We'll wait at the boats," Illume agreed with a nod.

John's avatar disappeared. Illume turned to Nari, who had already begun to leave the field. Illume followed close behind her as they returned to camp.

"We're not waiting for your brother, are we?" Nari asked.

"No, we are not,"

4

SWAMP

FOR ILLUME AND NARI, it took almost a week to cross the remaining land. On the seventh day, they arrived at a series of boats. There were dozens of them and one guard was assigned to three boats. Illume had spent the travel trying to learn the Barnogian language while Nari studied their armor.

Urtan had already initiated trade with the soldiers. He'd traded knick-knacks of his for non-essential equipment. He had come up with a rudimentary series of hand gestures that helped them communicate. Trillian spent most of his time hunting the fields for foxes, rabbits, and the occasional wolf that got to close. He had grown to roughly the size of a Tibetan Mastiff.

Illume began to inspect the boats. They were rowboats, but they were broad with a flat base. Oars were inside the boat that indicated they were designed for a six-person rowing team. Illume found the commander. He had what looked like white oak inlaid into his armor.

"We are leaving," Illume said slowly.

He made hand gestures as he spoke to help relay his point. The commander shook his head and let out a hiss. Illume nodded persistently.

"Yes, we are leaving now," he replied.

The commander shook his head once again. Illume had begun to grow frustrated. He turned to Nari and the rest of his people and waved them over.

"Come on!" he called out. "We're going to Moot."

"Is that a good idea?" Nari asked. "Your brother said to wait."

She walked over to Illume. Urtan and the other traders were behind him.

"If my brother says he'll be right back, that means he'll be back when he wants to be back," Illume explained. "He never was the most punctual of individuals and tends to move on his own time when not in the hospital. He could easily be gone for months at a time, if not years. Hastur grows stronger by the day. I don't want to give him any more time to prepare."

Nari took several seconds to mull over Illume's reasoning. Urtan and the other traders had already nodded their support. Nari shrugged.

"We have maps and you have ice," Nari reasoned

to herself. "Anything attacks us on the water and you could freeze it solid. And the coder for this section wasn't big into the whole enemies level with you. Hastur could easily out-level us to the point of no catching up. I guess we really don't have much of a choice. We wait for your brother at Moot!"

"I agree," Illume replied.

With that, Illume moved to the nearest boat. His part of the group climbed in while the Barnogian army stood without a word. Nari and Trillian took up the rear and were the second to last on the boat. The commander hissed at Illume several times. It almost seemed like he was pleading for Illume not to go.

With a single, strong push, Illume sent the boat out into the waters of the swamplands. The NPCs all grabbed an oar and began to row. Nari sat down and stared off. Her eyes darted from left to right. She must have been looking at the map. Illume took point on the front of the boat while Trillian curled up in the middle and fell asleep.

"We need starboard rowers to stop for a second!" Nari called.

The traders on the starboard side stopped rowing. It allowed the boat to turn around a small embankment of trees. Illume glanced around the world before him. He looked for any form of threat that could be lurking beneath the deep green water that now surrounded them. He looked in the trees that protruded from the water and even the small pieces of land that managed to break the water's surface.

Illume saw no threats. If this swamp was anything like the one he would go frog-digging in with his cousin in Louisiana, then danger could be just under the surface. Illume glanced back at Nari. She gave him a thumbs-up.

"Okay, we need to go straight now," she called out.

Everyone started to row again. Illume spotted a ripple in the water. He kept a close eye on the murky depths. The boat drifted through moss covered trees. Some were rotting, others had a lush canopy that hid the sun from them.

"We need to be as silent as possible," Illume warned. "Nari, tap your knee once for port, twice for starboard. I don't want to attract alligators."

Illume glanced back to see Nari held up her thumb to him. The trader's oars were silent as the boat moved through the swamp. Nari would tap her knee once, then twice, and once again. Illume made hand signals to indicate the locations of trees. They were successfully navigating the swamp. Illume had begun to feel something about ten minutes prior.

Something wasn't right, but he couldn't put his finger on it. Ahead, a strange fog began to roll in. The way it moved seemed unnatural. A chill ran down

Illume's spine as his gut screamed that something was definitely wrong. Trillian jolted and snarled. Illume glanced back to see quills had begun to protrude from the fluffy parts around his neck, feet and tail.

"Turn around," Illume whispered.

Illume opened his map. There was no fog that he could see. He closed it again. The traders tried to turn the boat, but it moved too slowly.

"Nari, did you invest in magic at all?" Illume asked.

"I didn't," she confessed.

Illume looked forward again. The fog was closing in.

"Doesn't matter. Get up here and focus all of your mana into your hands," he instructed as he planted his feet in the boat. "Urtan, grab the rudder and push it as far away from you as you can."

Nari moved up next to Illume as Urtan slid back and followed Illume's instructions. Trillian continued to growl as Nari moved past him. Once she reached Illume's side, he put his hands up to face the port side of the boat.

"Shoot fire port side at shoulder height," Illume said.

He focused all his mana into his hands. Both of them burned orange before each erupted in a fit of flames. Nari kept an eye on his mana as it fell. She followed his example, but after three seconds, her tiny burst of flame sputtered out.

That little bit was all he needed. The boat turned much faster. Illume spun as they were about to complete their 180-degree turn, then used the last of his mana to stop the rotation.

"Row now!" Illume commanded. "As hard as you can!"

Nari ran back to the rudder and took over. Urtan slid back to his seat and started to row as hard as he could. Illume sat across from Urtan. He picked up an extra oar and rowed as well.

Illume used all of his strength. He'd begun to cut into his stamina just to balance Urtan's mighty strokes. Illume glanced backward, the fog was bearing down on them. It moved at an unnatural speed and seemed to follow them.

"Can we go any faster?!" Nari yelled.

"I'm givin' it all she's got, Captain!" Illume called back with a Scottish accent.

"Stop quoting TV shows and get back here!" Nari yelled.

Illume glanced at his mana. It was almost fully charged at this point. His stamina on the other hand, was running dangerously low. Illume dropped his oar and tapped one of the traders who sat in front of Urtan. The trader moved to Illume's seat.

Stepping up on the rear of the boat, Illume threw his hands out and summoned his frost magic. The fog was mere feet away from them now. A wall of thin ice formed from tree to tree. He froze some of the water as well to support his wall.

The wall did nothing but shatter as the fog touched it. Illume took a sharp breath. He glanced at Nari. She had the same worry on her face that burned within Illume's gut. Illume threw his hands out once more and made a wall of ice directly behind the boat. This time, he made it much thicker.

Illume's mana should have been gone by now, yet he continued to unleash torrents of ice. Trillian moved up next to Illume. Soft blue light flowed from him into Illume's body. It danced like graceful solar flares.

New Dragon Level Reached.
Level 2
Trait learned: Share mana.
Trillian is able to share his vast mana pool with those who have a strong bond with him.

Skill unlocked: Frost breath
Cost: 1 Skill Point.
Attribute Points: 5
Skill Points: 1

Would you like to activate frost breath?

Yes! | *No!*

Illume hovered his vision over the *yes* prompt. It clicked and the message disappeared. When it vanished, Illume noticed his wall had begun to crumble. A deep growl filled Trillian's throat. He planted his feet, reared back, and threw open his mouth with a loud roar.

A torrent of blue, what Illume thought was fire, erupted from Trillian's mouth. Smoke rose from Trillian's body and danced off of the blue beam that surged from his mouth. Illume noticed the water around the boat had begun to freeze. As Trillian's blast hit Illume's wall, it was immediately fortified.

"Everybody off the boat!" Nari yelled.

Looking back to see that they were only a few feet from one of the land masses, Illume froze the water and created a bridge from the boat to the land. Nari slid past Illume and Trillian as the traders leapt from the boat to the ice before they ran to the land mass.

Once Illume felt they were far enough away, he glanced at Trillian, who showed no signs of slowing his ice breath. The blue light that danced from Trillian to Illume began to fade. Illume's mana plummeted once again. Eventually, it hit empty and Illume's magic sputtered out.

"Come on, Tril!" Illume yelled.

He dropped his hands and turned. He ran off the back of his boat and jumped onto the soggy ground. Trillian followed closely behind. The frost that Trillian emanated froze where his paws landed. He took off after Nari. Illume moved onto Trillian's tracks. He glanced over his shoulder to see the ice wall crumble and the fog closed in.

Illume ran after Trillian. He pulled his bow from his back and nocked an arrow. As they ran, Illume noticed movement within the fog as it closed in around them. He fought the urge to take a blind shot at whatever it was as he didn't have unlimited arrows.

Panting and fearful shouts rose from the traders behind Illume. They weren't far ahead. Trillian managed to outrun Illume as his stamina was still refilling. The fog overtook Illume and obscured his view. Fortunately, a bright pillar of blue light erupted from the fog before him.

Illume followed the blast. Within seconds, he was with his group. Urtan drew his mighty war axe. Nari held a sword in one hand and a throwing knife in the other. Trillian hopped from place to place and blasted ice into the thicker fog. His ferocious growls and puffed up wings made him look bigger. Trillian was only the size of a Saint Bernard, but Illume wouldn't want to be in his sights.

"Protect traders!" Urtan yelled to Illume.

Illume threw his hand out and formed a cylinder of ice around the other traders. It stood nearly twice their height and was several inches thick. Illume half expected the fog to shatter the ice, but it didn't.

"Illume!" Nari shouted.

Her voice shook with terror as the sound of her sword falling to the ground filled the air. Trillian stopped with his ice breath and let out a whimper. He tucked his tail and bowed his head slightly as he backed toward the frost pillar.

Illume glanced at Urtan. He was frozen in fear. The head of his axe was on the ground as the handle laid loosely in his palm. Illume followed his gaze. Nari backed toward the ice pillar as well. Illume stepped forward. He bent down and picked up Nari's sword.

As he raised his head, Illume saw that the fog had begun to disperse before him. A massive being in a yellow hooded cloak stood before him. The hood obscured its face from view. A pendant the size of Illume's palm rested on a gold chain that hung around its neck. Illume couldn't see the eyes, but he could feel them watching him.

"Don't look at its face!" Illume called. He dropped his vision to the pendant. "It's Hastur!"

5

HASTUR ROUND I

ILLUME TOSSED Nari's sword back to her. Before her weapon even reached her, Illume had his bow drawn and frost had formed over the arrow and the bow itself.

"Why Urtan not look at face?" Urtan asked.

"It'll drive you mad!" Illume replied. "Hastur, if you can understand me, let us be! We will kill you if we have to."

A deep, unearthly rumble left the hood of the yellow-cladded being. Illume felt an otherworldly fear grip him.

Fear Induced
All stats drop by 10.
You never should have come here. Flee, you fools!

Illume released his arrow. Half of his mana had been drained into the attack, more than what was used to kill the Dark King. The arrow struck Hastur in the darkness of his hood.

Frost Shot Successful
Headshot Successful
Bypass Armor Successful
Critical hit x10

Hastur's life bar faded into view. There was no visible health missing. A green cephalopodial hand reached out from behind its yellow cloak. His thumb index and pointer finger were humanoid while the remaining two were tentacles. His fingers gripped the arrow tightly and yanked. A spurt of yellow blood spewed from the hood as he threw the arrow away.

"How are we going to kill that thing?" Nari whispered.

"I have no idea," Illume admitted. "You want to say it?"

"We should have listened to your brother," Nari added.

Two more arrows were nocked by Illume. He drew and fired. Hastur vanished with a burst of wind. The arrows missed and disappeared into the fog.

"There it is," Illume replied. "Knuckle up!"

Illume jumped backward. Nari moved so her back was to his and Urtan closed the gap on the third side. Illume looked up to see Urtan run a green fruit over the edge of his blade.

"Woompa fruit poison to any who are not orc.," Urtan explained. "Also make good jam."

Illume drew his sword and held it out. Urtan ran the fruit over Illume's weapon then passed it to Nari. Illume placed his bow on his back and gripped his sword tightly with both hands.

Trillian paced back and forth around Illume and his team. He sniffed the air and would occasionally fire a blast of ice into the fog. Another deep laugh rumbled through the mist. Illume felt the same chill down his spine. Instantly, he could feel his stats drop by ten again.

The laughing continued until it sounded like it came from directly above them. Illume looked up to see a figure hanging upside down in the trees. Tentacles stretched out in all directions from under the cloak to support its weight. Illume used his extremely high dexterity to shove Urtan and Nari out of the way. He tried to use it to dive clear himself, but the ground gave way under the force of his leap.

Illume's feet slid out from under him and he fell. He rolled to his back just in time to see Hastur fall toward him. Channeling his electric magic into his sword, he held it straight at the beast. Just before it hit in a blur of blue, Hastur was tackled to the ground. Illume rolled over and clambered to his feet.

Trillian and Hastur tumbled into the water. Trillian blasted Hastur's hood with a ball of blue flame. Illume noticed Hastur's health drop ever so slightly. Illume's sword sparked as he spun it into a reverse grip.

"Trillian, get clear!" Illume yelled.

Immediately, Trillian flapped his wings and landed on the boat that was just behind him. Illume slammed his sword blade first into the ground. A surge of electricity bolted from it and into the water. As the water became electrified, Hastur seized up, and a deep roar of pain echoed from him. His health dropped ever so slightly once again.

Illume released his sword and sent torrents of ice out of both his hands toward Hastur. The ice around the Lovecraftian nightmare anchored it in place. He struggled to free himself, but with Trillian joining in and freezing the water, Hastur was entombed from the waist down.

Trillian shared mana with Illume once again. This allowed him to continue his barrage of magic. Illume glanced over his shoulder. The traders had been freed.

"Get in there and poison him then run!" Illume yelled.

Both Nari and Urtan gathered their courage then

charged at the thrashing monster before them. Urtan buried his axe deep into Hastur's chest. Nari slid hers into his side. Both blows damaged him, but his health was still near ninety percent.

Illume dropped his hands. He drew his sword from the ground and tried to dash at Hastur. His feet slipped once again and he went nowhere. Illume grumbled and ran at Hastur full force. He hit the ice in an all-out sprint, and with a swing of his sword, cut Hastur's head clean off his shoulders.

Hastur immune to poison.

Sliding to a stop, Illume turned to see Hastur's hooded head bounce across the ice and left a trail of yellow blood as it skidded to a stop. Urtan removed his axe from Hastur's chest, Nari pulled her sword from his side. Illume sheathed his weapon as he stood up.

"That wasn't very hard," Illume replied with a huff.

"Unk tass du lak moor! Fu ha di lak door!" A disembodied voice rumbled the swamp.

Illume glanced around. The traders had made it into the boat and Urtan was well on his way to them. Nari had started to walk toward Illume. She kicked Hastur's head into the swamp.

Hastur's health bar began to refill. It hadn't dropped to zero. In his cockiness, Illume didn't realize it, but the ice had started to crack. Illume's stomach dropped. At the base of Hastur's neck where Illume had made his cut, a small primordial membrane sac formed. It grew until it was the size of his hood.

With a *splurt*, the sac ruptured open and showered everyone with a yellowish mucus. It all happened so fast. Had Illume blinked, he would have missed it. The ice shattered, throwing Nari forward. Illume managed to catch her. Before he could even check if she was okay, Nari was ripped out of his arms.

"Han das hee koo," The same voice rang out, this time from Hastur himself. "Nichh hala foo san too."

Hastur peered over Nari's shoulder. He appeared to have a face like a man with cracking yellowed skin. Sickly green tentacles draped his face. His eyes locked on to Illume's and flashed bright yellow.

Madness of Hastur induced
1% affected
The longer you go without treatment, the faster
*   you'll go mad.*

Trophy Earned
Name: Haita the Shepherd
Type: Bronze
Requirement: Have a perfected class madness spell
*   cast on you.*

Why would you do this to yourself? Welcome to the
Minds of Madness.

Illume felt something tick within the depths of his mind. His health bar became visible as it dropped by a tiny fraction. The remaining bit was replaced with a sickly green color. This stunned him for a moment. Tears streamed down Nari's face as time slowed down for Illume. Trillian lunged from the boat at Hastur.

A massive tentacle shot from the water and wrapped itself around Trillian's neck. Illume lifted one hand to blast him with magic while the other went for his sword. Three tentacles burst through the ice. Two grabbed each wrist and drew his outstretched arms to his sides. The third wrapped around his throat and squeezed.

Struggling to breathe, Illume clawed at the slimy tendril as it coiled around his neck. His health wasn't dropping, as he was able to get just enough air to stay conscious. Hastur held Nari up before him. She was kicking, clawing, and stabbing anywhere she could. It wasn't harming him.

"I have heard of you Cryomancer," Hastur's deep voice rumbled within Illume's mind.

It was so powerful that Illume's health dropped just from hearing it. Illume charged each hand with shock magic and unleashed what he could. It didn't even faze Hastur.

"You wish to show your strength to me," he continued.

Illume's health dropped more. Illume changed his magic to healing magic and flooded himself with it. His health began to restore.

"Many have sought the blessing of Hastur," he continued. "They have been punished for their hubris. As will you be!"

Hastur opened his mouth. Needle-like fangs protruded from behind his lips. Hastur pulled Nari toward him and bit into her neck. She let out a cry of pain. He withdrew his teeth. Nari's neck healed instantly. Hastur dropped Illume. Illume caught himself and stood up in the waist-deep water.

Illume opened his arms to catch Nari as Hastur threw her at him like a rag doll. Illume managed to catch her. As he did, Hastur waved his hand as a tentacle returned his hood to him. Hastur placed the hood back on his head. It seemed to become one with the rest of Hastur's robes.

Hastur moved back into the water. He seemed completely unfazed by the attacks made against him. He disappeared into the depths of the swamp's water. Illume turned to Nari, who was desperately grasping at her neck.

"You're okay," Illume said softly. He took Nari's hand. "You're not bleeding."

Illume walked Nari to the land. He wanted to check her out with more scrutiny before they got onto the boat. Nari held on to Illume like her life depended on it as they made their way to the soft ground. Trillian shook his head as he rose to his feet.

One Handed Level up x2
Endurance now available.
Sharper now available.

Two Handed Level up x2
Bone Crusher now available.
Meat Bag now available.

Level Up Available x2
2 Skill Point Available
4 Attribute Points Available
Madness has decreased attribute point availability.

Illume blinked the screen away. That wasn't important now. Nari clawed at her neck as if ants were under her skin. Illume struggled to hold her hands back.

"No!" she whimpered, her voice trembling in fear. "Get it out of me! Get it out of me!"

Nari looked at Illume. The whites of her eyes gradually turned yellow. Her golden hues changed to a sickly green. Illume used his healing hands on Nari. The light flowed from him but seemed to be stopped from reaching Nari by a sickly green field that surrounded her.

Nari's throat tightened. She tried to speak but was unable to. Her breathing became labored as tears streamed down her terrified face. Horror cascaded through Illume. His vision began to blur as the thought of losing Nari crept into his mind. He ran his fingers through her hair and stared into her eyes.

"Stay with me," he pleaded. "You're going to be okay, I promise. Just stay with me."

Nari's body relaxed as her eyes rolled to the back of her head. Her eyes shut, she would have fallen to the ground had Illume not caught her. Illume immediately felt for a pulse. She had one, but just barely. It was so weak, he had to double check to make sure he hadn't imagined it altogether. He focused on her so her health bar would appear. It was full, but it flashed green.

Trillian limped over to Nari. He sniffed her head before he let out a low, sad howl. Illume stood and walked to the island's edge. Urtan made sure the traders waited for them. He helped Nari onto the boat.

"Will Nari be good?" Urtan asked.

"I don't know," Illume said softly. "But we need to get to Moot."

Illume grabbed a blanket and laid it over Nari. He gave her forehead a soft kiss as he ran his fingers through her hair.

"I'm so sorry, sweetie," he whispered. "I'll fix this, I promise. You were right. We should have waited. This is all my fault."

Illume stood, a light-headed sensation grabbed him. He swayed for a second before he caught himself. Urtan looked at Illume with concern.

"Is Illume okay?" he asked.

Illume shook his head as his vision began to blur. He fell forward as everything went black and he passed out.

Madness 2%

6

TOXINS

You've been poisoned.
-30 Health 190/220

ILLUME'S EYES BOLTED OPEN. A sharp pain stabbed at the back of his skull. He groaned as he sat up. The musky stench of the swamp seemed lighter, the breeze stronger. Illume glanced around. None of his people were rowing. Urtan gave a nod to Illume as their gazes met.

"Urtan got help," he said softly.

Illume stood up in the boat. Hooks gripped the inside edges and were attached to long ropes. Each rope was attached to another boat. Dozens surrounded Illume. It was the Barnogian army he'd left behind. The boats weaved silently through ruins of a city that had long since been claimed by the swamp.

Stone that was once white was now green with moss and algae. Brass bells that hadn't rung in centuries were muted in their shine by mud. Lizards, alligators, and other creatures, the likes of which he'd never seen before, climbed around the ruins.

A soft breeze flowed over the water into Illume's face. It was accompanied by a fine mist. Illume looked up river. Between the outcrops of land masses, the water grew from a mossy green to a soft blue. The sound of a waterfall filled the air. As they followed the bend in the river, Illume gasped.

A waterfall that would put the Niagara Falls to shame stood before him. Halfway up the falls, an outcrop of trees broke it into an upper and lower falls. From those trees poked brass rooftops and white stone. It was a citadel within the falls. White stone bridges connected two land masses where water interrupted the swamp's flow.

Illume was frozen in awe at the sight before him. He didn't move, even as the boats disappeared into the falls under the city. Illume braced himself as his row boat moved toward the wall of water. He looked down and shut his eyes as they passed through. Everyone on the boat got soaked head to toe, Illume included.

Opening his eyes, Illume looked up to a massive cavern that had docks built against the stone. Lime green flames illuminated the inside of the falls. The docks were busy. The humanoid reptilians known as the Barnogian took supplies off of ships from normal-looking humans.

Several smaller people caught Illume's eye. They had a slightly different tint to their skin but had pointed ears like an elf's. They held Illume's attention for several seconds.

"What are those?" Illume asked.

"Urtan don't know," Urtan replied.

Illume glanced around. He intended to redirect his question to Nari since she'd actually worked on the game. She wasn't sitting with any of the traders. Now that he looked, Trillian wasn't on the boat either.

Illume felt the boat jerk forward slightly. He turned to see several Barnogian soldiers pull on the ropes. As they approached the docks, John marched down a flight of stairs. He looked angry. As the boat reached the docks, Illume climbed out. John continued to walk at him at full pace and gave Illume a powerful shove. Illume staggered back.

"What's wrong with you!" John roared. "I told you to wait for me!"

"I didn't know when you were going to be back," Illume yelled. He stepped forward and gave his brother a shove right back. "You're the one who said Hastur grew stronger by the day!"

"Thanks to your impatience, Nari is fighting for her life," John snarled. "Hastur injected her with venom."

The news hit Illume like a hammer. His stance relaxed as his frustration for his brother evaporated into concern for Nari.

"Where is she?" Illume asked. "I have healing magic. I can cure her."

John shook his head. He gave Urtan a hand out of the boat.

"I already tried that," John reported. "Healing magic did nothing to help her. She is with Moot's best toxicologist."

"They have toxicologists here?" Illume asked.

"No!" John replied in an annoyed tone. "They're called healers. You should know that! This one just specializes in toxins. Now follow me and I'll bring you to her."

Following John around the docks, Illume spied several beings who appeared to be smaller Ents help unload heavier boxes. They had bark for skin, leaves for hair, and moss for beards. Some seemed to be able to extend themselves like a growing tree.

"John look, a Groot!" Illume pointed out.

"Those are Kapre." John replied. "Keep up!" he said harshly.

Illume kept a good pace behind John. They climbed a set of stairs that were wet from the constant mist that filled the cave. No one seemed to mind the water. As Illume and John reached a dry part of the cave system, Illume channeled his heat magic around him. It drained most of his mana, but the water that had soaked him evaporated.

"Where is Trillian?" Illume asked.

"Trillian is with Nari." John explained. "He's the only thing keeping her alive right now."

This made Illume's heart jump. Was she really in that bad of shape? She was a coder, a real person, and the bite healed immediately. Did it really cause that much damage?

"Had we not found you, she'd probably be dead already," John added. "Trillian refused to leave her side."

John's pace quickened as they continued to climb stairwell after spiraling stairwell. Torches of green flame lit their path. Eventually, they broke out onto the white cobblestone streets of Moot. John glanced around and pointed to his right.

"This way!" he declared.

Illume didn't pay any attention to the city around him. He kept his eyes on his brother and every movement he made. The tone in his voice and the urgency of his walk hammered home the severity of the situation. The last time Illume had seen John walk like that was when their parents had been in a car accident.

The walk only took about five minutes. They reached a house made of stone. Black soot covered the former white rock, which made it stand out. Unlike the other houses that had doors, this one had only a curtain.

John pushed the curtain aside and entered. Illume followed. The crashing of the waterfalls vanished as they entered the house. It was illuminated by orbs that glowed from the walls. Roots appeared to have taken over the inside of the house. It felt more like they'd walked into a tree rather than a stone building.

Poison effect -30 health
Health 160

Illume felt a wave of nausea wash over him. He staggered forward, grabbing the wall to steady himself as the room spun for several seconds. He summoned his healing spell and attempted to cast it on himself. His health rose back to full for a split second before it dropped again.

Poison must be dealt with before healing can be successful.

"Illume, are you okay?" John's voice sounded far away.

"I've been poisoned," Illume replied.

He looked up at John. The room stopped spinning,

but his vision darkened for a brief moment. As his wits returned to him, Illume pushed off the wall and stood under his own strength.

"Good thing we're here, then," John said.

John pressed forward. Illume followed farther back into the house. Shelves of items displayed prominence the farther back they went. Most of them gave off the slight glow of magic. A soft rhythmic tone echoed from the back of the house, accompanied by a sickly orange light.

John stopped as he entered the back room. Illume followed. Inside, a woman with a staff of gnarled wood stood over a book. The books pages flipped on their own as the orange light he'd seen flowed from the book and into her. She had a thin yet strong frame. She wore a tattered red dress that was adorned with beads, bones, and beetle carcasses.

The dress hung off her shoulders that had long braids, dreadlocks, and strands of loose hair draped over them. Her skin was grey. Her face was so cracked and dry that it looked to be made of stone, a stark contrast to the soft skin of her shoulder that peered from behind her hair.

She bounced forward and back as she chanted. Her eyes were completely blacked out. Her mouth was more gum than teeth and what teeth she did have were rotten. As the light entered her, she closed her eyes and stood straight up. She inhaled sharply. She spoke in a language that sounded like that Hastur had spoken in.

The light coursed through her body and down to her hands. Her left hand gripped her staff tightly while her right hand, which shared the same skin as her face, had the appearance of an open bird's claw. She walked over to Nari, who lay on the ground, unconscious. Illume moved forward toward her. John threw his arm out and stopped him.

"Don't interrupt," he whispered with a sharp tone.

Illume fought all of his instincts and forced himself to stand still. The woman continued to chant as she placed one of her talon-like fingernails on Nari's forehead. She dragged her nail across Nari's skin and formed two crescent moons that connected in the center of their curve. She drew small arrows that pointed into the crescent shapes with straight lines at the base of the arrows.

As the orange light faded, Trillian's soft blue mana started to dance into Nari. The symbol the woman had drawn pulsed softly and gradually turned blue as Trillian's mana flowed into Nari. The woman turned and looked straight at Illume. Her gaze froze him in place. What should have been the white of her eyes was crimson. Her irises were a pale blue, almost grey. A bruised red encircled both eyes; it stuck out, even against her stony skin.

"You have been gazed upon by the great old one!" the woman hissed.

Her voice crackled with age and dark magic use. She slammed her staff on the wooden floor.

"The madness will take you if the poison doesn't first," she added.

"Mighty Hecate," John said. "We have come to buy your services."

"I know this boy," she snapped. "I see more than your men tell me! You wish me to heal the girl?"

"I do," Illume nodded.

"I cannot," Hecate declared. "The venom of the King in Yellow is a death sentence. Only mana may slow its spread."

Illume felt his heart race. His body strained as stress washed over him like the waterfall.

Madness 3%

Illume's health bar dropped permanently a little more.

"Do you know anyone who can?" Illume pleaded.

"Only a god may cure this poison," She cackled. "But you will die long before you find him."

Hecate walked over to one of her shelves. She pulled an old, sickly green book from the shelf. She turned to Illume and held the book outstretched. It had a magical sigil on it that was reminiscent of a biohazard warning.

"Only by learning this can you hope to survive," Hecate cackled.

Illume reached out for it. She drew it back and shook her head.

"Nothing in this world is free," Hecate added. "Thirty-five thousand polis."

"That's robbery!" John almost yelled.

"Only four of these remain," Hecate rebutted.

"We don't have that!" John blurted.

"I do!" Illume said with hope in his voice. "It's at Cryo's Quarry, but I have that much."

"Bring it to me and the book is yours." Hecate relented. "But I warn you. The distance is far too great for you to travel, frozen one. She will be gone long before you get back, as will you!"

Illume looked back at John. The little spark of hope that had ignited ever so briefly was extinguished.

"What are we going to do?" Illume asked.

7

OMNI-LINGUAL

"I CAN FAST TRAVEL," John replied. "I can't take anyone with me and it may take a few in game hours, but since I've been to Cryo's Quarry, I can travel there fast."

"How can you fast travel?" Illume asked with a jealous scoff.

"I'm not trapped inside the game," John reminded him. "According to Mr. Matsimoto, some of the rules that apply to you don't apply to me and vice versa. I can only carry about ten thousand polis at a time, so it'll take several jumps."

"When will we be able to get going?" Illume asked as he glanced at Nari.

"First thing tomorrow morning would be my best guess," John replied.

"Do it," Illume instructed with a nod.

John nodded. His face went blank as he entered his menu. Several seconds later, he completely vanished. Illume turned back and gazed upon Nari. He moved over to her and knelt down. He ran his hand over her forehead and into her soft hair. She was burning up.

"Is there anything I can do to help her now?" Illume asked again.

"The swamp is a dangerous place," Hecate replied. "Such heavy armor and weapons will weigh you down, frosted one. Find new garments if you wish to survive this journey."

Quest Added:
Obtain New Equipment

With that, Hecate shooed Illume away. Illume gave Nari a kiss on her sweltering forehead.

"I'll be back soon.,You make sure nothing happens to her." Illume told Trillian.

Trillian huffed and nodded. He laid his head back down and gently pressed his nose against Nari's arm. His mana continued to flow into Nari. Illume turned to leave. Just as he was about to exit the room he glanced back at Hecate. She waved the book at him.

"Don't waste time," she warned. "Poisoning

doesn't take long and this is the only remedy in the city."

Poison effect -30
Health 130

Illume felt himself grow lightheaded for a few seconds. He held on to the wall to steady himself. As his vision focused better, Illume released the wall and made his way back to the street.

There had to be a square near this shop where he could find what he needed. Several people of the Kapre, human, Barnogian, and what he assumed was a small elf carried supplies toward a large square structure with a bulbous roof.

Illume followed the group. He listened in on what they were saying. He couldn't recognize the language; it was different from any of the other languages he'd heard so far. Now that they had gotten closer to more people, Illume deduced it had to be this land's "native tongue."

Looking up at the massive structure, Illume noticed the intricate carving in its masonry. From the images within the structure, Illume guessed it was a standing history of the city. Images of men and women made of scales and wood working together to make a village started on the left side of the building.

His eyes followed the intricate carvings. Their city grew, and from what Illume could tell, they were attacked by an invading army. The attackers appeared human. Despite this, the natives seemed to be able to fight them off. From the looks of it, this war went on for generations as the city grew.

A little over halfway across the structure were images of men using magic. They destroyed a cliff face behind the city and brought a massive lake down on their enemies. It looked like many of the natives died, but what was left was modern-day Moot. Near the end, a group of men approached Moot with a white flag. It was a new generation.

The new generation appeared to offer peace and advanced technologies to the inhabitants of Moot. The final panel was mankind being welcomed into the city of Moot to live peacefully alongside its inhabitants.

"If only we humans could really pull something like that off," Illume murmured to himself.

He approached the massive wooden doors and pushed on one. It creaked open, and as it did, the vast noise of the market escaped. Illume entered to find a market not dissimilar to the one in Lapideous. It had food on the left and transitioned to smithing on the right. At least some things were constant.

Illume stepped in to a flurry of noises that seemed to be different kinds of communication, none of which he understood. In the center of the market, Illume saw Urtan standing tall above everyone else. He looked lost and concerned. Illume pushed through the crowd. He dodged the treemen and stumbled over what looked like a cat made of moss and even got hit between the legs by one of the short elves. Illume stopped as the sharp pain jolted through him like electricity.

"You must be a south pole elf!" Illume groaned as he grabbed his crotch.

"That is no elf," A husky voice cut through the noise. "That is a Sprite. Usually, they have wings, but they retract them in enclosed spaces."

Illume glanced over his shoulder. A weathered man stood leaning on a walking stick. He wore a traveling cloak that hid his figure. Illume could tell that his hair at one time was a dark brown, but now grey had begun to take hold. The lines in his face accented his strong features. Illume shook off the strike and approached the man.

"Please tell me your name is Sean?" Illume asked, as the man looked identical to Sean Bean.

"I am Mercator." he replied. "I am on the council of Moot and my domain is trade. You, being human, I imagine can understand little of the many languages of Moot. There is a merchant in here that sells items that can change that."

"Where is this merchant?" Illume inquired.

Mercator lifted a large hand. Illume got a glimpse of an inhumanly large sword tucked within his cloak. Illume followed Mercator's finger to a small setup on the far side of the market. A mousy-looking man stood behind the table and glanced around nervously.

"That is Wayson, the merchant of tongues," Mercator said. "He will have what you need."

"Thank you, sir. What do I owe you?" Illume asked.

He reached for his coin purse. Mercator lifted his hand. He shook his head and leaned back onto his staff.

"My job is to make sure this market runs smoothly," Mercator replied. "I do not accept money from its citizens."

The weathered man turned and made his way back into the crowd. Illume walked over to Urtan and the other traders. They didn't seem to know what they were doing, since they couldn't communicate with the would-be patrons.

"Urtan, grab some money and follow me!" Illume said.

"Where Urtan go?" he asked as he reached for a small chest of coins.

"We're going to see if we can't get you something to help with the language barrier," Illume replied.

"Good! Urtan needs to sell," the orc exclaimed.

Illume continued to push through the crowd. Urtan

stayed by Illume's side. No one seemed to pay them any mind except for the Sprites. They were hateful little creatures. One tried to pick Illume's pocket, another attempted to steal his dagger. It wasn't until one tried to steal the ring off his finger that Illume decided to use his frost magic.

A wave of cold shot out of Illume's hand. The Sprite who was trying to steal from him immediately pulled back his little hands. Frost covered them like gloves and he shrieked a hateful-sounding tongue lashing in his native language, which Illume couldn't understand. He scampered off and screeched some more.

No Sprites came close to Illume or Urtan after that. They were able to navigate the crowd and reach the merchant. He took one look at Urtan and gulped hard. His already pale features seemed to turn whiter in contrast to his curly red hair.

"What can I do for you sirs?" he asked in a nervous tone.

"Little man seems scared," Urtan pointed out.

"That he does," Illume agreed. He turned back to the merchant. "Don't worry about Urtan here. He's quite the softy. We have a little problem. My friends and I don't know the local languages and Mercator pointed me in your direction."

The merchant visibly relaxed as Illume mentioned

Mercator. He let out a sigh of relief and nodded in approval.

"Mercator's a good man. He's kept me in business when I should have gone under." He pulled out a box from under his table that was adorned in different kinds of jewelry. "I'm assuming you'll need linguistic magic?"

The merchant opened the box. Inside were many different rings made of wood and necklaces made of silver. Illume noticed a golden shine to each of them. They were imbued with magic.

"How much for a ring?" Illume asked.

"Rings are three hundred. Necklaces are five," the merchant added.

Illume glanced back at Urtan. The orc opened the chest and counted the money. He shrugged.

"Urtan only have enough to equip us," he whispered. "Urtan and traders unable to buy anything for home."

Illume nodded. He glanced into his own coin purse. He had maybe enough to armor and arm himself as well. Even if John brought more money back with him, they would still need extra for bribes, supplies, and magic.

"I still have to armor myself," Illume said softly. "My traders only have enough to establish a healthy trade here. If I buy a ring for myself and I tell my guys to start their trade with you every time they come in, would you be willing to give them the items they need?"

The merchant hesitated for a moment. He shook his head and closed the chest.

"I'm not in the habit of giving things away." The merchant gazed hungrily at Illume's armor. "You give me one piece of that armor and you can have everything you want!"

"The armor stays with me!" Illume attempted to use as much charisma as he could. "They will have new wares from all over the plain-lands. You will have first pick of it all."

"I would need payment first," the merchant declined. Unfazed by Illume's charisma, he tapped long fingers on the wood counter in front of him.

Illume huffed. He needed to put more points into charisma. He turned to Urtan and held out his hand. Urtan pulled one of his little figurines out and placed it in Illume's open palm. Illume turned and faced the merchant once again.

"How about I give this to you in good faith?" Illume asked.

"That's just a glass bird," the merchant scoffed. "What about the necklace? Don't get cheap on me now."

"This necklace stems the effects of poison. I'm

poisoned right now, so I'm pretty sure if I take it off, I'll die," Illume said. "And that's true, it is a little glass bird. A little glass bird that was made by my really big friend here. A friend who knows how to imbue magic into his work."

"What good will a magic bird do me?" the merchant asked. "I am not amused, if you can't tell."

"You're a small guy. I bet you are a target for muggings and people who try to intimidate you, am I right?" Illume asked.

"I do get robbed a lot," the merchant confessed in an embarrassed tone. "I'm a lover, not a fighter. Mother says there is no shame in that."

"Okay, so we toss one of these into the first ten trade deals." Illume glanced at Urtan.

"Urtan like bird!" he replied.

Urtan's voice had a whine to it as he shut the chest and set it on the table.

"I know you do, Urtan. It is a beautiful bird and I promise I'll make it up to you," Illume pledged.

"Fine, show little man what Urtan makes," the orc relented.

Urtan took the axe off his back as well and set it on the table. He took several steps back and held his hands out to make a clear circle around him. Urtan nodded as he stiffened his body.

"Urtan ready," he called.

Illume threw the bird at Urtan's feet. A flash of light followed by a massive gust of wind and a small vortex threw Urtan nearly twice his height into the air. Urtan landed on his feet with a hard *thud*. Illume turned to face the merchant, who stood there stunned.

"You've got yourself a deal!" he blurted as he extended his hand.

8

RE-EQUIP

ILLUME REMOVED his ring of clarity and slid it into one of his pockets. The wooden ring he had paid for had a slight glow to it until he slid it onto his finger. The glow flared then danced over the ring. It left an artistic swirling pattern in the dark wood.

> *Superior Ring Found*
> *Ring: Circle of the Alltongue*
> *Weight: +1*
> *Worth: 100 polis*
> *Circle of the Alltongue allows its wearer to both*
> *understand and be understood by all but the most*
> *ancient of languages.*
> *Look at you, Mr. Omnilingual! Rosetta Stone should*
> *hire you.*

Scrutinizing the ring, Illume couldn't help but notice the beautiful craftsmanship was certainly of a higher quality, but he paid three times what it was worth. With his current speech skill, he'd only be able to sell it for fifty, maybe seventy-five polis. He shot the merchant a cold gaze.

"You know I can see how much these things are ACTUALLY worth, right?" Illume asked.

"I don't know what you're talking about!" The merchant tried to play dumb.

Illume lifted his hand and showed the thin man his new acquisition. He pointed to it.

"This is only worth one hundred polis," Illume revealed.

The merchant's already pale face went even whiter. He swallowed hard and shook his head.

"It-it really isn't!" he stammered unconvincingly.

Illume stepped forward. His jaw clenched as he felt a deep frustration brew within him at being cheated.

"You're lying to me now?" Illume snarled. "You're going to give my people a FAIR price from here on out, otherwise, our deal is terminated. Do I make myself clear?"

"Of course. Yes, sir!" the merchant blurted as what little color remained drained from his face. "I'm just trying to make a living here."

Madness: 4%

Taking a deep breath, Illume calmed himself down. His health bar was just over half and the "permanent" damage to his health bar was beginning to show. Illume left the merchant to think about his actions before he moved through the market. Urtan returned to the traders with their own "translation rings."

The roar of random languages merged together and became recognizable to Illume. The ring around his finger was warm and glowed softly as it allowed Illume to hear the proper translations.

"Armors of all kinds!" one merchant shouted.

"Items from the east!" another cried.

"Weapons, get your weapons here!" a third yelled.

That third one caught his attention. Illume walked over to the Barnogian forger. Judging by the curves in the dragon scale looking steel armor, this particular merchant was a woman. She had leather shoulder armor that was inlaid with metal plates for more protection and a cloak with the hood pulled back.

Illume couldn't quite tell the difference between a male and a female Barnogian just yet from their facial features. To him, they all looked like a broader-headed velociraptor from *Jurassic Park*. The main theme song from the franchise played in his mind. He couldn't tell if that was part of the madness wearing on him or his own normal nerd factor kicking in. Fortunately for Illume, his charisma with women was significantly higher since the end of his last adventure.

He approached the merchant's table. Behind her were racks of weapons of all shapes and sizes. Several lay on the table for him to see as well. Illume folded his arms as he gazed over the beautifully ornate weapons.

The Barnogian merchant leaned over her table. She set her hands close together to make her breasts more apparent, a clear sales tactic that undoubtedly worked on most.

"From the looks of it, you don't need a new bow," she said in a soft voice. "How about a new dagger?"

"I'm more than happy with my dagger," Illume replied.

He didn't completely shut down her avenue of flirting. He might need it to get a better price.

"I have been told I will need a faster sword for the adventure I am about to go on," he added.

"Mmmm, that sounds like so much fun," she purred as she walked over to a weapons rack.

Illume had seen plenty of displays like this at bars with well-dressed men. He had to admit it was a useful tactic. He'd seen it work more times than not. The Barnogian pulled a single-handed straight sword from the rack.

"You know I used to be an adventurer like you until

I took an arrow to the knee," she said in a sultry tone as she set the weapon down.

Illume picked up the weapon. He gave it a few spins. It was balanced perfectly and had a manageable weight, but he didn't like the feel of it in his hands. Illume set the sword on the table and shook his head.

"I'm sorry. I'm used to handling something a little bit bigger," Illume replied as he leaned against the table. "I'm going up against something very... VERY dangerous. Do you have anything specialized?"

She offered Illume what he assumed was a sultry smile. He couldn't really tell with the stiff-scaled complexion she had. She knelt, and Illume heard the creak of a chest from under the table. As she stood up, she had a cloth in hand.

The cloth was wrapped around what he assumed was a weapon. She set it down and unwrapped what was inside. A hilt wrapped in onyx leather was the first thing he saw. The handle had a slight curve to it with a sharp claw-like hook on the end. Its circular cross guard was made out of what looked like bone, which had an intricate carving of a dragon's face on it.

The merchant lifted the sword free from its covering. It was in a long black sheath that was only a few inches shorter than Illume's current weapon. She grabbed the hilt and gave it a twist. Two dark red, almost black blades shot out from the cross guard. They looked like they would leave a nasty cut.

With a single, fluid draw, she pulled the sword from its sheath. The blade was clearly inspired by a scimitar. It had waves in the metal that appeared to be flames. The blade itself was the same dark red, near black color as those that protruded from the cross guard.

"This is Dovabane," she pronounced loudly. "It was forged in the breath of a dragon and used to slay a great serpent, one that was said to be destined to consume the world! Its bones were used for the cross guard and the sheath while a claw was used for the weapon's hilt. It is a beautiful blade."

Illume couldn't deny that it was a beautiful weapon. Undoubtedly, it would be expensive. If dragons were as powerful in this world as they were in other fantasy worlds, he couldn't pass up the opportunity to get his hands on this blade. He offered her his most flirtatious smile as Illume turned on his charm.

"It's nothing compared to its wielder," Illume played along. He could swear he saw her blush. "And how much would such a fine piece cost me?"

"Maybe just a drink or two at the nearest tavern," she leaned in and whispered.

Illume gently took her hand, which still gripped the sword. He gracefully slide it from her hand into his. Illume surprised himself at his level of smoothness. He was getting better at this whole talking to the opposite sex thing. He held the weapon between them.

"I have an elder god to kill. But maybe after that, I'll get you the drink," he playfully flirted.

"It's three thousand polis," she said softly. "But for you, I think I could let it go for fifteen hundred."

Illume reached out and grabbed the sheath. He slowly slid the sword into its home.

"How about this? You let it go for a thousand, and when I return, I'll bring you the head of a Hydra," he offered, hoping this place even had one.

Her scaly eyebrow raised. She nodded and held out her hand.

"You have yourself a deal," she offered.

Illume gave her hand a shake before he paid her. Illume turned to walk away. He felt like he needed a shower for flirting with her like that. He was shocked that he managed to pull off a successful bargaining.

You're a dirty boy, he said to himself in his head. *A dirty, dirty boy.*

Speech Level Up
Speech increased by 2%
Matched with your intelligence, it looks like you
    finally got all the help you needed!

At this rate, you'll be able to talk anyone into anything at any time!

Rolling his eyes, Illume had a feeling that the leveling information was still being sarcastic toward him.

Poison effect Health -30
Health: 100
You don't have much time left!

Side-quest Started:
Bring the Lusty Barnogian a Hydra Head

Illume attempted to use his healing magic once again. His health bar filled as he held the spell. Once his mana ran out, it collapsed back to one hundred. He tried a healing potion. It did nothing. Unfortunately, he didn't have any anti-poison potions either.

He stopped by a potion peddler and took a look at his wares. There were no anti-poison potions there either, none that didn't have horrible side effects to humans anyway. The way Illume saw it, his only chance was to quickly finish his shopping and get back to the witch.

Illume made his way to the armorer who wanted to buy the armor Nari had made him. There was no way he'd surrender this armor, even if better protection came along.

"I'm sorry, this armor is not for sale," Illume replied to the Kapre.

"Fair enough," it replied slowly.

Unlike the Barnogians, the Kapre had no physical features to give away if they were male or female. They were just humanoid treelike entities. Thankfully, from the looks of it, the Kapre had armor of all different kinds for all different species.

"I heard you tell the lusty one you would fight the King in Yellow?" the Kapre asked.

"I am. He already nearly killed a close friend of mine and cursed me," he explained. "The only way to save her and myself is to kill him."

Illume glanced back over to the Barnogian merchant. She was flirting with yet another male customer. A brow raised as he pointed to her.

"Is there a book written about that one?" Illume asked.

"Several!" the Kapre scoffed.

"Yeah, I've come across some of them," Illume chuckled. "A little too graphic for my taste."

"As for mine!" the Kapre replied. "How much money do you have left? You only haggle that well if you are low on money."

Illume glanced into his pouch. He had about two

thousand polis left. It would be enough to get good armor, but it wouldn't be enough to get the top of the line he'd need to complete his quest.

"I know how this works," Illume said softly as he shut the purse. "I tell you how much I have left and you say that it's just enough for this really great piece of armor that's worth half of what I'm going to end up paying for it."

The Kapre merchant nodded some. It pulled a satchel off the ground and placed it on the table. It offered him a friendly smile, and even though its eyes were pure black marbles, they seemed kind.

"That is how most work around here," it agreed. "But you are taking on the King in Yellow and I guarantee the armor I wish to sell you is worth more than you have."

The Kapre continued, "There are things I need and depending on how much is in that purse of yours will depend on what I send you to fetch. So how much do you have?"

Sliding his coin purse off his side, Illume dumped the remaining money onto the table. The merchant nodded in approval and slid the satchel over to Illume.

"This is yours," the Kapre said.

Illume cautiously took the satchel. He slung it over his shoulder as the merchant slid all of the money into a chest. Illume glanced inside. A series of robes were folded together nicely within the pouch.

"What do I owe you?" Illume asked.

"The heart of a Dziwozona," the Kapre revealed.

"Bless you," Illume said.

"No that's not a sneeze, boy! A Dziwozona," the merchant repeated. "Also known as a Mamuna or Boginka. They are deep within the swamps and their hearts make an excellent forging material."

"As soon as I find one, I'll remove its heart for you." Illume nodded.

Side-quest Added:
Retrieve the heart of a Dziwozona/Mamuna/Bognika
  for the Kapre Merchant

Illume left the market and returned to Hecate's house. He stopped in the main room as she whispered to or with something in the back room. Illume held the sword in front of him and drew the weapon. It let off a deep *shing* that sounded like it was accompanied with flames.

New Sword of Legend Discovered:
Name: Dovabane
Damage: +10
Weight: +7

Worth: 5000 polis

(Got yourself a steal, good job!)

This literal sword of legend is thought to be a myth
even by those who wield it. Forged in the fires of a
dragon and quenched in its blood this
unbreakable blade causes +10 fire damage and
ignores armor made from natural resources. It
will heat up metal armor for an additional +3
damage.

Nodding in approval at the impressive stats for his new weapon. Illume set it down for a moment and pulled out the cloak from the satchel.

New Armor Discovered:

Robes of the Kapre

Armor: +25

Weight: +5

Worth: 3000 Polis

Kapre robes allow a +25 resistance to poison.

They reduce bursts of dexterity and speed by 50%.

Gloves of the Kapre

Armor: +7

Weight: +1

Worth: 1000 Polis

*Kapre gloves enhances your strength and grip
by +10.*

*Blessing of the Kapre prevents you from having your
weapon knocked from your hand.*

*Protection of the Kapre will allow a shield to form on
your non-weapon hand should it be needed.*

Boots of the Kapre

Armor: +7

Weight: +1

Worth: 1000 Polis

Kapre boots allow for a Feather Effect.

*Feather Effect: So long as there is ground under your
feet you will not sink. Be it mire, muck, sand, or
snow.*

Hood of the Kapre

Armor: +5

Weight: +1

Worth: 750 Polis

*Kapre hoods increase intimidation by +10 when up.
Allows for protection from elemental damage by
+5%. Prevents critical hits for headshots.*

Special Kapre Ability:

*When worn in a full set Kapre armor, robes, or cloaks
prevent enemies from landing a critical hit and*

adds +5 armor for each piece worn. Full armor allows a 50% grounding perk.

New Armor Stats: +64

New Stats:
Strength: +40 Getting near superhuman.
Dexterity: +20 Back down to a normal person.
Incumbrancer: 110.5
Poison Effect: -30
Health: 70
I'd get help now if I were you!

9

POISON CONTROL

REMOVING his Dwarven armor Illume donned the Kapre robes. He immediately felt lighter and more energized as they briefly glowed a soft green. Illume placed Dovabane on his left hip. He left the sword Nari had made him on his back attached to his quiver. Bloodlust sat just over his butt and his chimera bow was slung over his shoulder.

Poison Effect: -10
Health: 60
The Kapre were good to you!
Quest: Acquire New Equipment Complete.

Illume picked up his armor and made his way to the back room where Nari was being treated. Upon entering, he set his armor down next to Nari's supplies.

John had returned and was just finishing up counting the Polis for Hecate. She appeared pleased. As John finished his count, Hecate made her way over to Illume.

For someone with a walking staff and slightly hunched over, she moved surprisingly gracefully. She had the spell tome in hand and stopped just before Illume. She held the book out to him and he graciously took it.

"Looks like you arrived just in time," Hecate taunted. "Thank you for your business."

Taking the tome, Illume opened it with a little resistance as the spine popped and cracked with age. A green light swirled through the air from the book and into Illume. From the outside, he imagined it looked like a Disney witch's magic. The light flowed into him rather aggressively. It felt like his body was being washed from the inside out.

As the light faded, the tome fell apart like an old dry leaf. Within seconds, it was nothing but dust that floated lazily to the ground. Illume's vision was a soft green for several seconds. He attempted to blink it away, but to no avail. He looked around the room, as the green eventually faded away completely.

Poison Cured

Poison Control Skill Tree Discovered:

Poison Heal: Healing spells and potions can now
hold their effects. Does not remove poison.
(Passive ability)

Poison Cure: Cures poison from yourself costs 1 skill
point.

Poison Cure Others: Cures others that are poisoned.
Costs 2 skill points.

Toxicologist: Grants full immunity to all poisons,
venoms,or toxins. Costs 5 skill points.

Illume immediately summoned his healing hands. The soft glow of white light filled the room as Illume's health increased. His mana fell, but it stopped at the halfway point. His health had completely regenerated, minus the small portion taken from him for madness.

"Was it worth it?" John asked.

Illume's magic faded and he dropped his hands. He nodded to his brother as his mana recharged.

"Most certainly," he replied softly turning his attention to Hecate. "How did I get poisoned in the first place?"

"You are an outsider," Hecate explained. "The waters here are deadly to outsiders. And you were submerged in it. Now take your new power and find the one who can save your friend."

Looking down at Nari, Illume took a deep breath

and moved to her side once more. He took her soft hand in his and gave it a gentle squeeze before he brought it to his lips for a soft kiss. His eyes burned and his vision blurred at the thought of losing her.

"Stay strong," he whispered to her. "I'll be back as quickly as I can."

He leaned down and whispered softly in her ear. Something that was meant only for her and no one else. A silent tear rolled down his cheek as he pressed his forehead against hers. Illume raised his head and gave Trillian a scratch behind the ears.

"He can't go with you," Hecate pointed out. "His mana flow is the only thing that stems Hastur's venom. The power of a dragon is a rare and beautiful thing."

"How do we know you won't try to steal or sell him when we're gone?" John asked.

Trillian gave Illume's hand a lick before he lay back down. Illume could tell that the dragon was concerned for Nari.

"It is a dragon," Hecate snapped. "There are very few powers in this world that can outclass a dragon and I assure you none of them are in this city. Now go!"

Hecate lifted her hand and her staff. Both began to pulsate with orange light. She threw both arms out and Illume felt himself pushed back. He closed his eyes for only a split second, but as he opened them, Illume found himself on the dock next to John.

"Did she just Doctor Strange sling ring us?" Illume asked in a baffled tone.

"I think so." John scoffed.

John looked around for several seconds until he saw one of the boats he'd sailed in on. He waved for Illume to follow.

"Where are we going?" Illume asked.

"Hecate said the one who granted her magic could rival Hastur," John explained as he hopped into the boat. "She's confident that he has the power to cure Nari."

Illume followed his brother to the boat while he listened intently. He hopped in, sat down, and grabbed an oar.

"So where do we start looking for this being?" Illume asked.

John untied the boat and pushed off the docks. He sat down before his eyes glazed over for a few seconds. Illume received a soft ding and notification.

Noobmaster68 wishes to send you a waypoint.
Do you wish to accept?

Yes! | *No!*

Illume focused on *yes.* Immediately, his map was pulled up. A cave was marked directly south of Moot. It was a little over halfway to the coast and had the name Sunken Castle attached to it.

"You think we should add to our party before we actually go there?" Illume asked.

He closed the map and rowed in unison with John, who had sat down next to him. John shook his head.

"NPCs are a little too unreliable for me," he replied. "They always jump into your line of fire and end up dead anyway."

"That may be true, but what happens to me when you have to log off?" Illume wondered out loud.

"Not going to happen. Not today anyway," John informed him as they rowed through the waterfall. "Sarah and the kids are at her mom's house for the weekend, so it's just you and me like the good old days."

"Just like the good old days." Illume replied.

Madness 5%

He was less than enthused. In the good old days, they could stop the game whenever they wanted and go outside to play. Illume wouldn't be gradually going mad and the one person who meant the most to him wouldn't be dying slowly on some witch's floor.

"Those are interesting and expensive robes," John pointed out. "Where did you get them?"

They rowed past the ruins and back into the swamplands. Illume pulled up his map briefly to see if they could dock on land at some point and walk the rest of the way.

"I made a deal with a Kapre," Illume replied. "What I had left in my coin purse plus the heart of a Dziwozona."

"A what!?" John exclaimed with a laugh.

"I'm assuming some sort of swamp demon," Illume shrugged. "The merchant said their hearts are good for forging."

"Well then, this'll be a fun trip," John retorted sarcastically.

Both men continued to row for several hours in silence. Illume pulled up his map a few times. After numerous failed attempts, he found a portion of land where they could "dock" and make the rest of the way on foot.

"Think you have enough weapons?" John teased to break the silence.

"They're like a gun. I'd rather have them and not need them than need them and not have them," Illume replied.

John rolled his eyes.

"Oh, I'm sorry. I don't see you armed with any weapons!" Illume snapped.

"It's because I AM the weapon," John sneered. "That's what happens when you put everything into magic stats AND have robes that enhance that magic."

"And what happens when you run out of mana?" Illume asked.

"I never will. My mana regen is through the roof and magic damage is like being hit with a freaking cannon," John defended himself in an offended tone.

"A glass cannon maybe," Illume deadpanned.

"Bite me," John huffed.

Illume roared with laughter and nearly fell out of the boat.

"Bite me? What is this? The mid-nineties?" Illume managed to squeeze out between laughs. "All I'm saying is it pays to be more than a one-trick pony."

"I'm more than a one-trick pony, Ray," John taunted. "And I'll prove it to you."

"It's Illume here," Illume replied.

"Then it's Obscuritas for me!" John snapped.

"Obscuritas is a stupid name! It's a mouthful, it's really long, and…"

"Oh, and Illume's not?!" John yelled.

Illume punched John in the shoulder.

"And no one wants to have to keep repeating it!" Illume finished. "So I'm calling you John."

"Your name doesn't make any sense either!" John yelled as he punched Illume back.

"Yes it does!" Illume retorted with a sarcastic laugh to his voice. "Illume means ray of light. My name is Ray and I always play the non-homicidal maniac good guy in games, unlike someone I know!"

"Oh, look at me. I know how to translate my name into other languages," John mocked.

"You're a doctor!" Illume blurted. "You're supposed to be smart. How do you not know simple stuff like this?"

"I'ma punch you in the throat," John threatened with his brows raised.

"Oh yeah?" Illume challenged. "Just go ahead and try it."

Illume reached across the boat and slapped John in the face. John's jaw clenched and his face turned red.

"Are you serious right now?" John replied as he slapped Illume back.

"Hell yeah, I'm serious!" Illume replied.

He slapped John's other cheek. There was a brief pause before the oars were dropped into the boat and both men broke out in a flail of arms and hands. Each one slapped the other as often and as quickly as possible. Both aimed for each other's faces but only occasionally made contact.

The boat rocked in the water as the siblings

continued to slap "the living crap out of one another" as their mother used to say. After several minutes of slap-fighting, both men dropped their arms in exhaustion. Nothing but their panting and the natural sounds of the swamp around them filled the air.

"My God… Are we there yet?" John asked.

Illume gave his brother one more powerful slap across the face.

"No," he replied.

10

HEART OF THE ISSUE

ILLUME TOOK over the rowing as John "logged out" to grab lunch. With the time dilation, Illume managed to get the boat aground and secure it firmly. He picked John up, carried him out of the boat, and set him next to a tree, where John sank into the mud.

Looking at his boots with pride, Illume jumped up and down. He didn't leave so much as a footprint in the soft ground. Illume returned to the boat. Small metal rings protruded from its sides as holders for the oars. Use had built up a layer of dark oil. Illume rubbed some on his pointer finger.

Walking over to John's avatar, Illume made a circle around one eye. Under his nose, Illume drew a large, curled mustache, the kind that would have made the monopoly man proud. Illume stood back and admired his creation. He smiled to himself and even laughed. That was, until John began to move.

Illume quickly pulled up his map. He plotted out a land route to the sunken castle. There was a small village located between them and their destination, but other than that, the path looked clear. It wasn't far, and if they made good time, they could reach their way marker by nightfall.

"So I have some good news and bad news," John stated.

Closing his map as John stood up, he looked at the mess on his robes and wiped it away as best he could. John trudged over to Illume, the grease on his face still clear as day.

"The Dziwozona isn't a species," he divulged. "It's a singular being and a NASTY piece of work."

"It's an actual thing?" Illume asked as he fought back laughter.

"Yeah, it's a swamp 'demon' from Slavic mythology," John explained. "Has a nasty habit of stealing children and replacing them with her own. Not really sure what she did with the children, but I'm positive it's not good."

"Where'd you find this? Wikipedia?" Illume asked.

"Yeah, looked it up while eating lunch," John replied. "Why are we on land?"

"I found a path that leads to the sunken castle. I figured it'd be faster on foot than by boat," Illume explained. "Especially if the fog starts to roll in again. So how do we kill something like that?"

Illume walked into the thick marsh. Trees, vines, and moss were overgrown everywhere. Illume used his sword to slide away the foliage in their path.

"Website didn't say, but I'm assuming we cut the heart out and that should do the trick," John replied. "People would try to ward her from their towns by tying red ribbons on the structures and the children. Apparently, she is described as an ugly old woman with long grey hair that covers her body. According to legend, she also has a huge set of…"

"Shh!" Illume cut John off.

A soft rustle caught Illume's ear. He stood frozen in the thick overgrowth. Illume's eyes darted around in search of what had moved near them. Straight ahead, Illume saw something dash across their path. His hand instinctively began to chill.

"What are you looking at?" John whispered.

"We're not alone," Illume murmured. "There's something ahead."

Out of the corner of his eye, Illume caught something move as well. It made no noise and had progressed so slowly that had he not seen it move, he wouldn't have noticed the being. A large reptilian head slid from the mess of vines and trees that were next to Illume.

It was a Barnog. Its eyes were wild and had a hint of sickly blue to them. Its lips snarled back to reveal rows of razor sharp teeth. A light foam had formed around its lips. Illume offered the being a smirk.

"Clever girl," Illume whispered.

Just as it was about to lunge at Illume and he was about to blast it with a torrent of ice, a light green flash strobed from behind Illume. The vines around the Barnog lashed out and wrapped around its body. In an instant, they completely constrained the beast. Its health bar came into view along with the title of the character.

Feral Barnog

The health bar fell rapidly. Illume glanced back to see John's hand outstretched. He slowly turned and closed it. The beast's health dropped as steadily as John's hand moved. John clenched his fist tightly and a spine-tingling crack rippled through the marsh. The Barnog's health dropped to zero. John then relaxed his hand and the beast fell to the ground, lifeless.

Several loud shrieks echoed from the depths of the

marsh. The sounds of large creatures running faded into the distance. Illume crouched to inspect his would-be attacker. It was slightly misshapen and didn't look like the normal Barnogian. It also didn't have any weapons, armor, or clothes of any kind.

"Hmm, never noticed that before," John huffed.

"What?" Illume asked as he looked up at his brother.

"There has been an increase in the local populations turning feral," John explained. "Some said those who suffered from it were misshapen. Maybe even twisted by some dark power."

John moved to Illume's side and kneeled. He turned the beast over. It was a female. John opened its eyes. The pupils were dilated. He lifted its lip to reveal the rows of teeth.

"That's what I thought," John added.

"What are you thinking?" Illume asked.

"The Barnogs only have one row of teeth like a komodo dragon." John opened his victim's jaw. "This one has rows of teeth like a shark. I don't think this is a Barnog. According to lore, the children that Slavic swamp witch would steal would be replaced by look-alikes. The problem was those look-alikes were often deformed, misshapen, or mutated in some way."

John looked around at their surroundings.

"You're thinking that these feral locals are her children?" Illume asked.

"Maybe so. That means she has a small army out there and she could be working with Hastur."

"Then how do we take out her army?" Illume asked as he stood up. "Because we don't have time to organize an offensive."

Illume slashed his sword into vines that blocked the path. They walked forward once again.

"That is the good news," John replied. "With beings like Dziwozona, if you kill the mother, the children die."

"Every cloud, I guess," Illume mused.

Throughout his cutting of the vines, Illume's stamina gradually dropped. Their pace had been steady enough that Illume was able to stretch out his stamina usage for a longer period. Now that they had gotten closer to the village, the vines had grown thicker, which resulted in his using the last of his stamina.

Illume stopped for a minute. He'd been channeling his frost magic back onto himself in an attempt to prevent himself from overheating. Surprisingly it had worked. Illume leaned against a tree as the moldy stench of the swamp filled his lungs with each labored breath. The look of John's face paint dulled the exhaustion slightly.

"Move aside. Let me show you how it's really done," John said gloatingly.

John stepped forward. He put his hand out, which produced the same green light as before. The vines, branches, and roots all fell away like a curtain being pulled open. The plant-life formed a natural arch opening and allowed for clear passage to what looked like the village a few hundred yards away.

"You could have done that this whole time?" Illume demanded.

"Yes," John replied with a haughty tone.

"Then why'd you let me exhaust myself for the past two hours!?" Illume yelled.

John pointed to his face. His right eyebrow cocked up slightly as his finger made circular movements.

"Even if I'm away from the game and it's paused, I can still see what you're doing if you're within my character's line of sight," John informed him. "Consider us even."

"Fair enough, I guess," Illume conceded.

He sighed and shook his head before he pushed off the tree. Illume looked down the path his brother made. The roots formed into a solid path for John to walk on so he'd stop sinking into the muddy earth.

The village ahead was mired in a thin fog. It was translucent, unlike Hastur's fog, and bore a natural feel to it. Eerie outlines of houses and buildings could be seen. With the gnarled branches of trees that hung overhead, the village had a very Tim Burton feel to it.

"What are the chances there is something in there waiting to kill us?" Illume asked.

"Oh, one hundred percent," John presumed. "And whatever it is will certainly be something nasty."

With that, John walked through his little self-made tunnel. Illume followed closely behind. He put his sword away and drew his bow, nocked an arrow and brought his weapon to the ready.

"Why don't you carry any weapons?" Illume asked in a near whisper.

"When this character was brought in, almost all of my skill points were returned to me," John replied. "Like I said before, I have more mana than most opponents have health. All my points went into giving me pretty much unparalleled power in the form of necromancy."

"How were you able to control the plant-life like that, then?" Illume asked as they crept forward.

"We're in a swamp." John put his hand up and the tunnel behind them closed off. "Most of the plant-life here has some form of rot to it and since it's not as complicated a structure, say, as a once living being, I am able to control it with greater accuracy than a body."

"That is actually really cool," Illume replied.

"I know, right!" John said as they reached the end of the tunnel.

"Either way, you may end up needing a weapon," Illume said.

Illume handed his bow to John. John took the bow and shook his head.

"You know I'm a terrible archer, right?" John asked.

"Oh, you're the worst!" Illume smirked. "I'm not giving you my bow."

Illume unstrapped his sword from his back and held it out to his brother. John returned Illume's bow as he accepted the sword.

"I am just loaning this to you until we get through this and can get you one of your own," Illume explained.

"How do I use this?" John asked.

"Are you serious?" Illume scoffed.

"It's not like I just press 'x' anymore!" John rebutted.

Illume shook his head. He readied his bow once again as he started to make his way to the village.

"Stick them with the pointy end," he deadpanned.

"Yes, Lord Snow," John called back in a taunt.

Walking closer to the village, Illume's eyes darted here and there in hopes of seeing an actual person. The first tree he passed Illume noticed had something dangling on it about halfway up. It was small. He paid it no mind. As he moved forward, Illume noticed that other trees had the same small items hanging on them.

Illume pressed forward, entering the town. The fog was thickest here. He could only see a dozen or so feet in front of him, but the menacing outlines of the buildings surrounded him with an ominous aura. Illume moved closer to one of the buildings that had a forecourt to it.

Stepping onto the forecourt, Illume noticed fog was slightly thinner closer to the buildings. He could hardly see the forge attached to the side of the building. Its fires were long since extinguished and weapons still hung on the racks, rusted and dull.

"Illume," John called.

His tone was worried. Illume turned to see his brother standing next to one of the forecourt building's pillars. A small trinket was wrapped around it like those on the trees he'd passed.

"It's a ribbon," John added.

John used his thumb to wipe away the moss that had grown on it to reveal a bright red that contrasted starkly with the forest green. Illume felt his stomach drop. John moved two pillars along. It had a similar ribbon on it. John wiped the moss away to reveal a bright red. Illume swallowed hard. In the distance, dozens of high-pitched screeches filled the air. Illume rushed to his brother's side and tried to look through the fog.

"John?" Illume asked.

"Yes," John replied.

"Has your mana replenished itself yet?" Illume's tone was stern. "I think we're going to need it."

11

THE CHILDREN

JOHN FLUNG both his hands out to his sides. They shone a soft green, as did his eyes. Illume watched as his brother's glowing hues glanced around the area as if he were seeing things that Illume couldn't. The screeches grew louder and louder as the sounds of heavy footfalls began to stampede.

"Vitium voco invandus!" John chanted. "Vitium voco iuvandus!"

The light of his spell grew brighter. Illume caught a glimpse of movement within the fog. He drew his bow and aimed it into the haze. A loud screech erupted as a disfigured human burst through the curtain of mist. Illume released his arrow. It embedded itself into the being's eye before it fell to the ground, lifeless.

Illume nocked another arrow while his brother continued to chant. His head swiveled in every direction as the sounds grew louder. Illume fired blindly into the fog based on a scream. He saw a life-bar flash before it dropped to zero with a critical hit notifier in his view.

"What is that? Latin?" Illume asked.

"Shut up. I need to concentrate," John snapped before he continued his chanting.

Five more creatures rushed from the fog at Illume and John. These appeared to have massive tumorous growths that covered their bodies. Their grotesque features were contorted by their screams.

Stepping in front of John, Illume drew his bow and focused his ice magic into the arrow. Illume lowered his aim and fired at the attackers' feet. The frigid blue arrow struck the ground and exploded in a flash of blue. Ice encompassed the attackers and froze them solid. Illume's mana bar dropped by a third.

Illume grew nervous. He looked around to see that they were surrounded. Dozens of mutated, rotting, or near zombie beings had stopped at the edge of the brothers' eyeline. They just stood there and stared at Illume and John as if waiting for some sort of order. John continued chanting behind Illume, eyes closed.

"Please tell me you're almost done," Illume snarled.

He was good, but he wasn't fast enough to kill them all with his bow. Illume lowered his weapon and slung both his bow and the arrow he'd drawn back into their resting places.

"Just a few more seconds," John groaned. The spell had begun to put pressure on his body.

Illume took a step forward. He looked at the ground. Most of it was ankle deep in water and other parts had about an inch of coverage. Illume stepped off the wooden deck that he and his brother had been standing on and walked into the clearing before him.

Madness 6%

"You want us!" Illume roared as he looked around. "Come and get us!"

A single humanoid mutation stepped into view. Its eyes were black as night and its skin pale as the moon. Oozing pustules decorated its rotting body. It held up a rusted sword and pointed it at Illume.

The creature's jaw seemed to unhinge and opened to an inhuman width while its eyes bulged. An unearthly scream erupted from the creature unlike any of the others Illume had killed.

Madness 7%

Taking a deep breath, Illume focused on keeping his heart rate steady. The entire circle began to charge in on him, as Illume assessed the angles of his opponents. He dumped all of his mana into his hands as he summoned every amp of lightning he could.

Illume's hands sparked and crackled with energy as his mana bar hit zero. He held the magic back as the monsters closed in around him. He waited until they were five feet from him before he unleashed his magic.

A blinding flash of light accompanied by a deafening *BOOM* ripped through the small village. Bluish white arcs of electricity shot out through the water in all direction. The closest attackers were almost immediately turned to ash. Some of the more pustular beasts a little further out literally exploded.

Past them, the would-be attackers froze with shock, while they took serious damage. Beyond that, the damage was minimal and hardly slowed the group down. Illume's health dropped by half as the lightning struck him through the water as well.

Kapre grounding perk offers 50% shock resistance.

Illume would have let out a sigh of relief, but he saw movement behind John. Drawing his dagger, he threw it as hard as he could in John's direction. The dagger passed an inch away from his brother's face and embedded itself into one of the smoldering mutated beings hard enough to kill it.

Illume placed his hand on Dovabane. He'd killed or seriously injured half of the attackers, but there were still a lot of them left. Illume looked up to activate his leveling screen.

Level up Available x2
New Mechanic Available
The Marshlands have unlocked the option
for the player to level up only once should
they have more than one level available.
Would you like to use both?

Yes! | No!

Illume selected no and decided to use just one level up. He placed both his attribute points into health but left his skill points untouched.

New Stats:
Health 240

Closing his leveling menu, Illume's health filled up to the point where his madness meter was at zero. His mana filled up as well. Illume gripped Dovabane and drew it. A low growl accompanied the *shing* of the sword as it was drawn. The blade immediately burst into flame as he held it at the ready.

Mana Burn
+5 Damage
+5 Fire Damage

A mutated Kapre swung its massive trunk-like arms at Illume, who swung his sword at the beast. The flaming blade sliced through the Kapre's arms as if they were made of butter. Illume's wooden attacker immediately burst into flames and fell back. He noticed his mana bar dropped as he attacked.

Critical Strike x3

Illume wasn't surprised, as it was wood against fire. Illume quickly blocked a battle axe from slicing him in half. He punched the Barnogian in the face then slashed him twice across the chest. Illume's mana dropped some more.

"John, a little help!" Illume yelled as he cut down another. "Any time now!"

Illume blocked an attack from a broad sword. His vastly superior blade cut halfway into his opponent's weapon. They locked together. Illume tried to pull free, with no luck.

A shadow flashed behind Illume. It was a short-sword that was being swung at his head. Illume tried to free his weapon but was unable to. By instinct, he threw up his left arm and prayed that his armor could take the hit.

A shield of roots exploded out of Illume's left glove in a circle about the diameter of Illume's torso. A jolt shook Illume's arm, but his health stayed intact. Illume let out a snort of surprise and used all his strength to wrench his weapon and his shield free.

With a spin, Illume cut the head off his would-be attacker while he bashed the former owner of the broad sword with his shield. By now, the remaining attackers had closed in on Illume. They were all within reach and Illume didn't have the speed, skill, or mana to take them all out.

"Now or never, John!" Illume roared.

"Got it!" he shouted.

Dozens of roots shot from the ground, all of which had a faint green glow to them. Each root skewered an attacker through their lower body and exited at different places around their upper body. Black ooze poured from their wounds as the roots pulled themselves back out violently.

Each fell to the ground, lifeless and without a sound. Illume turned to his brother, who smirked and shrugged. A mutated attacker leapt from the roof in front of John. John drew Illume's sword and stabbed it through the neck. The attacker's health bar became visible and fell by two-thirds. John, in shock, released the sword. Both John and the mutated being fell to the ground.

"Your sword skills suck!" Illume taunted.

He walked over to his brother, ran Dovabane into the mutated being's chest and killed it, then pulled his sword from its neck and offered it back to his brother. Both men sheathed their weapons.

Level Up Available
Active Skill Points: 3
Active Attribute Points: 4

"Think it took you long enough to cast that spell?" Illume asked in a sarcastic tone. "I wasn't sure if I was going to die of old age out there waiting for you or one of these mutated freaks to get to me first."

"It's a legendary level spell," John rebutted. "It took up all my mana, but it killed everything, didn't it?"

Illume looked out at the lifeless bodies that were strewn around the road. He shrugged. There was no way to argue with the results.

"Good point," Illume conceded. "If I were you, I'd put some skill into swordplay next. That stab would have killed him if you had even one set of stats improved in the sword skill tree."

Illume retrieved his dagger from the corpse behind John. He sheathed it onto his lower back. His mana had begun to regenerate as the shield that produced itself was retracted back into Illume's left glove.

"Well, that gave me three levels, so I'll be doing that," John replied. "Without Nari, we could use more swords."

Illume huffed. He had been so distracted by the battle, his worry for Nari had evaporated. Needless to say, it was back in full force now. He looked around at the town and shook his head.

"How many people do you think died here?" Illume asked.

"Not sure." John shrugged. "But if I've learned anything from games like this, it's that finding out about local lore is important."

"No duh," Illume tossed back. "Chances are one of these poor souls has information on what we're hunting that could come in handy."

"Split up and meet back here in ten minutes?" John asked.

"The second we hear any more of these, we cut our search short." Illume pointed to one of the corpses near him.

"Sounds like a plan," John replied.

John entered the structure attached to the forge. Illume crossed the mire. He stepped over the bodies of the recently deceased. They looked as if they had already begun to decompose.

Illume made his way into a small two-story log house. As he pushed on the door, it fell right off its hinges with a crash. Illume flinched at the loud noise and froze in place. He listened for any other noises that indicated he tipped off someone. There was nothing.

Moving into the house, Illume winced as the stench of mold filled his nostrils more and more with each step. Illume drew Dovabane. The soft growl accompanied its unsheathing. It ignited once again and bathed the musky house in a dim light.

Everything was rotting, rusting, or spoiled. In the corner were two skeletons, each with shattered ribs and a crushed skull. However this town had become a ghost town, something told Illume it wasn't done peacefully.

Illume searched in drawers, cabinets, and chests downstairs. Anything that didn't immediately fall apart at his touch had nothing of value in it. Illume moved his way upstairs. Each step creaked as he climbed them. His sword stood poised at the ready as it illuminated his path.

He reached the second storey. Illume looked around to find more of the same. Rotten wood, broken drawers and chests, and rusted weapons. There were several beds upstairs. Their mattresses were in decent shape.

Illume flipped the first mattress. Nothing. The second also tumbled with no effort. Still nothing. He wasn't surprised; he just thought he'd be thorough. When Illume flipped the third mattress he saw that underneath it was an old, weathered leather book that was tied shut with several strands of rope.

Picking up the book caused the frail ropes to break and fall to the ground. Illume lifted his sword away from the pages. He sat on the bed frame, which groaned under his weight, and opened the book. Illume decided to start from the back, as he expected to find most of the interesting additions there.

The fifth day of my twenty-third harvest.

We had such a lovely few months, Brandon and I.

I thought he was one of the few good men in the surrounding villages. He was not. He left me today by the little lake where we had our first date.

Today was much like that day, sunny and warm.

The forest, grass, and crops never looked so beautiful. Perhaps because I thought he would propose today. Instead, he left me. He taunted me in front of everyone from the other villages.

It was all a joke to him. A cruel prank. A kind man dressed in yellow found me crying in the woods.

He told me he could help make the pain go away if I went with him.

Mother, Father, if you find this, know that I am

okay. I leave only because if I don't, I will take revenge on Brandon and those that mocked my pain.

I love you and I will return one day.

-Ibura

Closing the book, Illume coughed as a plume of dust kicked up in his face. He coughed again and waved the dust away from his face. Illume then got to his feet and looked out of the shattered window to where John was.

"John, I found something!" Illume yelled across the road.

12

DUNGEON OF GOD I

ILLUME LEFT the house and waited for John in the middle of the village's main path. He flipped through the book some more, but nothing written within it was of any use, as anything of interest was disfigured or erased by mold or even the humidity of the swamp. John walked out of his structure. He had a ledger in hand as well. He flipped pages as he approached Illume, stopping about five feet from his brother. He offered Illume a smile before he lowered the ledger to the side.

"Apparently, this place didn't used to be a swamp-land!" John declared. "A hundred years or so ago, this entire area used to be like the kingdom you came from."

"I got that same feeling from this," Illume shared as he held up the journal. "A girl named Ibura wrote about blue skies. She also wrote about some mean kids and a man in yellow that offered her peace."

"The name Ibura came up in the book I found too!" John replied.

He reopened the book and flipped through it. The ledger appeared to be a standing "police report" for the town. About halfway through the book he placed his finger on one of the entries.

Twenty-fifth day of Snowfall, Ibura was brought in today for harassment.

The locals have been experiencing more and more issues with her. She had manipulated, humiliated, or insulted most of the people in a five-mile radius.

She is staying in the cells tonight for shoving a new healer in town. As captain of the guard, I do need to see that this woman is okay. Ibura keeps saying we shouldn't pity the "stone faced woman."

She will be released to her parents' custody in the morning.

"So this Ibura woman…" John started.

"Probably working for Hastur," Illume finished.

"And judging from the entries, she was a nasty

piece of work before he got his tentacles on her," John added.

Illume tossed the diary away. He opened up his map to see if there was anything obstructing them from their waypoint. The path ahead was mostly clear. Illume closed his map just as John tossed his book away as well.

"Think we can make it to the castle before nightfall?" John asked.

"This place is overcast and dark all day long, John," Illume pointed out. "Does it really matter?"

John nodded as both men walked to the opposite end of the village. Several houses had mostly collapsed. From the looks of it, the only two structures that had been left standing were the ones they both had investigated and found nothing of real importance in.

Illume and John walked side by side for some time without saying a word. The ambient sounds of the swamp filled the air as they held branches out of the way for one another. Eventually, they reached a wall of trees that had been entangled together. Illume reached for his sword until John stopped him.

"I'll get this one," John said in a soft tone. "I'll do it the old-fashioned way and save my mana for when it really counts."

John drew his borrowed weapon from his back and

hacked away at the trees. It took several swipes to cut through each knot of branches, but he eventually sliced his way through. They moved forward and John continued to hack their path clear.

"I do have to say, Illume," John huffed between sword swings, "I owe you an apology."

John was sweating profusely as he turned to Illume. His face was beet red and he panted for breath. John wiped the sweat from his face, taking off the mustache and monocle Illume had drawn on earlier, before he leaned against the sword.

"I was dismissive when you said this place was real to you," John continued. "To me, it's just a hyper-realistic virtual reality game. I didn't fully appreciate the consequences of your decisions here. Killing those things... It's, it's heavy."

John pulled the sword from the ground and swung again.

"I bought the whole immersion kit," John explained. "The scent add on for the headset. The vest that hits you when you are struck in the game. Even though the vest adds weight and tires you as your character becomes exhausted."

"You bought a lot of stuff," Illume replied.

"That's not the point," John added as he cut through the last piece of tree that blocked their path. "The point is that, with all this stuff, I am extremely immersed in your world. It's not even a fraction of what you are experiencing. Killing those things, even though they were monsters, carries a heavy toll."

John sheathed his sword and huffed once more. "Fact of the matter is, I didn't respect you, I didn't respect Nari, and I didn't respect the true danger of this place. For that, I am truly sorry. I will show more respect in the future."

Illume followed in John's path as he hacked and slashed his way through. Once they were freed from the blocked path, Illume moved in next to his brother while John spoke.

"All is forgiven, John," Illume replied. "I can imagine it was hard for you to understand my view. I appreciate the lengths you went to in an effort to better understand my predicament. You're a good brother. I know you're here because you're worried about me. The reason you're doing any of this at all is to put down any threats that could endanger me."

Illume gave John a pat on the back. John pushed forward followed closely by Illume.

"Yeah well, getting to see you safe here is better than not being able to see you at all. Hey—there'd better not be a handprint on my back," John proclaimed.

"There isn't!" Illume replied.

"I'd say we're about an hour away. You want to stop and rest?" John asked.

"I'm good to keep pressing on. I don't want to stay in one spot for too long. It could make us an easy target to track," Illume huffed.

"True, don't want the Hydra to pick up our scents," John replied. "Pop quiz, how do you kill a Hydra?"

Illume climbed over a fallen tree as John ducked under it. Illume mulled the question over in his head.

"Well, if you managed to crush it, that would do the trick," Illume decided. "If we had a weapon that could pierce its scales, just about any other kind of attack would work, but their armor is nearly impenetrable save for the necks,"

Illume thought through the process out loud. "Cutting the heads off won't work, and according to the mythology, it's the middle head that's vulnerable. You have to cut the center throat."

"You are correct, sir!" John praised as he gave Illume a thumbs-up while his brother brushed by.

"Can you do me a favor next time you log off?" Illume jumped over a small knee-deep puddle. "Can you look into Ambrose Bierce and H.P. Lovecraft?"

"Sure thing. Why do you ask?" John asked as he jumped over the puddle too.

"You remember how our fourth grade teacher Mrs. Sawyer was a little off?" Illume asked.

"Yeah, but she was really cool!" John defended.

"I'm not arguing that. I wished more of my teachers were like her. Fact is she made us read Bierce, where there was a character referred to as 'The King in Yellow.' Lovecraft borrowed from Bierce forty years later. Maybe in their mythos they could hint at a way of killing Hastur," Illume speculated.

"How do you know all this?" John wondered as the ground grew slightly more solid.

"One of the first games I covered was called 'The Mind of Madness,'" Illume explained. "It was a cosmic horror game inspired by H.P. Lovecraft's book by a similar name. While doing research for the game, I came across a few things that seem familiar in this part of the map."

"That won't be a problem," John responded. "It may take a while, but I'll find something. Out of curiosity, how badly did he beat you?"

Illume shook his head. He didn't feel like re-living the memory of his failure to protect Nari.

"You saw the aftermath," Illume replied.

"I did," John said.

"It spoke for itself," Illume added.

Illume fell silent. He drew his sword as well and helped John cut away the overgrowth.

"Maybe I should make a clearing?" John asked as he hacked away.

"No," Illume stated. "If we get ambushed again, your mana needs to be full."

John nodded in agreement and kept cutting away. The overgrowth began to thin once again. This time, there was no fog that fell into the clearings, rather beams of sunlight that cut through the tree canopy.

For the first time in several hours, Illume and John were not walking in water, but rather on dry ground. Regular bushes and not swampy tendrils decorated the path ahead. John looked at Illume with an eyebrow raised.

"Are you seeing what I am?" he asked as he nodded ahead.

Illume's eyes narrowed. He looked around at the ground before him.

"I don't see anything," Illume said.

"Come on, nerd!" John prodded. "Think back to that geology camp you made Mom and Dad send us to."

Thinking back to that summer when he was twelve and John reluctantly joined him at geology camp, Illume couldn't help but smile. One of the classes was how to identify natural geological disasters by differing rocks in the same place.

Illume noticed a slight color variation in some of the stone. A sedimentary boulder sat on its side with thin lines that pointed vertically. Illume glanced at John.

"That stone has been upturned," Illume pointed out.

He looked up to see if there might be a hidden cliff it could have fallen from but there wasn't. Illume walked around the smallish clearing, where several different kinds of rocks were stacked in an arch across the clearing. The ground below his feet was firm yet uneven.

"Remember what the professor said?" John asked.

"I do! This is evidence of an upheaval in the tectonic structure... Something SANK here!" Illume shouted in excitement.

"Very good. Now what do you think it was?" John asked.

Illume opened his map. Both men were right on top of their waypoint. He closed the map and looked around the grounds. Some moss, but mostly grass grew in the clearing.

"Judging by our waypoint the god Hecate told us about should be around here," Illume replied. "If history has taught me anything, it's that gods are typically kept underground."

John knelt. He placed his hand on the ground and closed his eyes. Illume felt the ground tremble. He braced himself as he looked at John.

"What are you doing?" Illume asked.

"I'm looking for the entrance," John answered. "But this is burning through mana. I hope I find it soon!"

The ground continued to rumble for several more seconds before it fell silent once more. John opened his eyes. His face went pale as he climbed to his feet.

"What's wrong?" Illume questioned.

"Something bad happened here," John replied.

"Obviously, there's a god somewhere under us and chances are he's not friendly," Illume pointed out.

"It's not that," John rebutted. "There are thousands of dead buried here. I could hear their screams when I reached out. It was a massacre. They all died at once, in agony."

Swallowing hard, Illume sheathed his sword and drew his bow. The ground began to rumble once more. Illume looked at John, who shook his head. Illume felt the rocks under his feet shift. He leapt toward his brother just as the ground under him gave way.

John grabbed Illume by the forearm. The sinkhole spread out past Illume's jumping range. By some mad luck, John stayed on solid ground. Illume swung as he fell and slammed into a rock wall. Illume held John's forearm tightly. He let out a grunt from the impact before he looked up at his brother.

"You okay?" John asked with a strained voice.

"Perfectly fine!" Illume sneered.

John looked past Illume. His jaw dropped and his eyes grew wide.

"Holy crap!" John whispered in awe.

"What? What is it?" Illume asked in a panic as John's hand slipped.

Illume looked over his shoulder into the sinkhole. His stomach dropped just like John's jaw. Illume released his brother's forearm and fell three feet to a ledge underneath him. He looked over the side at the thirty-plus-foot drop.

"John!" Illume called up without moving his head. "I could be wrong, but I don't think we're in Kansas anymore!"

13

DUNGEON CRAWL

THIRTY FEET below Illume was a massive door of metal. It had intricate swirls hammered into it with spikes that protruded at asymmetrical intervals. A soft red glow danced through the swirls that gave the door a truly malevolent appearance.

John dropped down next to Illume. The door was easily five to six times their height. Had it not been at a lower angle, it would have been truly intimidating. Illume glanced around for a path to get down. There was a thin passageway that would require some jumping, but it looked to be traversable.

"You really think this is it?" John asked in awe as the lights grew brighter.

"It has to be, unless the god of chaos and mischief is above us," Illume replied.

Illume made his way down the path, hugging the

wall as he did. John followed behind several seconds later.

"How do we know he's down here, though?" John continued.

Rolling his eyes so hard they nearly fell from his head, Illume let out a sigh of annoyance before he replied.

"Remember that game that came out in 2011 where you played as a mortal with the soul of a dragon?" Illume asked.

"Yeah," John replied.

"In the fifteen missions where you dealt with one of the gods, how many took place above ground?" Illume asked as he leapt to a lower portion of his path.

"I'm not really sure," John replied.

"At least thirteen of them," Illume replied. "And at least half of them were in some sort of buried shrine."

Illume walked up to the massive doors that were at a ninety-degree angle from him. He pointed at them and offered John a sarcastic smirk.

"With how revolutionary that game was and how many others it influenced, I'd like to point out…" Illume looked back at the doors. "The glowing demonic-looking doors that are buried underground in the heart of a desolate swamp that is overrun by malformed demon people. THIS is where it'll be, I promise you."

"I bet you we find something else that will lead us to this god," John protested. "I'd bet almost anything we will have to bounce around the map at least two more times."

Illume glanced at his brother with a raised brow. He offered his hand to John.

"The usual bet?" Illume asked.

"The usual bet," John confirmed.

John shook Illume's hand and nodded. Illume stepped out onto the doors. They didn't budge. Illume looked around for handles for him to pull on. Nothing. Crimson light washed over Illume as the spells in the doors grew brighter.

"Any idea on how to open this thing?" Illume asked.

"Yep!" John called back.

The tone in John's voice was reminiscent of when he'd typically prank his brother. Illume turned to see that John stood near a pedestal. John's hand sat on a brass button with an emerald top and dropped several inches as he pushed it.

A low groan rang out from under Illume's feet, he glanced down just as a gust of stale air shot from between the doors and into his face. Illume took a step back and waved the putrid scented air away.

Looking back to his brother, Illume sighed. John had an ornery grin on his face as he waved at Illume and the doors dropped open. As in a popular coyote cartoon, Illume didn't immediately fall. He looked at John, who was laughing, while Illume's stomach was launched into his throat as he finally fell.

Illume had been standing a little over halfway up the doors when they'd opened. The angle at which the castle had sunk into the ground meant that he had way too far to fall, meaning the impact would most likely kill him.

The younger of the two brothers drew his sword and slammed it into the ground. Sparks flew as Illume's stamina started to drain. He decelerated and finally came to a stop a little under halfway through the main hall. Illume's stomach dropped back into his gut, making him laugh as the adrenaline of his drop began to wear off. He looked up to see John step into the sunken castle.

John approached Illume, standing upright at a ninety-degree angle to him. Illume's brow knitted together in confusion for a brief moment, before he fell through the air and slammed into the ground. Gravity had shifted for Illume. He groaned from the impact before he rose to his feet.

"Why'd you do that?" Illume groused as he pulled his sword from the ground.

"Because it was funny," John smirked.

Illume looked at the massive stone carved hall. Soft

blue flames ignited by themselves on staggered pillars, fully illuminating the hall. Rusted chandeliers dangled above Illume at such an angle that gravity should have been pulling on them.

"Crap!" Illume huffed softly as he put his sword away and drew his bow.

"What is it?" John asked as he summoned his magic.

"Last time I saw self-lighting torches this color of blue was to fight a lich," Illume explained. "A vampire lich."

"Well then, I won't be of much use," John admitted. "I'll kite him if it is one and you can take the experience."

"Thanks," Illume replied sarcastically.

Illume opened his map. The room they were in had a grey outline to it. There appeared to be a door parallel to the brothers that led to a corridor, but it and everything beyond was blacked out, since they hadn't reached there yet.

Illume dragged around his map to see how large this place was. It wasn't terribly large. Their waypoint hovered in the blackness of the map, as far away from John and Illume as it was possible to be.

"Ready for some dungeon crawling?" John asked.

"Always," Illume replied as he closed the map.

Nocking an arrow, Illume drew the bow halfway as

he moved forward. With knees bent he walked silently over the old marble floor. As they approached the doorway Illume had seen on his map, he moved diagonally across the door and scanned the inside for any enemies, then cautiously moved forward through the opening.

"Watch it!" John yelled.

Illume glanced back at his brother. Both of John's enormous feet took up Illume's field of view as John's kick struck Illume like a freight train. He was lifted off the ground by the blow. His robe armor protected him from taking any damage, Illume and John both hit the ground just as a spiked battering ram crashed down from the ceiling directly at chest height in the doorway.

"You okay!" John shouted.

He rolled over and looked at Illume. The battering ram was in its resting place above him.

"I'm good!" Illume replied. "Are you hit?"

"I'm alive," John replied.

Illume pulled himself to his feet. A thin rope lay under John. It had been stretched across the doorway. Illume shook his head.

"I'm sorry about that," he apologized. "That was a rookie mistake."

"I'll say," John panted as he leaned against the battering ram. "Rule one of dungeon crawl…"

"Don't talk about dungeon crawl?" Illume interrupted jokingly.

"Ha-ha," John rolled his eyes.

John stepped into the room and looked around. Illume followed his brother's gaze. There were several old, worn chests lining the walls illuminated by two blue flames. In the center, there was an intricately carved circular stone. Illume looked at the ceiling to see several spikes that protruded from the ceiling directly over the circle.

"I'd keep to the edges," Illume advised.

He pointed to the center of the room. Illume moved to the nearest trunk and knelt in front of it.

"Think there are any mimics in here?" John asked as he moved to another chest.

"Why did you have to say that?" Illume replied. "I didn't, but I am thinking it now."

Illume threw the lid of the trunk open. It was mostly empty, but a bar of gold was sitting next to multiple gems. Illume grabbed them and placed them into his coin purse. There were several old daggers that were worn and dull. He left them behind.

Gold Bar Added
Weight: +5 Worth: 500 polis

Flawless Diamond.

Weight: .05 Worth: 1000 Polis

Flawed Sapphire
Weight: +.05 Worth: 100 Polis

Garnet
Weight: +.05 Worth: 300 Polis

"Find anything good over there?" Illume asked as he moved to the next trunk.

"Some worn out weapons that aren't worth anything," John replied. "There are a few ancient arrows of frenzy if you want them."

Opening the other trunk, Illume saw several books. He picked up one whose cover read *The Lusty Barnog Vol. 13.* Illume shuddered and dropped the book as he shook his head. He wiped his hand off on his lapel as he reached back into the chest and felt a chill grip the room.

Illume looked over his shoulder to see John holding a staff in one hand and a book in the other. The book let off condensed smoke as it danced to the ground. Illume pointed at the book.

"What does the cover of that book say?" Illume arched his brow.

John looked at the tome and scoffed.

"God of Ice Volume: 3," John read. "What's that supposed to mean?"

Illume smiled widely. He walked over to his brother and took the book.

"HEY!" John snapped. "That's my loot!"

"This book series belongs to me," Illume interjected. "I don't know what'll happen if you open this one."

"And what will happen if you do?" John wondered then added, "I'm keeping the arrows!"

Illume cracked open the book. Blue light and ice erupted out of the volume and poured over him. His body temperature dropped so rapidly, it felt like he was encompassed in ice. Illume's sight faded to a light blue for several seconds. He felt the book dissipate from his hand.

God of Ice Volume: 3 Learned
Able to temporarily increase armor rating by
enhancing current worn armor with ice.

Illume's vision returned to normal. He looked at his hands. His armor had a thick layer of ice that covered it. He moved his arms and hands and the ice moved with him as if it were part of his own clothing. The ice that covered him fell to the ground around him and melted almost as soon as it hit the stone.

"What was that?" John marveled.

"It's the reason I'm called the Cryomancer," Illume replied. "These books enhance my frost abilities exponentially. Let's keep moving."

Grabbing his bow string as he pushed past his brother, Illume moved to the exit of the room. He knelt at the doorway to see another tripwire. Illume followed it and could see that it connected to a trap that dropped boulders. At the bottom of the stairwell, he could hear scuttling.

"Stay here," Illume whispered to John.

Stepping over the tripwire, Illume snuck down the mostly collapsed stairwell. He managed to navigate around the boulders and get to the bottom of the stairs. Pressing himself against the wall and glancing around the corner, Illume saw four armored insectoid creatures in the next room. They moved from one side of the room to the other. Illume drew his bow and leaned out from his cover.

Illume fired his arrow which struck one of the armored insectoids. The arrow bounced off and then all four creatures let out a high-pitched squeal and turned to Illume. They charged, each of their six legs letting out a barrage of tapping sounds as they ran towards him.

Turning, Illume bolted the stairs while the insectoids charged after him. Illume was significantly faster and reached the top of the stairs in a hurry. He ran through the tripwire, which dropped all the boulders. They tumbled and landed on Illume's would-be attackers, splattering them like June bugs when stamped on.

Trophy Earned
Name: Turned Tables
Type: Bronze
Requirements: Use a trap meant for you to kill your opponents.
You've got a bug on you!

He glanced down at his shoulder to see a piece of the creature's exo-skeleton had lodged itself onto his shoulder. Grabbing the goopy grey chitin, he threw it to the ground. Illume turned to face John, who held out the arrows he'd found.

"That was pretty cool," John said. "I think you've earned these."

John held the arrows out to his little brother. Illume took the arrows from his brother and placed them in his quiver.

Ancient Arrows of Frenzy x20 Added
Enemies up to level 15 will start attacking everyone and everything around them.
Damage -8

14

THE GUARD

THE BROTHERS MADE their way past the pile of insectoid corpses that still twitched and were scattered all
over the stairwell. Several loose boulders rolled at their
disturbance. John started to laugh as Illume stepped
over one of the twitching legs.

"What's so funny?" Illume asked.

"Remember when we lived in Oklahoma?" John
enquired. "Every June, those massive beetles would
just swarm the house?"

"Oh yeah!" Illume declared. "And we would
dissect them in the backyard. The ones we'd decapitate
would still hop around and fly in circles."

"We were little monsters, weren't we?" Illume
asked.

Reaching the bottom of the steps, they rounded the
corner into a smaller round room. Old suits of armor

lay on the ground half eaten by rust. Broken swords littered the room as well. A long-dead carcass which had a massive spear dug into its side sat in the corner of the room...it was the same creature that Illume had just killed.

"I wouldn't say that," John disagreed. "We were curious kids who wanted to experience life. It got me curious about how nerves worked, which led to the head smack, and we all know that's why I became a doctor."

He added, "Besides, at least we didn't have our faces buried in a screen."

Illume glanced back at his brother, rolling his eyes and then shaking his head. He approached a series of spiked bars that blocked their path. Next to the bars was a chain with a thick ring on the end. Illume pulled on the ring. A soft grinding filled the air as the bars lowered themselves.

"Lot of good THAT did us," Illume replied sarcastically. "You have a screen attached to your face right now while I'm literally living in one."

"This room is some sort of armory," John pointed out. "Should we loot it?"

"No." Illume shook his head. "Rooms like that have little of value. Anything that might have stood the test of time wouldn't outclass what we already have."

Pushing forward and down the dark corridors,

Illume strained to see into the darkness. Soft blue flames illuminated their paths once again. Both men hugged the walls. Neither wanted to trip a floor trap. Illume stopped from time to time to cut tripwires that were placed here and there, his caution preventing an accidental triggering of such a trap.

"Check that out!" John whispered as he tapped Illume's shoulder.

Illume followed his brother's finger. A massive iron gate was fastened against the wall. Enormous spikes protruded from the front of it. Illume looked over the gate closely. There were springs wound tightly where the gate met the wall. Perfectly parallel to the gate was a round stone that stood out from the traditional square stones that covered the ground.

"Remember that trap," Illume said in a hushed tone. "If we meet something that out- classes us, we could kite it this way and let the gate do the work."

"Good idea," John replied.

The corridor attached to the gate was a dead end. Only a skeleton leaned against the walls with several spikes from a trap running through it.

"Let's press on," Illume said.

Both men pushed forward once again. They passed bed chambers that were in a severe state of decay. Inside, Illume only found a few ancient bags of polis here and there. They eventually made their way into what was once a set of barracks that was lined with beds on both sides.

Skeletons lay in their beds with their swords, spears, bows and arrows while magical burns had scorched the bodies.

"What do you think happened here?" John asked.

Stopping at one of the few bodies on the ground, Illume leaned forward to inspect it. Its skeleton was deformed and misshapen. The hump on its back was reminiscent of the hunched humans they'd fought at the village. Illume nodded to the mutated corpse.

"Do you really need to ask that?" he replied.

"No, I guess not," John added.

Illume slung his bow back over his shoulder. He drew his sword with his right hand and his dagger with his left.

"Keep an ear out. Something tells me we'll hear a threat before we see one here," Illume instructed.

"Roger that," John replied as he drew his blade.

"I see you!" a deep voice whispered.

"Did you hear that?" Illume asked.

"Hear what?" John replied.

"The Sauron voice that said 'I see you' just now," Illume persisted.

"Can't say I did," John replied.

Madness: 8%

"Press forward, son of ice," the voice echoed once again. "I am waiting for you."

The voice was deep and rumbled through Illume like an avalanche. The voice was not his own, yet it seemed to come from within his own mind. Illume continued to move through the dungeon as silently as he could with John close behind.

"Are you feeling okay?" John whispered. "You seem a little off."

"I'm just worried about Nari," Illume replied as he pressed forward.

Soft screeches filled the corridors once more. The brothers were careful to sidestep any boobytraps they came across. The noises grew louder the further they pressed on. Parts of the ceiling dripped with water as they snuck through the dimly illuminated corridors.

They passed numerous bodies in various states of decay. Some had been hacked and slashed, others had arrows protruding from them, and some seemed to have their very life essence sucked from their bodies. Illume harvested as many usable arrows as he could until his quiver was full once more.

Illume pressed himself against a wall as they got to a turn in the musty dungeon. He peered around the corner to see several mutated beings shuffling around in circles. Their movements were zombie-esque as they screeched at one another like squabbling siblings.

Pulling one of his frenzy arrows from his quiver. Illume nocked it and drew the new projectile back. Crouching, he moved into the center of the corridor, taking aim at what looked like an orc that held a massive slashing weapon.

Illume watched and waited. The monsters circled each other in a pattern, and eventually, the orc would be in the center once again. Illume bided his time. The second the orc was in the center once more, he released his arrow.

Target has been poisoned.
Sneak attack critical x5

The orc's health dropped by a third. A soft green washed over its pustule-ridden skin, as it straightened up and let out a low growl. Its breath caught in its throat as its eyes widened and its body trembled as if it were enraged.

Target Frenzied

The orc roared and swung its sharpened hunk of metal around wildly. The mutated Barnogian next to it was immediately cut in half in a spray of yellow and black ooze. The humanoid, catlike, and other Barnogs that surrounded it all screeched and attacked the orc like rabid animals.

Health bars for each mutant faded into non-existence as each was damaged by the orc. Their fight didn't last long as the orc was ripped to pieces and thrown around the room like an unfortunate victim of a horde of zombies.

"Looks like meat's back on the menu, boys!" John proclaimed with a laugh.

The remaining mutants all looked at Illume simultaneously. Illume shot John a cold glare.

"I'm all for quoting that movie, but could you please keep it down? Some of us are on our last life here!" Illume whisper-yelled in frustration.

"Should we run again?" John asked as the mutated enemies shambled toward them.

"Uh, yeah," Illume replied.

The mutants charged at Illume and John. Illume stood up and shoved his brother. Both retreated as fast as they could down the dark tunnels of the buried castle. They leapt over the tripwire, but the mutated hit it, causing rocks to fall from the ceiling. Unluckily missing the mutants, who moved too quickly.

"Can't you freeze them?" John yelled at Illume.

"I have no mana potions!" Illume shouted. "If I burn my mana out and we're still in combat until we reach their mother, we're screwed."

John and Illume triggered a trap. Both men dropped to the ground and did a baseball slide as a blade swept from the wall, narrowly missing their heads.

"You're the necromancer. Bring some of these corpses back to life," Illume rebutted.

"That kind of magic takes too long to summon," John replied. "It's not like I'm a magician at a kids party and can just pull things out of my hat with a snap of my fingers."

They leapt over another trap. The first mutate hit the trigger. The second passed by unscathed, but the third got hit in the face with a falling mace. Its health, already low from the orc, dropped to zero.

"One down, two to go!" Illume called.

"The gate is up here!" John replied.

"Hit the switch for it," Illume instructed.

Illume was right on John's tail. John stepped on the trigger as both men ran past the gate's range. Illume stopped and turned. He nocked and drew two arrows. As he took aim, the gate snapped shut. It caught both the mutates in its range and slammed them into the wall in a glorious fountain of gore. Their life bars dropped to zero.

Level Up Available
Skill Point: +1

Attribute Point: +2
Active Skill Points: 6
Active Attribute Points: 12
Overall Level: 21

Friendly reminder:
You have several levels that require activation.
    Strongly recommend using them soon.

Illume shook off the extra messages. He was beginning to level bloat. Illume huffed. He didn't like having all those available skill and attribute points just waiting to be used, but if his first fight with Hastur taught him anything, it was that he'd need all the "cheaty" help he could get.

"Oh, that's awful!" John choked on the smell. "I can taste it in the back of my throat."

"You get used to it," Illume replied. "Death here is not as clean as the hospital."

Illume started to backtrack as he heard John gag behind him.

"You've been around death in the game and in real life before," Illume pointed out.

"Deaths at the hospital aren't like this," John rebutted. "I'm taking the scent visor off, one second."

John's avatar froze for a few seconds. It glitched

and twitched some too before John took control once again.

"Okay, I'm back," John called.

He didn't have any gagging to his tone now. He seemed perfectly fine as he caught up to Illume.

"Whoever came up with these smells is a horrible person," John muttered.

"At least you can get away from it," Illume replied. "I have it all the time."

"Yeah, I guess I didn't think of that," John said quietly. "I guess I don't want to think about a lot of things. How you're down to your last life. How you're stuck in this game. How there's no actual body for you to go back to, even if we could get you out."

"Well, when you put it like that." Illume tried to bring levity to the moment. "I don't know if ever going back is an option for me. I mean, even if I do beat the game, if that's even possible. I miss you and the rest of the family, but just sitting down and missing them isn't going to bring me back. I'm here now. I have to make the best of it whether I like it or not."

"When did you get so mature?" John looked at his brother sideways.

"Don't tell anyone," Illume said with a finger to his lips. "I have a reputation to keep up."

Together, the brothers walked back down the corridor. They passed the pieces of the mutated beings they had killed.

"This is always the annoying part of dungeon crawling," John huffed.

"The backtracking?" Illume asked.

"All the backtracking!" John amended.

"At least we can use traps," Illume added.

They passed through the area where the orc had been ripped apart. Its body parts were strewn all over the softly blue lit room. Illume ignored the chests and potential loot in the room around them.

"Aren't we going to look for loot?" John questioned.

Shaking his head, Illume reached the far end of the chamber. The next cavern. It was massive. There were no sounds like before, but Illume noticed a handful of potions were scattered on the ground. Some were for health, others were for mana, and only one or two were for stamina.

"Boss room," Illume pointed out. "We can loot later."

15

THE FATE OF IBURA

THE SOFT GROAN of Illume's bow string filled the air. Echoes of water droplets as they fell to the ground reverberating off the walls. As Illume silently entered the massive chamber, his breath seemed stolen from him.

On the far side of the massive empty room was a wall of blue crystal. It completely blocked off whatever used to be on the other side of the chambers. The crystal glowed softly. It pulsated with a warm light.

"What do you think is behind there?" John asked.

"If I had to make a guess based off of a programmer's mind, I'd say Ghidorah," Illume mused.

"Oh my God, I remember that movie!" John whispered with a laugh. "Dad used to make us watch that entire series once a month, remember?"

"How could I forget? It was his favorite," Illume replied.

Illume stared into the pulsating crystal. It seemed to draw him in. His body relaxed without him telling it to, as a series of dark whispers echoed into the back of his mind. Illume took note that his health was nearly ten percent gone as he rocked back and forth.

"Above you," the voice echoed in Illume's head.

Illume snapped out of his trance. Without looking, he drew his bow, which still had both arrows nocked. He didn't know how he knew where his attacker would be, he just did. Illume rotated and made eye contact with John.

"What are you doing?" John asked.

"This," Illume replied.

Without breaking eye contact with his brother, Illume fired both the arrows at a forty-five-degree angle above him. The hum of his bow string reverberated off the walls as his arrows whistled through the air. A wet impact splatted out a second or two later.

Critical Hit x2
Target Immune to Chimera Poison

Illume's eyes widened as he read the immunity. John summoned his magics as a blood-curdling scream ripped through the forsaken halls of the once mighty castle. Illume drew and nocked another arrow as he turned with John to face the source of the scream.

From the darkened corner of the ceiling, a creature writhed into the blue light. Whatever it was now, the Dziwozona was once a woman. Long grey hair covered her body. It did nothing to hide the thickness of her mid-section. She appeared almost like a greyed, nappy "Cousin It" only her hands were visible.

The screaming beast released the wall with one hand. Long, black razor-sharp nails released themselves from the rock that they had sliced into like butter. She gripped the arrows and yanked them from her body before she let them drop to the ground.

"Ooooookaaayyyy," John's voice trembled in fear.

"Easy," Illume instructed.

Illume watched as his arrows fell to the ground. He drew back another shot. The Dziwozona leaned forward. The long, matted hair that fell in front of her face seemed to part, which illuminated her chalky skin. Her eyes were all white, but Illume could feel her gaze pierce his flesh like that axe the first time he died.

She stared Illume down for several seconds without blinking. Her lips were sealed with a pale flap of flesh. With a violent jolt, the surface where her mouth was ripped open in a deranged smile that spread from ear to ear. Jagged teeth were visible from behind the strands of skin that still connected her mouth.

She let out another horrifying scream. Her breath caused the connected tissue to flap like a sail in a toxic wind. In a flash, she scuttled across the wall. Illume fired at her. His shot narrowly missed.

"That's straight up Regan!" John yelled as he crossed behind Illume.

"Then pull out your holy water and see if that stops her!" Illume demanded.

Illume fired several more times. The Dziwozona spun around on the wall and dodged his shots once again.

"CRANIUS IGNUS!" John roared.

A skull of pure white fire launched from John's hand and spun through the air with an infernal scream. It was on mark to hit John's target. Illume blinked and the beast was gone. The spell impacted the wall with a blinding explosion that rocked the chamber.

Dust and rubble fell from the ceiling as Illume's ears rang. He caught something move out of the corner of his eye. He threw his left arm up. The root shield immediately formed in front of Illume's head.

The impact was like being hit with a wrecking ball. A wrecking ball with ten stiletto daggers attached to it. Eight of his attacker's nails pierced his shield like it was tissue paper as he slid nearly ten feet backward.

"Why does it always have to be claws!" Illume ground out. "JOHN, A LITTLE HELP HERE!"

"Ignis vitis!" John yelled.

Illume's shield sprang to life. It sparked with embers as it bent out toward his attacker. As his shield morphed away from him, Illume made eye contact with the cursed woman. She screamed at him once again. Reaching deep within himself, he summoned the ice at his very core.

Illume let out a roar that was accompanied with cracking ice. It caught the Dziwozona off guard. She hesitated, and in that moment, Illume's shield struck out at her like a nest of vipers. Each pierced her throat, face, and chest with brutal precision.

As each spell-infused branch struck her, Illume saw her health drop. It didn't take long for her health to drop to one HP. The shield withdrew back into Illume's glove as the cursed woman fell to the ground. Soft whimpers drifted from her gaping maw, which hung inhumanly wide open.

"That was easy," John chuckled as he walked to Illume's side.

"Where'd the speaking spells come from?" Illume asked.

"If I say the spells, it cuts down on casting time," John replied. "I just lose a little control over the magic when I do."

Looking over at his brother with a laugh, Illume shook his head at John's ridiculous tone.

"Well, at least it did the jo…" A warm splash of blood cut Illume off.

Illume wiped the blood from his face. Crimson stained his fingertips.

"Hey, little brother," John sounded winded. "I'm not feeling so well."

Illume looked at his brother. John's hands were on his stomach. He tried to hold his bowels in from the gaping wound that had opened him up like a tin can. John's intestines poured out of his hands like Niagara Falls and onto the ground. His eyes rolled back as he fell to the ground and his life bar dropped to zero.

Shock hit Illume like a bolt of lightning. He froze in disbelief at the sight of his brother's dead body. Behind John's corpse, the Dziwozona stood with parts of his brother's guts dangling from her hand. Her health bar was full once again.

Illume felt a rage fill him with the heat of a dying star. His hand gripped his bow tightly as the temperature of the room dropped rapidly. So much so that the water droplets that fell from the ceiling turned to ice and shattered as they hit the ground.

The Dziwozona charged Illume. He used his bow to deflect her slash. She still hit with enough force to knock the bow free from his hand. That didn't deter him. His rage caused his body to shake uncontrollably as he marched toward her.

Madness 9%

"That was my BROTHER!" he roared.

"You will pay for that," Illume's voice dropped to a snarl.

She attempted to charge Illume once again but slipped on the ice. Illume threw his hands out and released a torrent of electricity into her. She convulsed and screamed and smoked as billions of joules of electricity flowed from him into her.

"I will make sure you suffer," he snarled as his mana pool dropped in unison with her health.

Just as his mana was about to run dry, he stopped his assault. Illume stepped back from the seizing, smoldering, matted pile of hair and flesh. He walked over to John's corpse and kneeled next to him. Illume slowly closed his brother's lifeless eyes.

"I'm sorry, John," he whispered, his voice caught in his throat.

Illume reached to his brother's back and let his fingers coil around the hilt of his original blade. Illume drew the weapon free before he turned to face his brother's killer. Illume pulled Dovabane from its sheath. This time, the sword let off a roar that rang out with the rage that burned within Illume.

His eyes locked with the animalistic woman who stood across from him. Black ooze dripped from her body as she circled Illume. As the ooze hit the ground, it began to writhe and grow into humanoid shapes. Within seconds, she had spawned six of her "children." Illume clenched his jaw and gripped his swords until his knuckles turned white.

"Come on," he snarled.

The mutated beasts charged. Illume flexed every muscle in his body and dashed at them. His speed was held back from his new armor, but he didn't need his full speed. With brute force, Illume plowed through all six mutates. His swords danced through the air.

Illume slid to a stop. The Dziwozona and her "children" turned to face him. All her children fell to the ground in several pieces each. Illume pointed Dovabane at the woman who was as tall as she was wide.

"No more children," Illume commanded. "Just you!"

Illume spun Dovabane as his mana refilled. The red blade burst into flames as it fed from his mana. The beast charged at Illume. He ducked under her swipe and dragged the flaming sword across her belly. She screeched as her health dropped.

By the time Illume got his sight back to her, the health bar was full once more. Illume imbued his other sword with frost.

"Good, I didn't want you to die too easily," Illume grunted out.

Illume dashed at her, she charged at him. Both beings clashed together like two lions fighting over a kill. Illume was able to move just fast enough to stay ahead of her claws, but her healing rendered most of his attacks useless.

Something within Illume enjoyed the fight. He liked slicing into her knowing it wouldn't kill her. Knowing that each frosty or scorching cut caused her agony. At this point, he didn't care he didn't know how to kill her. He reveled in his torture of her.

As he continued to slash and hack, Illume's mana ran down slowly, as did his stamina. He wasn't feeling the rigors of the fight as it raged around the chamber. Her fleshy maw snapped at him as she spun and slashed at Illume. Her razor-like nails managed to jam themselves into Illume's chest.

Frost lifted from Illume's cloak. A thick layer of ice formed between her nails and his body. Illume offered her a smirk as he ran Dovabane through her gut and out the other side. She lashed out and slung her other hand at Illume's face. He'd been so tunnel-focused on her that he hadn't seen her attack coming.

Illume flinched, her nails stopped less than an inch from his face. It took a second, but as his eyes focused, he saw a bloodstained hand held her hand back. Her arm was yanked to the side as she was pulled away from him. A second arm coiled around her elbow, and try as she might, she couldn't fight the grip.

John's lifeless face slid out from behind her into Illume's view. His eyes glowed a bright yellow. Illume looked down to see John's intestines still on the ground.

"Cut the heart out!" John's voice echoed from behind Illume.

Illume glanced over his shoulder to see his brother standing at the entrance of the chamber. John's eyes glowed yellow, as did his hands. He held his arms in a pinned-back motion like his corpse did with the Dziwozona.

Illume drew Bloodlust from its sheath. With a single and violent jab, Illume stabbed her so hard that his hand jammed into her chest cavity. She roared as he ripped her heart out with Bloodlust from the hole he'd made.

The Dziwozona's life bar dropped to zero. Her body fell to the ground lifeless as her heart stopped beating in Illume's hand. John's corpse collapsed to the ground where it turned to dust and left behind a pile of his supplies.

Dziwozona Heart Added
This item's effect on alchemy is profound yet
    mysterious.

"How did you?" Illume stammered.

"I re-spawned at the beginning of the dungeon," John shared.

"What about…" Illume continued with his stuttered.

"My body?" John asked. "Necromancer."

Illume offered John the sword Nari had made him back. John retrieved his supplies and donned his gear before he put the weapon on his back once again. Just as the sword fell into place, the ground shook. Illume glanced back at the blue crystal. It had a massive crack in it.

"You have freed me!" the deep voice echoed in Illume's mind.

16

GODS

THE ENTIRE DUNGEON shook as the crack in the blue crystal started to spread. Illume felt John grab his arm and pull on it to run. Something within Illume told him to stay put. He watched as the crack continued to grow

"It's not safe here. We have to go!" John yelled.

"This is the only place that is safe," Illume replied.

The blue crystal shattered and fell all around them. Upon impact, the crystal dissolved into a fine sand that covered the chamber floors with almost an inch of blue. John stopped fighting as the crystal fell all around them, but not where they had been standing.

"What is that?" John asked in a breathless tone.

Before them, in what was the heart of the crystal, stood a humanoid figure shrouded in darkness. The shroud turned. Illume could feel its eyes lock on to his.

"That is what we came for," Illume whispered.

Its eyes glowed the same blue as the torches that illuminated their path. Its body squared off with them. The being was enormous. Big enough where even The Rock would have to look up to him.

"You have freed me, boy," the voice rumbled, audibly this time.

"I was told a god dwelt here!" Illume called. "Someone very dear to me has been infected with the venom of Hastur. Your disciple said you could help."

At the mention of Hastur's name, all the torches dimmed. The figure seemed to grow even more imposing. John took several steps back. Illume stood his ground. If this god shrouded in darkness was the only way to help Nari, then Illume would make sure he helped, be it by convincing him or by force.

"You dare speak that name!" the being roared.

"You sound like you're scared of him," Illume replied. "I am not. And if you help my friend, I swear to you, I will bring you Hastur's head."

The shadow danced around the room, growing closer to Illume as it did.

"You should fear him. You have been cursed with his madness," the voice rumbled. "Then again…"

The shadow towered over them for a brief moment. Its intense gaze was unnerving, even for Illume. His hands gripped his weapons tightly in anticipation for another fight. The shadowy figure shrank down. It lowered to Illume's height and dropped several more inches.

"…you did manage to kill my brother."

As it grew smaller, the shadows around it dissipated until there was nothing left but a short, portly man with a bald head. He was an unassuming man in fine clothing. His cheeks were rosy as if he'd run up a flight of stairs and struggled to catch his breath.

"Well, you're not so scary," John commented off handedly.

"Your brother was Trillian?" Illume asked, putting two and two together.

"He was." The man nodded. "God of darkness, corruption, and power." He added, "I am Khal'sol's-latz, god of chaos and mischief. It's a pleasure to meet you."

He offered Illume his hand. Illume didn't reach out and shake the man's hand in return. John pushed past his brother.

"Illume, don't be rude," John huffed.

John took the man's hand and shook it. Sparks flew from Khal and into John, which sent him flying across the room in a flash of light.

"God of mischief and chaos. He literally JUST told us," Illume called to his brother as he pulled himself to his feet.

"Wise man!" Khal pointed out.

"Will you help us?" Illume asked sharply. He wanted to get back to Nari immediately.

"No," Khal replied without hesitation.

"If this is about Trillian, he was like a brother to me too. I di…" Illume was cut off by Khal.

"It has nothing to do with Trillian," Khal interjected. "He wished for a release of his nightmare, you granted it to him. For that I am grateful and bless you with my name."

The darkness that had shrouded the little man danced out of him now. Like a serpent, it coiled through the air before encircling Illume. It was rough as it touched his skin, like sandpaper. He didn't fight the darkness, mostly because he didn't want to. He wanted the power of this god above just about anything.

It took several seconds and Illume experienced a strange discomfort as the sandy darkness washed over his body. He could hear voices echo through his mind from the past, present, and future. Screams of agony, hisses, and roars filled his head until the darkness finally fully entered him.

Blessing of Khal'sol'slatz added.
User may invoke the god's name in the form of a
*   shout. This shout will summon the god's power to*
*   aid you in battle.*

The shout may only be used three times.

As the words faded, Illume could hear Khal's name being chanted by disembodied voices. He bent down and picked up his bow that was near his feet and slung it over his shoulder.

"I released you. You WILL help us cure Nari," Illume demanded.

"I would love to, but I can't! I'm a god," he rebutted, his voice growing squeaky. "That THING is an elder god… way past my power level. It would take a small army of gods to undo what he did and a medium army to kill him."

Madness 10%

Illume felt his anger rise. He pointed his sword at Khal's throat. It frosted over. This caught Khal's attention. His eyes widened and a smile spread across his face.

"I can't heal your girl, but I can point you to something that can," Khal blurted in excitement. "Follow me."

Khal put a single finger on Illume's weapon. He pushed it to the side with no effort whatsoever despite Illume trying to hold it in place with all his might. Khal walked toward the entrance of the room. Illume sheathed his weapon and followed with John close behind.

"What can save her?" Illume asked.

"There is a coastal city south of here," Khal explained. "Mire. In that city is a man named simply 'The Boat Man.' Give him these and he'll take you where you need to go."

Khal tossed two coins over his shoulder. Illume caught one, John the other. Illume looked at the coin for a brief moment. It was solid gold and a little smaller than the palm of his hand.

Traversal Coin added
Weight: .01 Worth: 0 polis
This coin has one use only, to pay the Boat Man.
This may just help you find something off the map's
  edge.

"The Boat Man?" John asked. "Pay the Boat Man and get taken to the underworld. Remember the history of the Greeks? He is the god of chaos and mischief. How do we know this isn't a trap?"

"I do," Illume assured him. "And it's not."

"How can you be so sure?" John pressed.

"Because your brother over here granted my brother something he wanted for thousands of years," Khal called out as he continued to march down the corridors. "Because your brother killed the Dziwozona who held the magical barrier that imprisoned me. And because your brother wants that squid-faced bag of tentacles dead almost as much as I do. For that, I will never fight against you."

John jogged up to Illume. He glanced at his younger brother. They were approaching the exit now.

"You killed his brother?" John inquired.

"Trillian, yes." Illume confirmed. "He was the closest thing I had to a real friend, but he was a threat to the land and the final boss of last game."

"Isn't your dragon named Trillian?" John asked.

Khal stopped in his tracks. He turned to face Illume, his silvery eyes glistened with a malevolent orneriness.

"You have a dragon?" he asked.

"Frost dragon," Illume replied.

"Well, where is it?" Khal pressed.

"He's with Nari, holding the poison at bay." Illume explained.

"You raise that dragon to fight," Khal instructed. "Get him big and strong and I doubt any could stand against your combined full potential."

He clapped his hands like a school child. "So exciting."

Khal turned and continued to lead Illume and John

out of his prison. It wasn't until then that Illume realized they'd forgotten the potions.

"Wait!" Illume call. "I forgot something a little ways back."

"No you didn't," John replied. "I looted the chests; a few polis, nothing of note like you said. I also grabbed the potions before helping you."

"Well, that was astute of you," Illume noted. "Khal, what do you know of the madness Hastur casts on people?"

"That's a nasty little spell he's got there," Khal attested as he approached the door that was now blocked by rune magic. "The more madness an individual has, the less healthy they become. Don't get me wrong, their magic drains slower and their stamina does last longer, but they have less health..."

He paused for a moment as he placed his hands on the runes. "...and when you hit 100 percent madness, you'll turn into Ibura back there. One of Hastur's mindless slaves."

Khal moved his hands to a different spot on the runes. His palms shone, which made the runes slowly rotate clockwise, then counter clockwise. He glanced back at Illume. From the look on his face, Illume knew Khal could see what he would become should the madness overtake him.

"She turned immediately, though, because she was

a nasty piece of work before her madness," Khal divulged. "The more pure of heart a person is, the longer it takes for the madness to take over. The trick is to stay calm. Things like anger'll drive you mad faster than anything else."

With that, the rune spell shattered into shards of light before it disappeared into nothingness. The door jarred open slightly and Khal pushed on it. The door swung open all the way before it fell back and crashed against the ground.

"That slimy yellow sack of tendrils!" Khal roared. "He sank my castle!"

"Oh yeah!" John laughed. "Forgot about that for a second."

Khal exited the structure and went to the sinkhole. John and Illume followed closely behind. As Illume stepped out and onto solid ground, his stomach dropped. The change of angles felt like he arched a curve on a roller coaster. Illume looked around the sinkhole. Something didn't quite feel right.

"Didn't you say you spawned at the entrance?" Illume asked as he looked around the edge of the sinkhole.

"Just inside the doors," John replied. "What are you looking at?"

"Something just doesn't feel right," Illume explained.

"It does not," Khal added. "And I can tell you why."

His finger rose and pointed to the opposite edge of the sinkhole. Illume followed his finger to see Hastur's yellow cloak. It lorded over them in a haunting manner. Illume drew his bow and nocked an arrow of frenzy. He drew and aimed at Hastur's head.

"John, whatever happens, don't look at his face," Illume instructed.

"I already know that," John replied in an irritated tone.

"Khal?" Illume asked.

"Yes," he replied in a squeaky tone.

"How is your battle prowess compared to your brother's?" Illume added.

"Eh," Khal shrugged. "We all have our strengths."

17

HASTUR ROUND II

THE SLIMY TENDRILLED hand of Hastur rose and pointed directly at Illume. Squawks and chirps echoed from the marsh lands above in a sea of noise. Illume noticed John moved back away from their group as Khal turned invisible. Illume huffed and shook his head.

"You all are jerks," he murmured.

"Bring me the cryomancer," Hastur's voice rumbled.

From the shadows, men in robes emerged. Their faces were shrouded, hidden by their hoods. They all chanted as they held out their hands.

"Oh great, a Gregorian chant," Illume growled as he drew his bow. "John, Khal, want to give me a hand here?"

The hooded figures continued to chant. Illume felt

woozy. He released his arrow. It missed his target and buried itself in the wall. Illume's legs buckled as he fell to his knees. His vision started to blur. His health bar started to drop.

You have been poisoned.

Illume looked up as his health dropped to below half. His skill tree and leveling screen became visible. Illume scanned over to his new skill tree and dropped down to the Toxicologist skill. He had just enough points, but he'd be forced to activate all his remaining levels to access the points.

Illume didn't have much of a choice and poured five of his six remaining skill points into his Toxicology skill so he wouldn't have to worry about poison for himself anymore. He used his last skill point to activate his "quick on your feet" perk.

Moving over to his attribute page, Illume could feel the madness creeping up on him. He'd need to increase his survivability. He put six of his points into health so he could take more hits. Three went into his stamina so he could fight longer. He slid over to constitution and placed the remaining three into it as well.

Illume closed his menu. His health maxed out at the edge of his madness meter. His queasy feeling dissipated and his vision focused once more. Illume's attention went straight to the man directly in front of him as his new stats appeared in his field of view.

New Stats:
Health: 300
Stamina: 260
Constitution: +33
You now take marginally less damage.

New Skills:
Toxicologist: Immunity to toxins, poisons, and
venoms.
Quick on your feet: +20% Light armor effectiveness.

Player Level:
Congratulations you can drink now!

"Oooo yaayyy, I can drink," Illume mocked.

Illume drew Dovabane and Bloodlust. The low growl of his flaming weapon gave the hooded figures pause. Now that Illume had a chance to get a good look at them, there was something familiar about their garments.

"Stand aside!" Illume commanded. "I have no quarrel with you."

"It is we who have quarrel with you!" they all replied in unison.

Hesitating for a moment, Illume felt chills cascade over his body as they spoke. Their monotone response had a very *The Shining* vibe to it. The leader lifted his hood. Upon seeing the man's face and helmet, he let out a groan.

"Are you ffff…. Come on!" Illume yelled. "The Order of Light is involved with Hastur? Aren't you guys all about the purity of the human form?"

"Humanity is the pinnacle of life true enough," the leader replied.

"Then why are you in service to Squidward up there?" Illume barked. "He will drive you mad and corrupt your human forms!"

"Some evils need to be tolerated for the greater good of all mankind," the leader retorted.

The grey-haired man summoned a strange spell unlike anything Illume had seen before. He dashed at the man. Illume judged by the look on his face that he hadn't anticipated Illume being able to move as quickly as he did. With a single, powerful swipe of his blade, he decapitated the leader. As his head fell to the ground and the light from his spell dissipated, Illume turned to the remaining three members.

"The true Order of Light would help me fight Hastur," Illume pointed out. "Should you serve him, you are his cultist and the exact thing you've set out to destroy. I will give you one last chance, leave or die."

The remaining members of the order reached into their cloaks and all drew long, curved, nasty-looking swords. They had the clear aura of Hastur to them. Illume sighed and shook his head.

As the enemy prepared to charge, an arrow pierced one of the men's shoulders. He let out a scream of pain as his health hardly dropped at all from the impact. Illume glanced over to see John with his bow up.

"Only a sith deals in absolutes," John called.

Since John only had a single arrow to fire, the weapon was useless now. He swung it over his shoulder. A soft glow danced off of him. Illume recognized the pattern of John's mana as it focused around him. He used the opportunity to throw Bloodlust at one of the members behind him.

The knife found its mark and the Order of Light member staggered back as his health dropped by a third. Illume charged at the two men in front of him. The order member John had shot staggered. His health dropped rapidly from the poison of the arrow.

Illume body-checked him to the ground as he swung Dovabane at the last member with full health. Their swords clashed with the ring of a bell. In a blade lock, Illume drove the cultist back several paces. The look in his opponent's eye was one of pure hatred. Illume almost felt sorry for the man as his sword burned red from the blade lock with Dovabane.

Shoving the man back, Illume imposed his will. The entire mid-section of his weapon looked like it had just come out of the furnace. With one mighty swing, Illume cleaved the cultist's weapon in half before he ran Dovabane through his gut.

His health dropped almost completely. Illume ripped his weapon from his opponent's gut, which allowed him to drop to the ground. Dovabane cauterized the wound so he didn't lose health to blood loss.

Illume turned to see the last remaining member, who posed a threat running in terror. The last enemy screamed as he moved to the shadowed place from whence he came. He was brought to a violent halt as a tentacle hand shot from the darkness and gripped the cultist by the throat.

The man kicked and screamed as he was lifted off the ground. His body convulsed as the sounds of his choking echoed off the walls of the sinkhole. His body emaciated until he was nothing more than a slab of jerky.

Hastur yanked Bloodlust from the cultist. His body was tossed to the side as Hastur emerged from the shadows. He put his hand out and lifted the cultist with the sliver of health left with his mind and tore out what little life force he had within him.

"John, look away!" Illume yelled.

Hastur turned his gaze to Illume. The yellow mask still covered his true face, but Illume could feel the madness emanate from the being before him. Had he not been cursed already, there was little doubt that he would have been now.

"You will come with me," Hastur commanded. "You will free my children and help me consume this world."

Illume smirked as the last gasps of the poisoned cultist wheezed into nothingness. Illume's grip tightened on Dovabane. He wasn't sure what John was planning, but if he could buy his brother enough time, perhaps they could end it all here.

"I will never join you," Illume snarled.

Madness 11%

"You will. It's just a matter of time," Hastur vowed.

Charging at the writhing mass restrained by a yellow cloak, Illume's grip on his weapon tightened. Hastur moved much faster. Before he could have closed the distance between them, Hastur moved out of reach.

Illume turned to greet a large tentacle with his face. His head snapped back and his health dropped from the blow. Illume staggered backward and let out an audible grunt. Another cephalopodan limb struck out at Illume. He sidestepped the attack and drew Dovabane up from his low stance.

The burning blade sliced through Hastur's limb like

a wire through cheese. Hastur didn't respond to the dismemberment. His health bar became visible, but it did not drop. Hastur's severed limb fell to the ground and twitched as it shriveled into near non-existence. Before the damaged base was fully withdrawn, his limb had regrown itself.

"Oh come on, do you have to regenerate to such a ridiculous degree?" Illume complained with a huff.

"You don't have the power to defeat me," Hastur stated. "You will never know such power, mortal."

He drew his hands together, out of the swamplands above snakes to pour into the pit by the hundreds. Illume wanted to summon lightning, but the wet floor would conduct it and harm his brother. He didn't have enough mana to freeze them all with the distance that separated them. He fell back.

"I do have a god on my side," Illume challenged. "And he is no fan of you."

The serpents circled around Hastur, and he lifted one off the ground with a delicate touch.

"I have defeated that god before. I can do it again," Hastur boasted. "He was far too simple last time…"

Hastur was cut off as the snake that he held turned into Khal. The god clearly had caught Hastur by surprise as he grabbed Bloodlust and stabbed Hastur in the neck with it.

"JOHN, NOW!" he yelled as he yanked the dagger free.

Hastur's health dropped from the attack and didn't immediately regenerate. This caused Illume's jaw to nearly hit the floor. Khal's stats had to have been off the charts. Hastur flung Khal across the sinkhole, where he bounced to a stop with Illume's dagger still in hand. A pulse of mana erupted from John and encompassed the sinkhole.

All the snakes turned and fled back into the swamp above. Illume looked back at Hastur, who had just begun to heal from Khal. Illume shook his head and prepared for another attack. His mana burn already chewed through half his magic reserves.

Hastur looked directly at John, whose eyes were closed. He moved toward Illume's brother, who was locked in place as his spell continued to be cast. Illume charged. He didn't make a noise, no screaming or call outs to draw Hastur's attention. His armor and sneak abilities were so high that even his footsteps didn't make a sound.

Leaping at Hastur, he drew his left arm back into a striking pose as he soared through the air. Illume felt the shield kick open just as he came down at Hastur. Illume slammed the edge of his shield into the side of Hastur's skull. As Illume followed through, he tucked his shoulder and body-checked the elder god to the ground.

As they hit the ground, it shook like an earthquake. Parts of the sinkhole walls began to collapse. Hastur hesitated, clearly shocked by Illume's blindsided attack. That split second was all Illume needed. A skeletal hand shot out from the ground and grabbed Hastur's hood.

A second, third, fourth! Dozens, if not hundreds shot from the ground. Visages of men pulled themselves from the earth. Their eyes glowed and roots and vines covered their bodies as if they were the decayed corpses and skeletons' musculature systems.

Illume felt a strong hand grab his shoulder and rip him off Hastur. He staggered back to see Khal with one hand on his shoulder. The other offered Illume his knife back. The cryomancer sheathed Bloodlust back in its home.

"The dead have a score to settle," John said softly as he approached Illume's side.

"True, but this is not enough to stop him," Khal replied. "You're going to want to take a deep breath."

Illume couldn't take his eyes off the writhing mass of bones and vines that covered the struggling elder god. Illume was overcome with a strange sense of falling as the world warped around them. As it fell back into focus, Illume found himself in a boat with John and Khal.

"Keep moving south," Khal said in an urgent tone. "I can cloak you from Hastur for a short time, but if you want to save your friend, you have to go to Mire and find the Boat Man."

"What about you?" Illume asked.

"I'm the god of mischief and chaos," Khal chuckled. "I will do what I have been prevented from doing all these years."

Illume reached for Bloodlust. Khal tilted his head and offered Illume a smirk.

"I am not malevolent like Trillian," Khal pointed out. "My mischief is harmless and my chaos is brought only to those who've earned it. Plus if you kill me now, my blessing is no longer useful, and believe me, you will need that blessing."

With that, Khal vanished into thin air. John handed Illume his bow and Illume put all his weapons back in their rightful places. Both men grabbed the oars inside the boat and started to paddle.

18

MIRE

ILLUME AND JOHN rowed in silence for a while. Illume wasn't really sure how long. All he knew was that he didn't really feel like talking. The swamplands were silent with only a few *plops* that sounded as fish would occasionally jump through the air. John glanced over his shoulder at Illume.

"I'll be right back," he said softly.

With that, John's avatar stiffened. The oar sat in his lap as he jumped offline. Illume continued to paddle through the thickly green coated water. The silence was so complete that Illume's ears began to ring. Gradually, that ringing turned to what he could have sworn were whispers.

Illume jerked his head around. His eyes darted from tree to tree in search of anyone who could have been watching them. With Ibura dead, Illume wasn't worried about any of her "children" springing a trap. The Order of Light didn't seem like the kind to hide and spy. Which left the Kapre.

Kapre were the only other species Illume could think of who could be spying on him right now and he not be able to see them. He bore equipment made by one of their kind, so the worry of attack lessened. Illume turned back forward and continued to paddle.

Opening his map, Illume navigated the swamp-lands. Khal had fast traveled both men over halfway to their destination and for that he was grateful. He continued to paddle, the whispers persisted at an inconsistent rate. Sometimes, it sounded like they were a long way off. Other times, they sounded like they were right in the boat with them.

John's avatar twitched before it came fully back online. He commenced rowing once again. He scanned the surroundings ahead of them as he rowed and always kept a firm grip on his oar.

"You remember Tablerock lake?" John asked.

"And the camp we went to that one summer," Illume answered.

"That was probably the best camp we ever went to," John added.

"Yeah, I really wish Dad would have sent us there more," Illume said. "Triathlete was a lot of fun."

"And that water was warm!" John continued. "Better than Taneycomo."

"Taneycomo was only that cold because it came from the bottom of Tablerock, though," Illume replied. "It was great for the polar bear club."

"Which we both missed by five minutes," John interjected.

"I think I could handle it now, though," Illume rebutted.

"Now doesn't count. You're a magical being who can almost turn himself into ice," John argued with a laugh.

"Good point," Illume acceded.

Both men fell silent once again as they continued to row. Illume could tell by how tense John's shoulders were that he was worried about something. Illume pulled his oar out of the water and rested it on his knees before he leaned forward.

"What are you worried about?" Illume asked his brother.

John didn't reply for a long time. When he did eventually break the silence, his voice was hushed.

"How can you speak that language?" John asked.

"What language?" Illume wondered.

"Hastur's," John clarified. "The infernal tongue of the eldritch gods."

"What are you talking about?" Illume asked in a confused tone as he sat up and furrowed his brow.

"When Hastur spoke and you replied, it was in a language I couldn't understand," John explained. "The words seemed to echo and shake the very foundations of the earth. How could you speak it?"

"I wasn't," Illume insisted. "We were speaking English."

John pulled his oar out of the water and set it in the boat. Very carefully, he turned around to face Illume as the boat gradually slowed its forward motion.

"You're telling me that you think you were speaking English back there?" John asked.

"I was," Illume insisted.

"But that's the thing, you weren't," John's tone had a bit of a sting to it. "I have heard mention of madness several times since I've loaded up into this game. You have told me several times not to look Hastur in the face. Did you look him in the face?"

Illume hesitated for a few moments. He didn't want to lie to his brother, but there were bigger things at stake, and if there was something he'd learned from being a bit of a cinephile, it was that a secret like this had the potential to turn allies into enemies.

"I have been afflicted with madness," Illume replied in a hushed tone.

"Madness? What does that mean, you've been

afflicted with madness?" John asked in a confused tone.

"Hastur hit me with his gaze on our first encounter," Illume explained. "Since then, I've had a meter that gradually rises. I don't know what makes it climb aside from Hastur's presence."

"Well clearly, one of the side effects is that you can understand and speak eldritch," John pointed out. "Has anything else accompanied the madness meter?"

"My health drops a percentage every time my madness rises," Illume explained. "I still have plenty of health left, but if my meter goes up too much, I won't be able to take a hit from even the lowest level enemies."

John nodded. He folded his hands in front of his face and rested his elbows on his knees. He fell silent for a few minutes.

Finally breaking his silence, John said, "I'll help you find some kind of cure or a way to manage this, but you have to keep me posted on your progress."

"Will do," Illume replied.

John turned back around and rowed as well. Illume pulled up his map to see that they were maybe fifteen minutes away from being able to see Mire.

"What kind of necromancy was that you used back there?" Illume asked. "I've never seen corpses reanimated like that."

"It costs less mana and the spell lasts longer if I use dead plant life to bring the deceased back," John explained.

Illume smirked. The smirk turned into a snicker. After several seconds, he leaned almost all the way forward and burst out in explosive laughter.

"What's so funny?" John questioned in an irritated tone.

"You're Poison Ivy!" Illume pointed out. "Your girlfriend is a harlequin!" He continued to laugh. "Please... PLEASE tell me you have a set of green armor."

Illume added. "I'm sure we can find someone to turn your hair red too!"

Illume was nearly bursting at his seams.

John shook his head and raised his right hand before he gave Illume the finger. After a few seconds, he lowered it and continued to row. It took a few minutes, but Illume's laughter died down. He stifled his chuckles as best he could since he'd begun to cramp in his side.

"I'm sorry," Illume replied between chuckles. "In all seriousness, the resurrection is really cool. I'm just so tired and overwhelmed by everything, anything seems funny."

"Yeah, it's cool!" John nodded. "Do you have any

idea how many years it took of experimenting with my skill trees to be able to do that? Way too many!"

"Well, it paid off," Illume said as his laughter subsided.

As they rounded one more small island, Illume noticed the water seemed to be a little bit thicker. Illume leaned to the side and looked around his brother. In the distance, among a field of mud, sat a small village.

The outskirts of the village were broken down and the structures had largely collapsed. As they rowed closer, Illume noticed that the center of the village consisted mainly of damp wooden buildings with moss roofs.

Mire almost appeared to be a ghost town save for the handful of people who bustled from cart to cart. Illume and John continued to row closer as each paddle became more and more of a fight to push their boat through the gradually thickening water.

Illume stopped paddling and leapt over the side of the boat. He sank maybe an inch into the mud. John jumped over the side and sank knee deep. Illume walked over to his brother with a sly smirk on his face.

"I told you Legolas had useful traits," Illume taunted.

"I hate you so much right now," John shook his head.

Illume turned and left John to get unstuck by himself. As he moved closer to the village, he noticed that the inhabitants scurried away and entered into the mold-covered buildings.

Stepping onto one of the roads that was made from logs laid side by side, Illume stretched and moaned. A thin layer of mud covered all the logs. A few carts were strewn about. Some had fish in them, others had furs, but most were empty.

The ground rumbled a little. Illume looked back to see John walk on a runway of dead plant life he'd brought back. As John approached Illume, the roots sank back into the mud. John limped as the mud had pulled off one of his boots. He held the caked shoe in his hands as he scowled at Illume.

"Are you sure you're a necromancer?" Illume teased. "Because you seem more like Luther Burbank than a conjurer of the dead."

John stopped. He dropped his boot and slid his foot back in with a squishy splat. His lips were pursed as he shook his head at Illume.

"Who is Luther Burbank?" John asked in a frustrated tone.

"Famous botanist?" Illume asked. "Personally responsible for over eight hundred varieties of plant life including dozens of fruits?"

"No idea," John shrugged and shook his head.

"You're an intellectual; how do you not know this!" Illume blurted.

"You're a video game journalist. How do you?" John probed.

Illume let out a frustrated sigh. He grumbled and turned away from his brother before he walked farther into Mire.

"I read a lot! Pick up a non-medical book every once in a while," he murmured under his breath.

Pushing farther into the village, Illume noticed the air increasingly smelled like fish and fog seemed to thicken the further in Illume went. He could hear John's mud-covered boots as they smacked the street behind him. The fog turned more to a mist that swirled around them and rapidly coated both men in a layer of moisture.

Illume could faintly smell the ocean through the stench of fish. He glanced back to see John's silhouette in the mist. Something moved behind John. In the blink of an eye, Illume had his bow off his shoulder, an arrow nocked, and the string pulled back.

He kept his eye sighted down his arrow as he tracked the shadow in the mist. At about ten feet, John became visible once again. The moment he saw Illume, he threw his hands up.

"Whoa!" he called out. "Hold your fire. I'm a friendly."

"It's not you," Illume murmured. "Something else is out there."

"We are in a village," John pointed out. "Probably one of the villagers."

"I don't trust anything that lives in a place mired in such an unnatural mist," Illume replied.

"HA! Good one," John replied.

Madness 12%

Illume heard whispers filling the air once again. Illume spun around as his eyes darted from left to right in a desperate hope to find the source of the whispering. It was impossible for him to see through the mist.

His heartbeat pounded in his head. It pounded so hard against his chest that it sounded like war drums in his ears. His breathing grew shallow as the whispers grew louder. Illume could feel his body begin to cool in anticipation for an attack. His bow frosted over as well.

"Lower your weapon, cryomancer," a slurred voice cut through the mist. "No harm'll come to ye in Mire. We be told of your comin' for years now."

Heavy footsteps echoed through the mist behind Illume. He kept his weapon drawn and turned to see a man with an eye patch standing right behind him. The man's other eye was oceanic blue. The mist matted down his long brown hair.

The man looked Illume up and down and scratched his scruffy chin with a hand that was full of rings. The glint of two small gold earrings caught Illume's eye, which led to a tattoo that peeked out from behind his massive shirt lapels. They were tendrils that had an eerie familiarity to them.

"Who are you?" Illume asked as the frost built up on his weapon while his mana fell.

"I be Corazon de Ballena," he managed to squeeze out without slurring. "I be the governor of Mire."

Illume's brow furrowed. How did this man know of him? He'd only been playing for a year in game time and it was not like the game coders could have anticipated the events that led him here. Could they have?

"You both be tired," Corazon grumbled. "Best you come with me 'fore you continue on your journey."

Corazon pulled a massive sandwich out of his pack. He took a bite and all manner of crumbs and condiments stayed on his face as he turned and disappeared into the mist.

19

PAYING PIRATES

ILLUME AND JOHN followed Corazon up to a ramshackle inn. Corazon opened the door for both men as he took another bite out of his meat heavy sandwich. Illume followed Corazon's nod and entered the building.

The main hall was set up in a very similar fashion to the other inns he'd seen so far. This one was damper and held the distinct scent of fish. Illume re-quivered his arrow as he slung his bow over his shoulder. He looked back at Corazon, who had the go-to appearance of a pirate if he'd ever seen one.

"One room's not flooded. It's yours," Corazon said as he headed to a bar that sat across from the fireplace. "If you want some grog, it'll cost you. I'm not trying to run a charity here."

He poured himself a large cup of frothy dark liquid

and took a massive swig before he leaned against the bar. Illume nosed around the main hall for a few moments. Water dripped from the ceiling in more than one place. He peered into some of the immediately adjacent rooms. They had a bed, a night stand, and about ankle deep water.

"What happened here?" Illume asked.

Illume turned back to Corazon to see John pay for a meal. Corazon pulled another sandwich out of his pouch and handed it to John. The pirate then poured John a cup of grog.

"This once be a peaceful tradin' town," he murmured into his mug. "Then ol' fish face came trudgin' outta the sea. Mire was the first to fall."

Corazon added as he took another swig. "Good mosta us died that day. Most who survived followed the King in Yellow."

Walking over to Corazon, Illume pulled a few polis from his purse and placed them on the bar. Corazon drew a mug from under the back of the bar and slammed it in front of Illume. He proceeded to pour grog into the mug.

After the cup was almost overflowing, Corazon stopped pouring. Illume lifted the mug to his lips and drank down the bitter dark liquid. He was never much of a drinker, but he did recognize a custom when one was presented to him. After Illume reached the bottom of his mug, some of the grog spilled down his chest. Illume slammed the mug down.

"And what about those who stayed?" Illume asked with a loud burp.

"Good one," Corazon complimented the belch. "Those who stayed behind changed. Now I trade for 'em so the world won't come sniffin' round here."

"Forgive my forwardness, but you don't seem like a trader," John interjected.

"I be more of a pirate, I know," Corazon acknowledged. "These people protected me when I needed it most. At the very least, I owed 'em this much."

Illume bit the inside of his cheek as he thought about his next move.

"Corazon, how did you know that I specifically was coming?" Illume asked.

"There be a legend round here that when the elder god wakes, a being of great power would come from the east to bring a stop to him," Corazon explained.

"Yes, but how did you know that it would be me?" Illume asked again. "How did you know I am called the Cryomancer?"

"Didn't," Corazon shrugged as he took another drink. "Small strange bald guy came in and said the one who was promised was on his way. Said I'd know him by his frost."

He pointed to Illume with the mug. "Then you

come wanderin' round here turnin' yourself into a snowman…"

"How do you know what a snowman is?" John asked through his mug.

"I may be a seadog," Corazon replied. "But I've my fair share of adventures. One such adventure brought me to the frozen north of Valka. Hidden city in the ice called Sigtuna. Few who venture there ever come back."

He chuckled to himself. "Had lots of fun. Anyway, figured you be of whom the fat little man spoke."

"Corazon," Illume's tone dropped as he slid into a stool, "my brother and I are looking for a being known as 'The Boat Man.' He is supposed to bring us to a lost island so I can find something to save a friend of mine. Do you know who he is?"

"Shiver my mud-soaked boots," Corazon grumbled before he took a swig of grog. "I know of whom you speak. Most unpleasant man to tend the seas. He only be helpful should you pay his price."

"You mean this price?" Illume inquired.

He pulled the Traversal Coin from his pouch and slammed it onto the table. Judging from the look of dread on Corazon's face, the coin Illume had just revealed was the one they needed.

"That be the price," Corazon replied in a defeated

tone. "You best get some rest. Tomorrow be a long day."

The pirate pushed away from the bar. He waved for Illume and John to follow. Corazon led them up a set of stairs that wound around the back of the desk. It had mead, a few bags of gold, and from the looks of it, a loaded crossbow tucked away out of sight.

Illume glanced back at John then nodded to the crossbow. John followed Illume's gaze and gave Illume a nod back. Illume continued to follow Corazon up the stairs and around the corner to a rickety second floor. Corazon stopped at one of the rooms and pointed to it.

"This be yours. Wouldn't go snooping after dark if I be you." he warned before he disappeared into a room a little farther down the hall.

Illume entered the chamber Corazon indicated. It was set up just like the one downstairs, only this one had two beds and a chair inside. Most importantly, there was no water on the ground.

"Well, this is better than the one downstairs," Illume said softly.

"You think we can trust him?" John asked.

Illume's brow raised at his brother's question. A wide smile formed on his face as he turned to face John.

"Look at you!" Illume declared with a chuckle.

"Learning to question the motives of NPCs, good man!"

"Look, Illume," John's voice was glum. "When I died back in that dungeon, it hurt. It hurt a lot! Everything I was wearing went haywire. It honestly felt like I'd been shot. That's why I logged out on the boat. Even the VR pack gave me a nasty shock."

Making his way to John's side, Illume pulled his older brother toward him and yanked his cloak back to look down his right shoulder blade. Two crimson red birthmarks ran down John's back. The same kind that Nari had, the same kind that he had.

"John, you only have two lives left," Illume informed him in a stern tone.

"What does that mean?" John asked with a hint of fear in his voice.

"I-I don't know," Illume stammered.

"Best guess then!" John demanded.

"Best guess?" Illume repeated. "I would say best case scenario, your avatar has perma-death."

"And worst case?" John probed.

For the first time in Illume's life, he'd seen true fear inhabit his brother's face. They could always tell when the other was lying. Illume took a deep breath as he voiced his worst potential fear.

"Worst case scenario, your VR set kills you," Illume

said softly. "You have a family, John. I don't want you getting any more involved than you are. It's way too dangerous for you to stay here. Log out and let Mr. Matsimoto or the developer for this region of the game know what's going on. See if you can find a way to make it safe."

John grabbed Illume by the forearm. His expression was resolute. John shook his head at Illume's command.

"You're my family too," John replied. "If what you're saying is true, then I have one more free life. At the very least, I'm staying with you until I'm down to one, okay?"

Illume recognized that look. It was the look John would get when he had set his mind to something. At this point, not even a train could stop him.

"Fine," Illume sighed. "But while I go to sleep, you are going to give yourself a full physical. I want to make sure that last shock didn't cause any real damage. Also do some research on the developer. See if he mentioned anything in interviews that helped inspire him for this game. There might be something there that will show us how to kill Hastur."

"Okay," John nodded. "But you clean my boots while I do. These things weigh twenty pounds each."

"You're exaggerating," Illume huffed.

"No I'm not," John argued. "It's showing on my

encumbrance. My boots are literally +20 in weight each."

Illume laughed and waved for them to be handed over. John slid both his feet from his boots and handed them to Illume before his avatar locked up once again. Illume sat on the side of one of the beds and began to scrub the mud off them.

As he worked, he kept an eye on the door. Corazon seemed friendly enough, but he was still a pirate and they were not to be trusted. He unsheathed Bloodlust and placed it on the bed next to him as he worked.

Nearly an hour later, Illume finished John's boots. He sheathed his blade and walked over to his brother and slid the shoes back onto his feet. Illume picked his brother up and walked him to the bed before he laid John down. Illume returned to John's chair and used it to jam the door shut.

Walking over to the other bed, Illume lay down. He nocked an arrow and placed his bow next to him in his bed. He leaned Dovabane against the headboard where he could grab it with ease and he placed Bloodlust on the nightstand. If anyone managed to get through that door, it would be the last thing they ever did.

That night's sleep was restless. Swirling images of Hastur and countless other entities who looked like him filled Illume's mind. Some rose from the mountain tops, others from the desert, and one massive winged beast erupted from the ocean.

All the monsters laid waste to Valka with little difficulty. Every mage, warrior, and monster that called the continent their home rose up to fight them. When the dust settled on the scorched remnants of Valka, only the elder gods remained.

Madness 13%

Shooting up out of his bed, Illume wiped the sweat that cascaded over his body away as he tried to calm himself. His breathing was labored and the whispers he'd heard outside flooded his ears. Illume grabbed Bloodlust as he looked around to see his brother was gone and the door was open.

He sheathed both his bladed weapons and grabbed his bow. Illume made his way out into the hallway. He glanced back to see if anyone could be behind him. No one was. He made his way down the stairs as voices echoed up from the main hall. Illume didn't recognize one of them and drew his nocked arrow.

As Illume reached far enough down the stairs where he could see, he aimed his weapon into the great hall. John had his back to Illume on the far end of the great hall. Corazon stood across from John and faced

Illume. A third figure dressed in all black with his hood drawn stood between them off to the side.

Illume caught Corazon's gaze. He put his hands up and took a step away from John. John clearly noticed the reaction and turned. His eyes widened and his hands flew up.

"Hold on!" John yelled to Illume. "Everything's okay. We're just working the logistics of our trip!"

Illume lowered his bow. He put the arrow back in his quiver and slung the weapon over his shoulder. After Illume finished descending the steps and approached John, he nodded toward the man in black.

"Who is he?" Illume asked.

"I'm the Boat Man," the man replied.

His voice was raspy as if aged beyond any natural lifespan. Illume noticed a glint of light catch off one of his fingers that clutched a walking stick.

He turned to Illume, who took in a sharp breath upon seeing the man's face. Scales stretched up his neck and covered most of his visage. It was narrow and came to a point near his nose, which resulted in his bulging eyes appearing to be almost on the side of his head.

"Do you have my payment?" the Boat Man asked as he extended one of his web-fingered hands.

20

THE BOAT MAN

ILLUME FISHED through his coin purse. He retrieved the Boat Man's payment and placed it in his scaly hand. Illume watched as the Boat Man bit into the coin. He scrutinized it before he placed it in a purse on his hip.

"You wish to go to the islands of ash, I take it?" the Boat Man asked.

"If there is something there that can save my friend, yes," Illume replied.

Corazon grumbled and put his hand to his face as he shook his head. Illume turned to the pirate with a raised brow.

"The Boat Man is taking us," Illume pointed out. "Why are you so glum?"

"Because," Corazon replied with a huff. "Despite

bein' named the Boat Man, can you guess what he has not?"

"A boat?" John replied.

"Aye, he hasn't a boat." Corazon pointed at John as he spoke. "Which means I be your captain."

Illume turned his gaze to the Boat Man. He counted his tokens as his large eyes bulged even more at the sight of his gold.

"How do you not have a boat?" Illume asked.

Corazon pushed between all three and walked over to the bar. The Boat Man looked around for a moment before he shrugged.

"Monsters dwell in the depths," the Boat Man replied. "Some of those monsters hunger for the living, others for the dead, and even some for the salted wood of a good ship."

"Is that something we need to worry about, then?" John questioned.

John turned his attention to Illume. Illume shrugged. He didn't even know there was a seafaring part to the game.

"We needn't worry about the matter of monsters," the Boat Man pointed out. "The *Woeful Damnation* isn't a high quality ship."

"Don't be bad-mouthin' my ship," Corazon snapped. "At least she still be afloat."

He pushed past everyone once again. This time, he

had a small barrel of grog tucked under each arm. He'd donned a three-pointed hat with a flamboyant feather that protruded from it.

The Boat Man shrugged at Corazon's comment then followed Corazon out of the inn. Illume glanced over at John, who shrugged and fell in line.

"Guess we're doing this," Illume muttered under his breath. "Because nothing bad could happen on a ship called the *Woeful Damnation*."

"Did you say something?" John asked as he glanced over his shoulder.

"No." Illume shook his head.

As Illume exited the inn, Mire's mist encompassed him once again. The streets were dark with just enough light to make everything hauntingly terrifying. Illume closed the Inn's door, which extinguished the warm light from the fire and candles that burned within. The city retreated into a pale grey.

Stopping for a moment, Illume turned around. Just out of clear sight stood dozens of people. Illume could only assume they were just as "fishy" as the Boat Man. The silhouettes just stood there like ghosts who couldn't quite remember who they were.

An unsettling feeling tore through Illume's gut as he stepped onto the muddy path before him. The Boat Man held up a lamp that gave off an orange light. Its warmth was suffocated by Mire's dreary setting almost before it left its home. Illume fought the urge to draw his weapon. He could tell John was doing the same.

Even the soft lapping of the unseen ocean had a melancholy dread to it. Illume glanced over his shoulder as he forced his way forward through the wall of mist. The soft orange of lanterns accompanied the silhouettes. He swallowed hard as a lump formed in both his throat and his chest.

Illume tried to force himself to stay calm. He didn't want to trigger another spike in his madness meter. He took a deep breath and pressed forward. Ahead, the shadow of a large ship with three sails became visible.

The ropes on the pier filled the air with a sorrowful groan as the impact of the ship against the docks had a loneliness that Illume could relate to. It was the sound; of an empty apartment, of a long airplane flight to an exotic land with no one to share the experience with, of a dinner table and theater ticket for one.

Illume stopped for a moment. The loneliness of his life outside this world hit him like an anvil would hit Wiley Coyote, only this kind of hurt. He'd left on this quest to save Nari, not really thinking he'd fail. The stark reminder of his empty, lonely life before her caused Illume to freeze in the fear that he might.

What if he failed? What if she died before he got back? How could he forgive himself? It was his fault she'd been poisoned in the first place. Had he listened to John, he wouldn't be in this city that sucked hope from everything that entered.

Madness 14%

Illume felt his legs go weak as he became light-headed. The whispers gradually returned as he fell to his knees. Illume's mind raced as time warped around him. He felt his stomach turn as the unimaginable terror of losing Nari finally fully grasped him.

Illume's breathing was quick and shallow as his vision began to narrow. His heart raced like a grey-hound at the tracks as it desperately tried to go some-where and went nowhere instead.

No! Illume thought to himself. *You will not lose her!* Illume forced his breathing to slow. *You will bring her back.* He felt his heart rate return to normal. *She will help you defeat Hastur.* Illume pushed off the ground and rose to his feet. *You will not be alone anymore.*

"You okay?" John yelled from the mist ahead.

"Yeah, just missed my footing," Illume lied.

"Well, stop being clumsy and get up here!" John commanded.

Illume took a deep breath as he steadied himself. He forced the thoughts and feelings of the sheer empti-ness of his previous life out. He hadn't even realized how alone he was until he met Nari, Trillian, and Urtan.

It was as if concrete were attached to his boots. Each step forward took more effort than he thought he could give. His stamina bar didn't drop as the whispers subsided. With each step, he thought of Victor and Kassandra, Uthrandir and Buthrandir, about the twins Abdelkrim and Halfdan, and of Khal.

With each step, his feet grew lighter and the whispers grew dimmer. His senses sharpened and breathing became easier. Dread was replaced by confidence, doubt by hope. Illume knew that he would press forward, that he would succeed. Not for himself but for his loved ones.

Illume climbed onto the docks to see John and Corazon ascend up a ladder onto the *Woeful Damnation*. At the base of the ladder stood the Boat Man. He leaned on a long staff, one he didn't have before. As he peered at Illume from behind his hood, the cryomancer could have sworn he saw the Boat Man's face turn skeletal for a brief moment before it reverted to its fishy form.

Hoisting himself up the ladder and onto the main deck, Illume let out a huff when he saw John and Corazon waiting for him. Corazon had set down the kegs and had a map out that he looked at closely. He rolled it up and stuffed it into his coat as the Boat Man climbed over the edge as well.

"I have three rules on my ship," Corazon commanded. "I be your captain. If I tell you to do somethin', you do it." he said with a scrutinizing glare from his un-patched eye.

"Should there be singin' that comes from the waters, tie yourselves to the mast." Corazon added as he held up two fingers. "And no matter what happens, no matter what, you do not go to the water."

Corazon lifted his hand. The sails unfurled by themselves and seemed to fill with a breeze Illume didn't feel. Corazon lowered his hand and placed it over the map in his jacket.

"Where we go, there be monsters," he added with a word of warning.

With that, Corazon made his way up to the wheel of the ship. He pulled a compass from his waist and opened it. Corazon turned the wheel ever so slightly. A groan rumbled throughout the ship as it lurched forward. Both Illume and John staggered as the ship sliced through the water.

"Ooo, don't have my sea legs yet," John whined. "One second."

John's avatar stopped moving once again. Illume walked over to the edge of the boat. He leaned against the railing and looked back as the docks of Mire disappeared into the mist. The grey began to thin out as light from the sun started to illuminate the ship.

"That's better," John called out.

His avatar glitched then started to move once again. He approached Illume and leaned against the banister as well.

"Take off the VR set?" Illume asked.

"No, the game won't play on anything but VR," John replied. "I turned off the settings that registered the ship as rocking. Otherwise, I probably would have thrown up all over myself and you."

"I'd appreciate it if you didn't throw up," Illume murmured. "I don't want a repeat of Six Flags."

John let out a boisterous laugh, one he could hardly control. Illume watched as his brother nodded.

"Yeah, that was a bad day," John agreed. "I'm still not entirely sure if we're allowed back to that particular park."

"If I were the owner, I wouldn't let us back, that's for sure," Illume replied.

The mist started to thin as the air grew less and less wretched. Illume glanced up. He was actually able to see the colors of the sails. They were a bright purple. Illume turned to Corazon, who was facing him already.

"They used to be black," Corazon yelled preemptively. "Smugglin' trip went wrong, now they be purple. I don't want to be hearing 'bout it."

"Fair enough!" Illume replied.

Illume pushed off the rail and walked to the bow of the ship. It gently bobbed up and down as it sliced through the water. The ship itself was sturdy, but its planks were clearly aged.

The Boat Man walked up to Illume and gazed into the ever thinning mist. After about twenty minutes, it fully burned away to reveal a wide open ocean with crystal blue water as far as the eye could see. Little puffs of white speckled the otherwise clear sky.

"So why do they call you the Boat Man?" Illume asked his new fishy friend.

"There are places in this world guarded by ancient magic," he replied. "They may only be opened by those older than those places themselves."

The Boat Man added, "I am one of the few still alive that old. They call me the Boat Man because I used to ferry people to such places."

"So you're immortal?"

The Boat Man shook his head with a scoff. His scaly hands gripped his staff as he leaned against it. Illume watched his bulgy eyes as they scanned the ocean with a strange desire and sense of loss.

"Un-ageing and immortal are two very different things," the Boat Man corrected. "Immortals don't forget things with age."

"Like their own names?" Illume asked.

"Like their own names," the Boat Man nodded. "There is one other thing you should know, cryomancer. Something I doubt even the history books remember."

"What is that, Boat Man?"

The Boat Man held out his hand. He pointed to the horizon where a strange series of clouds seemed to be locked in place while others lazily floated by them.

"Those are the crystal shallows," he replied. "There you can't use that ice magic of yours."

"Why not?" Illume asked.

"A god be trapped there!" Corazon interrupted. "You be tellin' our passengers tales once again?"

"It's not a tale," the Boat Man argued.

"It be a tale!" Corazon urged. "He be tellin' this tale to any soul'll listen. I've sailed with him through the crystal shallows n'er more than once. There be no eldritch horrors trapped in the deep by the frosted powers of the eldest god."

"Azathoth sacrificed her life to keep the elder gods at bay!" the Boat Man snapped. "With her dying breath, she cast her power to the four corners of the world that only a worthy vessel could wield them once more. Problem is…"

"Shut up!" Corazon snapped.

"I will not be disrespect…" the Boat Man started.

"No, seriously, shut up!" Corazon interrupted one more time.

Corazon's accent had vanished as he walked to the ship's edge. He lifted his eye patch to reveal a second, fully functioning eye underneath. His face went white as a sheet as a soft melodious tone rose out of the waters.

"Now would be the time to tie yourself to the mast," Corazon whispered with a hint of terror in his voice.

SIRENS

BOTH THE BOAT Man and Corazon dashed from the bow of the ship. The Boat Man grabbed a rope. He tied it off on one of the pegs on the mast and ran a quick circle around the pillar of wood. He drew the rope around his chest and tied himself off.

Illume watched as Corazon tied the wheel in place before he joined the Boat Man at the mast and tied himself down as well. Illume descended the steps to the main deck. John had a mild look of concern on his face. He leaned over the edge and looked forward before he glanced back.

"What's going on?" John asked.

"Sirens," Illume replied.

"You mean like the Little Mermaid?" John scoffed.

"They are known as mermaids yes," Illume

explained. "But these aren't like Disney where everything is happy. They'll entice you with their song, drag you to the depths, and kill you. It's basic mythology."

"How do we fight them?" John asked.

"I already suffer from madness, so their singing shouldn't have an effect on me," Illume replied.

Illume drew Dovabane. It growled once again but did not burst into flames. He walked over to John and pulled him away from the edge of the boat.

"You turn down your audio input so you can't hear them sing. That way your avatar won't be compelled to jump over the edge and die." Illume suggested.

John's avatar froze once more for a few seconds. Illume looked over the edge. Behind them was a seemingly impenetrable wall of mist that completely covered the land. Before them, the water churned with the oncoming sirens.

"OKAY, I THINK I GOT IT!" John yelled at the top of his lungs.

Illume flinched at his brother's deafening tone. He turned to John and held a finger up to his lips.

"Does he have to yell?" Corazon asked.

"He can't hear anything," Illume explained. "He's trying to compensate. It's mostly involuntary. Now both of you shut up and let us work. And Corazon? We are going to be having a conversation about just ALL of this."

Illume indicated to Corazon as a whole.

"You just pointed to all of me," he replied.

"Yep!" Illume said without hesitation. "Now you stay there. Hiccup and let the grownups work."

Running to the bow of the ship, Illume leapt onto the railing and grabbed a rope with one hand. He leaned out over the water as the wind blew through his hair and his cloak billowed behind him. The churning water of the sirens grew closer and closer as the rushing wind filled Illume's ears like the crashing of a waterfall.

Illume sheathed Dovabane and raised his hand up as high as he could. Sparks formed around his fingers as his mana started to drop. The sirens bore down on the ship. They were only a hundred yards away now. Their songs grew louder as they closed in. Once Illume's mana hit the halfway mark, he opened his hand to the ocean before him.

A bright flash of light accompanied and a deafening crack of thunder shattered the song of the sirens momentarily. The bolt of lightning erupted from Illume's hand as if it were cast by Zeus himself. In the blink of an eye, the electric bolt slammed into the water ahead of them. Upon impact, it diffracted into thousands of smaller arcs of electricity.

Steam rose from the ocean as the water heated up from the energy of his electric blast. Dozens of health bars became visible from under the waves. They didn't drop very far.

Sirens are heavily resistant to magic.
Burns inflicted on targets.

"Great," Illume mumbled to himself.

Pulling himself back onto the deck, Illume leapt down the stairs to the main deck. He drew Dovabane as he made eye contact with John. Illume opened his hand and flared magic then shook his head before he made a "no go" signal with his hand. John nodded and drew his sword.

"Hey, um... buddy," Corazon whispered as the siren songs grew louder. "Wanna cut us free?"

Looking back at Corazon and the Boat Man, Illume shook his head. Corazon pulled against the ropes as hard as he could. This yanked the Boat Man, who was tied up on the opposite side, against the mast. He groaned.

"Humans are always so quick to fall to the sirens," the Boat Man grunted.

Illume leaned over and punched Corazon in the face. His health bar popped up and dropped by almost half as he slumped against the rope, unconscious. Illume looked at his hand in shock for a moment. How low level was this guy?

"Thank you, cryomancer," the Boat Man said softly. "I'd look behind you if I were you."

Illume whirred around. On the deck was a woman whose lower half was a long, slender, and strong tail of scales that shimmered blue. From the waist up, she had the body of a Victoria's Secret model, lean yet strong.

Her long black hair stuck to her wet skin and hid any part that could be deemed inappropriate. She had icy blue eyes and full, pouty red lips. Pointed ears poked from the hood of her dark hair as she writhed onto her tail. Her body moved as if she were trying to seduce him.

Glancing over his shoulder, Illume saw John was slack jawed over her appearance. *Come on, man, you can't be THAT desperate!* he thought to himself as the most beautiful sound floated from her lips as if it were honey from the gods themselves. Illume heard the Boat Man begin to struggle against the bonds as well.

"Keep it down over there or I'll knock you out too!" Illume called.

Illume turned his attention back to the siren. She was now accompanied by a blonde with a green tail, who was somehow more beautiful than the first. Illume gripped Dovabane tightly as his mana finished filling up. A third leapt onto the ship's deck, her hair was bright red and her skin as pale as the moon. Both of them joined their sister in song.

Hastur's Madness resisted the Siren's Song.

Smirking, Illume pointed his blade at the three women who were trying to seduce him. He initiated the mana burn, and with a low growl, his sword burst into flames. Illume dug deep, and with the intimidating voice of cracking ice, he snarled at them.

"You are but monsters and I will take your heads!"

Instantly, all three stopped singing. The white of their eyes turned black and their irises gold. Their skin shifted to grey and more fishlike than human. When they opened their mouths this time, only layers of razor sharp teeth could be seen, reminiscent of a shark.

Their melodious songs shifted to those of horrifying screeches. Illume gripped his blade with both hands as John staggered back in disgust at their sudden change. The dark-haired one lunged at Illume with her clawed nails. Illume was able to bring his sword to bear against her arms. Dovabane cut through them like tissue paper.

The siren's life bar dropped significantly. Before she had a chance to vocalize her pain, Illume decapitated her. A strange sense of pleasure warped through his body at seeing her headless body flop around on the deck.

Illume watched John for a few seconds as he struggled with his siren. She used her blonde hair as a whip against him to keep him on the defensive. He was holding his own, but it was only a matter of time before she landed a blow. Illume fired a bolt of electricity from his hand. It did nothing to damage her, but it distracted her enough for John to run her through. Her life bar only dropped by a third.

Turning to the redhead, Illume took a deep breath as she slithered across the bannister as if she were a serpent. She hissed several times. Illume extinguished Dovabane and drove it into the wood of the deck.

"Look at these swords," he partially sung as he pulled his bow off his shoulder. "Aren't they neat?"

He drew Bloodlust. "Wouldn't you think my armories complete?"

Illume held both the bow and dagger in the same hand. He nocked a frenzy arrow as he turned his side to her and drew his arrow. "Come on, Little Mermaid, let's do this." he snarled.

The redhead lunged at Illume. He fired his arrow at her right shoulder. The sirens were humanoid. He didn't want to hit a main artery. The arrow found its mark and the siren jolted back onto the deck with a shriek. Her health bar dropped by a quarter.

Illume glanced over to see how John was faring. He had gone full frenzy on the blonde siren, and even though she looked like a fish filet at this point, she'd only just died. Illume laughed and shook his head.

"You really need to invest in swordsmanship," Illume teased.

A birdlike screech sounded from above. Illume looked up to see a siren with leathery, bat-like wings swoop down at him and prepared himself to dive out of the way. Just as he was about to move, a blur of red tackled the flying siren out of the air. It was the frenzied one. The redhead ripped into her flying sister like a hungry dog being given a bloody steak.

Illume drew two more frenzy arrows. By his count, he'd have sixteen left after this. Sirens hopped onto the sides of the ships. Some had wings, others didn't, but all of them had discarded their attractive sides. Illume fired both the arrows at two flyers who were distracted by John. Both were hit.

Crystal Shallows entered:
Cryomancy no longer costs mana.

Illume smirked at the sight of both the flyers as they went haywire and ripped into every siren they could get their hands on. Illume slung his bow over his shoulder and grabbed his sword. Without a second thought, he lunged into the fray of flesh, hair, teeth, and scales.

He loved it, the flash of his sword. The splatter of blue sirens' blood and the screeches they made as each fell to his hand or to their sisters. Illume was in a trance as he fought. He didn't know where Corazon and the Boat Man were. He didn't know where John was or if he was even okay. In this moment, he didn't care. All he craved was what violence he could bring on these seductresses.

As the crowd of sirens thinned, Illume found himself against one of his frenzied. With two fluid swipes, Illume cut her wings off before he kicked her in the chest so hard, she stumbled overboard. Illume swirled around to catch his breath. His stamina was nearly gone, but he only yearned for more blood.

In the center of the deck sat the redheaded siren. She had taken her human form once more as she looked around in horror at the carnage surrounding her. Her eyes welled up and tears streamed down her face.

"What have I done?" she stammered in horror.

"My bidding," Illume growled.

She looked up at Illume. Terror gripped her young face as she tried to back away. Her tail had been injured and dragged limply behind her. Illume caught up to her in no time and stepped on her tail to prevent her escape. She winced at the pressure of his boot.

"My sisters, they're gone," she whimpered.

"You kill innocents," Illume stated.

"We only kill what we need to survive," she rebutted. "We've been starving, and we only needed one of you!"

Illume leaned forward. He placed more pressure on her tail, which made her cry out in pain. It was strange, but he enjoyed the look of agony on her face.

"The rest of your kind will die when I have completed my mission," Illume said tauntingly.

"Leig leis an ton thu!" she snapped.

She spat at Illume, who dodged her saliva. The dodge to his side gave her enough room to slide free from his foot. She frantically clawed against the wood to make it overboard. Illume drew Bloodlust and threw it into her tail and pinned her to the deck. She screamed in agony.

"Illume!" John barked.

Illume looked over his shoulder to see his brother approach.

"She's beaten, release her!" he commanded.

Illume stepped forward and pulled the dagger from her tail.

"As you wish." he murmured.

"Thank you!" the siren cried gratefully. "Thank you, stranger, for your…"

The siren was cut off by Illume's sword as it separated her head from her neck.

Madness 17%

A deep rumble filled the air. Illume heard the Boat Man call out in fear. Illume turned to see a darkness on the horizon that grew.

"What is that?" John asked.

22

FIRE & ASH

WALKING TOWARD THE MAST, Illume slashed the rope, which freed Corazon and the Boat Man. Corazon whimpered as he fell to the ground, while Illume pointed at the ever-growing tidal wave on the horizon.

"Corazon, get us away from that," Illume commanded.

Corazon was still in a daze and groaned as he shook his head. Illume leaned down and pulled the dazed man to his feet. He turned the "pirate" around and pointed him toward the wall of water as it rapidly approached.

"That! Right there!" Illume persisted. "Get us out of its range."

"There is nothing he can do," the Boat Man informed, his tone resolute. "Even if you had not nearly killed him with that punch, that wave is magic.

It is a curse placed on us by the sirens. None who have been cursed have ever lived to speak about it."

Illume's brow arched at the Boat Man's comment. He glanced around and noticed a large rope ladder rigging that went to the crow's nest.

"Then how do people know about it?" Illume asked.

"There have been witnesses," the Boat Man replied.

"Everyone, focus all your magic on that wave," Illume commanded.

"Brother, we don't have enough to slow that thing down, let alone stop it," John opined as he approached the railing.

"Just do it," Illume ordered.

With that, Illume climbed the rope ladder as light shone from both the Boat Man and John. The wind picked up as the wave grew closer. Illume made it to the crow's nest in a matter of moments but his stamina took a hit from the climb.

As Illume faced the wave, he could see flares of magic as they danced over the hundred-foot swell. It was only a few miles away, but it closed in fast. Illume summoned his mana with all his might as he brought to life his frost magic.

As he threw his hands out in front of him, a massive beam of blue frosted light shot from his hands. He had to admit he felt a little like Arnold

Schwarzenegger's frost gun, but it was intoxicating. Illume separated his hands as the center of the wave began to solidify.

With both hands slowly separated from one another, Illume was able to continue to freeze the impending wave. His mana didn't drop due to his proximity to the crystal shallows, but the cost of unleashing a torrent of frost cold enough to rival Pluto took its toll.

A sharp pain struck Illume's mind. He smelt the blood before he felt it drip from his nose. He gritted his teeth as his vision blurred and his heart pounded. His knees weakened, but the wave wasn't frozen yet and it was now less than a half mile away.

Illume felt a wave of cold wash over him, as his vision went white for a few seconds. The cold seemed to be absorbed into his very core. He could feel the crystals form throughout his body as he grew colder and colder. Pressure built up within him to the point where he felt he might explode. .

Finally, Illume felt all the cold within erupt outwards in front of him. His vision went black for a few seconds,before fading into blurred obscurity. Illume was lightheaded but the rail of the crow's nest prevented him from falling. His head throbbed and his mouth was dry, yet Illume managed to pull himself to his feet as he blinked his vision back into clarity.

Less than fifty yards away, the massive wave stood in a thick layer of ice. The *Woeful Damnation* rocked ever so slightly from the disruption of Illume's spell. He wasn't sure how it worked, but he was fairly certain it defied most of the laws of physics.

Level Up x2
Active Attribute Points: 2
Active Skill Points: 1
Overall Level 23

A snowflake danced down in front of his field of view. Soon the entire surrounding area experienced snowfall. Illume felt his strength return before he looked over the edge of the crow's nest and down to the main deck.

"What have you done?!" the Boat Man yelled.

"I just saved your life!" Illume replied.

"At what cost?" the Boat Man yelled as he pointed to the other side of the boat. "Look and pray your actions were not enough to wake him!"

Illume turned to the opposite side of the frozen wave. It was then why he understood this place was called the shallows. The water was only a few yards deep. At the bottom was a massive crystal that stretched as far as Illume could see. The boat shook and the water rumbled as the sound of a muffled cannon ripped through the air. Illume noticed a massive crack lance across the face of the crystal.

The "ground" under the crystal shifted. It didn't take long for Illume to realize it wasn't sand that shifted but rather an enormous eyelid. A massive eye with bluish-black marbling was revealed. The pupil was ovaland horizontal like a goat's. A deep rumble emanated from whatever was trapped under the crystals as its eye darted straight to Illume.

Madness already imparted.

Swallowing hard as the eye seemed to stare into his very soul, Illume fell back and into the crow's nest. Under him, he could hear the Boat Man barking orders, though he couldn't hear what they were. He did feel the boat as it increased its speed from its almost complete standstill.

Illume glanced over the crow's nest edge once again. The massive eye continued to watch him as the boat pulled away from it. The crack in the crystal had stopped about halfway up the eye's height. Illume clambered over the edge and clumsily descended the rope ladder, returning to the deck.

The Boat Man marched over to Illume and gave him a powerful shove. Illume staggered backwards. Anger flared within him and his hand instinctively went for his sword, but John's hand clamped down around Illume's and held the weapon in place.

"You have awoken him!" the Boat Man yelled. "We are lucky you didn't use enough of that magic to free him."

"What did Illume wake up?" John asked, his voice at a normal level now.

"Hastur's little brother," the Boat Man replied.

"That's his LITTLE brother?!" Illume scoffed in disbelief.

"Yes, locked away by the Azathoth, and only THAT power can release him," the Boat Man urged. "Now that he's awake, he will use Hastur's disciples to find a way to free him."

"How do we stop him?" John asked with a level tone.

"His species is hierarchical," the Boat Man explained. "If they don't devour each other, they strictly obey the hierarchy."

"Then we kill Hastur before he has a chance to free his sibling," Illume decided. "We take Hastur's place and we can put him back to sleep."

The Boat Man paused for a brief moment. He shook his head.

"It's worth a try," the Boat Man replied. "But because you don't have all of Azathoth's power yet, you wouldn't be able to lock him away."

Crystal Shallows Exited:
Cryomancy now costs mana.

"One problem at a time!" Illume pleaded. "Our plates are already full enough without the mess I potentially made being added to it. Let's just get to where we're headed and worry about saving Nari. Then we'll take care of Hastur and the Order of Light. THEN we'll come back here and put this being back into an eternal slumber."

"LAND HO!" Corazon yelled.

Everyone looked back at him, then followed where his finger pointed. On the horizon, there was an island that seemed to phase in and out of view. He climbed to the bow of the ship and squinted. His eyes did not deceive him - what he saw was in fact an island.

A THUD brought Illume's attention back. John lay on his back with bits of siren surrounding him. He had slipped on one of the amputated fins. An appearance of disgust filled his face as he looked at the blood that covered him.

"Can we clean this up, please?" John pleaded with a cracked voice.

The Boat Man helped John up. Illume kicked the lower half of a bisected siren off the ship. It took a while, but eventually, most of the evidence of the slaughter that took place was cleaned up. Illume couldn't explain it, but he had a macabre urge to keep the head of the red-haired siren, albeit hidden from view.

While the others were distracted, Illume took her head and placed it in a bag under one of the stairwells. He snickered to himself at the thought of Corazon finding it and screaming.

Corazon yanked a rope free from its knot and started to pull. Illume climbed up the steps behind him and assisted. Each tug pulled up the main sail until it was completely furled once again, slowing the ship's speed down.

"Sorry about the face," Illume said with remorse in his voice.

"I was putting us in danger," Corazon replied. "You did what was necessary to save lives. For that, you have no reason to apologize."

Corazon rubbed his jaw briefly and laughed to himself before he moved to another rope. He knew he was able to man the ship single-handed if he wanted.

The ship continued to slow as they approached the island.

"Illume, grab the wheel and turn it hard to port," Corazon yelled from across the ship.

Illume did as he was instructed. The old wheel squeaked with each turn he made. The ship turned as it prepared to stop and they could see that a series of docks dotted the island's edge.

Massive rocky cliffs made approach from anywhere but the docks impossible.

The island appeared to be abandoned, as no one waited or worked on the docks. There were no sounds aside from the surging of the ocean and the incessant screeching of the gulls overhead.

Corazon walked to the center of the deck, kicked a lever and a series of splashes rang out as the ship's anchors were dropped. Illume descended the steps as both Corazon and the Boat Man grabbed a long plank of wood and set it on the edge of the boat. It slanted down to the docks and both men descended, followed closely by John, then finally Illume.

"Welcome to the Isle of Flame and Ash," the Boat Man greeted them. "We may venture no further. But if you follow the path ahead, you will find what you seek."

"Thank you," Illume said softly.

John and Illume pushed forward. They traversed the surprisingly well kept docks and climbed a series of steps that had been carved from the rocks.

"What happened back there?" John asked as they climbed.

"What do you mean?" Illume inquired.

"With the sirens," John supplied. "You looked like

you lost yourself. You cut through them without mercy or remorse. They didn't stand a chance against you. And the redhead."

"They tried to kill us!" Illume snapped back, his voice as sharp as a tack. "If every single one of them wasn't cut down, they would have continued to pose a threat to us."

John stopped climbing. He looked back at Illume, who could see that John wanted to believe him, but wasn't sure if he could. John let out a sigh.

"If you really believe that then I trust you," he relented after several seconds.

"I do believe that," Illume maintained.

"So be it," John replied.

They continued to climb up windy stairs that had been haphazardly hacked into the cliff. Some of those stairs went through little tunnels where Illume used Dovabane's flame to light the way. As they climbed, Illume's stamina dropped steadily. From the way John slowed down, Illume could tell his had begun to drop as well.

After almost an hour of walking, the brothers finally made it to the top of the island. Not all of their climbing had been upward progress. Some tunnels twisted and turned, while others were straightaways. It seemed at times like the stairs were a deterrent for the lazy.

Both men emerged from a narrow corridor onto a large flat stone mesa. Grey rocks protruded all around the flat area. A massive gate was off to their right by about two hundred yards. It was set with its top level with their feet and had been carved into the earth itself.

A strange red light seemed to be emitting from the gate and the stones that surrounded it. While John was transfixed on the gate, Illume looked around to see a throne made of blackened stone that faced it. The throne had what appeared to be flames carved into it, and in front of the seat was a pedestal.

Illume walked over to the throne and ran his hand over the charred/ashy rock, inspecting the fine craftsmanship before he sat down. Suddenly, a book became visible on the pedestal in front of him. The cover read:

The Book of Azathoth

Illume ran his fingers over the coarse leather. The book was as thick as half the length of Illume's forearm and had a familiar stench to it. He couldn't control himself and with a flick of his wrist, the thick book opened up and slapped onto the pedestal.

The words within were written in a thick, dark crimson. If Illume wasn't mistaken, it had the color and texture of blood. Illume touched the heavy pages as he read the words scrawled inside.

> *"When Azathoth arises from the dark the foundations*
> *of the world will tremble.*
> *Only the great cold one may stem the tide of gold."*

"What are you doing?" John barked.

His words broke Illume's concentration. He looked up to see a woman standing behind John.

"John, look out!" Illume yelled.

Illume jumped to his feet, drew his bow, and fired an arrow at her in the blink of an eye. The woman threw her hand out and the arrow turned to ash before it made it halfway to her.

"I have been waiting for you for a long time, Illume of Valka." Her voice was soft yet stern and her eyes burned into Illume's very soul.

23

THE MUSE

JOHN STAGGERED AWAY from the woman. She was taller than either of them and wore a white robe that had been smeared by ash. She had short dark hair that was curly and hugged the sides of her head as if she were from the 1920s. Her form was slender, as was her neck and her skin was olive.

Tarnished gold disks held her robe together at her shoulders. Her face was relaxed yet had a sense of disappointment to it. But her eyes, they glowed with living fire as if the very light of her soul shone through.

"How do you know his name?" John stammered.

"She's programmed to," Illume replied.

"I have seen your deeds as they stretched far and wide," she interrupted. "You have committed evil against some, yet goodness to most. The mission that brings you here is one of purity, for you seek out the power hidden here not for your own use, but for that of another."

Her gaze burned into Illume's soul. He felt a tinge of guilt for his actions against the sirens on the boat. Illume felt her mind as it rooted through his own. He staggered backward into the podium and collapsed as his legs gave out.

"What are you doing to me?" Illume gasped.

"I am purging your mind of the corruption that dwells within," she replied.

She walked toward Illume. The closer she got, the hotter his body became. Illume summoned his frost magic to cool himself, but her power was beyond him and melted the ice before it fully formed.

Illume saw John attempt to move in and assist, but with a flick of her wrist, he was frozen in place. She moved closer to Illume and gently placed her hand on his head. It was cold. Illume closed his eyes and leaned into her soft touch as his body felt like it was burning from the inside out.

Her cool touch soon washed over his body like a refreshing river. His body rapidly cooled back down and he relaxed back against the pedestal with darkness no longer clouding his mind.

"The madness of Hastur could not be cured, but its effects could be made void," Her tone was that of a loving mother.

"Who are you?" Illume asked.

Illume looked up to the mysterious woman's face. Her eyes were an almond brown and full of kindness. She gently lifted Illume to his feet. With a wave of her hand, John was freed.

"I am Melpomene, guardian and prisoner of this land," she replied matter-of-factly. "I am glad that you have survived the sirens and did not awaken the sleeping one."

"You said that you knew why I was here?" Illume asked.

He glanced over to John, who kept his distance. From his stance, Illume could tell he was ready for anything. He made eye contact with the slender yet very tall woman before him.

"You are here for the last feather," Melpomene replied. "The only thing that can render the venom of an elder god harmless."

"Where can I get this feather?" Illume pressed.

Melpomene put her hand up and shook her head. She offered Illume a smile before she gracefully walked over to the throne and sat on it. Her long slender fingers flipped each page of the *Book of Azathoth*. As she reached an empty page, blood began to stain it.

Illume tried to read what was written, but it was in a strange language he couldn't decipher. In fact, all the pages she'd flipped were in the same language.

Melpomene nodded to herself as she read the pages before she shut the book. She looked up at Illume and rose from her seat.

"It has been decreed. Illume, you will be permitted to enter the labyrinth within to retrieve the feather," Melpomene said. "But you must go alone and face your challenges without the aid or conscience of another. Should you succeed, your friend will be saved. Should you fail, the power of Azathoth will be scattered for another to find."

"What are you talking about? I'm going with him!" John interrupted.

Illume put his hand up to his brother and shook his head. John stopped in his tracks.

"You can't come with me," Illume reiterated. "Even if you could, I won't let you. Whatever I face down there, I won't risk another one of your lives. I alone got Nari into this mess. I alone need to get her out."

"I should go," John insisted. "I still have two lives left. Plus I still have a body in the real world. Even if I do lose both lives, that doesn't mean that I die there."

"It doesn't mean that you don't," Illume answered. "Who knows what happens to you? I don't even think the creators of the game know. It's a miracle in and of itself that you were able to get onto the server to play."

Illume looked back at Melpomene. There was something about that name that seemed very familiar. He couldn't quite put his finger on it, but now wasn't the time. Her hand rested on his shoulder, light as a feather.

"What waits for me below?" Illume asked.

"Only what you take with you," John cut in.

Illume shot his brother a stern glance. Usually, he was all about puns and pop culture jokes, but Nari's life was on the line. Losing her was too great a risk to play around. John took a step back and closed his mouth while he offered Illume a thumbs-up.

"I can't tell you," Melpomene said. "For I have never been. The door is open to all but me. What dwells below will try you, mind, body, and soul. Some might be real, others may not be. But all will be dangerous."

"Will this be one of those Aladdin things where I'm not allowed to touch anything inside?" Illume asked.

"Of course not," Melpomene replied. "Any treasure within was brought by others who sought out the feather, only to fail. You may claim anything but be wary of greed. Strong warriors would have succeeded had their greed not overtaken them."

"Then lead the way," Illume instructed.

Melpomene offered Illume a gentle smile. She wrapped her arms around him and hugged him close as a mother would an overeager child.

"You are tired, Illume," she whispered. "You must

rest should you wish to succeed in your endeavors. Please, sleep."

Illume felt his body go limp as she told him to sleep. Everything went dark, but it was unlike anything he'd experienced before. It was peaceful, serene. Even in this resting place Illume felt at peace and not at all like he HAD to do anything.

Illume didn't know how long he'd been out. It felt like he'd been asleep for months as he finally woke up. He was refreshed beyond anything he'd felt before. He let out a groan as he turned over on the flat rock he'd been sleeping on and pushed off of it.

The whispering of John and Melpomene caught his attention. Illume looked over to see them inspecting one of John's spells. She appeared to deconstruct it and re-form it into something different. Illume rubbed his head.

"How long was I out?" Illume asked.

"Time is a relative concept to me," Melpomene replied.

"About an in-game day," John replied.

Illume clambered to his feet. A whole day? He didn't have that kind of time to waste. Nari didn't have that kind of time.

"I need to get that feather now!" Illume yelled at himself.

His sword, dagger, and bow had been placed next

to him on the slab. He gathered up his gear and approached Melpomene.

"How do I enter the place below?" Illume asked.

Melpomene turned and motioned to the massive reddish door on the other side of the clearing. Runes glowed around its edge, followed by a deep rumble. The door split down the center and slowly opened.

"This is your doorway. Remember your path, as we can't aid you once you cross the threshold," Melpomene said.

"Thank you," Illume said with a nod as his impatience got the better of him. "By the way. How did you read the book? I read from it, but when I looked again, I didn't recognize the language."

"Not many can read the words of the ancients," Melpomene replied with a kind smile. "Unless they use a device made by one, like my throne."

Illume nodded, impressed at the concept. He then made his way over to John and placed a hand on his brother's shoulder.

"Now would be the perfect time to attempt to find the coder of this part of the game to see if he can help," Illume suggested. "I don't know how long I'll be gone, but I can tell you that you're going to be really bored just sitting here waiting for me."

John placed a hand on Illume's shoulder. He laughed at Illume slightly and shook his head.

"I'm going to miss you too. Be careful and I'll be here when you get back," John instructed.

John pulled the sword Nari had made for Illume from its sheath and offered it to his brother.

"You might need it while I'm gone," said Illume, as he waved farewell to John. "And please put some skill points into your swordsmanship. It's just embarrassing the bad way you use such a beautiful weapon."

Illume turned and descended toward the crimson lit door. He took a deep breath and drew his bow before he nocked an arrow. Frost formed on his fingertips and danced over the string of his weapon before it spread to the feathers of his arrow.

The ground trembled as the massive doors opened with an echoing grind of stone against stone. Ahead, everything was pitch black, apart from a soft crimson light, that pulsed almost a hundred yards into the labyrinth.

Illume passed the massive doors. He looked up at the enormous stone structures. Jeff Goldblum's voice echoed in his head as he passed through the doors. *Who've they got in there King Kong?*

The darkness enveloped Illume. It was tangible, almost as if it had a physical presence. A sense of unease and dread filled him from without,. due to the darkness that surrounded him. He couldn't tell if the pressure or the disturbing silence was worse. He glanced back at the doors that had already begun to shut. From inside this strange place he couldn't hear the grinding of rock or the slam as they closed.

Complete darkness enveloped Illume while the pulsating red light did nothing to illuminate the path ahead. Illume released his bow string and threw his hand up. He summoned flames and shot a pillar of fire ahead .

The darkness seemed to feast on the fire, so it illuminated nothing and was extinguished before reaching five feet ahead of Illume. Each step he made was tentative, as he felt around with his foot to ensure his next step wouldn't be down a bottomless pit. So far, so good.

To cover the distance from the door to the light took what felt like hours. Patience was the game here, any impulsive move would certainly spell death for Illume as well as Nari. He was so close to what would save her that it took every fiber of his being not to just start sprinting.

Red flashes grew brighter and brighter as Illume got closer to the pulsating red sack. Now that he was close enough, Illume noticed that the light was being given off by what looked like a heart in a sack of fluid. Each beat created a pulse of light.

Illume passed under the heart. It stopped beating. Illume looked down at his hands, his bow. He could see himself as clear as day. A soft reflection of himself rippled in what looked like black water under him. He didn't sink, so looked around in confusion.

"Please don't let Eleven or a demigorgon come out and kill me," Illume whispered to himself.

"You found me," a voice called out from behind Illume.

Illume drew his bow and whirled around. He nearly released the arrow out of shock alone as his eyes fell on Nari. She wore clothing similar to Melpomene. Illume lowered his weapon. He felt like he'd just been hit with an anvil.

"You're supposed to be in Moot," Illume replied.

"The witch sent me here after you left." She looked around at the void around them. "She said this place would nullify the poison that ran through my veins. And it did."

Nari approached Illume. She offered him a sheepish smile as she placed a hand on his chest. She leaned in and gave his cheek a warm kiss with her soft lips.

"I'm safe now. You can stay with me here where we are safe from Hastur," she offered.

Illume wouldn't lie; it was tempting. The feel of her breath on his ear, the sultry tone of her voice. Her scent, the way she held herself. Everything about her felt real, but something in his gut told him not to trust her. Nari wouldn't slink away into a void; she would have faced Hastur by herself if she had to.

"Who did you forge the armor you made me with?" Illume probed.

"What are you talking about?" Nari asked in a confused tone.

"You forged me the most beautiful set of armor that could withstand blows from some of the most powerful beings you knew of," Illume said. "Who did you forge it with?"

Nari gave Illume a shy smile. She ran her fingers through her hair and batted her eyelashes at him.

"I would only forge the best for the one I love," she replied. "And only Domacius could help me forge your armor."

Without a word, Illume swung his sword in a flash of flames. Black oozed from the wound he placed across her chest. A life bar formed over her and dropped to zero almost instantly.

Critical hit x10

Fire is extremely effective against Shifters.

24

DUNGEON OF GOD II

NARI'S FORM turned to a mass of black goo that slumped to the ground and dissolved into a puddle. Illume looked around the black void and pursed his lips. He couldn't remember where he'd seen something like this before, but there was psychic ooze involved and its creations lived in a nest.

Illume sheathed his sword. He looked around for a few more seconds before he summoned fire to his hands. His mana fell as the flames licked up his arms. He increased the heat of his magic, which caused the black ooze around his feet to back away slightly. This revealed stony ground.

"You're in my mind," Illume spoke with a threatening tone. "You know what I'm about to do. Remove yourself from me and leave me to my mission. Or don't. I could always use the experience."

The fire grew brighter as Illume poured more mana into his hands. The blackness around him withdrew, letting out a small hiss as it did. Illume kept a close eye on the retreating beings. Several piles of black ooze formed around the outside of a massive room made of red dirt, reminding Illume of Oklahoma.

One of the blobs shifted into John's form. He took several steps forward until Illume held up his flaming hand. The replicant of John stopped in his tracks and held his hands up.

"We accept your terms," John's doppelganger blurted. "You will not be bothered by us in your labors ahead."

"Why should I believe you?" Illume narrowed his eyes.

"Look around you." He motioned towards dozens of skeletons that littered the floors.

"None of these brave knights gave us the choice to surrender. They all wished us dead and so we wished them dead." he instructed. "You are the first to offer mercy - as a token of our gratitude the ones your people have called shifters will not plague your path."

Illume closed his hands and extinguished the flames. He nodded to the being who held his brother's form.

"Thank you," Illume replied in a hushed tone.

"Please, press forward," the shifter offered. "But be

warned, there are things far worse than us in the lower depths."

He indicated to the far end of the room. A hatch lay open with two planks of wood that protruded from the hole. Illume looked around at all the skeletons in armor. Illume stepped over the bodies as he made his way to the open hatch.

At the entrance lay a skeleton in mage robes. His skeletal hands clutched a scroll which he held open. It was clearly something important enough to consider a last resort. Illume kneeled next to the skeleton and got a glimpse of the scroll. He gently took it from the body. Its hands fell off.

"Sorry about that, buddy," Illume murmured as he opened the scroll.

Scroll of the Nameless Mist
This one time use spell summons a thick mist to
*   confuse your enemies. They will not be able to see*
*   through it but you can.*
If used in the presence of existing mist or fog this
*   spell will allow it to side with you.*
Weight: +.05 Worth: 1500 Polis

Illume rolled the scroll back up. He picked up an empty satchel. He slung it over his shoulder and slid the scroll inside. Illume looked down a hatch in the floor nearby. A rickety-looking ladder stretched down the twenty-foot drop below, so Illume climbed onto it and made his way down.

As he descended, the temperature cooled slightly. The air became crisper and smelled more of winter than of the mouldy crypt. Illume looked around the large room which was similar to the one above, but with a throne in the middle instead of darkness or shifters. Bodies lay cast to the side in perfect lines approaching the throne.

Illume reached the bottom of the ladder. The second his foot touched the ground, he felt an unseen force lock him in place. He had been ready for anything, or so he thought, but he was not ready for this. Words filled his eyeline:.

What belongs to you, but others use it more than you do?

Illume paused for a moment, then smirked. Riddles were one thing that he'd learned to enjoy at his first job in a coffee shop. His manager would put out a "riddle of the day" every morning. This happened to be one of the riddles his boss used.

"My name." Illume called out.

The words disappeared and Illume stepped forward. As his second foot hit the ground, he felt his body locked in place again. He tried to step forward again, but couldn't.

I live beneath a roof yet am never dry should you hold me I shall not lie.

I cut deeper than steel, poison worse than a bite; should you unleash me all will take flight.

This one stumped Illume for a few seconds. He bit the inside of his cheek as he searched his mind for the correct answer.

"My father always said that nothing in this world is more wicked or cuts deeper than the tongue," Illume called out.

The words disappeared. Illume nodded as he recognized the use for this room. He stepped forward and came to a stop a third time. Then the next riddle appeared.

When you need me you throw me away.
When you don't you bring me back.

"Hmm. Not sure about this one," Illume murmured to himself.

He sat and thought about the possible response for quite some time. Nothing he could come up with quite fit the description. After nearly an hour, he thought he'd come up with the right solution.

"A fishing line." He proclaimed with confidence.

The room turned red. Puffs of air struck him followed by a sting. Illume reached for his neck and pulled a dart out. His health bar dropped.

Toxicology prevented poison.

The wall to Illume's right continued to spit out dozens of darts. He crouched and lifted his left arm. His shield asserted itself and blocked most of the darts. Others sailed past and only one or two more hit Illume.

When the darts stopped shooting at him, Illume summoned his healing magic. His life bar hadn't fallen by much, but with over ten percent of it missing already, the little damage the darts had done stacked up. Illume healed himself as he stood back up.

"Okay, an anchor." Illume guessed.

The magic that held him released. Illume looked at his hands and moved them around. He stepped forward, then back.

"Are you kidding me?" he scoffed to himself. "Should have thought of that."

Stepping forward once more, Illume was almost within reaching distance of the throne. The bodies were burned beyond recognition, almost completely reduced to ash. Illume looked around himself, to see small holes with scorch marks were on either side of him.

Illume extended each arm to his side. He called on his frost magic. He used all his mana to create two walls of ice on either side to protect him from the flames.

What can run but cannot walk,
  has a mouth but cannot talk,
  has a head but never weeps,
  has a bed but never sleeps.

"A river," Illume called out with confidence.

The magic released him, so Illume stepped forward. He glanced back at the pillars of ice that had already begun to melt despite the cooler temperature of the room.

Illume approached the throne and placed his hand on the smooth marble chair. He couldn't see clearly from the base of the hatch, but it was almost like glass, carved from a single piece of stone. As Illume touched it, his vision went dark.

Throne of Chaos Discovered

Images filled his head of conquest. Hastur falling to his hand. A woman who seemed to be half made out of rotting wood, who (Illume somehow knew fed on the souls of the innocent), was reduced to ash. An army of the Order of Light fell before him in a glorious storm of swords and magic.

Illume sat on the black throne in Trillian's armor, with a crown made of what looked like dragon's teeth and molded metal, carrying two swords on his back and a massive golden spear in his hand, Valka being consumed by natural disasters left, right, and center, yet when Illume raised his hand even the slightest bit, they all came to a stop.

Hordes of men, elves, dwarfs, giants, every race living and dead chanted his name. Illume felt a swell of pride roll over him like a wave in the ocean, making a satisfied smile form on his face. Something about it seemed off to Illume. It seemed like dark magic.

Just as quickly as it had come, the vision was gone. Illume found himself still sitting on the throne. Before him was the crown from his vision and a tome that appeared to be some kind of spell book . Illume tried to push himself from the throne, but he couldn't. He was held in place by the same magic that had held him previously.

"I wield great power, yet am brought to my knees? A king above all, yet slave to these, corrupted, the incorruptible now all men pays, brings light to darkness at the end of days?" Illume whispered to himself.

The riddle seemed to flow from the crown and out of his mouth and caused Illume's brow to become furrowed. He would be what was brought to his knees. He would be a slave to the immeasurable power the crown could give him. The light at the end of days would likely be him using dark magic to destroy everything.

Absolute power corrupts absolutely, Illume thought to himself as he grabbed the book.

Spell Tome: Scale Skin
Weight: +5 Worth: 350 polis
Costs 150 mana to cast. Turns caster's skin as tough
*   as dragons' scales for sixty seconds.*

Cracking the book open, Illume heard a low growl from the book similar to one his sword. Fire engulfed his face, it was warm but didn't burn. He felt a strange sensation wash over his body, making it feel hardened, as he imagined wearing armor would.

As the fire subsided, the book was gone. Illume looked at his hands to see that they had translucent scales covering them. The scales retracted from his fingers and palms as his normal sensation returned.

Player Has Learned Scale Skin.

The wall ahead of Illume fell to the ground. Inside the opening a massive boulder sat on a narrow ledge before him. That ledge inclined to a bowl three dozen yards above. Illume let out a defeated sigh and shook his head.

"I'm not Hercules!" Illume grumbled.

He pushed forward. As he exited the room with the Throne of Chaos, the wall slid up behind him. Illume looked at the boulder that was a good foot taller than he was. He shook out his arms and pushed against the giant rock. It hardly moved.

Illume attempted to use ice to create a ramp that would run up the boulder. The ice melted before it could even form. He wasn't strong enough by himself to move the boulder. He didn't have enough attribute points to make a difference in moving it either.

With no tools around to help get the rock to its resting place, he had only one choice left. Illume summoned his new Scale Skin spell. As the magic never left his body, the spell actually worked. His mana dropped by about half, but he felt immensely stronger.

Illume leaned into the boulder with all his strength. To his surprise, the giant rock moved. He planted his feet and pushed as hard as he could, making his stamina drop rapidly as he started to make progress. He was about a quarter of the way up when his spell wore off. Instantly, the boulder slid back down. Illume used the last of his mana to cast it once again.

He kept count this time. He used as much of his energy as he could to press forward until his stamina failed again. Illume stopped moving completely - at least he could hold the boulder in place for now.

Illume opened his skill and attribute trees. He left the skill alone but placed both his attribute points into wisdom. His health was as full as it could get and didn't move. His near empty stamina and mana both filled completely.

New Stats
Wisdom: +42
Mana: 320
Look at you, getting wiser by the day!

Closing the menu, Illume continued to push. He recast the same spell as he reached the last few seconds. Sweat beaded on his brow. He'd never worked so physically hard in his life. His heart pounded, his legs burned and his back ached, but he didn't give up.

He kept pushing the boulder with all his might. He recast the spell one last time as he approached the apex of the incline. He had no idea how he'd managed to keep it on the narrow path, but it wasn't something he would concern himself with right now. Just as Illume reached the top, he dropped the stone into its bowl.

His spell dissipated as he collapsed into it. Illume looked all around the square room he was in. It was made of the same grey stone as the island, which didn't surprise him much. There didn't seem to be a way out until words burned into the rock.

Intelligence, compassion, strength.
These tests have you passed.
Rest now warrior for your greatest labors are yet
    ahead.

25

DEEPER

ILLUME OPTED to relax for a few minutes to catch his breath and regain his mana and stamina. His mana started to restore itself. He chilled his hand and placed it on his sweating forehead.

As his body returned to its restful state, Illume pulled himself to his feet. He wasn't sure how to activate the next room, but voice commands seemed to work so far.

"I am ready to move on!" Illume said to no one in particular.

Part of the wall disappeared into thin air, which revealed the path ahead. Illume maneuvered himself carefully to the next narrow bridge and slid down.

As he reached the bottom, a skeleton lay on the ground. Every bone was shattered to near dust and a large round dent was in the wall. The feet still had boots on them that were Kapre boots.

Illume reached out and grabbed the higher quality boots. The legs separated at the knees as Illume held the boots in his hands to inspect them. They were still in perfect condition and the dead body hadn't seemed to damage them in any real way either.

Boots of Water Dash (Fine)
Armor: +10, Weight: +1 Worth: 1500 polis
Boots of Water Dash have the same effects as regular
    Kapre boots. They have the additional perk of
    allowing the wearer to move along the surface of
    water so long as they don't stop.

He looked up at the ball above him. It probably wouldn't have, but Illume couldn't help but picture that thing turning him into a pancake too.

Illume entered the doorway which closed right behind him. After he glanced around to ensure the coast was clear, Illume sat down and swapped out his boots. These ones seemed to fit even better than the first pair, which he placed in his satchel.

An orb of light formed over Illume's head. It shone in a dim circle all around him. A flight of stairs descended into the darkness below that grew wider and wider with each step. Illume drew Dovabane. Its growl echoed through the corridor before him. From the sounds of the echo, the room was massive.

Dovabane's echo eventually faded into silence. Illume was surprised that he hadn't seen any bodies. At this point, he couldn't help but wonder what "labor" awaited him here. The stairs continued to descend and grow even wider. They turned to his left and led down into the dark room below.

A deep growl echoed from the abyss before him. Illume stopped in his tracks. He gripped his sword tightly. The bow wouldn't do any good if he couldn't see his target. The orb or light above him rose into the air. As its circle spread, Illume finally saw what hid in the dark. Hundreds of dead bodies littered the abyssal room before him.

Pillars decorated the cavern-like walls which stood dozens of feet high. Illume descended the stairs with caution. He moved as silently as he could, although he doubted there was any point since he had a literal beacon of light over his head.

The stench of death filled the air as Illume spotted movement on the edge of his light. A python-like head slithered into the light. A long forked tongue flicked at the air. Three spiny frills with a fleshy membrane that ran down its neck shot up and rattled.

Its head whipped around. It still hadn't seen Illume, despite him standing in the center of the light. Clearly its eyesight was poor. *Great, a basilisk,* Illume thought to himself. When the creature opened its mouth and hissed, Illume spotted teeth that belonged to a dragon, not a snake. He swallowed hard.

How did Harry Potter kill his basilisk? Illume wondered to himself. *That's not going to work Illume, you're not in the same universe!*

Two more heads that looked exactly the same slithered from the darkness as well. Illume let out an internal groan. One basilisk would be hard enough. He wasn't sure he could take on three.

One of the giant serpentine creatures opened its mouth wide and slammed its teeth into the stony stairs. It raked its teeth across the dead bodies. A sickly purple light left the monster's teeth and entered the bones. Illume sheathed Dovabane and drew his bow.

Each skeleton that the creature's teeth touched lurched to life. They pulled themselves to their feet like shambling zombies. Zombies with purple magic that flared from them.

I don't remember basilisks being able to do that!

The beast on the other side did the same. Between them both, they managed to resurrect eight zombies. Illume drew two frenzy arrows. Fourteen left. Illume nocked one arrow and fired. Before the first reached its target, Illume fired the second at the other group.

Both arrows struck their targets. Two of the eight

zombies let out a screech to rival Ibura's children. Both zombies hacked and slashed at the other six. It was a violent, untrained mess, but they managed to kill the three that had been raised with them.

Each frenzied zombie turned to the darkness and charged the enormous snake heads. A massive, heavily armored clawed foot shot from the darkness and crushed one of the zombies flat. Its stomp shook the entire chamber. Pebbles and dust fell from the ceiling. A second claw crushed the second.

Illume staggered back a few steps. His stomach dropped as his heart skipped a beat. It wasn't one basilisk; it wasn't even three. The heavily armored monster stepped into the light. The trio of heads looked directly at Illume with angry serpentine eyes.

"Hydra!" Illume stammered. "You've GOT to be freaking kidding me!"

Illume's voice echoed throughout the cavern as he drew three arrows from his back and fired them as quickly as he could at each of the Hydra's heads. The first arrow hit the beast between the eyes. It snapped and fell to the ground without harming the beast. The second arrow struck the Hydra's center head in the eye. Same effect. The third hit the final head in the mouth. None of the shots even brought up the health bar.

Illume slung his bow over his shoulder. A green fog

formed in the center head's mouth. It struck out and fired a ball of smoking green ooze at Illume. Illume threw his shield up to block the attack. The impact threw him back against the stairs. Green fog encompassed him. The stench of rotten eggs stung his nostrils.

Toxicology Prevented Poisoning

"Money well spent!" Illume grunted.

Illume's shield arm started to warm up. He looked down to see the tree shield dissolving on his arm. Green liquid dripped from his degrading shield onto the stone floor, which began to smoke. Illume looked around and saw a vial of glowing blue liquid a few yards ahead of him on the ground.

"Poison acid spit?" he blurted. "So not fair!"

Illume's shield fell from his forearm before the acid had a chance to reach his arm. He turned his attention to the Hydra as it stomped toward him. Each of the three heads hissed and snapped. The other two heads charged shots as well.

As both fired at him, Illume dove and rolled down the steps. Both acidic shots splattered against the stairs. Illume glanced back to see a massive hole where the shots landed.

Illume's dive took him within striking distance of

one of the heads. It took the opportunity and struck at Illume. Still on the steps and without a shield, he couldn't dive out of the way in time. Illume rolled to the side as the strike narrowly missed him.

The Hydra crashed into the steps with such force, it reduced the stone to pebbles. The first head struck at Illume as well. Lucky for him the first head didn't seem very intelligent. Its strike slammed into the neck of the third head's neck.

The center head let out an angry hiss and struck at the first head. The third head hissed at the first as if to scold it. Illume took the opportunity to scramble to his feet. He clambered up a few steps to one of the pillars and slid behind it for cover.

He heard each head snarl and hiss at the others, as Illume tried to remember his Grecian mythology. He knew Heracles managed to kill one, but all he could remember was that the cartoon version crushed one with a cliff.

Illume couldn't bring down the cave on top of the Hydra. It would kill him as well. If he cut off a head, it would grow two more. *What if I shatter a head?* His thought was interrupted when one of the heads peered behind a pillar two gaps away from Illume.

Illume scooted away around the pillar. His back hugged the stone as he glanced at the Hydra's body.

The first head searched the other side while the center head lapped at the air as it sniffed for him.

Out of nowhere, the head that he'd just dodged slammed into the pillar in front of him, which caused it to crack. Illume held both hands out and unleashed the full might of his cryomancy. The shock of the cold must have stunned the beast. It didn't withdraw its head before Illume successfully froze it solid.

The other two heads screeched and lashed around the cavern. The frozen head banged into the pillar that Illume stood against. It shattered into several larger pieces and dozens of smaller ones. The Hydra's health bar finally showed up and dropped by a third. Both remaining heads struck at Illume. Illume dashed to the side and used another pillar as cover as each of the remaining heads slammed into the walls on either side of him.

Igniting Dovabane with the last of his mana, Illume swung it down on the Hydra's neck. Maybe if he didn't completely sever the head, just the spine. It would do the job as well. A spurt of red mist sprayed from the Hydra's neck, which caused the two heads to recoil in agony.

With another dash, Illume attempted to get behind the Hydra. Its body was way too armored for his weapons to pierce, but maybe he could get the remaining head to damage the body. Illume leaped onto the beast's heavily armored back. The tail whipped around, which caused tremors to reverberate throughout the cavern.

Illume drew Bloodlust from its sheath and attempted to drive it into the creature's back. The dagger glanced off its armor. Bloodlust slipped from his hand and clattered off the side of its body. Illume grabbed one of the spines that ran down its back.

As he steadied himself, Illume looked up to see the shattered stump writhe and snap from left to right. Two heads erupted violently from the stump. The "sprout" showered the stairs in slime and goo that seemed to eat away at everything it touched.

The health bar filled almost all the way back up and grew higher in the process. The newly sprouted heads turned to Illume. They let out a hateful hiss and struck at him. Illume dove out of the way. Both heads struck its own body making razor sharp teeth glance off of Illume's armor. Luckily, not even they could penetrate its protection.

Illume dove at the neck with Dovabane ablaze. With a powerful swipe and the last of his mana, Illume slashed the neck with two heads. A loud sizzle filled the air as Illume fell off the beast's body. He attempted to catch himself but ended up falling to his back under the monster's neck.

The two headed neck crashed down past Illume,

with a violent sound like thunder. Illume kept his eyes locked on the base of the Hydra's neck. It sizzled as the wound was cauterized by Dovabane's flame. The Hydra hesitated, stunned at the fact that its heads weren't growing back.

"Right! That's how he did it!" Illume yelled to himself.

The Hydra's health bar dropped by a third and didn't refill. Illume couldn't help but smile. He thrust off the ground and dove to a body that was next to him. Both remaining Hydra heads slammed into the ground where Illume had just been.

Illume grabbed the mana potion he'd seen earlier. Dovabane erupted into flames again so Illume dashed at the heads. The middle one withdrew, but the first was too slow and Illume sliced its head clean off. His sword cauterized the wound closed. Its health bar dropped by another third.

The first Hydra neck fell limp. Its mouth snapped as it rolled down the steps. Illume rose to his feet and faced the final head of the Hydra. The wounds Illume inflicted on it had healed, but he didn't have his sword ablaze the last time. It reared back in preparation to strike. Illume gritted his teeth as he readied both himself and his sword.

"Come on!" he snarled. "Let's end this."

The Hydra struck at Illume. He threw his hand out

and created a shield of ice. As the creature hit the shield, it glanced off and slammed into the ground. Illume sliced through both his shield and the Hydra's neck. Its decapitated neck coiled back. Its body twitched and writhed as the beast fell to the ground, lifeless.

Level Up x2
Attribute points: 4
Skill points: 2 (3 available)

Trophy Earned
Name: Lernaean
Type: Silver
Requirements: Kill a Hydra by decapitation.

"SILVER!" Illume complained as he sheathed Dovabane. "I just killed a Hydra. That's a gold at least!"

Grumbling to himself, Illume walked over to one of the Hydra heads. He grabbed the head and picked it up. Walking over to a body that had a chain, Illume tied the head to his back. Illume grabbed the empty mana vial and walked over to the body of the Hydra.

He slid around the edge of the hulking body and scanned the ground, looking for Bloodlust. Eventually, he found it among a pile of destroyed bones. Illume leaned down and grabbed his dagger. He walked around back to the front of the Hydra corpse. He jabbed the torso with his dagger. It didn't break the skin.

Illume stabbed the flesh a few more times. The dagger did no damage to the body. He sheathed the dagger and reached for Dovabane, when a glint of white light caught his eye.

He turned to see the hilt of a sword protruding from the Hydra's chest. Illume grasped the soft leather handle as tightly as he could and ripped the blade out with all his strength. The sword fell free as blood oozed from the wound. Illume used the mana bottle to catch the blood being careful to not let any of it touch him.

As blood dripped on the ground, it ate away at the stone. Illume capped the bottle off and placed it in his satchel. He looked down at the blade he'd pulled from the creature. Its handle was ornately twisted with red jewels in the cross guard and at the base of the pommel was shattered to a razor's edge about a foot off the cross guard. The weapon had a ghostly sheen to it. Illume tilted it to one side then the other and could see that Nordic runes were carved into the side of the blade.

Hydra Head
Weight: +10 Worth: 5000 polis

The head of a Hydra is full of magical items used in
*   alchemy and forging.*

Blood of the Hydra
Weight: +1.5 Worth: 2000 polis
The highly toxic blood of a Hydra can be used to
*   poison even the most toxic weapons.*
Shattered Blade of Valcoth
Damage: +12 Weight: +5 Worth: Unknown
This sword of legend was said to have slain so many
*   "unholy" beings that it exists in both the physical*
*   and spiritual plane. Any damage dealt affects the*
*   victim's very soul.*

Illume grabbed the long piece of leather. He tied it around the shattered blade in a makeshift sheath. He secured it snugly before he slung it over his back. He positioned his new weapon on his back right next to Dovabane. The next room behind the Hydra's corpse lit up.

"What's next?" Illume asked as he rose to his feet.

26

LIBRARY

PRESSING on past the Hydra body as the light faded above him, Illume moved to the next chamber. Upon entering, his adrenaline finally wore off from the previous fight and he collapsed just past the doorway.

Illume closed his eyes for a few minutes so he could catch his breath. It took a few minutes, but eventually, his heart rate slowed and the adrenaline that coursed through his body subsided. He opened his eyes once more to see the room before him fully lit.

Torches were ablaze on either side of the dozens of pillars that supported the room. Illume pushed forward and let his gaze wander. The room was full of books. Walls upon walls of shelves filled with leather bound, fabric bound, or just cheap string bound books.

The air was old and stale. It smelled of dust and mold. At least it wasn't damp or hot, but instead a crisp and cool temperature that matched the perfect fall morning. Illume pressed forward after he didn't detect the scent of death, corpses, or putrefaction like he had with Hastur, Ibura, or even the Hydra.

Set to the side were tables and chairs where many a skeleton sat with piles of books on either side of them. A few leaned against pillars with an open book in their laps. Almost none of them were armored, but rather, wore robes. Illume pressed forward through the room.

Being dyslexic and not much of a reader, this room held little temptation for Illume. Or so he thought. As he pressed through, he spotted a bright red and orange book whose cover seemed to dance with flame. It sat on a table next to a pillar.

Illume approached the book. A skeletal hand sat on its cover as the dead body lay slumped over the old rotting desk. Illume grabbed the hand and slid it off the cover. The body fell to the ground with a loud clatter of old dry bones.

He sat down and ran his fingers over the cover. It was warm to the touch. As his fingers ran over the front, words seemed to appear in flames. *Legends of the Phoenix,* the cover read. Illume flipped the book open. A wave of welcoming heat radiated from the volume.

"Oh, there is no way this won't cause cancer." Illume mumbled.

The book of the stories of every Phoenix from first to last.

The inside cover read. Illume nodded, that sounded like a pretty cool book. He flipped through a few pages to find a chapter head that would have caught his attention. He stopped at one title that promised to be of interest.

The Dark Phoenix

This phoenix loved humanity with all its heart.

It flew around the world to learn of the cultures, customs and lifestyles. The phoenix shared her knowledge with every settlement, town, and city she came across, until one day, she was captured.

Clapped in chains forged by the dwarven gods, the phoenix could not escape. Forced to take her human form, she was abused, paraded around, and treated like a piece of property by a corrupted sorcerer.

His magics held hers at bay and for centuries suffered the abuse at the sorcerer's hands.

Her heart grew hardened against the people of the land. The people who she'd helped who now just stood by and did nothing to aid her.

One day, a young man, sympathetic to the phoenix,stole the key from the sorcerer and freed her.

She was not grateful for this kindness; no, she was filled with rage that it had taken two hundred years for someone to assist her.

The young man was the first to be turned to ash by the phoenix's power. She proceeded to burn down the palace and everyone inside as she took flight. The heat from her wings cracked the very ground beneath her as she flew, leaving only cliffs and spires of rock for miles.

The kingdom she'd been held in suffered a similar fate. She flew from town to town scorching those who she shared knowledge with until the once lush and prosperous kingdom was nothing but a barren wasteland.

The dark phoenix was only stopped when a group of survivors who called themselves The Order of Light rose up to defend the few remaining people of the kingdom.

The Order of Light used arcane magics to summon an ancient demon to combat the phoenix. What came through was worse than the phoenix herself. Their battle raged for months until, finally, the phoenix flew the demon into the sky and exploded, killing them both.

"Okay, Jean," Illume scoffed.

He flipped a few more pages. Nothing on them grabbed his attention like the previous story. He was interested to know where the Order of Light came from now. Much like the Baldknobbers of the Ozarks, they started out good. Things just happened to take a left turn somewhere along their line.

Illume scanned the end of each story. He saw a pattern. Each and every phoenix was killed in such a way they could not be reborn. This wasn't a book of legends. It was an obituary anthology.

Finally, Illume made it to the last chapter of the book. He stopped on this one that he had to read. The title was *The Last Phoenix*. Illume couldn't help but feel an overwhelming sadness at the title. The phoenix was a beautiful, benevolent creature. It seemed like each one suffered fates none of them deserved. Most of it was at the greedy hand of man.

This is the story of the last phoenix. I do not know how many people will read this, as the route we sail is a dangerous one. If we make it, I pray she will have the strength to thrive there.

Who I am is not important. What is, is that after searching my entire life, I have found the last surviving phoenix. Hidden in plain sight while being hunted like a ravenous beast.

She is kind-hearted and has saved my life more than once on this adventure. She is now gravely wounded. I only hope I can return the favor.

I have been working tirelessly to save the phoenix over the past few days. It has taken every ounce of my considerable knowledge and magical abilities just to stem the spread of the poison that kills her.

I have found a spell among my books. One that can pull the phoenix force from her and negate the poison in her. I pray it works, I pray it saves her.

Illume flipped the page to continue reading. The handwriting changed to something a little more feminine.

I know no one will likely read this, but I must write this down. The great chaos mage Azathoth saved my life at the cost of his own. He pulled the fire from within me using his cryomancy magics.

The ritual pulled the magics from his body and killed him.

With what little power I have left, I bound his magic into four books and have scattered them to the four corners of the world. I take my feather and place it in the depths of this place, guarded by labors and monsters so that only he who wields the power of my savior may retrieve my power.

Illume closed the book. He ran his fingers over the back cover as he closed his eyes. The story moved him more than he thought it would. It was as if something inside of him wept with joy in the knowledge she survived. Illume placed a hand on the book before he took it and placed it in his satchel.

Melpomene may want to read the anthology, Illume thought to himself as he moved on through the library. There were many rare and amazing books that were scattered around the room as well as spell tomes and magical artifacts.

Illume ignored them all. He had no use for them. There was no way to realistically get them to Cryo's Quarry to help his people. If he tried to carry it back, he'd likely become over-encumbered, which could risk his life later.

As he pressed on, Illume noticed that the bodies around him weren't just skeletons anymore. Some of them had a stone-like appearance and others looked like a bad rock jigsaw puzzle put together by a drunk toddler.

Just ahead stood a statue of a large man in heavy armor looked like an ancient Greek hero. As Illume approached, his stomach sank. In the man's hands was a shield. A real shield that was a bright silver in color and polished so completely, Illume could probably start a fire with it.

Illume looked into the next room. Heat rose from its depths as statues dotted the rocks and paths that delved into the cave structure below. An eerie orange hue illuminated the cavern from far below.

Closing his eyes, Illume hit his forehead against the shield. His gut knew exactly what this was while his mind screamed for it to be wrong. Illume looked up at the statue. He was a handsome, strong man who undoubtedly thought he'd make it out with the prize below.

Illume looked around the back of the shield. Its leather straps were firmly attached to the statues body. It held the shield against its chest. Illume moved back to the front and grabbed the large round shield by either side.

He gave it a quick yank. Nothing. He planted his feet and pulled with all his might, to the point that his stamina fell. Again, nothing. Illume moved to the side of the statue. He looked it over before he closed his eyes and shook his head. He didn't like where his mind had gone.

"Sorry about this, buddy." Illume mumbled.

Extending his hand, Illume summoned a small torrent of ice to encompass and chill the forearm and part of the chest of the statue. then moved back to the front and grabbed the shield once more. This time, with one final mighty pull, the frozen stone gave way.

Illume staggered back as the shield came free. A massive hole was left in the chest of the statue. Illume cringed at the sight as cracks formed all throughout the body. A few seconds later, the whole thing collapsed into thousands of little pieces.

"Sorry about that!" Illume whimpered.

Polished Shield of Athena

Defense: +20 Weight: +10 Worth: 6000 polis

This shield was forged by the greatest smith of the ancient era. She then polished it using an unknown technique so it would redirect magic back to its sender.

Illume slid his arm into the leather straps of the shield. He pulled his bow off his shoulder and drew an arrow. He dipped the tip into the Hydra blood inside his satchel. *Bow toxicity increased two fold.* Illume nocked the arrow and descended into the bowels of the island.

He drew his bow as he walked over the mounds of volcanic rock that lay beneath his feet. The stench of sulfur filled his nostrils once again as he pushed forward. Illume partially drew his bow as he stopped to listen for any movement that could give his target away.

Illume glanced over to see a statue with a bow in hand in the exact same position as he was. He shook his head before he moved on. A harsh rattling filled the air as Illume delved deeper. He closed his eyes and groaned. "Why did it have to be one of you?"

27

DEMOGORGON

ILLUME CONTINUED on into the depths of the island. A river of lava snaked around pillars that had long since cooled. Dozens of stone statues were scattered throughout the cave. Illume noticed that most of them were fully armored warriors. Only one or two wore mage robes.

It was a testament to the temptation of the library that so few mages got through. To Illume, the fact that so many had managed to get past the Hydra was baffling. Then again, snakes were notorious for their poor eyesight. From how they searched for him, Illume only assumed the Hydra had that same flaw.

A large vial filled with a swirling potion sat on the ground next to a mage frozen in place. Illume walked over to the mage, who was frozen with his hands up as if to shield his face. He grabbed the vial and placed it in his satchel.

Vial of Ultimate Restoration
Weight: +.05 Worth: 500 polis
Fully restores mana, stamina, and health.

Lying on the ground were several fractured arrows. They were made of black wood and were as thick as Illume's thumb. The heads were barbed hunks of razor sharp black metal and the feathers were tattered and worn. Illume picked up one of the arrows. It was so heavy that there was no way even his legendary bow would be able to effectively fire one.

Dropping the arrow piece, Illume continued to move forward. The rattling from a distance ahead grew louder, as he moved next to a stalactite that was twice as wide as himself. He pressed himself against it and shuffled along the edge.

Illume crouched. A boulder sat just a few steps away from his current cover. He swiftly and silently moved to the next cover. The orange light from the lava beds grew brighter as the entire outside of this chamber was encircled by it.

The temperature had risen considerably, but Illume's cryomancy prevented him from sweating. Illume pressed his back against the boulder. He lifted the mirrored shield and used its reflection to peer into the room.

In the center of the room was a gazebo made of stone. From what he could tell, the gazebo had a pedestal in the center. What was on it, he couldn't see. His vision was blocked by a man about his own height.

Muscles rippled down his bare back with only the leather of his shoulder armor and bracers hiding parts of his upper body. A bronze belt held up what looked like a Roman legionnaire's battle skirt.

Leather greaves covered his ankles up to his knees. In his left hand, he held a bronze shield; in his right, a black bow that appeared to be very heavy. Its thick arms curved outward with a rigidity that Illume had never seen before. On his left hip was a sheath for a short sword whose handle appeared to be made of bronze as well.

The rattling filled the room once more. This time, Illume could tell it came from the man. His shoulder-length flowing hair moved and writhed in a mass on his head. Suddenly, several pairs of yellow glowing eyes opened all over his head and began to rise up on their own.

Several of the snakes appeared to look directly at Illume's shield. They hissed and the man moved. He picked up a quiver from the pedestal filled with the same nasty-looking arrows Illume had seen earlier. The man slung it over his shoulder.

"You know how many people have tried to sneak up on me?" his voice echoed through the chamber.

His tone was soft, almost friendly. He picked up a metal helmet and slid it over his head. The serpentine hair lay down flat as it slid into place.

"I'm guessing everyone you've turned to stone," Illume called.

"And many, MANY more," the man replied.

Slowly, he turned around and showed Illume his face in the reflection of his mirrored shield. Objectively, the man had a wonderfully handsome face, which was wrapped in the calm repose of death. His body appeared to be built by the gods themselves and his shield was reminiscent of the shield of Achilles.

"I do not wish to fight you," Illume called out.

"Then why are you here?" the other asked with a hiss in his voice.

"I've come for the phoenix feather," Illume replied.

"I have been charged with its protection," the man rebutted.

"What is your name?" Illume asked.

The question seemed to take the man by surprise. He hesitated for a few seconds before he responded.

"No one has ever asked me that before," he said. "I

am Theon. Son of Stheno. Demi-gorgon and protector of the last phoenix feather."

"Okay, Theon, Son of Stheno. I am Illume of Valka. The one I love suffers from the bite of an elder god," Illume explained. "The only way to save her is with THAT feather. May I take it?"

Theon waited for a few seconds. He sighed and shook his head, as best Illume could tell through a reflection.

"My fate is tied to this feather," he explained. "Should it be taken from this cavern, I will certainly die."

Illume closed his eyes and hung his head. He gritted his teeth. He couldn't let Nari die, but if he saved her, Theon would have to be sacrificed. He took several deep breaths.

"Tell me, Theon. Have you ever been in love?" Illume asked.

"Once," Theon called out. "A beautiful young woman as tall as I and with eyes that pierced your soul. She was my muse, the only one immune to my gaze. The only one who never feared me."

Illume took a deep breath. He lowered his shield and stayed leaned against the boulder. He looked at the bow in his hand and the arrow tipped with the Hydra's blood.

"What would you be willing to do for her, if her life were in danger?" Illume asked.

Illume heard the soft moan of his bow grip, as Theon must have squeezed it. There was another long silence followed by the echo of a sigh.

"I would do anything to save her," Theon replied.

"Is there any way to remove that feather without it killing you?" Illume asked.

"There is not!" Theon responded. "I have pored over every book in the library and found no way out."

Illume punched the ground. Anger filled him. This demi-gorgon was not like the other perceived monsters he faced. He hadn't tried to turn Illume to stone, he hadn't even nocked an arrow yet. Every kill he had made up to this point must have been in self-defense.

"Are you still there, Illume of Valka?" Theon asked.

"I am," Illume replied.

"Then what are you waiting for?" Theon asked. "The woman you love needs the feather. Should the feather leave this chamber, I will die. I cannot allow that to happen."

"I don't want to fight you," Illume admitted. "You seem like a good man."

"I do not wish to fight you either," Theon retorted. "You are the first in thousands of years to not attack me on sight. You seem like a good man too."

"I have to fight you. I can't let her die," Illume replied.

The low familiar grind of an arrow being dragged against other arrows filled the chamber. The soft groan of a bow string as it was being pulled soon followed.

"So be it," Theon called out in a resolute tone. "Whomever falls this day, let them do it in such a way the muses will sing about it until the end of time."

Pulling an arrow from his quiver, Illume nocked it as well. He partially drew his string. There had been no footsteps, which meant that he hadn't moved. Without knowing how Theon's arrow would ricochet, Illume didn't want to sneak a peek with his shield.

Illume took several deep breaths as he positioned himself on one knee so he could stand up quickly. He drew his bow just a little more before he let out a remorseful sigh.

"I won't hold back," Illume warned.

"I would not want you to," Theon replied.

Illume stood up as quickly as he could. He used his peripherals to see where Theon was then closed his eyes, fired his arrow, and held the shield in front of him. Illume felt a kick to his shield as if it had been hit with a hammer. It smashed into his face, opening a cut along the ridge of his nose. Blood spurted out, covering his lower face.

Illume ignored the pain racing across his nose. A

large dent in his shield showed where the arrow had impacted.

Illume dashed toward the stalactite and took cover as another massive arrow whistled past him. It struck the ground and ricocheted off before it embedded itself into the far wall. He glanced at Theon's position from behind the pillar and saw his massive health bar.

"Word of advice, Illume of Valka," Theon yelled. "Do not waste your Hydra blood on me. We are kin and cannot be harmed by one another."

"Thanks for the pointer!" Illume called out. "Best to even the field, I guess. Don't waste any of your poison on me either. I'm immune."

Illume nocked and drew another arrow. He heard Theon's footsteps move away from him. The moan of Theon's bow filled the air once more.

"Do not let anyone tell you that you are a bad sport," Theon called out.

Illume stuck his foot out on one side of the stalactite. He pushed off and spun to the other side, dropping to a knee just as an arrow whizzed over his head. Illume released his arrow. It embedded itself into Theon's shield. Illume dove to the side behind a pillar and nocked another arrow.

"I have seen nearly every battle tactic," Theon called. "Every feign, every deceit over my nearly two-thousand-year life span. A simple dodge will not fool me. You need to do better!"

His voice rang out as if he had begun to enjoy the fight. Illume drew a second arrow and held it between his pinky and ring finger. He lined up the nock in the arrow with his string.

Illume took a deep breath as his heart raced. He spit out blood that still poured from his nose into his mouth. The metallic tang was the last thing on his mind. The pain he felt was an afterthought.

He pushed off the ground and moved back into the open. He fired his first arrow. Theon's split it in two and whistled past Illume's head. Before he even had a chance to blink, Illume fired the second arrow.

He charged Theon as fast as he could. The second arrow caught Theon off guard. He sidestepped to dodge Illume's attack as Illume leapt at Theon. As he flew through the air, Illume moved his shield up. He saw Theon's eyes start to glow gold.

Just as his shield covered his face, a flash of golden light erupted around all sides of Illume. The shield did its job. Illume landed and threw his entire body into the back of his shield. Like a gong, both men's shields slammed together.

Theon grabbed the top of Illume's shield. He attempted to pull it down to expose Illume's face. Illume pushed against Theon with all his might. His arms trembled as his muscles started to burn. Illume took deliberate deep breaths in a desperate effort to maintain control. His stamina dropped as he attempted to hold Theon at bay.

Illume grabbed the Shattered Blade of Valcoth. He relented to Theon's pull. Illume closed his eyes as his shield dropped. He felt a warm light bathe his face as he spun and brought the pommel of the broken blade down on Theon's head.

Illume opened his eyes briefly as he continued with his momentum and spun. Before Theon could right himself, Illume brought the edge of his shield down on Theon's helmet. Theon dropped his bow and staggered backward, a smirk of enjoyment on his lips.

"It has been a long time since someone has struck me," Theon praised. "Well done."

Theon's eyes shifted to gold once again. Illume held the shield up as yet another flash of light reflected around the room. As Illume lowered it, he saw Theon's short sword sliding straight toward his face.

Illume threw his body to one side and deflected the sword toward the other. He spun the weapon around and brought it down on Theon's neck. The demi-gorgon blocked the attack with his shield and slashed in for Illume's side. Using his shield, Illume deflected the blow.

Both men raised their right foot and proceeded to

kick one another in the chest. The blow sent Illume flying back and into the stalactite. His impact shattered it and dropped his health by a third as well as Dovabane. He bounced off the ground and slammed into several statues.

Pain lanced through his chest. Agony tore at his muscles. Breathing was a labor that brought new definitions of pain with every gasp.

His body ricocheted off the stone warriors. Each impact let out a purple blast of light. Illume's chest hurt from the kick. It was like getting hit by a truck. His spine ached and his fingers tingled and began to go numb. Illume's hands glowed with his healing magic. His health bar filled as his mana drained.

Illume looked up to see Theon marching toward him. Shield on one arm, sword in the other. His health was down by a quarter. As he approached, a stone soldier stepped in behind him and stabbed him in the back with a dagger.

Theon roared in pain. The serpents under his helmet hissed. He turned, and with a headbutt, shattered the first stone soldier. The second didn't get so lucky as a single blow from his shield shattered it as well.

"The teeth of a Hydra," Theon pointed out with a nod, impressed. "I didn't think they could bring my creations back."

He ripped the dagger out of his back; his health had dropped a little more. "I guess I was wrong."

His eyes began to glow once more. Illume held up his shield to deflect the stone gaze. He felt the ground tremble from a powerful leap. Theon's sword passed Illume's shield and knocked it away. Illume barely got his other arm up in time to prevent the gaze from turning him to stone.

Illume's health dropped to half as Theon slammed his shield into Illume's chest and knocked him into the ground. Air was expelled from his lungs with such force that they burned as if Illume had inhaled fire. He let out a groan of pain as he rolled to his side. His health was low, his mana dropped, and his stamina had started to wane.

Illume reached into his satchel and pulled out the potion. He rolled out of the way of one of Theon's attacks and quickly chugged the glowing magical elixir. All his reserves filled back up completely.

By the time he'd finished, Theon was jabbing at him. Illume used the empty bottle to knock away his blade before he slammed it against Theon's chin. His head snapped back and his helmet flew off. Illume kicked Theon's sword hand and knocked the weapon free.

He drew Valcoth's blade and swung it at the staggered demi-gorgon. Its sharp edge sliced a deep gash across his chest. A pale light flashed from the sword and consumed Theon for a split second. Theon's health dropped to just above half.

Illume didn't relent. He struck Theon in the chest with his shield before he placed another slash across Theon's bicep. Theon attempted to block with his shield once again, but Illume used his own to knock it away before he slashed Theon's leg.

The demi-gorgon fell to his knees. He summoned the magic for his stone gaze once more. Illume held the shield up. Theon let out a scream that was straight from the underworld as the golden light erupted from his face like a thermonuclear bomb.

Illume felt the heat spike in the chamber. He summoned frost over his body in an armor to protect himself from it. The heat was so intense that his armor began to melt. The center of his shield had started to turn to stone as well. It grew heavier by the second, and by the time Theon's stone gaze dissipated, his shield turned to stone.

Illume dropped his defense. It shattered into dozens of pieces. Kneeling before him was Theon. His eyes whited out with a look of serene peace on his face. A hint of a smile tugged at his lips.

"I truly have been bested," he whispered as the snakes on his head coiled in pain. "I am glad my death could pay for the life of another and that it came by the hand of someone as skilled as I."

Illume kneeled before Theon. He placed a hand on Theon's shoulder and gripped his broken sword tightly. Illume looked at Theon's health bar. It was almost completely gone.

"My brother is a necromancer. Is there any way I can save you?" Illume pleaded.

"No." Theon shook his head. "Take my head when you leave," he whispered. "I wish to serve an honorable man, even in death."

Theon coughed as he leaned forward into Illume's chest. Illume held the noble warrior close and nodded.

"I will make a shrine for you that you will not be forgotten," Illume vowed.

"Thank you, my friend," Theon replied.

With that, Illume shoved his blade into Theon's heart to give him a painless and quick death. A white light erupted from Theon and was drawn into the blade.

Shattered Blade of Valcoth has earned a perk.
The blade now has a 10% chance to turn enemies
      level 10 or lower to stone.

Illume followed Theon's request and took his head from his shoulders.

Head of a Demi-gorgon

Weight: +20 Worth: 90000 polis

Even a Demi-gorgon can cast the Stone Gaze.

In death, should the head be kept, the ability of Stone
    Gaze can be used three more times.

28

FEATHER

SHEATHING HIS BROKEN BLADE, he placed the head in his satchel as well. It was now too full to fit anything else in. Theon's body disintegrated into a writhing mass of snakes that scattered. Illume picked up Theon's sword, shield, and armor, and walked into the main chamber.

In the center of the chamber where Theon first stood was the pedestal with a soft red glow at the top. As Illume approached, he saw a small red feather that floated in the air. It was no longer than a pencil and as unassuming as a pigeon feather.

Illume kneeled before the pedestal. He drove Theon's sword into the ground. It was so sharp, it slid into the stone with ease. Illume placed the greaves in front of the sword. He folded the battle skirt and placed it in front of the greaves.

Taking the bracers, Illume placed them at the foot of the greaves. Lastly, he set Theon's helmet on the handle of the sword. Illume leaned the shield between the sword and the greaves with his quiver slung at an angle on one side.

He looked for the bow. Rising to his feet, he approached the weapon. As he picked it up, he attempted to draw the string. It hardly budged. He pulled harder. Nothing. Illume pulled with so much force, his stamina dropped. He couldn't even get the weapon to a quarter draw before his muscles surrendered to the will of the bow.

"Theon, you were a lot stronger than I thought," Illume chuckled in embarrassment.

Illume picked up his sword and sheathed it as he returned to the shrine he built for Theon. He slung the string across the shield in an X pattern over the quiver.

Illume turned his attention to the feather. He stepped forward and it burned brighter. Illume gently grasped the small item. It was warm and inviting. Illume could feel energy pour from it greater than Theon's Stone Gaze.

Phoenix Feather
Weight: .01 Worth: Priceless
The feather of the last phoenix. Its true power is

unknown. There were few in existence who could rival the power of a phoenix.

Level Up
Active Skill Points: 4
Active Attribute Points: 6
Overall Level: 26

Illume cradled the feather in his hands as if it were precious cargo. On the top of the pedestal was a small button. He moved to press it before he looked back at Theon's helmet. Illume stepped forward and gently grasped it and brought it close to him.

He turned back to the pedestal and pressed the button in the center. The cavern trembled as the small circle around the pedestal rose into the air. Illume stood close to the center. He planted his feet as it started to lift into the air.

Illume looked up to see the illusion of the ceiling fluctuate and disappear to reveal a large shaft that rose straight up. Illume looked back down at his prize. He wanted to be excited about it. He could now heal Nari. His joy, however, was tempered by the death of a good man.

As the pillar rose, the ceiling rolled back to reveal the blue sky. Illume squinted as the bright light of day poured down the shaft and washed over him. The rumbling ceased as the pillar stopped. Illume turned to see the throne an arm's length away from him.

"Did you get it?" John called from behind Illume.

He turned to see John and Melpomene standing a few yards behind him. Melpomene had a look of sorrow on her face as she saw Illume. John's face glowed with joy. Illume shook his head subtly at John to hint for him to stop.

John took the hint but looked confused as he did. Illume slowly walked over to Melpomene. A silent tear rolled down her face as Illume presented Theon's helmet to her. She swallowed hard and nodded as she took the piece of armor.

"I know who, what you are, Melpomene," Illume whispered. "I am so sorry about all your tragedy. I do thank you for the unimaginable sacrifice that you both made for me, a stranger. If there is anything I can do to repay my boundless debt, please tell me."

Melpomene ran her fingers over the helmet. Her brow furrowed as if it brought back countless memories for her. After several moments of silence, she looked back up at Illume.

"Did he fight well?" she asked.

"Best I've ever faced," Illume replied.

"Did he suffer?" Melpomene added.

"I made sure it was quick and painless," Illume murmured.

"Will you free me?" she asked after a few moments of silence.

Melpomene lifted her hands and pulled them apart. As she did, a golden string of light formed around her wrists. It bound them together with a strand that went up and around her neck, then down and around her feet.

New Side-Quest Added
Free Melpomene.

Illume grabbed his newer blade. He placed it under the golden string and tried to cut it. A weapon that could pierce Hydra flesh had trouble with cutting a piece of string. Illume pulled on his sword harder. The blade glowed with its spectral white light and let off a soft whine.

As the light shattered, Illume felt the weapon slice through the string. The gold light that bound Melpomene dissipated in an explosion of glittering light. Illume sheathed his sword as Melpomene rubbed her wrists.

Side-quest complete
You have earned Melpomene's loyalty

"Thank you, Illume of Valka," she whispered.

"It is the least I could do," Illume replied. "Where will you go?"

"I don't know. I have been on this island for a thousand years," She sighed.

"Well, if you wish, there is always a home for you at Cryo's Quarry," Illume offered.

"I might take you up on that," Melpomene nodded. "In the meantime, I think I am going to experience Valka. Sail the seas with Corazon and the Boat Man." She took Illume's hand. "Now that you have freed me, I can send you to Nari."

Illume looked at John. John stepped over toward Illume and nodded. Illume looked back at Melpomene.

"That would be greatly appreciated," Illume replied as his heart skipped a beat.

Melpomene tucked Theon's helmet under her arm. She reached out and took John's hand as well.

"Be weary. Moot has been visited by Hastur in your absence." Illume's eyes widened. "Nari is safe. She was protected by the witch you left her with. The city will not be the same as you remember. Be safe, Illume of Valka. I pray we meet again, and when you see Nari, place the feather on her chest."

With this, Melpomene gently squeezed Illume's and John's hand. An explosion of flames engulfed Illume's vision and wrapped him in a warm embrace of light. Illume's stomach dropped as he was flung forward. It was almost like travelling through fiery hyperspace before he came to a violent stop.

The brothers managed to catch their footing. Illume looked around to see that they were both in the witch's hut once again. Ahead in the back, the unmistakable blue light of Trillian's mana transfer filled the room.

Illume charged forward and burst into the back room. The witch stood over Nari with her hand out and her eyes closed. Trillian, who had grown significantly in Illume's absence, rested his head on Nari's stomach.

Nari was deathly pale. Sweat poured from her body as black veins stretched over nearly every inch of her. The witch looked at Illume and nodded toward Nari.

"Hurry, she has no time left!" Hecate commanded.

Illume rushed forward and pressed the phoenix feather to Nari's chest. It immediately burst into flames and disintegrated to ash. The ash danced around Nari as it settled in on her sickly skin. Illume gritted his teeth and rocked back and forth.

Heart pounding, mind racing, worry coiled around Illume like one of Hastur's tentacles. He prayed that this would work. She was so emaciated, she hardly looked like herself anymore. He hoped the power of the feather would be enough to bring her back. Illume took Nari's hand.

"Come on, you can fight this!" he whispered as he kissed her hand.

Nari pulled her hand away from Illume's. She gently placed it on his cheek. Illume looked up with a wide smile at her. She gazed at him through jaundiced eyes so lovingly.

"I love you," she whispered.

With that, Nari's eyes closed. Her body went limp and instantly fell cold as her health bar dropped to zero. Illume sat forward. He grabbed Nari by the shoulders and gave her a shake.

"Nari? Nari wake up!" he yelled. "No, no no no!"

Illume's vision blurred as his eyes stung from tears. Illume ignited healing spells on both his hands and placed them over her heart. He poured so much mana into the spells that his hands let off a light so blinding that even Hecate covered her face.

Illume's mana ran dry. He continued to try and heal her. He looked at Trillian, who gently nosed her cold hand. He gave it a lick and whimpered.

"Mana transfer with me," Illume commanded.

"He can't," Hecate replied. "He's used all his mana to keep her alive."

Illume turned to John as he rose to his feet. He took several steps toward his brother.

"Bring her back!" Illume barked.

"I can't," John replied sympathetically.

"You're a necromancer. BRING HER BACK!" Illume roared.

Madness 23%

Grabbing John by his robes as his adrenaline surged, Illume slammed him into a wall. Panic, pain, terror, heartache, rage, and countless other emotions crashed into Illume like a snow plow. John raised his hands in a defensive posture.

"I reanimate the dead, Illume," John blurted. "I don't resurrect them. She wouldn't be the Nari you loved if I brought her back!"

Illume released his brother and staggered back. His head swam. He swayed from a short spell of dizziness.

"I'm... I'm sorry, John," Illume whispered softly.

He fell to his knees and slumped over as tears rolled down his cheeks. A pulse of heat struck Illume in the back of the neck. Illume opened his eyes and turned to see the source.

It was Nari. She floated several feet above the ground as flames danced over her body. A spark of hope ignited within Illume as he rose to his feet and faced her. The fire grew brighter and brighter as it fully engulfed her.

There was no stench of burning flesh or hair and within a few seconds, the fire pulsed brightly and reduced Nari to ash. Her equipment fell to the ground as the ash rained into a small pile next to them.

As the spark of hope was extinguished, Illume staggered backward. He felt John grab him and hold him upright. It was the only thing that prevented his body from completely collapsing.

"I am so sorry," John whispered into Illume's ear.

Illume's mouth went dry as a sense of loss unlike anything he'd ever felt gripped him like the inescapable hopelessness of a black hole. His body went numb. Was this what happened when your last life was up?

John gently set Illume on the ground. Illume's eyes didn't leave the pile of ash before him as he collapsed to his knees. Trillian let out a curious whine. Illume looked at his dragon, who stared at the pile as if he saw something Illume didn't.

Illume followed his dragon's gaze back to ash. It moved slightly, then a little more. Illume's brow furrowed. A woman's hand exploded from it and slapped the ground.

29

FROM THE ASHES

LIKE SOMETHING out of a zombie film, the arm lurched from the ash and pushed off of the ground. John jumped back, his hands glowing, ready for anything. Illume threw up his arm to indicate for his brother to stop.

An ash-covered head of hair emerged from the pile that once made up Nari. Illume recognized the golden eyes as they fluttered open. It was Nari pulling herself from the ashes. Illume moved in to help her. Hecate blocked his path with her staff.

"Those reborn of Phoenix ash are far too hot to touch, even for you, cryomancer," she warned.

Nari continued to pull herself from the ash pile. The fine grey powder clung to her naked body as she fully emerged. Illume got a glimpse of her shoulder blade. She had one life indicator visible.

As she rose to her feet, Illume noticed she no longer had the scars on her body that she'd received in previous run-throughs. Her hands were smooth as if they'd never held a hammer. Every scratch and scar had been removed in her rebirth process.

Nari stood before them covered in nothing but ash. John turned away and Illume ignored Hecate's warning. The call to Nari overrode his self-preservation instinct. Illume marched over to her.

Sliding one hand around the small of her back, Illume let the other cup her soft cheek. Illume pressed his lips against hers in a tender yet passionate kiss. She still tasted the same as she returned his affections.

He had craved this for not even he could remember how long. Nari's body temperature was off the charts. His hands burned, as did his lips. His body even warmed up from being so close to her, but he didn't care.

Illume gradually broke the kiss. He leaned back and gazed deeply into Nari's eyes. A wide smile formed on her lips as she swayed a little bit from the passion of his kiss. Nari looked Illume up and down and raised an eyebrow in her seductive manner.

"That was… uh… wow!" she remarked with a gleeful tone. "Just one question."

"Go ahead," Illume replied.

"Who are you?" Nari asked.

It felt like a pike had been rammed through Illume's gut. His hands dropped to his side as he staggered backward. His mouth went dry as dozens of questions tore through his mind at a thousand miles an hour.

"I'm-I'm Illume," he stammered. "We've been together for a year now. Do you not remember me?"

"I'm sorry." Nari responded as she leaned down and grabbed her garments. "I know that I was a forger, that my name is Nari, and that these are mine, but that's about it."

Madness 25%

"The resurrection process is rough," Hecate remarked. "It may take some time for her memories to return."

"What if they don't?" Illume frowned.

"Then we find the phoenix that feather belonged to," Hecate suggested. "Her magics should be able to restore her memory."

Side-Quest Added
Find Melpomene and ask her to restore Nari's
     memories.

Nari began to get dressed. The weight of the Hydra head wore on Illume. He grabbed the chain connection at his chest and pulled on it. The head fell to the floor behind Illume.

"The phoenix is gone," John informed Hecate. "She went to sail the seas with the Boat Man and a pirate named Corazon."

"We don't have time to find them," Illume argued as he glanced at the map for a few seconds. "Hastur has already attacked Mire. He's moving north."

"You can stop by Traders Bay in your pursuit," Hecate suggested.

"But you have to stop him before he reaches the white cliffs of Arangduul," she warned. "Should he turn the griffins, he will be able to extend his reach to all corners of Valka and there would be nothing we can do to stop him."

"There're griffins here?" John asked in surprise.

Illume looked back at his brother. At a glance, he noticed Nari had finished getting dressed. Illume patted his leg and Trillion came trotting over and nuzzled under Illume's elbow. He had grown significantly. Trillian's front leg shoulders were the same height as Illume's.

"I have a dragon. We just used a phoenix feather to save Nari from Hastur's venom. On the floor is a Hydra head and I killed a demi-gorgon," Illume said with a layer of sarcasm to his voice. "Why wouldn't there be griffins as well?"

"Good point," John conceded.

"Who is this Hastur that poisoned me?" Nari asked.

Illume took a deep breath. He could feel tendrils gripping at his mind as he fought to stay calm. He felt Hecate's hand on his shoulder as she hobbled past him.

"Come and we will show you!" Hecate waved for them to follow her. "And bring that head with you."

Nari followed first, with John moving in second and Illume and Trillian taking up the rear. Illume grabbed the Hydra head on his way out. It was a tight squeeze for Trillian, but he managed to maneuver throughout the house without causing too much damage.

Once they exited Hecate's hut, Illume looked around in horror. Bodies were strewn all over the streets. The once white stone was smeared in the red of Hastur's victims.

Trillian let out a mournful whimper as he moved from body to body and sniffed them. Hastur's signature thick, unnatural fog had overtaken all of Moot. Illume searched the faces of the bodies to see if any were his people.

"Your friends got out before this happened," Hecate informed Illume.

He breathed a sigh of relief. His heart was still

broken at the lives lost, but at least his people had a chance to get out. They could warn the other kingdoms about what was happening here.

"Hastur did all this?" Nari asked in disbelief.

"And infinitely more," Hecate pointed out. "This kingdom used to be lush and beautiful. Its people thrived and lived in peace for centuries. When Hastur came, he corrupted the land and turned it into this life-less swamp you see today. He has slaughtered, turned, or corrupted anyone that has crossed his path…"

"Is that what happened to you?" Nari interrupted in reference to Hecate's appearance.

"This was not from Hastur," she replied. "This was my penance for meddling with magics I didn't understand."

"Then how was Hastur able to do THIS to a city but leave you untouched?" Nari interrogated.

"Nari," Illume called. She looked over at him. "Hecate serves a god of chaos and mischief. It was his power, channeled through her, that kept both you and Trillian safe when this was happening. She sent us on the journey to find what would save your life. It is because of her you are standing here right now. She isn't one of Hastur's,"

Nari's brow furrowed as Illume spoke. After a few seconds, she looked at John for confirmation.

"He's telling you the truth," John nodded.

"Help us!" a weak, mutated voice echoed from the fog.

Trillian leaped in front of Illume. The baby fluff around his neck and tail were gone and replaced by needle-like spikes of ice. Each quill stood up on end as his wings folded tightly against his body. He let out a deep snarl into the fog.

Illume moved up next to Trillian and placed his hand on the dragon's back. His head snapped back and looked at Illume. Illume offered Trillian a nod. He felt Trillian's body physically relax under his touch. Illume stepped forward to the front of the group.

"Who's there!?" Illume called.

From the fog staggered the Kapre merchant who'd asked for the Dziwozona heart for payment. She had scales and a deep rot set into her wooden body. She teetered forward before she collapsed.

Illume ran to her side and helped her back to her feet. He slung her arm over his shoulder and walked her to the safety of their little group. Illume laid her down. Her health bar became visible. It had a green tinge to it and fell rapidly.

Illume opened up his skill tree. He wanted to save some skill points for his intimidation shout, but the situation was dire. Illume could save lives or let countless die just to satiate a narcissistic fantasy.

Using two of his skill points, Illume activated *Poison*

Cure Others. He put one point into *Quick On Your Feet* to increase his light armor effectiveness by 20 percent. Illume used his last skill point to activate *Perfect Fit* to increase his armor rating by an additional 30 percent when he wore a full set.

Looking at his attribute points, Illume had six left. He wanted more than anything at this moment to rip something apart with his bare hands, to feel the muscle and sinew as it gave way under his own force. Illume put all six of his attribute points into *Strength.*

New Stats
Armor rating increased by 50% so long as you wear
    a matching set.
Strength increased by 6, overall rating +36; +46
    while wearing the Kapre armor.
You are approaching superhuman levels.
Overall Armor Rating (With Bonus): 114.5

That's half of my heavy armor. I need to get that back, Illume thought as he closed his skill tree. Illume placed his hand over the Kapre's heart. A soft green light flowed from his hand and into her. His mana drained relatively quickly.

As his magic entered her, the rot dissipated and her health bar gradually turned to the proper red color it needed to be. As he cured her poison, she sat up. The scales stayed put and her health was low, but she was no longer dying. She offered Illume a wooden smile.

"Thank you, cryomancer," she said in a hushed tone.

"I think I have something for you," Illume retrieved Ibura's heart and handed it to her. "As per our arrangement."

The Kapre merchant softly laughed as she took the heart from Illume. She observed it closely and nodded in approval.

"This is certainly what I sent you for," she said. "But you saved my life. That means more to me than the heart."

She offered it back to Illume, who shook his head.

"When I enter into business with someone, I make sure I keep my end of the deal," Illume said. "I healed you because it was the right thing to do, not because I wanted anything out of it."

Side-Quest:
Retrieve the Heart of a Dziwozona for the Kapre
    Merchant: Complete

"Are there others who need help?" John asked.

"The market is full of the survivors." The Kapre pointed into the fog.

"Illume, what are you doing?" Nari asked as she

approached him. "Hastur is ahead of us. We can't lose time healing the poisoned and the injured."

Illume stood up. He helped the Kapre up as well before he turned his attention to Nari.

"You may not remember, but before all of this, you would have wanted us to help in any way we could. Yes, Hastur is ahead of us, but there are only four of us versus who knows how many of him," he pointed out. "If we help these people, they will have our backs when the time comes and that could turn the tide of battle."

Nari hesitated for a few moments. Illume could tell she was chewing on the inside of her cheek, something she did when she mulled things over.

"We leave right after?" Nari asked.

"As soon as we are no longer needed," Illume replied.

The Kapre merchant led everyone through the mist. It didn't take long before they reached the doors of the market. Two of the guards stood watch. They were just as mutated as the fishy citizens of Mire.

They opened the door for Illume and his group. Inside, there were dozens of people poisoned and injured. The one thing every race had in common was that they were mutated into some scaled fish versions of themselves.

"Thank the gods you're here," Mercator's voice called out. "We could use the extra hands."

30

QUESTS COMPLETED

ILLUME SPUN TO see Mercator fully armored and right behind them. He was green at the gills, literally, but other than that, he hadn't mutated much. Mercator approached Illume, and the men shook hands.

"Hastur?" Illume asked.

"And others," Mercator replied. "Those who didn't die or get turned into Hastur's brood wound up here. I'm afraid we're all that's left. Is there any way you can help us?"

"Hecate and I will heal the poisoned. Nari and John can dispense potions and clean wounds. Trillian can do mana transfer. It helps slow the spread of poisons until Hecate and I can get to them," Illume pointed out. "But we have to be gone by nightfall. We can't let Hastur get much further ahead of us."

"Thank you," Mercator said before he turned and left.

John approached Illume as both men watched Mercator check on a few of the injured.

"Are you surprised that he's still alive?" John asked.

"A little bit," Illume replied. "Why do you think that is?"

"Probably because he looks exactly like Sean Bean and that guy can't make it to the mid-way point in anything," John replied.

"That is so true." Illume laughed as he nodded. "Let's get to helping people."

With that, John and Nari broke off into their groups. Trillian moved along as well. Hecate approached Illume and grabbed the Hydra head from him. In a display of incredible strength, she pulled ten teeth from the serpentine head with little to no effort.

"Before you give this to that Barnogian, I wanted to get a few of these," She muttered under her breath before she limped away.

Shaking his head at the crazy witch, Illume turned and went to the corner of the market. He sought out the poisoned and used his new poison healing magic to prevent them from dying in such a horrid manner. It took several hours, as each time Illume healed someone of their poison, it ate up most if not all of his mana.

Illume met Hecate in the center of the room. She was sweating nearly as much as Illume was from pushing her magical abilities as much as she had. She wiped her brow then leaned heavily on her staff.

"I have never seen poison as deep-seated as this." She looked over the injured.

"I wouldn't imagine you will again," Illume replied. "Once Hastur is gone and with no more elder gods loose, I imagine this kingdom will return to its natural state."

"By Khal, I hope so," she replied.

Hecate took a deep breath as she prepared herself to move forward. As she left Illume, he made his way to John, who dispensed potions where he could.

"You don't have any healing magic?" Illume asked as he grabbed a mana potion.

"Only to heal myself," John replied. "I never played a support role. There was no need for it."

Illume popped the cork out of the potion and drank it. His mana filled all the way back up. The fact that his health bar was permanently stuck at 75 percent had him worried, though.

"Thank you for helping anyway," Illume said as he healed one of the injured.

Illume then made his way across the room to Nari,

who knelt near a little girl and played with her doll. Her health was at half and she looked to be in serious pain. Illume kneeled at her side. Nari glanced up at him for a moment.

"I ran out of healing potions twenty minutes ago. There's nothing I can do for this girl." She looked up at Illume pleadingly. "Do you have any potions?"

"I don't." Illume shook his head. "But I can help her."

Placing his hand on her forehead, Illume summoned his healing magic and channeled it into the little girl. Her health bar filled rapidly, as she didn't have much health to restore. The wound on her leg closed and the festering stench vanished. Instantly, the color returned to the little girl's face and she smiled.

"Thank you," she whispered as she gazed at Illume.

"You're welcome," Illume replied as he looked back at her. "Nari, this is why we stayed. Has anything come back to you?"

"I know about my life outside of Valka," she said softly. "I know about my first two attempts to free myself from this place and I know that Balathor is a skeevy old man."

Illume stood to his feet. He offered Nari a hand up. She took it and stood as well.

"Balathor is dead," Illume replied. "He allowed Tanner's Folly to be attacked due to his greed. I took the displaced and brought them to the quarry north of Tanner's Folly. You and I built a settlement there the people called Cryo's Quarry."

"If I helped build a settlement, why would I leave?" Nari frowned.

"Because that kingdom was in danger and you wanted to save it," Illume replied. "Just like you wanting to save this kingdom."

Nari stood there for a few minutes. Her full lips pursed and her brow knitted together. Illume noticed she'd braided her hair back in a traditional elvish style, which allowed her ears to poke out. Nari finally shook her head.

"I'm sorry, Illume," she finally said. "I really am, but I don't remember any of that."

"It's okay," Illume said in a defeated tone. "We'll get your memory back."

Illume felt his eyes burn with tears. He quickly glanced around to see who else needed help. There weren't many others. Illume's sight caught the Barnogian to whom he owed the Hydra head. She had an arrow wound in her upper thigh.

"I still have work to do," Illume said quickly.

He turned his back to Nari so she wouldn't see and headed over to the Barnogian. The merchant's lizard scales seemed to have an additional shine to them, like thicker, harder fish scales. She had fins that accented her body now and gills on her neck.

As soon as she saw Illume approach, she arched her back and attempted to appear seductive to him. Illume kneeled next to her and placed the Hydra head by her side.

"Your Hydra head as per our agreement," Illume said.

Side-Quest:
Bring a Hydra Head to the Lusty Barnogian
     Complete.

"It looks like Dovabane served you well," she purred.

Illume caught a glimpse of her health bar. It had hardly fallen at all, which meant that not only was this arrow the only wound she had, but it was also superficial.

"It did. Thank you for selling it to me," Illume replied as he inspected her wound.

When he touched her leg, it felt warmer than it should have. An infection had begun to set in. She let out a groan of discomfort.

"It was my pleasure," she replied.

She emphasized the word "pleasure." Illume rolled his eyes, not in the mood to put up with her crap.

Showing no tenderness as he had the others he'd treated, Illume grabbed the arrow and violently yanked it out.

The Barnogian screamed in pain. She grabbed Illume's forearm and gripped it tightly. Illume used his free hand to heal her wound. Her health rose, his mana fell, and in several seconds, she was fully healed. The only place on her that wasn't covered in shimmering scales was where her wound had been. It was her natural skin.

"Thank you," she once again purred.

Illume didn't respond. He got up and moved to the opposite end of the market. By now, nearly everyone had gotten back on their feet and were completely healed. Their fishy features, however, remained. Illume ducked into the back of a small room and closed the door behind him to escape the crowd.

He had done a lot of good just now, but it didn't feel like it. He'd pushed his magical healing abilities to their limits. He murdered a good man to save Nari and for what? Nari didn't remember anything before him, conveniently.

John's bereavement leave would be running out soon and he'd have to log off. He'd been forced to kill the only true friend he'd ever had, and the itch in the back of his brain grew worse each passing day.

Illume slammed his fist into the marble stone wall

of the room. A loud CRACK rang out. Illume looked up to see that his fist had buried itself almost a quarter of an inch into the stone. The solid piece of white rock fractured in all directions from the floor to the ceiling.

The soft creak of the door broke the temporary silence. Illume pulled his hand from the wall and turned to see the Barnogian merchant as she entered the room. Her eyes widened as she saw the wall he'd punched.

"Big strong man, I see," she said softly as she shut the door behind her. "I never got the chance to properly thank you."

"There is no need to thank me," Illume grumbled. "Please leave."

He leaned against the wall then slid down to the stone bench that circled the room. The Barnogian sauntered over to him. She swung her hips with each step. Illume's head was splitting. He could feel his blood pressure higher than it had ever been.

The merchant placed one of her knees on the seat next to him. He looked up at her with a look of disgust on his face. He'd told her countless times he was uninterested. Why was she still pushing herself on him?

Whispering filled Illume's ears as the Barnogian lifted her other leg and straddled him. She placed her hands on his shoulders as she sat on his knees. Illume fought the urge to kill her right then and there.

"Shove her."

"Watch her splat on the wall."

"She wants it."

"DO IT!"

The voices all whispered at once to him. He felt locked in his own body. The whispers grew louder and louder as she got even closer. An image flashed in Illume's mind of Nari walking in on them. She had no memories and would misread the situation.

"I said I'm not interested!" Illume snarled as the image disappeared.

Illume grabbed the Barnogian by the throat and lifted her off of him. He stood up, turned, and slammed her into the wall so hard, it cracked again. Her health bar dropped significantly as he did.

"I told you to keep your scaly hands off of me," Illume snapped as the whispers grew louder. "I am NOT to be one of your conquests."

He squeezed tighter as his rage built. "You are a cold-blooded lizard. I wonder what would happen to you if I were to snap freeze this room with you inside."

Madness: 27%

"P-p-please don't!" she begged through Illume's grasp.

Illume turned and flung her across the room. She

bounced off the wall and hit the ground hard. She looked up at Illume with rage and hate in her greenish-yellow eyes. Illume took two steps forward and towered over her.

"If I see you again, I will use the teeth of the Hydra to kill you," Illume snarled as he used his intimidation voice. "I have seen what they do. Something tells me you know what they do. Then you will become a mindless slave."

With that, Illume left her on the ground and slammed the door behind him. Fighting the whispers that urged him to kill her, he used his cryomancy to seal the door shut and lock her in before he left.

Illume turned around to see the survivors all staring at him in confusion. Undoubtedly, she made sure that everyone saw her enter that room. Illume glanced back as the whispers subsided. He motioned to the door.

"She wouldn't take no for an answer," Illume finally broke the silence. "She'll be able to get out in a few hours."

Level Up Available

31

I HAVE 12% OF A PLAN

MERCATOR APPROACHED with his hand on the hilt of his sword as he looked at the door. He turned his attention to Illume and raised an eyebrow. A smile cracked on his stern face followed by a boisterous laughter. Over half of everyone else laughed as well.

Releasing his sword, he moved to Illume's side, threw his strong arm around the cryomancer's shoulder and walked Illume toward the main doors of the market. Mercator went so far as to wipe a tear from his eye caused by his laughter.

"We have been wanting to lock her away for years now," Mercator chuckled. "Thank you."

Mercator led Illume outside where John, Nari, Hecate, and Trillian were waiting for him. As both men exited, the doors shut. Mercator's smile gradually disappeared as he scratched his head.

"What is our next move?" John asked.

"Moot is no longer safe from Hastur or his growing horde," Hecate added.

"There is no place in this kingdom to safely take these people," Mercator said.

Illume pursed his lips for a few seconds as he thought things through. They would need as many expendable reinforcements as they could get. Illume looked around at the hundreds of bodies strewn around the city.

Opening his map, Illume zoomed in as far as he could. He studied the map as he formulated a plan. A smile spread across his lips as he nodded. He lowered his map and turned to Mercator.

"Hastur hasn't gone to the sea," Illume proclaimed. "He's gone BY the sea, but no one has mentioned that he's gone ONTO the water itself. If we're going to stop him, we will need an army to get in his way."

"Where are we going to get one of those?" Nari asked.

"It's not as if you can call your men, they wouldn't make it in time," John added.

"No, they wouldn't," Illume agreed. "But we have a necromancer and hundreds of dead here. If you can get those dead to the white cliffs of Arangduul, John can take as long as he needs to prepare a spell that will bring them back…"

"In a manner of speaking, they will not be themselves," John interrupted.

"I am aware of that," Mercator replied. "I know how necromancy works. That doesn't answer the question as to how the few survivors we have can move all these dead that far."

"The boats. Load everyone onto the boats and take them to Traders Bay. You can get to the ocean from here. There you can use the locals to get the fallen to the white cliffs. After that, you'll take their ships and evacuate everyone." Illume looked at John. "I mean EVERYONE and sail for Mire. From there, I will have people waiting to bring you as far from this kingdom as they can."

"Who?" Nari asked.

"The people of Cryo's Quarry," Illume replied. "I don't know what Hastur is truly capable of. He changed this entire landscape, and as far as I can guess, the second we start attacking him, anything he has influenced inside this kingdom could turn on us."

"How do we know your people will accept us?" Mercator asked.

"The captain of our night guard is a werewolf," Illume explained. "His right hand man is a lich vampire and his wife is our city's steward. We have an orc as head of our markets and trade and a dwarf forger who's been trained by the best blacksmith in the kingdom."

Illume looked at Nari.

"You can't fast travel," John pointed out. "I can. I should be the one to go to Cryo's Quarry and inform them about what's going on."

Illume shook his head as he looked at Trillian. The dragon was large enough to fly. He hoped he'd be able to ride Trillian that far.

"You haven't been anywhere north of us. You wouldn't be able to fast travel, catch up to, find us, AND start your spell in time," Illume rebutted. "I will fly with Trillian. It's not as fast as quick travel, but I will at least be able to get a bird's eye view of everything and find you on my way back."

"Can you fly on your dragon?" Mercator asked.

"He's large enough to carry Illume," Hecate informed Mercator. "That's our best chance of success."

Mercator shook his head in disbelief and then shrugged.

"Okay… I'll get everyone to start loading the bodies." With that, Mercator turned and entered the market once again.

Walking over to Nari, Illume gently took her hands and gave them a gentle squeeze. He gazed into her mesmerizing eyes and offered her a friendly smile.

"Nari, when these people return to Moot, I want

you to go with them. You are an amazing fighter and they will probably need your protection." He looked over at Hecate. "Hecate, I want you to go with her. Your magics might be useful as well."

Hecate's eyes narrowed and her thin lips pursed together. She let out a bit of a growl before nodding. Illume looked at Nari. She didn't even have her swords on her. She glanced over at Hecate before she nodded as well.

"We'll do it. But you might need this!" Hecate said.

She tossed a burlap sack to Illume's feet with a CLANG. Illume leaned down and looked inside. It was the armor Nari had made for him. Illume nodded and picked up the bag.

"Thank you," Illume replied.

Slinging the bag over his shoulder, Illume walked over to John. He set the bag down and drew Dovabane from his back. He offered it to his brother. John took a step back and shook his head.

"That is yours," John protested. "I'm not taking it from you."

"It feeds on mana," Illume replied. "I have only a fraction of what you do." He added, "It does more damage, is easier to wield, and it's overall better suited for you."

He held Dovabane out to John. After a few seconds of hesitation, John reached out and took the sword. It growled at him, causing Trillian to snarl at the weapon.

"But now you don't have a sword," John remarked.

"Oh my god! I'm trading you weapons, you dingus! You're hardly proficient enough to use one sword. Why would you use two?" He laughed.

A deep blush overtook John's face. Hecate and Nari chuckled. John stuck Dovabane into the ground. He drew the sword from his back and offered it to Illume, who grabbed the blade and inspected with a smile.

"Nari made this weapon for me. There's no way in heaven or hell that I would not wield it in the final battle." Illume slid it in next to Valcoth.

Dovabane Given
All Stats Lost

Mystery Sword: Great
Damage: +15 Weight: +10 Worth: 400 polis
This beautiful weapon ignores 10% of enemies armor rating. Enhances both single and double handed combat simultaneously. +20 damage to imps.

Illume smiled to himself as he looked at the stats of his weapon once again. He closed the information down and glanced over at Nari, who observed the weapon closely.

"I made that?" she asked curiously.

"You did," Illume replied. "Along with this."

Illume walked over to her and opened the sack to show her the armor. As she gazed inside, Illume pulled the sword from its sheath and handed it to her. Nari observed the flawless work in meticulous detail.

"I have gotten much better than I remember," she said softly as she scrutinized the blade.

"There is no dulling or damage to the weapon's edge... How did I do that?" she asked in astonishment as she handed the sword back.

"I couldn't tell you," Illume replied. "I'm not much of a blacksmith. But you made these specifically for me and they have not failed me yet."

"Then why do you wear robes?" Nari asked.

"The armor is heavy. I would sink in the swamp with heavy armor and I need to move quickly," he replied. "I would much rather wear your work."

"Thank you," she replied with a bit of a nod.

"John, I have something for you as well," Hecate cut in.

She hobbled over to Illume's brother. She fished within her robe and pulled out a necklace made from the Hydra teeth she'd pulled. He was impressed with how quickly she'd made it. The use of her magic no doubt.

John pulled Dovabane from the ground and

sheathed it the same time Illume sheathed his sword. He reached out and took Hecate's gift. His eyes widened as he saw the stats for it.

"The Hydra's tooth can raise the dead," Hecate explained. "An amulet of their teeth is a very powerful necromancy charm. You will need it in the battles ahead."

"Thank you, Hecate," John replied.

He slipped the necklace on as the market emptied with the townsfolk. Illume grabbed his armor and slung it over his shoulder. He looked back at Nari as the dead were retrieved and taken to the boats under the city.

"I promise I'll be back for you," Illume said softly to her.

He walked over to Trillian, who lowered the top half of his body. Illume climbed on just behind the spikes that made up his frill. As Trillian stood back up Nari ran over to Illume's side.

"I know you know me," she said softly so only Illume could hear. "But I don't know you."

"I understand," Illume murmured.

"You seem like a good man." Nari touched Illume's hand. "I want to remember you, I honestly do. While you are back at Cryo's Quarry, if you find something that might bring back some memories, will you bring it for me?"

"I will," Illume nodded.

Nari released his hand. He held on to Trillian's frills as he gave his dragon a gentle nudge with his heels.

"Let's go buddy," Illume whispered.

Trillian opened his massive wings and gave them a powerful flap as he jumped into the air. Illume leaned into the beast as it launched them both into the sky like one of his rockets at space camp.

His stomach dropped, but he held tight. Five flaps later and both he and the dragon were hundreds of feet off the ground. A soft ping filled Illume's ears.

You've now unlocked fast travel!

So long as you ride your mount, you may fast travel to any destination you both have previously been.

While riding your mount, you may scout out other areas on the map.

Fast travel by sight is limited to cities previously visited. You may return to your party outside of a city once every twenty-four hours.

"Okay, Trillian," Illume said softly as he looked to his right to see fields off in the distance. "Let's go home."

32

HOW TO TRAIN A DRAGON

A MAP of Valka became visible as Trillian soared through the air. Fluffy clouds danced around Illume's body as they weaved between the floating fluffs of cotton.

Every city Illume had been to was lit up like a Christmas tree. Cities like Traders Bay were a soft grey. Illume looked around. He hovered over Strang for a few moments before he looked at Cryo's Quarry. Illume focused on the city and a soft *click* could be heard.

The map closed. Trillian altered his direction and flapped his wings as hard as he could. Their speed picked up greatly. As both man and beast flew higher into the sky, Illume heard another soft ping.

New Dragon Level Reached x18

Overall Dragon Level 20

Available Attribute Points: 90

Available Skill Points: 18

Dragons reach full maturity at level 30

Dragon's max level is 100

Stats:

Health: 500 regenerates 5% of max health a second outside of battle.

Mana: 1000 regenerates 15% of max mana a second outside of battle.

Stamina: 750 regenerates 7% max stamina outside of battle.

Unique Traits: Godlike Mana. Due to extreme limits of the share mana skill being pushed Trillian's mana wells have grown exponentially as has its regenerative properties.

Frost Vacuum: Due to being a frost dragon and taking on the traits of his owner, Trillian is not only immune to frost damage but any frost magic used against him will temporarily increase his mana pool.

Attributes:

Strength: +150 Average for a dragon.

Intelligence: +300 Above average for a dragon.

Armor: +100 Below average for a dragon.

Flight Speed: +100 Below average for a dragon.

Attack: +400 Above average for a dragon.(Base attack stat is influenced by the dragons first fight.)

Skills:

Frost Breath (Unlocked)

Frost Storm (2 Skill Points)

Frost Fire (3 Skill Points)

Tail Attacks:

Tail Whip (Unlocked by default of having a tail) +25 damage

Tail Club (2 Skill Points) +50 damage

Tail Mace (3 Skill Points) +100 damage induces crush

Claw Attacks:

Grip (Unlocked by default of having claws) +10 pierce damage

Tear (1 Skill Point) +40 pierce damage

Dismember (2 Skill Points) +85 pierce damage

Wing Attacks:

Slap (Unlocked by default of having wings) +10

damage

Slash (1 Skill Point) +30 damage

Razor (3 Skill Points) +50 damage

Defensive Frills:

Quill (1 Skill Point) +5 defense

Spike (2 Skill Points) +45 defense

Projectile (3 Skill Points) +85 defense +20 damage

Jaws:

Bite (Unlocked by default of having mouth) +10
    Pierce/Crush damage

Chomp (2 Skill Points) +20 Peirce/Crush

Devour (5 Skill Points) +30 Pierce/Crush +50
    Health/Stamina/Mana

Dragons will learn new unique skills as they grow
    and experience events.

Illume closed Trillian's stat page. That was a lot to take in, but he was happy to know that he complemented Trillian perfectly. They would make a strong team, and if fostered properly, they could be unstoppable. Trillian cleared the thoughts that swirled around in his head.

Opening up his map to check their location, Illume was pleased to see they had made some great progress and were about halfway to Cryo's Quarry. He glanced down to see that they flew over great fields and plains. In the distance, Illume noticed an unmistakable dust cloud rising into the air. He looked at his forearm at the symbol of the centaurs and smiled.

Illume cycled to his dragon stats page. Just like with him, he knew that putting points into one thing could have minor boosts on multiple skills in the late game. He had a lot of points to mess with. The only questions were what would best suit the battle at hand.

Strength would need to be first. The stronger Trillian was, the faster he could move and the harder his physical attacks would land. Illume placed twenty of his attribute points into strength.

Flight speed increased by 2% Attack damage increased by 2%.

Nodding in approval, Illume would have preferred something more substantial than two percent, but he wouldn't argue with a free boost. Next he moved to the armor stat. Below average was unacceptable, especially going up against something like Hastur.

Illume placed fifty points into armor just to bring it up to the average for other dragons. *Clubbing and crushing damage increased by 5%,* Illume was informed. He nodded, impressed with that stat boost.

With twenty points left, Illume placed them in flight speed, the only remaining stat where Trillian was currently weak. There were perks to having a specialized "special unit." but Illume preferred to have a well-rounded one to fit his play style. He always had been able to outthink characters who were stronger, faster, better armored, or hit harder than he could. There was no point in changing that now.

Illume moved over to Trillian's skill trees. He had so many potentially useful attacks, he wasn't sure what he wanted to invest in outside of the "breath" skills. Illume placed two skill points in frost storm, which unlocked frost fire. Illume used three more to unlock that as well.

Next was Trillian's defenses. The base stat was well rounded, but every little bit would help. He attempted to unlock projectile off the bat. There was a low and aggressive buzz that rang out as the words *must unlock previous skills first* appeared in his view.

With a sigh, Illume relented and put one point in quill, two in spike, and used three to unlock projectile. As Illume closed out the defensive frill portion of his skill tree, he was greeted by another message. *Armor has increased by 7% across the board.*

Illume glanced at his skill point counter. He had seven points left. They were heading to the land of the griffins. If Hastur got there first, then Trillian would have to contend with flying beasts trying to take him down. He flipped to the skill tree for Trillian's wings.

He used four points to unlock the remaining skills. One for slash and three for razor. *Armor has increased by 3%. Offense has increased by 10%.* Illume sighed and nodded. He was happy with this decision.

With three points left, Illume ran into problems. Where would he put the last three? What combination of attacks would yield the highest possible damage output?

Eventually, Illume settled on unlocking chomp, as it did combine forty extra damage with the last point going to tear. Illume closed out the skill trees and returned to the game once again.

New Stats for Trillian

Attributes:
Strength: +170 Average for a dragon.
Intelligence: +300 Above average for a dragon.
Armor: +189 Average for a dragon.
Flight Speed: +122 Below average for a dragon.
Attack: +471 Above average for a dragon.

New Skills for Trillian

Breath: Frost Fire

372 JONATHAN YANEZ & ROSS BUZZELL

Tail: Tail Whip
Claws: Tear
Wings: Razor
Defensive Frills: Projectile
Jaws: Chomp

Trophy Earned
Name: First Timer
Type: Bronze
Requirement: Level up your mount for the first time.

Look at the fluff ball! Who's a good boy?

Illume closed the information that flooded his vision. As he did, he felt Trillian speed up ever so slightly as he flew. He looked down toward the ground patched by different crops that stretched as far as the eye could see.

Up ahead towered a citadel. A massive white wall the same height as Lapideous. Rows of people flooded in and out like ants on their way to and from their nest.

Squinting, Illume rubbed his eyes in disbelief. There was the land bridge, but nothing else looked the same. Every structure was made of polished white stone. Men in shimmering blue tinted armor stood on the wall.

Illume leaned to one side, causing Trillian to bank

left. They circled the city as he held tightly to Trillian's quills. Far below, people started to scream and scatter. A few of the guards jumped onto a massive crossbow. Illume's eyes widened at the sight.

"Trillian, bank right!" Illume yelled.

He pulled Trillian as hard to the right as he could. A massive arrow narrowly missed them both as they did a barrel roll. Illume heard voices scream for them to cease fire. It was too late for one of the bows. An arrow was already headed their way.

"Trillian, let's try out that frost fire." Illume suggested with a smile.

Illume turned the dragon toward the oncoming bolt. He raised his hands, prepared to block the attack with a wall of ice if need be. Trillian took a deep breath. Snow formed around them for a split second.

Trillian released his breath into a massive beam of near nuclear luminescent light. Blue flames danced off Trillian's central beam, which consumed the projectile. Trillian's shot lasted only for a second or two before he turned and spun out of the arrow's path.

The projectile flew past them at blinding speeds. It was longer than Trillian and thicker than Illume's thigh. Anything it hit would be a one-shot kill. Illume looked back and watched it strike the ground. It shattered into hundreds of smaller pieces.

Trillian and Illume continued their descent in a

circle like a vulture descending on its prey. This allowed Illume to get a better look at what Cryo's Quarry had blossomed into. The only structure he recognized was his own home, which hadn't been touched up to this point.

They grew closer and closer to the ground as the inhabitants of Cryo's Quarry all flooded to the center of town in front of Illume's house. Eventually, both Trillian and Illume landed to the roar of applause.

Illume grabbed his bag of armor and climbed off of Trillian, who gave himself a shake like a dog who'd just woken up from a nap. Scales, skin, and quills flew off of him in massive sheets. Illume put his arm up to block the sloughing-off skin. Some smacked him in the face and had a thick slime to it. Illume gagged as he wiped his face off.

"Come on, Trillian. That is disgusting!" he complained.

Illume turned his attention back to his dragon. He'd molted to roughly the size of a Clydesdale. His quills were thicker and longer than before and the horns at the crown of his head and the crests of his cheeks had grown by about seven inches.

The front edge of his wings glinted with razor sharp ice that whistled as the slightest breeze touched them. Trillian's claws had grown longer, thicker, and sharper as well. They had taken on the void-like properties of flawless black ice and his jaw became more pronounced.

"I guess what they say is true," Illume chuckled. "Be careful who you make fun of in grade school."

Illume gave Trillian a scratch under the chin. He seemed to smile and shook his body in enjoyment. Guards flooded in a circle around Illume with pikes and pointed them at both Trillian and Illume.

Placing his bag by his feet, Illume smirked. Trillian arched his back like a cat and growled as his mouth started to glow. Illume summoned frost to his hands as the temperature around them dropped so suddenly that everyone's breath became visible.

"Surrender!" one of the guards called out.

"You don't know who I am, do you?" Illume replied.

"STOP! WAIT!" Victor's voice shouted.

33

HOME SWEET HOME

VICTOR PUSHED through the guards and pulled one of the pikes away from the man who told Illume to surrender. He threw it to the ground before he stepped between Illume and the guards.

"You will all stand down this instant!" he commanded. "This is Illume the Cryomancer. He is the founder of Cryo's Quarry and the one who ensured you are all well paid."

Immediately, all the guards relaxed their stance. Victor took off his helmet and turned to Illume with a wide smile. Trillian relaxed as Illume gave Victor a massive bear hug.

"It's good to see you, my friend!" Victor proclaimed.

"Likewise," Illume replied. "What happened to this place. I hardly recognize it!"

"It's all Kassandra. She organized most of the treasures to be brought here from the Dark King's castle when we made it a garrison," he explained. "We used that to build as much as we could and hire the very best. As a result, Cryo's Quarry has become the unofficial capital of this kingdom."

Cryo's Quarry
Population: 600/1000
Annual income: 1M Polis
Cost & Maintenance: 600K Polis
Amount in Treasury: 850k Polis
Trade Established with four major cities over two kingdoms.
Status: Growing and Thriving.

Illume smiled and nodded to himself as he read the stats for Cryo's Quarry. It had grown nearly three times over since he'd left. He took in the beauty for a few moments before he turned back to Victor.

"Have Urtan and the others returned?" Illume asked.

"They have. They told us what was going on and about Nari," Victor responded. "Is she okay?"

"In a manner of speaking," Illume replied. "She's alive, but some of her memories are gone."

"Well, you have the full might of our army." Victor saluted Illume.

"Thank you, but that is not possible," Illume replied. "The only way to get where we'd need you are over the mountains or through the swamplands. There would be no time to traverse over those lands and make it to the white cliffs in time."

"What about under?" Buthrandir called out from the crowd.

Illume followed the voice to see Buthy push her way through everyone. She gave one look at Illume's armor and scoffed. She shook her head as she approached Illume.

"You call this armor?" she asked.

"I've been in a swamp," Illume protested. "I needed to wear something that wouldn't weigh me down. The armor you and Nari made for me is right here."

He indicated the sack. "I was hoping you could combine the two?"

Buthrandir looked at each set of armor closely. She pursed her lips together and shrugged.

"I think it could be done. It'll take a day or two, but I could get working on it right away," she accepted.

"Good!" Illume exclaimed. "Now what did you say about going under the mountain?"

"My uncle, Uthrandir, you remember him," she berated.

"I do," Illume replied.

"He cleared out the ancient passageways that stretched out from Strang," she said. She spun her hammer and gazed at it with a proud grin. "I have already sent word to him weeks ago. He had scouts all in those swamps and the dwarven people are ready to aid you."

Illume's brow raised as he chuckled at her ingenuity.

"Thank you so much, Buthrandir!" Illume proclaimed.

Illume moved in to give her a hug. She held her hammer out towards him in a threatening manner.

"Hug me and I'll break your fingers," she snarled. "Now gimme those robes and let's see what we can do."

"Give me a second!" He pulled away and waved for Victor to follow him.

Buthrandir grabbed the bag of armor as all three walked toward Illume's house. The children started to play with Trillian.

"I need you to send a full rescue force to Mire," Illume instructed. "There are going to be hundreds of people at least who will need evacuation. Bring them here."

Opening the door to his house, Illume entered,

followed closely by his blacksmith and captain of the guard. He walked into his bedroom and shut the door, and immediately took off his swords, bow, dagger, and satchel.

"And why are we bringing them here instead of fortifying their position?" Victor asked.

Illume grabbed a fancy garment meant for a lord and changed out of his cloak. He folded the cloth together as he slipped on a different pair of shoes.

"Because they have been influenced by Hastur," Illume replied through the door. "They have been forced to take on a fish-like appearance. Hastur is something called an elder god. He is powerful enough to change the very typography of the planet by walking across its surface. If he tries to activate them, I want as much distance between us and them as possible to help delay the signal and buy us time to kill Hastur."

"And how might you kill an elder god?" Victor called out with confusion from the door.

Opening the door, Illume poked his head out near Victor's. He looked at Buthrandir and tossed her his Kapre armor. She shoved it in a bag and left the room.

"I have a plan," Illume replied.

"Mind filling me in?" Victor asked.

"Sorry." Illume stepped from the room. "For my

mind only. I don't know where Hastur could have spies."

Illume grabbed the shattered blade of Valcoth and his sword before strapping them both on his back once again.

"Very well, my lord." Victor bowed. "When would you like the relief to depart?"

"Immediately. Those who aren't on guard, walking, or riding a horse can rest in the carts," he instructed. "When the shifts switch, those who've been walking will swap with those in the carts. I want them to be able to move day and night but still remain rested."

"Very well, sir!" Victor agreed. "I will send a group out within the hour."

With that, Victor left too. Illume walked around the main hall. He let his fingers run over the pillars, chairs, and tables. He even plucked a piece of fruit from the table and ate it.

The scent of burning wood filled his nostrils. It was peaceful. Something Illume missed if he were completely honest with himself. Not much had changed within the walls of his home, of that he was glad.

Illume leaned against the hearth of his fireplace and gazed into the flames. Their warm light danced on his face. He closed his eyes and took a deep breath. The crackling of the flames filled his ears. It was peaceful.

A warm smile spread across his lips for a brief moment. The crackling of the fire began to sound like the clanging of metal. The darkness of his eyes gave way to visions of a battlefield.

An army unlike anything he'd seen slammed into an ocean of blackness. They fought with all their might but were soon consumed by their enemy. Illume alone staved off the inky darkness as it swirled around him until a single dark tendril reached from the ink and wrapped itself around his throat.

"Prepare all you like, Illume of Valka," Hastur's voice echoed within his skull.

Illume grasped for the tendril that held his throat. It felt as if he were actually being strangled.

"I know of the phoenix fire you sought. It will not avail you," Hastur threatened. "Not even with the frost of Azathoth can you stand against me!"

Madness 30%

Illume laughed at Hastur. A small giggle at first before it swelled into a sea of hysterical mirth. He pulled his shattered blade and slashed at Hastur's tendril. It turned to stone and shattered.

Hastur's illusion withdrew as his tendril grew back. Illume unsheathed his other sword as frost washed over both his weapons and his body. He continued to laugh in the same vein of the Joker.

"You still think I'm trying to kill you?" Illume asked between laughs. "I wouldn't do that!"

Illume's laughing stopped. "Not until I take your power will you be allowed to die."

Illume threw his hands out and unleashed a torrent of ice onto Hastur's image. The light of his magic washed away the darkness of Illume's vision. As it faded, Illume dropped his hands. His fireplace was frozen solid.

Dropping his hands to his sides, Illume was struck with a wave of exhaustion. He looked around to ensure no one had been injured by his outburst. He was still alone.

Illume heard the sounds of combat echo through his back door. He rushed toward the commotion. Illume threw the door open, ready for just about anything. Just about anything except for what he saw.

Khal had a wooden sword. He flipped around what would be Illume's back yard like Yoda as he fought off Halfdan and Abdelkrim, who were both armed with practice spears. Even with only one weapon, Khal was able to outmaneuver and out-fight both the skilled warriors.

"Come on! Is that the best you got?" Khal taunted.

Sheathing his weapons, Illume leaned against the

door frame with crossed arms. Khal continued to taunt his opponents. Illume shook his head, wishing he'd stop. Khal might have been fast, but he didn't have the strength or stamina yet to be able to get away with taunting.

Just as Illume was thinking that, Halfdan hooked his spear under Khal's foot and pulled it out from under him. He fell on his back and both warriors placed the tips of their practice spears to his chest.

Illume started to clap, impressed with Khal's performance. All three looked over. When they saw that it was Illume clapping, they straightened up. The twins faced Illume and stood at attention. Khal pulled himself to his feet and charged at Illume.

Illume greeted Khal with a big hug as Khal wrapped his arms tightly around Illume's waist. Illume looked up at the twins and gave them a thumbs-up.

"It looks like they are taking to their jobs well!" Illume pointed out. "You are quite the fighter. Do you know how they beat you?"

"I taunted too much," Khal replied with a huff.

"Taunting works to throw your enemies off. Make them upset and force them to fall into making a mistake," Illume explained. "These two men, they know you, they care for you. Your taunts do not work on them aside to wear down your stamina and weaken your fighting arm so they can knock you on your back."

He smiled at the boy. "I have not seen fighting like that in a very long time. You've done well."

"Thank you!" Khal grinned.

"Is Nari here?" he asked, his voice laced with hope.

"I'm sorry, she isn't." Illume ruffled Khal's hair. "She is helping save a whole lot of people right now, which is why I'm here. Have you been practicing your potions?"

"If I may, sir," Halfdan interjected.

Illume turned his attention to Halfdan as he drank a strange banana-yellow liquid. He took a deep breath as yellow prisms shimmered over his body for a few seconds before disappearing.

Abdelkrim took a step back, and with all his strength, slammed his practice spear into Halfdan's back. Halfdan didn't flinch. The yellow light prismed once again and dissipated as Abdelkrim's spear shattered into pieces.

"Did you make a potion for a protection spell?" Illume asked with an impressed tone.

"I'm close," Khal replied. "I just can't find a way for it to hold. It breaks down after about three seconds."

"I believe in you. Why don't you talk to Urtan tomorrow morning and see if he doesn't have anything from the swamplands to help prolong that spell," he said. "In the meantime, go get cleaned up, get some dinner, and go to bed. You're going to need your rest because we are about to have a lot of guests and I expect you to make them feel welcome."

"Yes, sir!" Khal exclaimed before he ran into the house.

Illume approached the twins and bowed slightly to them both. They bowed back.

"I thank both of you for training Khal so thoroughly," Illume said softly. "He has progressed far beyond what I could have taught him. After this calamity passes, I will grant you whatever you wish."

"We are happy just to serve," Abdelkrim replied.

"Nonsense!" Illume rebutted. "You are being paid handsomely, and you clearly have a good home here, but there is no real land for you to own. Would you like land? Titles? A post of some kind?"

"I would like to be the warden of The Dark Tower," Halfdan replied.

"The Dark Tower?" Illume frowned. "I have never heard of it."

"It was the Dark King's castle," Abdelkrim clarified.

"So be it. Only so long as you do not enter the very top of the tower," Illume warned. "And you. What can I offer you?"

"I wish to join you in this fight," Abdelkrim requested.

"That cannot happen," Illume rebutted. "Trillian can only carry one right now. But I will bring you on my next adventure should you wish."

"I do," Abdelkrim accepted.

34

TRUE SKILL OF A DWARF

ILLUME MOVED THROUGHOUT HIS HOUSE. He used fire magic to melt the ice he'd made before grabbing some food to eat. After he heard Khal rustling around in his bed, Illume followed the noise to his adoptive son's bedroom.

Leaning against the doorway, he watched Khal toss and turn in the dark. Khal huffed and grumbled to himself about not being able to sleep. Illume pushed off the door frame and took a few steps in.

"Why can't you get any sleep?" Illume asked.

Khal spun around in his bed and looked at Illume from behind a scrunched-up face. Khal sighed and shook his sheets some.

"I just can't!" Khal blurted in frustration.

Stepping into Khal's room, Illume pulled a seat up

next to him. He tucked the boy in a little more before he leaned against his knees.

"How about I tell you a story, then. Will that help you get to sleep?" Illume asked.

"Yes," Khal responded with a nod.

"This is a story about how I met a god," Illume started. He sprinkled his voice with wonder. "Once upon a time, there was this great god of mischief."

"Khal'sol'slatz?" Khal asked, his voice laced with excitement.

"That's the one! This god caused all kinds of problems for all kinds of people," he continued, "but he had a sense of justice. He would only cause mischief based on what the individual deserved."

"So he's a good guy?" Khal's brow furrowed.

"He is," Illume confirmed. "But that means that when another god, one older than him came to the kingdom, the god of mischief was locked away behind a wall of his own magic."

"How did he get out?" Khal inquired with eyes full of wonder.

"He was freed when a brave knight and his brother stormed the dungeon that held the god of mischief!" Illume proclaimed. "They fought all manner of beasts, monsters, and demons just to get to the god."

Illume adjusted himself in his chair. It was not comfortable and his left leg had begun to go numb.

"But before the knight and his brother could reach the god, they were stopped by a female demon of the swamp," Illume continued. "She was as round as she was tall. She had long grey hair that covered her body like an ape. She summoned her children to stop the knight and his brother, but both men fought valiantly and won the day."

"Did that free Khal?" Khal asked.

"It certainly did," Illume replied with a nod. "The earth shook beneath the brothers' feet as the magic fractured and broke. From within emerged the god of mischief himself. He was so grateful that he gave the knight a blessing that allowed the knight to summon him three times for aid."

"What happened next?" Khal asked curiously.

"They were attacked by the same god who locked the man we rescued away," Illume replied as he tried very hard not to say his name. "The god of mischief took his dagger and used it to fend off his captor, and with the help of the knight and his brother, the god of mischief escaped."

"He didn't really use your dagger!" Khal stated in disbelief.

Illume unbuckled Bloodlust from his waist and offered it to Khal. Slowly, the boy took the dagger. His eyes widened as his fingers explored the blade. He drew it part of the way out of its sheath before he placed it back.

"He really did use this!" Khal exclaimed.

"Do you like it?" Illume asked.

"I love it!" Khal replied in an enamored tone.

"Then it's yours," Illume replied. "You're a man now. You need something to properly defend yourself with."

Khal leaned forward and wrapped his arms around Illume's neck. Illume hesitated for a moment before he returned Khal's affection. He felt a sensation of what could only be described as paternal love washed over him for Khal.

"Thank you! I love you, Dad." Khal cried out.

"I love you too… son." Illume's heart pounded against his chest. "Now you go to sleep and don't go through any of my things if you wake up before me."

Illume explained. "Some of what I brought back is VERY deadly. Good night."

Khal released Illume as Illume stood up and left, making his way to his bed. He removed his weapons and lay down. The bed seemed a lot larger and more empty without Nari. Eventually, he let the exhaustion of his trip take him.

Unconscious, Illume was plagued with hellish visions of Hastur and the brood who now followed him. Of unknowable evils of writhing masses of flesh and tentacles. Countless eyes watched Illume from the dark as he fell into what felt like oblivion.

The itch in the back of Illume's mind grew worse and worse with each passing second. Illume slammed into the ground, a ground he couldn't see. Confusion washed over him as he tried to stand, only to be knocked back by some unseen force.

Illume fell into the black ground. It sloshed around him like water but had an inky slickness to it. It burned as it filled his nostrils and lungs. He frantically attempted to summon the ice from within him to no avail.

The ink solidified around Illume. Gradually, it entombed him in oblivion, unable to move, speak, or even breathe. Yet something kept him alive. Some dark entity beyond that of even Hastur held him in the depths as madness swelled within him with the ferocity of the seas.

A violent blow rocked Illume awake. His eyes bolted open and he gasped for air. His lungs burned as if he hadn't been breathing. Illume felt his stomach violently churn. He rolled over and vomited into a bucket on the far side of his bed.

"Thought you'd never wake up!" Buthrandir taunted from behind Illume. "You feeling okay?"

Her voice softened as Illume vomited.

"I'm fine," Illume groaned as he threw up once more. "How long have I been out?"

Wiping his mouth with his sleeve, Illume turned to face Buthrandir, who stood at the foot of his bed.

"Three days!" she exclaimed. "We figured we'd let you sleep to regain your strength, but when you started to speak in that funny language, I thought it best to wake you up."

"You did the right thing," Illume replied. "Thank you."

"Where did you learn that language?" Buthrandir asked as she moved into the main hall.

"It's a long story," Illume sighed.

Illume stood up as Buthrandir entered the room once again. This time, she carried a chest with her. She set it down next to Illume's bed and opened it. Illume peered inside.

The armor that Nari had helped make him sat within. It was laced with scaled and wood accents from his Kapre robes. Illume picked up the armor. It was lighter than he remembered.

"Whatever your robes were made out of was impressive stuff. It was tricky to work, but once I got it going, it managed to both lighten and strengthen the armor. I hope it fits okay."

"Buthrandir, this is beautiful!" Illume exclaimed.

He marveled at the tiny details that accented each

piece and how they perfectly seemed to complement one another. Buthrandir grabbed the gauntlet for Illume's left arm and held it out to him.

"I noticed something cool with this glove," she explained. "I also saw that whatever was built in was destroyed. I used a little bit of dragon magic and what Trillian shed the other day to help replace what you lost."

Illume slid the gauntlet on. He closed his fist and held it up in front of him. A circle of dragon scales formed up in front of Illume. He gently ran his fingers over the scaled shield. It felt just like Trillian's skin.

Dragon Skin Shield
Weight: +.05 Worth: 10000 polis
Defense: +80 offers 75% resistance to magic attacks.

Illume closed the shield as he continued to marvel at her work. He shook his head as he kneeled before the crate.

"You are a goddess of the forge," Illume whispered. "You've grown so much since we left. I am proud to have you as part of my team."

"Don't mention it. If you're going to be saving the world, you need the best equipment imaginable. I'm just happy to be of service." She turned to leave the room. "I'll leave you to it, then."

Illume picked up the breast plate. As he did, the metal gradually changed to a frosted blue color. The longer he held on to it, the more it resembled ice.

Legendary Multispecies Armor:

Frost King's Armor.
Armor: +100 Weight: +25 Worth: N/A
Armor attributes increased by 30% when worn as a full set.
Bursts of speed and dexterity increased by 50%.
Frost magic costs 30% less mana to cast.

Frost King's Bracers.
Armor: +32 Weight: +3 Worth: N/A
Armor attributes increased by 30% when worn as a full set.
Sure grip of the Kapre prevents weapons from being knocked from your hands. Enhances non-armed combat strength by +10

Frost King's Boots.
Armor: +35 Weight: +3 Worth: N/A
Feather Effect lasts on all surfaces even when standing still.
If frost mana is channeled through the boot, the wearer will be able to glide.

Frost King's Helmet.

Armor: +35 Weight: +4 Worth: N/A

When worn, intimidation increases by +20. All elemental magic does 10% less damage. Prevents critical headshots.

Special Armor Set Abilities:

Critical hits can't be landed while wearing a full set.

+5 armor for each matching piece worn.

Overall Armor rating:

+360 Protection against damage

+440 With shield

+10% Protection against flame and shock magic

+85% with shield

+82% Protection against frost magic

Absorbs 30 mana per second with shield.

"Buthrandir," Illume whispered to himself. "You are a miracle worker."

One piece at a time, Illume donned his armor. It fit even better than before. It was lighter and seemed to flex and move with him. The silvery metal began to take on the full appearance of blue as Illume kept the protection on himself.

He grabbed his swords and slung them over his back where they settled in right at home. He snatched his quiver and bow and slung them over his shoulder in the opposite direction.

The ridiculously high-rated armor made Illume feel invincible. Something told him he'd need every bit of the protection he had when facing down Hastur. Illume picked up his satchel with the scroll and Theon's head.

Before he left his room, Illume glanced over at the bucket on the far side of his bed. There were no chunks of food, no spew of stomach acid. Only ink. The thick black ink that tried to consume him filled the bucket.

Illume felt the scratching at the back of his skull. He heard the whispers as they echoed throughout the room. His health bar was permanently a third of the way down.

"I don't have long." he whispered as he looked at his trembling hands. "Hastur must die!"

He spoke as if he were trying to persuade himself of that fact. He gritted his teeth and marched toward his door. Illume flung it open and made a straight line for his front door. As he opened it, half the city was waiting for him.

Khal sat on the back of the admittedly less adorable Trillian. Kassandra was with her children and Urtan stood next to them. Countless other faces he didn't recognize had all gathered to wish him well on his travels.

Urtan was the first to approach Illume. He held an amulet in his hands. As he grew closer, Illume recognized it. It was the exact inverse of Hastur's magical amulet.

"Short bald man came to Urtan's boat. He insist Urtan trade wares for amulet. He said to give it to you." Urtan held out the amulet. "Urtan proud to be Illume's friend!"

Illume took the amulet. He removed his Silver Necklace of Purification and slid the amulet Urtan had given him on.

Amulet of Sound Mind:
Weight: +1 Worth: 900 polis
This amulet can't prevent madness from overtaking
    you, but it can prevent you from reaching any
    higher levels.
The higher your madness meter, the less this will
    work.

"Thank you, Urtan. Please, take this for me." He handed Urtan his necklace.

"Urtan hold until you get back."

"Thank you. You are a good friend." Illume smiled.

Illume walked over to Kassandra and her children. He crouched and gave her son a high five and her daughter a hug. He stood up and faced his Lycan-thrope Steward.

"If I am not back in two weeks, take everyone and flee to the lands of the east," Illume said softly.

"Yes, sir," Kassandra responded with a hesitant nod.

"I could not have asked for a better Steward. For a more loyal friend or a more lovely family than your own. Cryo's Quarry's success is thanks to you. I hope you are proud of your work here because I am."

"You'll come back to us," Kassandra insisted with a nod.

Her eyes welled with tears as she gave Illume a huge hug. Illume returned her embrace. After a few seconds, he moved on to Buthrandir, who he didn't see behind Trillian.

"If I make it back, it's going to be thanks to this armor." Illume tapped the bracer with his knuckle. "It is the greatest armor I have ever had the honor of wearing. Thank you. And should I get back, you're teaching me how to smith."

Buthrandir said nothing. She only gave Illume a nod. Illume turned and walked over to Trillian. He looked up at Khal. The boy slid into his arms before Illume set him down.

"When are you going to be back?"

"Hopefully soon," Illume answered. "In the meantime, I want you to ask Urtan about the bald man who visited him on the boats."

Khal's eyes lit up like it was Christmas day. A huge smile overtook his face.

"Are you serious?" he asked.

"Completely," Illume nodded. "He got to meet the mischief god." He paused then added, "I love you and I will be back as soon as I can."

He gave Khal a tight hug. Khal returned his embrace. After Illume released Khal, he ran over to Urtan. Illume climbed onto Trillian's back and looked around at the city that he'd help make. It was tranquil and joyous.

Dozens of races lived here in peace with one another. He looked forward to adding more. Illume looked back at the twins. He nodded at them, they saluted back.

"People of Cryo's Quarry!" Illume yelled. "I know only a handful of you truly know me, but I swear to you, I would not be gone for no good reason."

His voice echoed over the stone structures.

"In the swamp kingdom is a threat unlike anything you've seen. I have faced him twice and trust me when I say the Dark King is much more preferable to him. I leave now. Not to abandon you, but to make sure that the cancer does not spread to you." Illume looked around as Trillian turned from here to there. "I will return!"

The crowd exploded in cheering and hollering for Illume. They chanted his name as well, over and over again. Illume leaned down to Trillian's ear and gently patted his dragon.

"Are you ready to go?"

Trillian nodded and let out a snort. Illume gripped his dragon tightly and leaned as close to the quills as he could.

"All right, let's go."

GRIFFINS

WITH A POWERFUL FLAP of the dragon's wings, Illume and Trillian were in the air once again. An audible gasp from the people of Cryo's Quarry rang out as they took off. It didn't take long for Trillian to reach his "cruising altitude." and by then, they had already flown over Lapideous, which looked sort of abandoned.

Illume scanned the kingdom as they flew. In the distance to his left, he saw a large group that moved at a steady pace. They were too far away to see any detail, but Illume could tell they were his. Illume looked down at the blessing on his forearm.

He wanted to summon the Centaurs to help, but he wasn't sure how good of an idea that was. Their stampede could easily trample entire lands under their massive hooves, and if Hastur managed to inflict madness on them, there would be nothing anyone could do to stop them.

Illume pulled up his map to see that there was a very specific colored blue waypoint already set. It was moving away from Traders Bay and toward the white cliffs. It had to be John, he was obsessed with that color. Illume closed his map and leaned so that Trillian was aimed at the marker.

As they flew, Illume kept an eye out in all directions. As he approached the border of the swamplands, he could see the ocean on the horizon. Several ships had begun their voyage. He looked for anything that resembled the *Woeful Damnation* but to no avail.

Over the sound of the wind rushing, Illume heard a deep rumbling that grew louder. Illume searched for the source. It didn't take him long to find it.

Up ahead, a few miles from John's marker, the trees from the swamp swayed violently. It moved at a steady pace forward and nothing seemed to slow it down. *Hastur!* Illume thought to himself as they flew over the commotion.

Clenching his jaw, it took everything in his power to not have Trillian do a strafing run on Hastur's position. The mere fact that the whispers had come back and were telling him to do it was the only reason he didn't.

As they passed over Hastur's position, something

in Illume's gut told him to fly higher. He grabbed Trillian by the frills and gently pulled up. Trillian leaned back and ascended ever so gradually.

Illume looked to his right. From this high up, he could see the original Trillian's citadel tucked in the crevasse of the mountains. His brow furrowed. On the march to that citadel, Illume saw griffins flying in this direction.

There had been warnings that Hastur couldn't get his hands on the griffins that lived on Arangduul. Where were they? He should have seen them flying around the skies by now. Or at the very least on the ground ahead. They were nowhere to be seen.

Illume's stomach sank. He swallowed hard as they continued to climb. A high-pitched screech rang out. It was strange, as if someone had mixed the call of a hawk and the roar of a lion. Illume leaned to one side, then the other, causing Trillian to sway as he flew.

From the swamps below, Illume saw five massive creatures flying towards them. They flew straight up and were climbing fast. Each flap of their wings let off a puff of yellowish spores. Illume pulled back on Trillian and gave him a nudge with his heel.

"We've got company!" Illume yelled.

Trillian kicked it into high gear and flew straight up as well. Illume looked back. All five were gaining on them quickly. Illume shook his head as the importance of flight speed now settled in.

"Try not to kill any," Illume yelled over the roar of the wind. "We may be able to use them."

With that, Illume leaned back off Trillian and released his mount. Weightlessness grasped him as he spun around to face the oncoming threat. Illume drew his broken blade. He began to free fall toward the griffins. They let off loud calls to one another and formed up in a staggering formation under Illume.

Frost formed around Illume's feet. He felt the boots begin to lighten as Illume took a step through the air. As he did, his trajectory changed ever so slightly. He was no longer in free fall.

Stepping through the air, Illume guided his descent as he spiraled down toward the massive beasts as they charged up at him, their front talons sharp and open. Their beaks were like massive curved swords waiting to devour Illume.

As both were about to collide with one another, Illume jumped. He rotated his body to the back of the lead griffin. Illume grasped for the edge of the wing near its shoulder, and by some miracle, managed to catch it and hang on.

His body jerked violently as his trajectory changed. The wind was forced from his lungs, but he held tight. Illume looked up to see that they were rapidly gaining on Trillian. Quickly, Illume made two shallow cuts on the beast with the blade of Valcoth. Each cut let out a flash of white. The griffin's health bar became visible and dropped slightly.

Griffin Immune to Stone Gaze.

The hybrid creature had a ridiculous amount of health and the fact that it was immune to the stone gaze effect was a bit of a relief. He gave it two more superficial wounds. Trillian was now only a few feet away from them.

"Trillian, now!" Illume yelled.

The griffins might have been faster, but Trillian was far more maneuverable. On Illume's signal, Trillian leaned back and rotated. Illume stretched as high as he could and held out his hand. Trillian tucked his wings as he maneuvered his fall to be just above the griffins.

As Trillian passed, he grabbed Illume by his hand. Illume fell from the griffin and sheathed his sword. He held on to Trillian tightly as they blasted past the sickly green-feathered animals.

Illume held his breath as they passed through the griffins' "spores." Each of the bird-lion hybrids struggled to get turned around but eventually started to dive after Trillian and Illume.

Climbing up Trillian's side, Illume sat on the back of his mount once more. It would be super easy for Trillian to just blast them with ice or scorch them with fire. He could even shock them and let them fall to their deaths, but the griffins were innocent creatures corrupted by Hastur.

It wasn't their fault and they didn't ask for this, so Illume wanted to try to spare them if he could. As he glanced back, Illume noticed the griffin he'd cut had begun to act strangely. It seemed to fight the desire to follow with the other griffins.

Turning his attention forward for a split second, Illume directed the dragon into a tuft of clouds. As they entered, Illume pulled Trillian to the side and started to hover. They heard four loud gusts of wind pass. They were the griffins. Illume gave Trillian a gentle kick. He flew forward once again.

As they moved from the cloud cover, Illume was struck by a dark blur. It hit him so hard, he fell from the dragon's back. Trillian lost his gait and began to tumble through the air as well. Illume's gut leapt into his throat as he fell. He searched frantically for Trillian as he left the clouds.

Illume focused his frost mana to his shoes once again to slow his descent. Trillian broke through the clouds above him and a few hundred yards away. Three of the griffins pecked and clawed at him.

Trillian roared in pain and fired his beam of frost fire into one of the griffins faces. The beast turned to ice almost instantly and plummeted to the swamp below.

Illume skated toward Trillian. His mana fell with each step he took.

Illume summoned frost to his hands. Electricity would probably have worked better, but he didn't want to run out of mana before he got back to his ride. Illume was about to throw the spell as a fourth griffin dove out of the sky and grabbed Illume by both arms.

The griffin clamped Illume's forearms so tightly, he couldn't move his fingers. The griffin's back legs scratched at Illume. He managed to prevent the creature from tearing him to ribbons, but a glancing blow kicked them away.

Illume and the beast tumbled through the sky. It let out a screech as it looped around and dive bombed the ground. Illume noticed his health dropped slightly from the claws that gripped him tightly. He attempted to use frost magic. His hands being unable to open prevented that from happening.

Illume ignited his hands on fire, but the wind extinguished it immediately. Illume summoned his last bit of magic, lightning. His hands crackled, but the sparks that leapt to the griffin served as little more than a mild annoyance.

"RELEASE ME!" Illume roared.

He used his intimidation speech. The griffin looked down at him, squawked, then pecked his helmet. The contact rang his ears and caused his health to drop even further.

Armor prevented critical hit.

Illume looked at the ground. It was approaching fast. There was no way he'd be able to survive that. Illume glanced over at Trillian, who had killed another griffin by filling it with the spikes on his neck. He was still being overwhelmed by the other. He had no other choice. Illume looked up at the beast as he decided to summon a god.

"KHAL'SOL..."

"KAAAWWWW!" Illume was cut off.

The fifth griffin crashed into the one that held Illume. It gripped Illume's attacker by its wings as it clawed its back to shreds with its lion's feet. Feathers, blood, and screeches of agony exploded into the air around them. The fifth griffin pecked Illume's attacker several times. Each peck dropped its life significantly.

Illume felt its grip on him waver as they got closer to the ground. Finally, Illume was able to open his hands. He gave the griffin a nasty bolt of electricity, which was all that was needed to kill it.

Slipping free from the corrupted beast's grip, Illume's savior swooped around and caught Illume on its back. Illume grabbed tightly as it pulled up with all its might.

The corrupted griffin that held Illume slammed through the trees and into the ground with a loud *THUD*. A geyser of water shot up above the tree line as the griffin Illume rode skimmed the tops of the trees.

Illume leaned back as far as he could. He held his breath as they both screamed over the trees at breakneck speeds. One clipped tree and they'd both be done for. Illume fired blasts of frost at the tree tops that they were about to hit, which helped them shatter with as little friction as possible.

Eventually, the griffin regained control and they both climbed once again. Illume saw the injuries his blade left on the bird. They were still bleeding. Placing his hand over the wounds, he used his healing magic to close the cuts. After the griffin's health refilled, Illume looked around for Trillian. He couldn't see the dragon anywhere.

"TRILLIAN!" Illume yelled as the griffin climbed higher. "TRILLIAN, WHERE ARE YOU?"

Nothing. Worry clouded his mind. Had that one other griffin gotten to him? Illume looked down to the swamp below as panic set in. Trillian's bright blue scales would contrast starkly against the brown and dark green ground. His heart beat in his chest and pounded in his ears.

The screech of a griffin ripped through the air like fingernails on a chalkboard. It came from directly above. Illume looked up as the final griffin descended on them with all of its claws, talons, and beak prepared to rip them both apart.

36

TRACK-DOWN

ILLUME GRITTED HIS TEETH. Time seemed to slow down as the griffin descended on them. Its legs were longer than either of Illume's swords. Should he kill it with the bow, it would undoubtedly crush him. With the distance between them, the griffin that had saved him wouldn't be able to outmaneuver the other in time.

Raising his right hand as the dragon skin shield deployed from his left, Illume pointed his hand at the beast as it dove toward them. He would only get one shot at this. Illume focused as much of his mana as he could into the electric spell in his hand.

Just as he was about to release it, a blur of blue screamed over them. There was a spurt of blood and the griffin's health bar dropped to zero. It tumbled past

Illume and his current mount, cut clean in half to the swamp below.

Illume looked up to see Trillian hovering in front of them. The griffin's blood stained his wing. Parts of his body looked rather beat up, but his health bar was full. Illume could see the anger on Trillian's face as he glared down at the body.

The dragon dove down, and with a roar that ripped through the air like a clap of thunder, he unleashed a torrent of frost fire so mighty that a thick layer of snow formed all around them. The water for dozens of yards in all directions froze solid and the trees shattered from the rapid expansion of the liquid within.

Trillian cut off his blast. He huffed then blasted it one more time for good measure. He flew back up next to the griffin. He let out what Illume could have sworn was a grateful sound, to which the griffin nodded.

The griffin let out a series of chirps to Trillian and changed directions. Trillian moved in behind the giant bird-lion hybrid. Illume could have sworn Trillian smiled at him.

Dragon Level Up
Attribute Points Available: 5
Skill Points Available: 1
Level Reached 21

Woo, he can drink now! Just kidding.
Don't give a dragon alcohol. That's how accidents
*   happen.*

Level Up Available
Attribute Points Available: 4
Skill Points Available: 2
Level Reached 28

Sighing softly, Illume nodded. Trillian earned that level up. He wasn't so sure he had. Illume glanced at his mini map. The griffin corrected their course to go toward John by itself. How did it know to do that?

Illume checked the satchel for Theon's head. It was still there. He felt so weird carrying around a demi-gorgon's head, but Theon did wish to be useful. He just hoped the stone gaze would work on Hastur.

Below, the swamp gradually shifted to muddy ground then eventually turned into rolling plains of golden grass that stretched over the yawning hills before them. To their right, the mountains offered ominous clouds that held flashes of lightning that stretched as far as the eye could see to the northeast.

Snowcapped, each mountain peak teased at the idea of winter all year around. Illume felt a deep desire to explore those peaks one day. They inspired awe like something out of Peter Jackson's work.

The griffin lowered its altitude, and Illume brought his attention forward. Before them was a large hill that dropped off to one side. The griffin turned west and flew over the ocean. It brought Illume to the outer ledge of the white cliffs of Arangduul.

Illume's breath caught in his throat. He let out a sigh of admiration as they flew serenely over the ocean. The griffin only took them halfway down the cliffs. Sea mist caught against the cliff faces gave their jagged edges a depth of mystery that intrigued Illume.

The waves lazily crashed against the base of the cliffs like a sleepy child reached for its mother. They were monoliths of titanic proportions, and even with all his power, Illume couldn't help but feel small in comparison.

Trees, grass, and bushes grew from any surface that was not vertical, giving the cliffs tantalizing splashes of color. The griffin and Trillian glided lazily over the crisp sea breeze for several minutes. Illume couldn't help but enjoy the sensation.

He closed his eyes and leaned back on the hybrid beast as the ocean from hundreds of feet below gently kissed his skin. He only wished he wasn't in full armor and could completely drink in the brilliance of it all.

The griffin gave a sharp cry. Illume snapped his eyes open as his body went on full alert. He summoned electricity to his hands since with all this moisture in the air, his frost could cause the cliffs to collapse into the ocean. Illume looked back at Trillian. The dragon didn't seem to sense any danger at the moment.

Illume let himself relax a little. His magic simmered down, but he still prepared himself for an attack from any angle. After several moments of the griffin's call echoing off the cliffs only to be drowned out by the ocean, Illume heard a similar call in response.

The griffin drifted around a large protrusion from the cliff and into a small cove. A wide smile formed on Illume's face and he couldn't hold back an audible chuckle.

Before them was an entire cliff face of massive nests. Hundreds, if not thousands of them. In each of these nests were one, two, and sometimes even three griffins. Some were smaller and still had their down feathers, which made their little eyes bulge.

Others were older with a little more grey in their feathers. The majority were of a healthy demeanor and appeared to be in their prime. The griffin he rode screeched once more. This time, all the griffins stood in their nests. Those that could spread their wings and leapt from the cliffs.

Like a waterfall of living brown feathers and golden fur, the griffins fell from the cliff face. Illume followed them. He peered over the side of his mount to see hundreds of griffins shoot straight up into the sky above them. They twisted and turned with the agility of small hawks.

The griffin Illume rode glided up the side of the cliff face. All the others circled about and fell in behind him. Illume had no idea what was going on, but they weren't being attacked, so he didn't much care.

The griffin crested the lip of the cliffs to reveal a field blanketed in purple blossoms that danced lazily in the wind. Illume tried to get the griffin to raise its altitude. He wanted to try to find his brother. It wouldn't stray from its course.

With Trillian and the other griffins in tow, Illume flew only about twenty feet off the ground. Each powerful flap of the griffin's wings caused the flowers to erupt in a shower of purple pedals and golden pollen.

Illume breathed in the sweet scent of the pollen. That was one of the good things about this world. No more allergies. On the horizon ahead, the swamplands loomed with a foreboding tone.

Halfway between them and the forest, Illume spotted three people surrounded by piles of dead. Illume leaned forward and pointed at the people. The griffin began to slow down as best it could.

Trillian moved up to Illume's side as they grew closer. The griffin reared back and flapped its wings hard several times before it landed on the ground, allowing Illume to dismount. Nari looked in amazement at the griffins. John ran up to Illume and gave him a massive hug.

"We saw the ambush. I thought you died!" John proclaimed.

Illume hugged his brother. After a few seconds, he broke the embrace and nodded to the griffin.

"I probably would have died had Hastur's hold on this one not been broken," Illume disclosed.

"Been broken?!" Hecate yelled.

She moved past Illume, shooting him an angry look. The witch approached the griffin and looked him in the eyes. She pried open his mouth and gazed inside like a curious child who'd just seen their first dog.

"Hastur's spell has not been broken," she snapped. "Part of his soul is gone."

Hecate marched over to Illume. "Why did you steal this creature's soul?"

"I didn't!" Illume backed away from Hecate.

"Not intentionally!" he added. "When they ambushed us, I thought if I hurt them, they'd leave us alone. Had I used the sword, it would have killed him."

"Had you used the sword, it would have been more merciful!" she sneered. "A griffin is meant to be free and you took that from him."

She shook her head. "Your will is tied to him and he is their leader. You have just enslaved an entire species."

"How can I free him?"

"You can't, not without relinquishing control back to Hastur, then all of them will be against us."

"Then after we kill Hastur, I will free him to be with his own kind."

"Do you know how many will die because of this?" Hecate hissed. "Too many! Far too many."

With that, she shook her head and walked away as she muttered under her breath. Illume looked at John, he shook his head in disbelief.

"I swear I didn't know." Illume confessed.

"I know that. She knows that. I'm sure it'll all be okay in the end." John patted Illume on the back. "In the meantime, Hecate is going to show me the spells that I'll need to pull this off."

John bobbed his eyebrows and sighed. He turned and followed the mismatched witch. Illume turned back to see Nari gently petting one of the larger golden-colored griffins.

The griffin nuzzled her hand and cooed as she pressed her forehead against the griffin's. Illume walked over to Trillian. He inspected his dragon closely. There were scrapes in his scaled armor and the skin between the scales had agitations.

Some of his skin had light bruising, but Illume didn't see any gashes or deep scratches. Illume looked up at Trillian's face and gave his chin a scratch then patted Trillian's neck before taking a step back.

"Don't worry about those, buddy. I'll take care of you," he whispered.

Illume used his healing hands to patch up Trillian's minor injuries. The dragon purred and licked him across the cheek. Illume laughed as he lowered his palms and patted Trillian on the head.

"Easy there, big guy." He chuckled. "I don't need my armor rusting up on me."

Trillian flopped on his side and folded his wings underneath him. Illume's brow furrowed. He shook his head and gave Trillian's belly a rub. His back right leg started to kick.

"One of the most powerful mythological creatures to exist and you only want a belly rub." Illume used both his hands to scratch Trillian's stomach some more. "You're really just a big dog, aren't you?"

Trillian looked at him with a huge smile. His pupils were fully dilated and his tongue flopped to the side out of his mouth. Illume patted Trillian's stomach before he moved to his head. He looked the dragon deep in the eyes as his smile faded.

"You sure you're ready for this, buddy?"

Trillian rolled onto his stomach and huffed. He

smacked his lips and looked into Illume's eyes. Illume couldn't help but laugh at the eyebrows his scales seemed to make and how expressive they were.

"Yeah, me neither," Illume replied. "But we have to stop him before he takes over any more lands."

Trillian whined a little. It almost sounded like an *I know*. The dragon looked over toward the cliffs. Nari stood at the edge, her swords on her hips. The wind blew the loose fabric of her clothes around.

Illume gave Trillian a final pat before he walked over to Nari. He stopped a few feet behind her and crossed his arms. He stood in silence for a few minutes then glanced back to see Trillian stare at him.

"So pushy," Illume huffed at his dragon.

"What did you say?" Nari asked.

Illume turned back around. Nari didn't even glance at him. He stepped up next to her and gazed over the peaceful ocean.

"How was the boat trip?"

"Stressful. I'm not really sure why, though. I just felt like something was watching me the entire time. Something evil."

"Believe it or not, that's a good thing," Illume told her. "It means that some part of you remembers Hastur."

"But I DON'T remember," she insisted.

"I know." Illume backed off some. "It's a good sign nonetheless."

Both fell silent for another few minutes. As Illume gazed over the beauty of both the cliffs and Nari, a poem came to mind, the only one he admittedly knew. He wasn't much of a poet either, but he didn't hold it back.

"O were my Love yon Lilack fair,
Wi' purple blossoms to the Spring;
And I, a bird to shelter there,
When wearied on my little wing.
How I wad mourn, when it was torn
By Autumn wild, and Winter rude!
But I was sing on wanton wing,
When youthfu' May its bloom renew'd.
O gin my love were yon red rose,
That grows upon the castle wa'!
And I mysel' a drap o' dew,
Into her bonnie breast to fa'!
Oh, there beyond expression blesst
I'd feast on beauty a' the night;
Seal'd on her silk-saft faulds to rest,
Till fley'd awa by Phebus' light!"

The words flowed from Illume's lips like honey. As he spoke, he hardly noticed Nari stare at him. It was only after he finished that he saw her eyes had welled with tears. A look of shock had overtaken her face.

"That was beautiful," she whispered. "Did you write that?"

"No. Don't know who did. I just heard a man named Ron Swanson say it while he overlooked the Cliffs of Moher in Ireland."

"You went to Ireland?"

"No," Illume replied. "It was from one of my favorite shows."

Nari let out a stifled laugh and shook her head.

"I'm sorry. I'm not laughing at you." she persisted.

Illume laughed as well. He realized how it sounded. Such a beautiful poem followed by saying it was from a TV show.

"No, it's okay," Illume started to laugh. "Because I'd laugh at me too."

It took a little while, but they both regained their composure. She turned and sauntered back toward Hecate and John. Illume walked alongside her.

"O were my Love yon Lilac fair," Illume finally said.

"What?" Nari looked at Illume with her golden hues.

"That's the name of the poem," Illume explained. "Over that ridge is a field of purple. That and a few other things brought it to mind."

"Will you write it down for me?"

"If we survive, I will," Illume promised.

Nari and Illume approached John and Hecate. John had his eyes closed and chanted in the same strange language Hecate spoke. Orange light flowed from Hecate and into his brother, whose magic danced off of him and into the medallion on his neck.

The medallion glowed a dark purple. The purple aura gradually expanded over John's entire body. Illume looked at Nari, she shrugged.

Illume felt the ground rumble, drawing his attention toward the swamplands. The trees trembled as another pulse shook the ground. He pulled his bow off his back and drew one of his arrows.

Trillian walked up beside Illume. The quills around his neck stood straight on end, and they gave off a rattle similar to that of a snake. He snarled as his mouth smoldered with chilled blue smoke.

Illume climbed onto Trillian's back. The golden-colored griffin moved up alongside Nari and she climbed onto his back. Illume looked down at Hecate. She was looking at the swamplands.

"Will the spell be ready in time?"

"It will be ready soon enough," Hecate replied.

"Shut up!" John snapped. "This is a tricky one."

Illume grabbed his bow string and looked over at

Nari. She drew both her swords and took a deep breath.

"You ready for this?"

"As ready as I can be," Nari replied. "Are you?"

Nari looked at Illume. He offered her a hesitant shrug as he heard the whispering once again in the back of his mind.

"More than you know," Illume decided. "Use the resurrected to draw Hastur's forces to the cliffs. The griffins and Nari will push them over the edge."

"What about you?" Nari asked.

Illume looked back across the field. From the forest all manner of mutated beings shuffled, scrawled and scuttled out of the tree line. An army flooded onto the field. They fell into formation as they waited for their leader to arrive.

It didn't take long. Hastur, in his yellow cloak emerged from the forest. Illume could feel Hastur's eyes on him. It felt like his soul was being set ablaze. Illume nocked a second arrow. John threw his arms out as his spell met its apex. A blast of purple light ripped across the field. It coursed into the bodies. Their eyes shot open with a purple glow. The dead rose to their feet.

"I'll take Hastur," Illume snarled.

37

WAVE ONE, THE FIELD

THE RISEN BODIES of the dead let out a wind-chilling wail. Illume kept his eye on Hastur, who extended his tendrilled hand. Like something out of a nightmare, his forces charged, scuttled, and slithered across the field. Illume gave Trillian a nudge and he took off.

John's risen ran toward the cliffs. Illume cut across the battlefield as low and as quickly as he could. Illume activated Trillian's shared mana. A blue light rushed off of the dragon and into Illume as they turned to cut a forty-five-degree angle across the battlefield.

Illume threw out his hand as Trillian fired a beam of ice from his mouth. Working in unison, both beings unleashed their full magical potential. A wall of ice formed. The grass frosted over on either side for nearly forty feet.

As they skimmed the ground, Illume saw Hastur's

forces closing in. Within several minutes, the wall reached nearly twenty feet high, over two feet thick and stretched over halfway across the battlefield. Illume used his fire magic to cut off a way around the ice wall as Trillian turned back.

Hastur's forces slammed into the wall. It gave off a violent shudder, but they were redirected. Illume glanced over his shoulder to see several attempt to go around the ice wall. They were incinerated by Illume's flames.

The fire wouldn't hold forever, but long enough to do its job. Illume swooped around the back of the wall. John's forces moved toward the cliff. From the looks of it, they had drawn a little over half of Hastur's army in that direction.

As Illume passed the edge of the wall, he drew his bow. Two beings who used to be human lunged at Illume. They were able to launch themselves nearly twenty feet into the air because of what Hastur had done to them.

Illume fired both arrows. Each projectile pierced the turned monsters gaping, spike-tooth-filled maws. Their emaciated, elongated, and scaled bodies fell limp to the ground as one of Illume's arrows went on to kill another of Hastur's soldiers. The other buried its head in the dirt.

Even while flying, the scent of rotting flesh filled

Illume's nostrils. The snarls and guttural roars of the turned drowned out even the rush of the wind in Illume's ears.

Illume quickly assessed the field. The majority of Hastur's forces were now headed toward John's. They needed a force on the ground, someone to drive the rest toward the cliffs. John's resurrected were nothing more than bags of meat compared to Hastur's mutated. They wouldn't stand a chance in the vanguard.

Illume pulled Trillian back toward John, Hecate, Nari, and the griffins. Nari and the griffin leader moved forward slightly. Illume waved them off as Trillian landed him halfway between the edge of his wall. It still rumbled with the impacts of mutated bodies against it.

He dismounted as several of the turned passed his wall. Illume drew the frenzy arrows. He started to fire the magical projectiles indiscriminately into the horde before him. Some arrows nicked their targets, some struck and caused serious damage while one or two actually killed their victims.

Reaching back for more frenzy arrows, Illume felt around the soft feathered tips of his quiver but found nothing as distinctly unique as the frenzy feathers. Illume slung his bow over his shoulder and drew the sword Nari had forged him and broken blade.

"Cover me!" Illume called to Trillian.

The dragon snorted and nodded. Illume charged forward with Trillian close behind. The frenzied soldiers attacked everything that moved around them. They tore into their own like sharks on a feeding frenzy.

Screams, hisses, and screeches filled the air along with a distinct muddled iron smell as black blood covered the field. Illume sliced through his first enemy with little effort. The second managed to catch his sword in a set of clawed hands. Illume swung his broken blade to sever its hands.

Upon contact, Hastur's victim turned to stone. Illume ripped his sword free as Trillian landed behind him and fired a blast of frost fire across the field, which obliterated a large portion of the corrupted.

A yellow-eyed Kapre lunged at Illume, its wood blackened and rotted. Illume threw up his shield and dropped to one knee. The Kapre slammed into the shield with such force that Illume tumbled backward.

The impact was like being next to a gong. It hurt his head and his ears but almost no health left him. He smiled at the durability of the armor as that blow would have killed him previously.

Illume's shield retracted as he rolled backward and onto his feet. The Kapre lunged at him again. Illume used his superior speed to dodge the attack and brought the sword to bear against its bark flesh. It bounced away and did almost no damage.

Diving forward, Illume rolled under a sweeping attack. He didn't want to use his magic just yet. He wanted to save it for Hastur himself. Illume gave the Kapre a slice with his broken sword.

The blade of Valcoth shone with a white light as it broke the Kapre's hardened skin. Its health went almost nowhere. Illume sheathed his main weapon and held the broken one in his dominant hand.

He held up his shield to deflect his opponent's blows. The Kapre fluctuated in size as it attacked. For long sweeping motions, its arms grew thick and long, and while moving more swiftly, it grew thinner.

Each large attack was easy for Illume to dodge. The smaller ones pushed him to his limit for speed. They came out of nowhere and in the blink of an eye. Each chance he got, Illume would slice and jab as he chipped away at the Kapre's health. A white light flared each time he made contact.

A shadow over Illume made him look up. A mutated Barnogian flew through the air at him. Illume changed his position and raised his shield. Just as it was about to impact Trillian dove over Illume and bit it in half.

As Trillian landed, he brought his weight to bear. He used his tail like a club, his claws like swords, and his teeth like daggers. He was a living Swiss army knife of death and any mutated that got near him fell quickly.

Illume felt himself lifted off the ground. His health bar blinked down by a fraction as he was forced backward. He hit the ground, tumbled to a stop and let out a groan as he pulled himself to his knees. The armor had done its job; he'd hardly felt the blow. Clearly, his strategy wasn't working. Illume sheathed his weapon and retracted his shield. As he exhaled, his breath became visible while he rose to his feet.

Illume's hands went cold. Several blasts of frost left him and shattered the mutated that charged at him. Illume turned his attention back to the Kapre, whose bark-like skin appeared to bleach from where Illume had wounded it.

Withdrawing his spells, Illume pulled his sword once more. He gave a loud whistle as the Kapre's bark completely bleached white. It turned and attacked the charging army with all its might. This effectively blocked the hole he needed to fill.

Trillian landed next to Illume and lowered his head. Illume quickly climbed on and both took to the skies once more. Hastur's forces had thinned out considerably over the distance they had been redirected.

His forces had already engaged John's. The resurrected fought well with rudimentary weapons but little armor. They were fast but lacked the sheer strength and speed of Hastur's forces. With no mutated weapons built into them like the fangs or claws, they didn't stand much of a chance.

As the cannon fodder was being ripped into, Illume waved for Nari to join the battle. She and the other griffins took off but stayed low to the ground. Illume and Trillian closed in on the troops that had amassed near the cliff being held by the flimsy reinforcements of John's spell.

Trillian grabbed several in his claws and pulled up. As he turned around, he released them over the cliff's edge. Even if they survived the fall, there was no way they'd be able to get back into the fight. As Trillian turned, he blasted stragglers with a beam of ice.

"Easy, buddy. I don't want to freeze the whole field," Illume whispered.

The griffins swooped through and grabbed as many as they could. They followed Trillian's lead and threw the bodies over the cliff as if they were nothing. With the number of griffins they had, it only took one pass to clear out the bulk of Hastur's forces.

As Illume and Trillian swooped back down to the sparsely concentrated forces, he leaned off the side of his dragon and fired bolts of lightning. As they hit, the mutated shrieked before they fell to the ground in a smoldering husks.

Each shot jumped over several mutated, killing more than one at a time. Illume circled back around to see that Kapre fall. It had been swarmed by what was left. A blast of orange light erupted from Hecate and consumed the last remaining mutated and reduced them to ash.

Looking over to Nari, Illume made a circular motion with his hand. They returned to John and landed around him. Illume dismounted and approached his brother, who had just finished chanting.

"That went smoother than I thought," John panted.

"Why didn't you use the root magic to bring them back?" Illume asked as he looked his brother up and down for sign of injury.

"They aren't skeletons. That only works on skeletons or decomposed corpses."

"What do we do now?" Hecate asked as she approached from behind Illume.

"We take the fight to Hastur," Nari informed.

Illume turned to face Hastur. He hadn't moved an inch and his imposing form towered over the field. He saw everything and showed no sign of surprise or panic. He stood fast, unmoving and shrouded in his yellow cloth.

"We don't," Illume rebutted. "This is a boss fight.

Since when do you only fight one wave of minions during a boss fight?"

"Then what do we do?" John asked.

"Trillian and I will scout. We'll fly high enough where he can't reach us and we'll report back what we find. But when the time comes, none of you get near Hastur. He's mine."

"So you can get all the experience points yourself?" John asked. "I don't think so."

"No, because I'm already going insane because of him!" Illume shot back. "Because he can't inflict madness on me like he can with you and I have a few tricks up my sleeve for this fight."

Level Up Available x2
Active Skill Points Available: 4
Active Attribute Points Available: 8
Overall Level: 30

Dragon Level Up Available x2
Attribute Points Available: 15
Skill Points Available: 3
Overall Level: 23

"We've got some leveling to do while you scout." John looked around as if he saw something no one else could. "We'll be ready when you get back."

Illume climbed onto Trillian's back once again. Taking off, Trillian climbed as high as he could and still be where Illume could see. They crossed the field and circled lazily over Hastur's head.

Illume saw nothing at first. That was, until the trees shook. A blur flew past Illume and Trillian followed by a loud *CRACK*. Trillian banked to his right so violently, Illume was almost thrown off.

As Trillian turned, Illume got a good look at what had been rumbling the ground and the trees. Massive, what looked like snail shells, broke into view. They had a hole in their center that was big enough for Illume to see from this high up.

The trees trembled as something flew from a shell. Illume turned Trillian and ejected a cloud of ice at it to slow it down. It's speed diminished enough for him to see the projectile. A massive spike as thick as his thigh and nearly twenty feet long reached to their height before it slowed down and fell back to the ground.

Illume watched it fall. It landed on the shell. The bio-organic artillery piece exploded in a scene of yellow entrails. Smaller beings, which he couldn't see in detail, were blown to the ground. Illume's eyes widened as he saw dozens more of Hastur's artillery rolled out of the forest and aimed their pikes directly at John, Nari, Hecate, and the griffins.

38

WAVE TWO ARTILLERY

ILLUME TURNED TRILLIAN AROUND. The dragon flapped his wings as hard as he could as the ground shook and a volley of spikes ripped across the battle-field. The griffins took to the skies, but not all of them were fast enough.

The spikes slammed into the ground in and around Illume's forces. Their impacts were so great that Illume could feel the shockwaves from nearly a hundred yards away.

Dirt flew into the air as each projectile impacted. Several griffins were skewered by the spikes. From the looks of the impacts, they felt none of their injuries.

Illume heard a soft winding sound as Trillian came to a hard landing. He leapt from his mount and threw his hands out. Ice erupted from his hands as Trillian joined in with his chilled breath.

Several more booms rang out. Another volley of spikes ripped through the air past Illume and killed more griffins. A few projectiles hit Illume's frost wall. The punctured through but were stopped before they could hit anything.

Illume looked back at Nari, John, and Hecate. They had huddled behind Illume and guarded their faces from the dirt that erupted around them. The sight of dozens of griffin bodies dismembered and twitching haunted Illume's vision.

"Get behind the wall!" Illume yelled to Nari, John, and Hecate.

They didn't hesitate. All three sprinted as fast as they could to the wall Illume had made as another volley flew past. By now, most of the griffins were off the ground and able to dodge the projectiles. Those that struck the wall glanced off due to the angle.

Illume looked up at the griffin he'd influenced and nodded at him. The griffin cawed and led the others over the edge of the cliffs and out of harm's way.

"What are you doing?" John yelled. "They were our heavy hitters!"

"Not against those," Illume shouted over the sound of the spikes as they pelted the walls. "Their armor is far too thick for a griffin to get through."

"Then how do we kill them?" Nari asked.

The wall where they stood cracked. They all moved

down the defensive barrier to a portion that had taken less damage in the fight. The attacks seemed to follow them.

"We've got back up coming," Illume replied. "We just need to buy them time."

"How much time?" Nari asked.

"I don't know," Illume replied as a spike whistled over their heads.

"What kind of back-up?" Hecate questioned.

Illume felt the ground shake once more. This time, it was different. The quake didn't originate on the surface but from under their feet. Illume drew his gaze to Hecate.

"The dwarven kind," Illume replied. "You three go around the far end of the wall. I'll draw their fire."

The portion of wall Illume and his team had just been standing at shattered into chunks of ice and fractured munitions.

"You can't!" John insisted. "You'll get killed."

"I'll be fine," Illume reassured his brother.

"Don't let him look you in the face," he called over his shoulder as he ran to Trillian and hopped back on. He waited until he heard the moan of the artillery as it prepared to fire once again. Trillian took to the air. He kept them low and flew as fast as they could.

Bolts whizzed past them. They were narrowly missed by each flying projectile, but Trillian's quick reflexes kept them out of harm's way. Illume had Trillian cut down the edge of the field to keep as much distance between them and the artillery as possible.

Out of the corner of his eye, Illume saw his team of three move through the scorched grass and to the tree line as they tried to get behind Hastur's forces. Illume drew his bow and nocked an arrow. Frost formed over his weapon as he noticed the artillery pieces begin to shake.

"Ready?" Illume asked as they got closer to Hastur's line.

A deep horn bellowed from the depths of the earth itself as the ground under the center artillery piece shifted then collapsed into the ground. Trillian immediately cut across the battlefield as everyone, including Hastur, turned to see what caused the collapse.

Dwarves flooded out of the hole. They wore brass-colored armor from head to toe. More like small walking tanks than anything organic. With axes, hammers, and crossbows, they made short work of the piece they pulled into the ground before they had begun to cut down its escort force.

Trillian lowered his head and held his wings out as straight as he could and flew directly at one of the artillery pieces. Illume fired an arrow and killed what looked like a goblin mixed with a squid.

They passed the piece without losing any momentum. Illume glanced over his shoulder to see a deep gash across its side. Yellow blood poured from the wound as ice gradually crept over the creature's surface.

Illume finally got a good look at the force that accompanied Hastur. They weren't like the half fish people he'd seen up to this point. They were fully mutated land beings that had been changed to accommodate the ocean.

Some looked like the crew of the *Flying Dutchman* from a movie he watched as a kid. Others just looked like a squid and another species were spliced together.

Illume fired his arrows indiscriminately. Trillian blasted as many of Hastur's soldiers as he could. Hastur kept his face pointed at Illume. Illume fired an arrow at him. It struck Hastur in the chest and damaged him. He pulled the arrow out and what little damage it did to his health immediately healed again.

The artillery continued to fire, but Illume and his teams were too close now to be accurate. They ended up hitting a lot of their own troops. Trillian sliced through another section of the enemy as the dwarves swarmed from the hole in the ground like a colony of ants.

They washed over the next nearest piece and shattered it with their more superior forged weapons. Illume saw, at the other end, roots erupt from the ground and wrapped around an artillery piece before it was crushed.

From the looks of it, Nari and Hecate played a defensive role to protect John. Illume continued to rain arrows down from Trillian's back until his quiver was dry. By then, there were only a few artillery pieces left, which John and the dwarves made quick work of.

Illume turned Trillian to join forces with the dwarven army. On their way, a crossbow bolt struck Illume in the chest. His armor deflected the bolt, but the kinetic energy knocked him backward.

Tumbling off of Trillian's back, Illume fell to the ground some twenty feet below. The impact jolted his body worse than his botched attempt at rock climbing. His bones cracked and his joints strained as Illume's health dropped by just shy of a quarter. Missing half his health already meant that Illume was down to quarter health.

Slinging his bow over his shoulder Illume summoned healing magic to patch himself up. As his health bar filled as much as it could go, Illume felt the itch at the back of his mind once again as well as heard the whispering.

He didn't draw his weapons as he looked around to see the oceanic mutated hybrids around him. They all had rusted swords, spears, and axes, all of which looked like they'd been under water for centuries.

Illume clenched his fists as a desire to hurt them plucked at his mind.

"Who wants some?" Illume snarled.

The first soldier that made a move toward Illume was obliterated in the blink of an eye. Illume dashed at him and closed the gap between them before his opponent could react. He used the strength that cracked granite to punch the soldier into a fine mist of black.

Illume turned his attention to the rest. They all took a step back for a few seconds. Their expressions suddenly changed as if something had entered their minds. They let out roars that sounded as if they were still under water as they charged Illume.

Channeling frost to his boots, Illume skated around the field. He dodged, countered, and ripped his opponents apart tentacle by tentacle. The few blows they did manage to land on his armor shattered their weapons due to their degradation.

Hastur let out a low bellow that rippled through the air like a shockwave. Illume looked over to see an unnatural mist begin to flood the area. It was so thick, that the instant it overtook someone, they disappeared.

Illume grabbed the last of Hastur's soldiers in his immediate area. He lifted the creature off the ground, and with one swift movement, he ripped the being in half like it was nothing before he tossed both halves away.

He was bathed in blackened blood and something deep down loved it in the most sadistic way. Illume reached into his pack as the fog overtook him. He glanced around in all directions. He wouldn't have been able to see his hand in front of his face.

A whistle rang out as a sharp pain engulfed Illume's leg. He looked down to see an arrow protruding from one of his legs. It had slipped past the armor. His health dropped as lightning pain surged throughout his body. Illume grabbed the arrow and yanked it out. Illume's health dropped a little more.

He brought up his shield as several more arrows bounced off of it. Using his chin to open the scroll, he held it up and channeled mana through it. As he did, the mist began to thin, and he was now able to see at least a few dozen yards ahead. The scroll disappeared in Illume's hand and became part of the mist.

In the background, Illume heard the dwarves as they fought for their lives. He could hear Nari as she sliced through targets while the explosions and groans of roots told Illume that John was still alive.

A spear screamed by Illume's face. He barely was able to dodge it in time. Illume followed the trajectory to the spear's source. From the depths of the mist marched the Barnogian merchant. She had a bow in her hand and several spears on her back.

Raising his hand, Illume launched a torrent of ice at

her. She held up her hand and the magic simply dissipated before it made contact. He switched to fire with the same effect before attempting electricity. Again she was able to deflect the spells with no ill effects.

"That's an interesting trick," Illume pointed out as his shield emerged from his forearm.

"You like it?" she taunted. "A gift from my king."

Illume drew his sword from his back. He planted his feet and held his shield up to protect himself from thigh to neck, just like Leonidas used to.

"How long have you worked for Hastur?" Illume asked.

The Barnogian laughed. She drew another arrow and fired it at Illume. He blocked it once more with his shield.

"I was the priestess chosen to bring him into this world."

She fired once again at Illume. He blocked the arrow and raced across the field at her, closing the gap before she could reload and grabbed her bow. He snapped it with a twist of his wrist.

A scaled hand slammed into Illume's helmet. It rang like a bell. The kinetic force of her punch sent Illume staggering to the side. He caught his footing and managed to get his shield up as she punched at him again.

Her blow made Illume slide backward several feet.

Illume peered over his shield to see a spear being thrust at him. He dodged the attack and threw his shield up to knock her weapon away while thrusting his sword at her. She dodged the attack and head-butted him in the chest.

Her attacks weren't quite enough to cause much damage through his armor, but she was certainly far more powerful than when he encountered her last. As she closed in once again, Illume scanned her during their brief engagements. She wore the same garments she had back in Mire.

Illume felt a sharp pain in his side. His health bar dropped a little more substantially. Illume reached down and grabbed her wrist. As he slowly pulled it away from him, Illume felt her dagger leave his body. She was accurate, having slid it between his armor plating.

That was when Illume saw it: a medallion that was exactly like the one around Hastur's neck. Illume head-butted her and sent her staggering backward. Before she could look up for another attack, Illume used his healing spells on himself, which brought his attention to his stamina. It was half gone.

The merchant pulled a second dagger from her corset. Illume sheathed his sword and pulled the broken blade from his back. This way, she couldn't get inside his range of attack.

Illume let her make the first move. She lunged at him as beams of Trillian's blue breath erupted from the mist. Illume dodged her first attack then he engaged her in close-quarters combat.

His shield was more a deflector than a blocker and his broken sword never truly tried to find a killing blow against her. Both exchanged savage blows with one another. She was faster, but Illume was stronger.

Illume swiped at her. She bent back to dodge the attack, which threw her medallion into the air. Illume cut the thin chain that held it around her neck. It flew off and disappeared into the fog.

The second the medallion left her, the merchant staggered backward and fell to the ground. It was like all her fighting prowess came from the medallion itself. An eruption of orange rippled through the fog as a massive fire whip became visible. A deafening crack tore through the air as the whip struck at some unseen foe.

"You think you were meant for this?" the merchant hissed in an exhausted tone.

"Why did you give me Dovabane?"

"I hoped you would retrieve the phoenix feather so I could give it to Hastur when he got to Moot. But you took too long and he wasn't willing to wait."

Illume paused for a moment. The fire whip cracked again, as did one of Trillian's frost fire beams.

"It looks like Dovabane's full power has been unleashed," she said with a confident laugh. "You have no fate here but death. And I long to see you fall."

"I don't believe in fate," Illume said softly.

He looked at the Barnogian and raised his hand. He pressed his thumb and ring finger tightly together. Frost formed on their tips.

"But I do believe in inevitability," he added. "And just like Thanatos, I am inevitable."

Illume snapped his fingers. The air around them dropped so completely that she froze solid before toppling over and shattering into hundreds of pieces. Illume turned away and followed the light of the whip. He kneeled and stabbed the medallion with his broken sword.

It shattered then turned to dust. Illume pressed forward through the mist. He cut down any who crossed his path with ease. Eventually Illume got to the foot of a hill where Nari, Hecate, and John held the high ground.

Swarms of Hastur's soldiers charged at them. Nari fought them off with ease. Hecate's spells held them back and atomized any who managed to get through. John held Dovabane in his hand. It had formed into a massive fire whip, which cracked with magic he used to clear out swathes of his attackers with each explosive swipe.

Tucking his lower lip, Illume let out a loud whistle. This caught not only the mutated soldiers' attention but also those of his friends on the hill. Since Illume was Hastur's main target, all of the attackers on the hill turned and charged him.

The cryomancer sheathed his blade and held his arms out for them to come at him. As they closed in and just before they could make contact, another high-pitched whistle filled the air before Trillian's frost fire breath wiped out the rest of the soldiers.

Ascending the hill, Illume looked Nari over. She had a few cuts and bruises but nothing fatal. Illume placed a hand on her shoulder and healed her wounds. He looked over at John, who sheathed Dovabane as the whip retracted.

"That was an interesting skill you learned there," Illume admired.

"I learned that one in balrog class."

"Can I sign up?" Illume chuckled.

"You shall not pass," John retorted with a head shake. "Now what do you say we go find and kill Hastur?"

"I say we meet up with Uthrandir and see what he knows," Illume suggested as he gave John a playful punch.

39

DUNGEON OF GOD III

ILLUME WALKED through the mist with John, Nari, and Hecate behind him. Although he couldn't see them, it was easy to find the dwarves. They sounded like an army of clanking pots and pans mixed with extremely heavy breathing.

"Elves would have so much fun with this," John whispered.

"Maybe if we were in Mirkwood," Illume murmured.

Illume weaved between broken and naked trees. They passed around piles of bodies of Hastur's soldiers. Dwarven armor protruded from the piles of corpses here and there.

"They lost so much for us," Nari's voice echoed up in a whisper.

"They did," Illume acknowledged. "They ensured our victory through their sacrifice."

Illume crested a hill to see the small army of dwarves surrounding the hole they'd come out of. Their brass armor seemed to glisten, even in the mist. Uthrandir, with a massive axe in hand, leaned over and gazed into the hole.

"Find anything interesting in there?" Illume yelled.

Uthrandir turned to Illume's taunt. His grizzled, dirty face lit up as soon as he saw Illume. He held up his axe.

"Frost boy!" Uthrandir yelled.

He shook his axe in the air as he pushed through his men.

"Move! Get out of the way!" he muttered and growled. "Urin, I will strike you!" he threatened one of the others.

Uthrandir managed to finally get through the crowd. Illume greeted the man by grabbing his forearm and gave it a firm shake.

"When my niece said you'd need my help, I could hardly believe it!" Uthrandir proclaimed, his voice boomed like a cannon. "After the way you handled the cave, I figured you could handle just about anything!"

"This one is a little different. Thank you for coming. Your people sacrificed a lot to save us."

"For every one of ours that fell, we killed a hundred of theirs," Uthrandir proclaimed. "Good numbers for any day."

"When were you going to tell us these guys were coming?" John asked from behind Illume.

"I'm sorry." Illume glanced over his shoulder. "It slipped my mind."

Illume turned back to Uthrandir. "This is my brother, John. This is Hecate, a sorceress of Moot."

Uthrandir moved past Illume. He gave John and Hecate each a firm handshake.

"It is a pleasure to meet you both." Uthrandir told them. "Any friend of Illume's is a friend of the dwarves."

Uthrandir turned and smiled widely as he saw Nari. He set his axe down and slowly approached her.

"Nari, you are as beautiful as ever. It is good to see you again."

Nari nervously took a step back. Illume noticed her grip on her swords tighten. So did Uthrandir. He stopped his friendly advance.

"Who are you?" Nari asked.

Caution danced in the tone of her voice. Uthrandir turned to look at Illume with concern on his face.

"Don't take it personally, friend," Illume replied. "She doesn't remember anything from the last two years. Hastur bit her and we used a phoenix feather to bring her back."

Uthrandir's brow raised as he nodded in understanding.

"And where is Trillian?" Uthrandir asked.

Trillian burst through the mist and landed on top of Uthrandir, knocking him over. He gave the dwarf a lick across the face as he screamed in terror.

"Trillian, get off him!" Illume commanded.

Trillian backed away. Illume gave Uthrandir a hand up, who picked up his axe in the process.

"I've heard of shape shifters, but nothing quite like that!" Uthrandir proclaimed in shock.

"This is my pet," Illume said. "He is named after Trillian who—who died fighting the Dark King."

As he spoke those words, it felt like a dagger went into his heart as he looked at Nari. She was one of the only ones who'd known Trillian. It felt like the light of his memory had faded a little more somehow.

"I'm sorry to hear that," Uthrandir sympathized.

"Thank you. We've wasted enough time as is. Have your men seen a giant in yellow?" Illume asked.

"I have!" Uthrandir proclaimed. "He looked at me, did some weird flashy eye thing, and disappeared into the hole we came out of."

"We need to go to Strang and cut him off."

"No we don't," Uthrandir countered. "We didn't want to leave anyone vulnerable to whatever could go into the tunnels. We collapsed it behind us. Hastur is trapped down there. Now what do you say we go down and kill him?"

Illume turned back to John. He held his hand out and looked at Dovabane.

"I'm going to need that back for a bit."

"I'm going with you," John contested.

"We are too," Nari added as she nodded to Hecate.

"No, none of you are," Illume countered. "Uthrandir and Trillian will be joining me for this job."

"Why them?" John asked.

"Trillian is bonded to me. I have already been cursed with madness, which means he can't be affected by Hastur's gaze. And Uthrandir has been exposed to it as well." Illume pointed out. "My cryomancy comes from an elder god like Hastur, which is why the madness didn't completely consumed me. Dwarves are of a hardy nature…"

"Stubborn, we're of a stubborn nature," Uthrandir corrected.

"Stubborn, okay," Illume relented. "Otherwise, he would be a thrall to Hastur right now as well. Hastur dies, his servants die, you go down there with us, you become his servant, then you die. We don't have time for this. Will you just give me Dovabane?!" Illume snapped.

The itch in the back of his mind flared as his frustration grew. John removed Dovabane from his back and handed it to Illume. He strapped the blade to his hip before he removed his bow and gave it to John since he had no more need of it.

"When I get back, we'll trade," Illume informed him.

Illume turned away from his brother and team and walked toward the hole with Trillian and Uthrandir close behind. He approached the hole and looked down. It was about twenty feet down until it branched off under them.

Leaping down the hole Illume landed hard. He pulled Dovabane from his hip and held it over his head. The sword ignited and lit the path for them. Trillian hopped down from wall to wall until he was next to Illume. Uthrandir hit the ground like a cannonball. The impact didn't even faze him.

"Are there any branches that could be used to surprise us?" Illume asked.

"No, it's a straight shot." Uthrandir looked up and yelled, "Post a guard down here! If something other than us returns collapse the entire tunnel!"

Illume pushed forward. His mana stayed full as the dragon shared mana with him. Trillian and Uthrandir moved in closely behind Illume. He heard Uthrandir draw a second axe.

"I have something in my satchel," Illume whispered as they moved silently. "If you see me reach for it or hear me tell you to close your eyes, do it immediately."

"If you say so," Uthrandir replied.

The three delved deeper into the massive tunnel the dwarves had created. The deeper they went, the higher and wider the tunnel became until Illume's light didn't even reach the ceiling.

The stench of death filled the air as they moved through the tunnel. A scuttling noise echoed around them. Without hesitating, Uthrandir threw an axe into the darkness. One of Hastur's soldiers fell into the light with Uthrandir's axe buried deep into its skull.

Illume looked over at Uthrandir as he went to retrieve his weapon. He pulled the axe out of the would-be ambusher's head and gripped it tightly once more.

"What? We live underground. We CAN see in the dark."

"Then what do you see ahead of us?" Illume asked.

Uthrandir looked forward. He shook his head in disbelief.

"There are no words for what lies ahead." he replied. "Whatever it is, it works fast."

With that, they pressed forward. The rotting corpse smell grew stronger with each step they took until finally the tunnel opened up into a chamber. It was cut in half by rubble and a soft greenish-yellow glow filled the room.

40

HASTUR ROUND III

ILLUME LOOKED AROUND. Luminescent sacks pulsated on the walls all around them. Hastur hadn't been down there for more than a few minutes. Illume was curious how he pulled it off.

"You with the power of Azathoth. Why do you persist to fell your own kind?" Hastur's deep voice echoed through the darkness.

"You have murdered countless innocents," Illume spat. "You will never stop until you have destroyed the world, and for that, you must be stopped."

"I do not wish to destroy this world. Merely remake it," Hastur contested.

"Into the image of the elder gods!" Illume fired back. "Into a writhing mass of tentacles that devours the minds, bodies, and souls of every living being."

"Not the souls. Those belong to another."

"Show yourself, you coward," Illume snarled. "Trillian, block his escape."

Trillian unleashed an inferno of frost fire, covering the tunnel's entrance at their backs. The light illuminated the room enough for Illume to see Hastur perched halfway up the wall. The second Illume noticed him, he lunged off the wall at him.

Illume dashed out of the way as Uthrandir rolled the opposite direction. Hastur landed between them with Trillian to his right. Hastur rose up in an attempt to intimidate Illume. He felt the magic of the amulet course through him and counter Hastur's psychological warfare.

"Round three," Illume smirked as his hand ignited with fire magic. "Fight!"

Hastur lurched at Illume.

"FALCON PUNCH!" Illume yelled.

He used every ounce of enhanced strength to strike Hastur with a flaming fist in the chest. Hastur's health dropped, then dropped some more as an axe buried itself into the back of his head.

Trillian darted forward and bit into Hastur's neck. He clawed at the god while his mouth glowed from his breath. A beam of his frost fire ripped through the far side of Hastur and opened him up like a can of beans.

Hastur's health fell almost completely as Trillian ripped away and landed next to Illume. Hastur writhed and twitched as he stumbled away from Illume and Uthrandir before he fell to the ground.

"That was easy," Uthrandir proclaimed.

"Don't be so sure," Illume replied.

He gripped Dovabane tighter as his shield opened up. Hastur's golden mask dropped from his face and spun before it fell to a wobbly stop. His body pulled itself back together as his health bar filled once more.

"There it is," Illume added with a nod.

Hastur's cloak writhed with the tendrils beneath. Illume increased the amount of heat Dovabane produced. Trillian moved in behind Illume and snarled.

"What's going on?" Uthrandir asked.

"Beings like Hastur have more than one form," Illume explained. "Each one is typically ten times harder than the last."

Illume swung Dovabane down and at an angle. A blade of fire flew from the weapon and slammed into Hastur with an explosion powerful enough to make Hastur roar in pain. His health dropped then immediately rose once again.

Hastur turned to Illume and showed his true face. Illume hesitated for a few seconds as time seemed to slow. He was stunned by what he saw. It was indescribable, like everything and nothing at once. As if he stared into the abyss itself and the abyss looked back.

Illume could feel Hastur attempting to creep into his mind. The magic of the pendant around his neck held him at bay but barely. Everything around Illume went muffled. He heard a roar and Uthrandir yell.

Time snapped back to normal as Illume was thrown across the room by a powerful impact. One of Hastur's tentacles had slammed itself into Illume. His armor bore the brunt of the attack while his health bar dropped by half.

He collided with the far wall so hard, the air was forced from Illume's lungs. He fell to the ground and let out a wheeze. He was getting tired of being thrown into things. Illume's hand flickered to life with healing magic as he cast it onto himself.

Groaning as his broken ribs snapped back into place and his double vision focused back to normal, he lifted his head to see Hastur whip another limb at him. He rolled out of the way just as the tendril struck the ground.

Illume shoved himself to his feet as Uthrandir hacked and sliced at the limbs Hastur sent after him. Trillian whipped his tail around and used his razor sharp wings to slash at Hastur.

Each attack did damage, but Hastur's regeneration was too advanced. There was no lasting damage they could have done to him. Hastur's limb slid at Illume.

With a powerful swipe, he cut the limb in half before he reached into his satchel.

"CLOSE YOUR EYES!" Illume yelled.

"Hey, Hastur!" he snapped at the mass that writhed under the yellow tunic.

Hastur turned and looked at Illume. He let out a deep growl as he too moved toward him. Illume pulled Theon's head from the satchel. He closed his eyes as he held it face first toward Hastur.

Illume heard a series of rattles followed by a loud hiss. Even from behind closed eyelids, Illume saw the flash of golden light and felt its warmth, which indicated Theon had activated.

Elder Gods are Immune to Stone Gaze.
Healing Factor Significantly Slowed.

Opening his eyes, Illume returned the head to his satchel. Illume held his shield up as he charged at Hastur, who had staggered back from the attack. He swung Dovabane as hard as he could while focusing as much mana as his body would allow into the blade.

A deep CRACK rumbled the cave as the blade of Dovabane melted into a whip of molten metal fused by magic. The whip scored Hastur across the chest. His health bar dropped by a quarter. It started to regenerate but significantly slower.

"Now!" Illume yelled. "Give him everything you got!"

Uthrandir practically turned into a bladed top as he spun and hacked at Hastur. Trillian got in close and used his claws and teeth to harm the elder god. Illume was siphoning so much mana to maintain the whip, he didn't seem to be able to use frost fire.

Illume snapped the whip at Hastur once again. It ripped across him from mid-chest to his neck. The blow caused the rest of his yellow cloak to fall to the ground, revealing what was underneath.

A thrashing mass of tentacles and eyes burst from the cloak like a water balloon breaking. It let out an ear piercing roar as its health reached the halfway point.

Tendrils struck out blindly in every direction. Trillian was thrown off first. Illume was able to use the whip to deflect those that closed in on him. Uthrandir took a blow directly to the face that sent him so violently into the frost wall that it cracked. He slumped to the ground unconscious.

Illume noticed his mana plummeted. He released Dovabane as he jumped into the air and "skated" around Hastur's thrashing limbs. Countless bulging eyes watched him as he danced around Hastur's attacks.

Drawing his sword, Illume sliced at anything that got too close. His trajectory had him aiming to come down right on Hastur's head. Illume turned his sword upside down as his mana ran dry and he hurtled toward his target.

He released a primal roar as every eye on the twitching mass locked on to him. Just as Illume was about to make contact, he was smashed into by another tendril. His health dropped violently as he crashed into the ground and bounced several times before he came to a stop.

That blow would have ripped him apart had it not been for Buthrandir's armor. Illume staggered to his feet. His mind swam as he climbed to his feet, swaying back and forth. He hadn't brought any potions with him. A foolish decision.

Hastur's writhing mass moved toward Illume and towered over him. It dropped a tentacle down on either side of Illume. The stench made Illume's eyes water as he glared at Hastur in defiance.

"You are too injured to attack." The voice emanated from the center of the mass. "You have no magic to use against me. Kneel and become my herald."

Smirking, Illume could taste iron in his mouth, so he spat blood at Hastur. Two tendrils snapped out and grabbed Uthrandir and Trillian. The dragon was secured by the throat while Uthrandir was completely encased. Trillian began to gasp and whimper at the attack.

"You have no moves left. Surrender or they die," Hastur demanded once more.

"I surrender, they die anyway. I have one move left."

The sound of fracturing ice echoed through the cave as Illume summoned his intimidation speak. Illume planted his feet as every muscle in his body tightened.

"Khal'SOL'SLATZ!" Illume shouted.

The words accompanied it with an unrelenting force that shot from his lips. The force of the shout made Hastur stagger backward as Illume used his first summons. Hastur righted himself with a demonic cackle.

"Is that all the god of mischief granted you? A shout?" Hastur moved toward Illume again.

"Ba'kawk!" a chicken called out.

Illume looked down between himself and Hastur. A chicken with a lazy eye strutted between the two and pecked at the ground. Illume laughed until he saw Hastur's tendril drop toward the chicken.

Illume dove behind the nearest rock as the ground shook from Hastur's impact. Illume's health and mana filled all the way back up again as everything fell silent.

"A chicken? Is that the best you have?" Hastur taunted.

"You shouldn't have killed it," Illume yelled from behind his cover.

"Why?" Hastur goaded.

The squawks of thousands of chickens filled the air. Illume looked around, but he didn't see anything. Illume got a glimpse of Uthrandir and Trillian, who both struggled to break free from Hastur but to no avail.

A blur of white dashed past Illume. Followed by another then another. The squawking of chickens started to sound like a tornado as it bore down on them. Before he could figure out what was going on, thousands of chickens assaulted Hastur.

They flew in from nowhere and disappeared just the same as they pecked and gouged Hastur's countless eyes. Hastur released Uthrandir and Trillian as he lashed out blindly at the chickens. Illume looked at his health bar. It was the literal equivalent of being killed by bug bites.

Each chicken that took an eye with it caused a miniscule fraction of damage. In the unbridled chaos, Hastur's heath dropped infinitely faster than it recovered. Before the chickens even cleared out, Hastur gave out one final screech before he fell limp to the ground and his life bar hit zero.

As the chickens disappeared into the walls of the cavern, Illume stepped out of cover. He looked at the heaping mass of Hastur that lay lifeless on the ground as he picked up Dovabane. Illume shook his head while sheathing his sword.

"Everyone knows you don't touch the chickens," he said with a mountain of sass in his voice.

"Did we do it?" Uthrandir poked the corpse.

Illume looked around. It was a final boss; these usually led to level-up screens. Why wasn't one coming up? It was then that he realized they'd only taken out two forms. Illume turned to Trillian and blasted him with frost magic. Trillian flinched initially before he started to enjoy it like a dog and a hairdryer.

"What are you doing?" Uthrandir asked.

"It's not over yet!" Illume replied.

Hastur's mass retreated back into itself. It grew smaller and smaller until it was roughly the size of a man. The mass coalesced into a humanoid about Illume's height.

He was far more muscular and his face was more octopus than man. His webbed fingers gripped a golden straight sword with an intricate tentacle grip and cross guard. His health bar not only refilled but grew larger.

Illume stopped using his frost magic on Trillian and faced Hastur with Dovabane in hand, imbuing the sword with frost magic, which changed the blade and the flame blue. Hastur pointed and stared Illume down with his strange ocean creature eyes.

"I challenge you to single combat," Hastur snarled.

"Let me think about that," Illume replied.

Flexing every muscle in his body, Illume threw Dovabane at Hastur with so much force that his stamina bar completely depleted. The blue flaming sword cleared the room so quickly that even Illume didn't see it fly.

Hastur jolted as the blade slammed into his chest. He stepped back as his health bar dropped. He gave Illume a shocked look.

"Trillian... Frost fire," Illume commanded.

Turning to his dragon, Illume unleashed every ounce of frost magic he had into the dragon as Trillian fired a beam of luminescent light directly into the hilt of Dovabane. The sword channeled the dragon's magic through the weapon itself, which surged into Hastur like a dam breaking.

Hastur attempted to charge Illume but only made it about three steps before he froze solid. Illume continued to feed Trillian until his mana was completely depleted.

"Don't let up!" Illume commanded.

Illume drew his sword and walked over to Hastur, who was still under relentless assault from Trillian. He looked at Uthrandir and held up his sword. Uthrandir approached and held his axe up on the other side.

Both men prepared to swing. Illume nodded to Trillian, who cut off his breath. Before he could blink, both Illume and Uthrandir smashed their weapons into the frozen solid Hastur. He shattered into a million pieces along with Dovabane as his health bar disappeared.

Level Up Available x10
Active Skill Points Available: 14 (+1 for hitting lvl.40)
Active Attribute Points Available: 28 (+2 for hitting lvl. 40)
Overall Level 40

Dragon Level Up Available x10
Active Skill Points Available: 13
Active Attribute Points Available: 55
Overall Level: 33

Once you activate the levels your dragon will molt one last time to his adult form.

Quest Complete:
Stop the Threat to Moot and its Surrounding Lands.
Madness lifted.

Illume watched in relief as his health bar became fully available to him once again. It filled up all the way for the first time in what felt like years.

Trophy Earned
Name: Mind of Madness
Type: Gold
Requirements: Obtain madness from an elder god then cure the madness by killing that same elder god.

Congratulations! You get to leave the cuckoo's nest!

41

GOODBYES

"WOULD YOU LIKE THE HONORS?" Uthrandir asked.

The dwarf lord held up a fuse to Illume. He looked around at the army of dwarves, his brother, Nari, and Trillian, who stood around him in the forest. They stood on dry ground as the swamplands had already begun to recede.

After he received several nods of approval, Illume touched the end of the fuse and used his fire magic to set it alight. In an instant, the fuse jumped to life and disappeared down the hole. Several seconds later, the ground shook. The tunnel that marked Hastur's final resting place collapsed in on itself.

"That ought to make sure no one gets in or out of there," Uthrandir declared.

Illume walked over to the loot they'd taken from

Hastur's body before they exited the tunnels. He grabbed Hastur's pendant. He was surprised at how heavy it was.

Partial Pendant of Hastur
Weight: +8 Worth: Unknowable
This pendant was forged by the elder gods for their
*   king.*
Those who wear this pendant can speak and
*   understand all languages. Parts of it have been*
*   chipped off by Hastur himself. No one*
*   knows why.*

Illume looked at his ring. It had a similar shine and grade to it as the pendant, which was harmless enough. It only acted as a translation unit. Illume walked over to Uthrandir and handed the pendant to him.

"For saving our lives and helping bring an end to Hastur, I want you to have this token of gratitude."

Uthrandir took the pendant and hung it around his neck.

"Thank you!" Uthrandir said. "But we dwarves find a good fight payment enough."

Illume turned to look at John. He held the hilt and the shattered blade in his hands.

"I'm sorry I broke your toy," Illume bantered playfully.

"Eh... I'll tell Mom later," John jested. "Plus I'm sure I can figure out a way to fix it."

John took the weapon and its shards. Illume looked around for Hecate. He didn't see her, only her staff.

"Where's the witch?" Illume asked.

Everyone fell silent for a few minutes. Nari stepped forward. She wrung her hands as she did.

"When you summoned Khal, she sacrificed herself so that 'the spell will be powerful enough to stop him.' I believe was her exact words," Nari explained.

Illume looked back at Uthrandir. He took off his helmet and bowed his head in respect to her.

"She saved our lives down there," Illume confessed softly.

"The dwarves will always remember the name of Hecate," Uthrandir promised.

"How do you plan on getting back to Strang?" Illume asked Uthrandir.

"I plan on returning to Cryo's Quarry with you. I need to pay my niece a visit. As for my men, they will accompany us as far as the mountains before returning to Strang."

Illume let out a sigh. He looked at Nari, who held Hecate's staff close to her.

"We'd better get going then," Illume said. "It's two months' walk to Cryo's Quarry from here."

"I won't be going with you," John interjected.

Illume turned to his brother. His brows knitted together in confusion.

"Why not?" Illume asked.

"The wife and kids will be back any minute now," John explained. "My bereavement at work is up tomorrow. I have to return to MY real world."

"Will you at least log in from time to time?" Illume asked in a hopeful tone.

Illume felt a lump form in his throat as John said he'd have to go. He would return to being alone again as the only other people who truly knew him were Trillian and Nari and she didn't remember their history.

"You bet I will. Just send messages to Cryo's Quarry on your whereabouts. When I log in, that'll be my spawn point and I'll come find you."

John approached Illume. Both men embraced in a tight brotherly hug. Illume's arms coiled so tightly around John that he gasped and patted Illume on the back.

"Okay, I can't breathe."

Illume released John, who immediately went over to Nari. He leaned in and whispered in her ear before giving her cheek a kiss. John turned and faced Illume.

"I love you, loser."

"I love you too, you big jerk."

John's avatar froze for several seconds. It glitched like it had so many times before then it vanished. Illume took a deep breath as he watched where his brother once stood for several moments.

A squawk from overhead snapped Illume out of his trance. He looked up to see the griffins returning. They landed a few yards away from Illume, Nari and the dwarves. They all lowered their heads as if to invite them on.

"How do you guys feel about flying?" Illume asked.

"We've never flown before!" Uthrandir exclaimed. "Could be fun."

Uthrandir and the dwarves walked to the griffins. Most were able to be alone on the majestic beings' backs. Others had to pair up. Illume approached Nari, who held the staff tightly.

"Are you okay?" he asked.

"Yeah, just a lot to process."

"I know," Illume nodded. "And thank you for joining us in the fight."

He hesitated then added, "When we get back to Cryo's Quarry, you can have your old post back as the city forger. I know you don't like to go on adventures because of your run-ins with the Dark King..."

"What ever happened to him?" Nari interrupted as she shuddered at his name.

"I'll tell you one day," Illume said softly. "You don't need to fear him anymore."

Trillian walked up to Illume and lowered his head. Illume picked up Hastur's mask and cloak. He climbed onto Trillian then offered Nari his hand. She didn't take it right away.

"You don't have to share the ride with me," Illume reassured her. "But would you rather share it with one of them?"

Illume looked at the mud- and blood-caked dwarves, who were clearly not comfortable on the griffins. Nari followed his gaze before she climbed up onto Trillian behind him and sat down.

"Okay, buddy. Take us home," Illume whispered to Trillian.

Trillian shook out his wings. He threw back his head and let out a deep roar. With a powerful flap of his wings, all three launched into the sky. Nari gripped Illume's waist tightly. She pressed her face against his back and squealed as they tore into the clouds.

Illume looked behind him as they climbed higher and higher. The griffins followed suit. The brown and green swamplands had continued to recede rapidly. Illume could see the soft yellow of a flower contrast against the earthy tones. A soft smile tugged on Illume's face as he turned back forward toward Cryo's Quarry.

———

The End

EPILOGUE

ILLUME STOOD ALONE in his house. Nari had moved in with Buthrandir. Khal had started to make friends with some of the newer families and was having a sleepover.

The fire's warm light illuminated the room and warmed Trillian, who was curled up in front of it. Its crackling was the only sound that broke the silent, chilly night. Illume picked up Hastur's mask and looked at the golden object.

Mask of Hastur
Weight: +5 Armor: +3 Worth: Unknowable
When worn, the Mask of Hastur hides the wearer's
  true form, allowing others to see only what the
  wearer wants them to see.

If worn by anything other than an elder god, the
mask enhances the wearer's worst traits.

Within the hidden compartment under the floor, Illume spied one of Buthrandir's magic trunks. Opening it, Illume placed the mask inside. He grabbed the yellow cloak as well.

Cloak of the King in Yellow
Weight: -12 Armor: 0 Worth: Unknowable
Whomever wears this cloak is king indeed.

Illume closed the trunk and secured the floorboard over the compartment. He held the cloak in his hand. Channeling his frost magic into it, the cloth gradually turned from yellow to a frosted blue. Illume walked over to his armor and draped the cloak over it.

Illume opened his leveling and skill tree. He flipped through what he wanted to learn. Most of what he had invested in was what he used. He hadn't used alchemy or any thief skills, so there was no point in wasting points on those.

He did, however, really want to see what the full intimidation shout looked like. Illume used all fifteen of his skill points. Five on *Shout level two* and then the other ten on *Shout level three.*

Shout level three unlocked.

Congratulations, you can now scare people to death.

Illume moved to his attribute tree. The strength had been useful. It was nice being noticeably stronger for once in his life. Illume placed four attribute points into *Strength* before cycling through his other attributes. His armor supplemented his magics significantly. He needed to focus on his health and stamina more than anything now.

Illume placed seven points into *Stamina*, followed by another eight into *Health*. If he'd learned anything in this last adventure, it was that he needed to have more health. Illume put the other nine points into *Constitution*. Hastur was thousands of times more powerful than the Dark King. He needed to be tough for whatever came next.

New Stats:

Strength: +40 (+50 w/ Kapre armor)
near/superhuman.

Stamina: 300 regenerates 5% of max stamina a second while not in battle.

Health: 300 regenerates 1% of max health a second while not in battle.

Constitution: +39 without armor, above average for a human.

New Level Reached: 40

Cycling over to Trillian's tree, Illume looked through it and did some quick math. A chuckle left his lips. He'd have more than enough to unlock all of Trillian's base skills.

Illume spent five skill points to unlock *Devour.* Two skill points unlocked *Dismember.* An additional five unlocked both *Tail Club* and *Tail Mace.* Illume zoomed back. Every skill was unlocked for Trillian as of now and he still had one point left.

Shifting to the attribute point tree, Illume had fifty-five points to allocate wherever he wanted. Illume placed eleven points into *Armor* just to get him to above average. He wanted to speed Trillian up, but he wanted his dragon to be prepared for whatever came next.

Illume placed thirty points into *Strength* to help Trillian in future fights. He then placed four points into *Attack* before he placed the last ten into Trillian's *Speed.*

New Stats:
Strength: +200 Above Average for a Dragon.
Armor: +200 Above average for a Dragon.
Flight Speed: +132 Average for a Dragon.
Attack: +475 Above Average for a Dragon.

As Illume closed the menu, he heard a wet splat from the other side of the room. Trillian had nearly doubled in size. His armor was thicker, his features more defined, and his horns just a little bit longer. Sheets of scales lay on the ground all over the place. Illume walked over and picked them up. They were lighter than his shield and as soft as silk.

Returning to his hidden compartment, he reopened it and placed the scales inside before he sealed it up once more. With that all taken care of, Illume made his way to his bedroom.

He crawled into bed and placed his hand where Nari used to sleep. Her pillow was still next to him. It even had some strands of her hair that she left behind. Illume sighed as he closed his eyes and went to sleep.

"Illume!" a voice whispered from the dark.

"He threatens us." It warped again into his dreams.

An image of a massive tree amidst the snow flashed in his mind. It was grey and overcast, but the tree had a hint of green tucked within the bluish white of the snow.

"He has come to devour us." The voice sharpened; it was that of a woman.

Another image flashed of a hauntingly beautiful woman. She had pale skin, white hair, and eyes that would rival the blue of ice itself. In her right hand, she had a staff made of gnarled wood that blossomed at the top. Her left hand outstretched to him.

"Please help us," her soft voice echoed.

The image shuddered and showed her standing among what looked like a volcanic wasteland. She was on a set of stairs and wore a long flowing dress that hugged her form. The collar of her dress was a large tuft of wolf fur.

An arch of ashen stone was behind her and what looked like a white silhouette of a human was within the arch. In the background, a massive beast moved. It was miles away but appeared to be hundreds of feet high. He couldn't tell what it was, just that it was colossal.

"Our souls are in your hands, son of Azathoth," she whispered.

The woman's skin browned and cracked as it turned to bark. Her eyes became two luminescent orbs as her flowing white hair hardened into branches. Her clothes fell away as her body morphed into a tree.

A flash of lightning and Illume felt himself being pulled backward. He came to a violent stop in a room he'd seen before. It was the room Trillian had died in. The entire sensation was surreal. He turned to look at the frost-covered mountains.

The sound of a door being rammed into caught Illume's attention. He snapped out of his dream and into the waking world. The door flew open as four fully armored guards entered.

They pointed their pikes at Illume, who blinked in confusion. He raised his hand at the sight of the guards.

"Hold!" Halfdan's voice rang out. "Illume? What are you doing here?"

"What are you talking about? I'm in… bed?" His voice was laced with confusion.

He realized he'd been standing and not in fact in bed. Illume looked around.

"Where am I?" Illume asked.

"Sire… You're in the forbidden room of the Dark Tower, my lord." Halfdan replied.

Illume turned around and looked out the window. In the distance, tucked behind the stretching peaks of the snowy mountains, Illume saw a dark cloud and flashes of lightning. He exhaled and could see his breath. Illume looked down at his body, he was still in his sleeping gown.

"How did I get here?" he asked.

STAY INFORMED

Get A Free Book by visiting Jonathan Yanez' website. You can email me at jonathan.alan.yanez@gmail.com or find me on Amazon, and Instagram (@author_jonathan_yanez). I also created a special Facebook group called "Jonathan's Reading Wolves" specifically for readers, where I show new cover art, do giveaways, and run contests. Please check it out and join whenever you get the chance!

For updates about new releases, as well as exclusive promotions, visit my website and sign up for the VIP mailing list. Head there now to receive a free copy of *Shall We Begin*.

http://jonathan-yanez.com

Enjoying the series? Help others discover *Legends Online* by sharing with a friend.

Made in United States
Troutdale, OR
09/24/2024

23070037R00304